THE IMMORTAL TRANSCRIPTS IV
GLIMMER

LISA BORNE GRAVES

AUTHORS 4 AUTHORS PUBLISHING
Marysville, WA, USA

Published by Authors 4 Authors Publishing
1214 6th St
Marysville, WA 98270
www.authors4authorspublishing.com

Library of Congress Control Number: 2024935282

E-book ISBN: 978-1-64477-182-2
Paperback ISBN: 978-1-64477-183-9
Audiobook ISBN: 978-1-64477-184-6

Edited by Rebecca Mikkelson
Copyedited by Brandi Spencer

Cover design ©2024 Practically Perfect Covers. All rights reserved.
Statue from cover image:
Marianne
post office of the National Assembly (Palais Bourbon)
Paris, France

Interior design and family trees by Brandi Spencer.

Authors 4 Authors Publishing branding is set in Bavire. Titles and headings are set in Goudy Trajan and Mr Darcy. Text messages are set in Source Sans Pro Semibold. Handwriting is set in Reey for Lucien, Architect's Daughter for Callie, Allura for Archer, Angel Delight for Aios, and Gatelo for Akila. All other text is set in Garamond.

THE IMMORTAL TRANSCRIPTS IV
GLIMMER

LISA BORNE GRAVES

Authors 4 Authors Content Rating

This title has been rated 17+, appropriate for older teens and adults, and contains:

- graphic violence
- strong language
- frequent brief implied sex
- mild alcohol use

Please, keep the following in mind when using our rating system:

1. A content rating is not a measure of quality.

Great stories can be found for every audience. One book with many content warnings and another with none at all may be of equal depth and sophistication. Our ratings can work both ways: to avoid content or to find it.

2. Ratings are merely a tool.

For our young adult (YA) and children's titles, age ratings are generalized suggestions. For parents, our descriptive ratings can help you make informed decisions, but at the end of the day, only you know what kinds of content are appropriate for your individual child. This is why we provide details in addition to the general age rating.

For more information on our rating system, please, visit our Content Guide at: www.authors4authorspublishing.com/books/ratings

DEDICATION

To Kelly, Stuart, Taryn, and Dylan,
thanks for your ongoing friendship, support, and positivity.

Despite the vast pond between us,
you are closer than friends—you're family.

WORKS BY LISA BORNE GRAVES

Celestial Spheres

Fyr
Draca
Bladesung
Wundor

The Immortal Transcripts

Quiver
Fever
Shudder
Glimmer

Stand-alone Titles

Apidae
"Dare"

TABLE OF CONTENTS

NOTE TO READER

The following is a faithful transcript for the use of the newly formed International Republic of Immortality (IRI) in its inquiry behind the altercations involved in the Olympian sector. As far as the signed witnesses state, everything was recorded with complete honesty, arranged chronologically, and written separately so as to not influence one another's accounts. ~~The IRI reserves the rights to this manuscript, and it is by no means to be reproduced nor shown to any creature mortal. Mortals who read may be subject to permanent silence.~~

In case we are executed for our "crimes," I pass this on to you, mortal, in hopes to continue our memories into the future. Welcome to our world.

CHAPTER 1

My husband, Archer, and I were lying in bed, exhausted and horrified but alive. After a war. After so much more. We both held onto each other, unable to speak about what had happened. Words were too hard. Archer and I had almost died after he basically killed his grandfather Zeus. And then (as if that weren't enough) our best friend had traded his soul to keep us alive—during a full-on god war.

But now, I was in a dream—or nightmare—blinding fog all around me, unsure of where to go or what to do. Then my feet moved. They were so determined on their course of action, I couldn't stop them. I should've been freaking out. What other nineteen-year-old has to deal with gods trying to kill her, becoming a goddess herself, and dreaming visions of the future? Most likely, this was one of those visions, but the fog was new (starting to hate all that is *new*).

Something came into my view: golden gates. I threw out my arms, feeling through the fog, and my hands brushed stone walls before I saw them. I let my hand follow along the rough edges to stay on course, knowing if I got scraped by the jagged edges, I would instantly heal. I'd learned the hard way that, despite having amazingly godly abilities such as healing, I could die; if I did, Archer would go with me. He'd had our souls bound, a foolishly endearing thing, because we could not live without each other. He did it to protect me, but I wish he had asked me instead of doing it behind my back by overly paraphrasing his translation of the Ancient Greek in our wedding vows. It was the custom, but he had not translated the soul-linking part. Sadly, I love him too much to chastise him over it or ever to see it as a mistake. Plus, I hadn't even known I was an immortal back then. Well, I did have my suspicions, ones I did not voice. (Yep, full-on hypocrite here.)

My hands touched the cool golden gates, and they swung open inwardly. As soon as I was inside and a few steps down a dirt path that cut through a field of grain, the gates clanged ominously shut behind me (only a dream, right?). My feet kept going, the cool mist around me dissipated, and the warm sun tried to come out. I let the light shine upon my face, and I swallowed hard, trying not to think of Lucien (originally known as Apollo), the sun god. In answer, the clouds covered the sun again to remind me of his sacrifice for me, for Archer, for something more

THE IMMORTAL TRANSCRIPTS: GLIMMER

I was not ready to face. I'd been mad at Lucien while foreseeing his betrayal, though conflicted when I foresaw his death, but in the aftermath, we learned the betrayal had been taken from him, by the very elixir of truth he had invented for mortals. His own mother had used it against him. He'd never wanted to betray Archer and me (my guilt burned).

Something in the dream caught my eye. I almost jumped out of my skin. A woman with bronze skin and dark brown braids stood in front of me (like came out of nowhere). The dark eyes looked familiar, but I couldn't place them. She gave me a half smile, as if her very thoughts were on the dead sun-god as well.

"Where am I? Why am I here?" I asked.

"I thought it was clear that this is the Elysian Fields, or Elysium. Take your pick. I can't keep up with the mortal world's jargon from here." Well, she wasn't very welcoming. "And you are here because *he* is not. Someone must take on prophecies."

"I thought the powers passed to his eldest child?"

"Prophecies do not belong to one god alone. Why you are here is not known to me. I simply deliver messages not safe for mortal oracles to carry."

"Who are you?"

"You're wasting time. Take my hand, and get your prophecy. Prepare yourself. You will not like it."

She felt like someone's very stern grandparent (not that I had a living one to know) with her brisk attitude and commands. I got the vibe the woman didn't really like me for some reason (who knew).

I grabbed her hand and forced myself to hold on, because the power of images being thrust into my brain was painfully overwhelming: *a place of darkness and ghosts, Archer yelling and slamming someone into a wall, pure rage in his face...me!* Then they sped up, and I tried to focus on the images: *a distorted-looking face with platinum blond hair, in a hospital? A scared-looking Linda, arrows and lightning flying through the sky,* and my grip was severed.

I opened my eyes to meet those dark ones full of compassion, just like Prometheus's. (A relative?) "Archer would never—"

"Things aren't always what they seem. Do not trust your eyes, but rely on your inner eye foremost. Now, go!"

I heard some kind of growling in the wind. Never having been a huge fan of big dogs, an angry-sounding one made me sprint. Thanks to immortal speed, I was out the gates and into the dense fog in seconds. Then I fell—into our bed, sitting bolt upright in our hotel room.

"Are you okay?" Archer asked me groggily.

"Just a dream," I told him. But the image of him attacking me was seared into my brain. "Just a dream." Only, the repetition didn't convince me that was true.

CHAPTER 2

When I tried to go to sleep, I felt sick to my stomach. Anteros and Himerus made ridiculous excuses to sleep out on the living room floor in our new apartment. Prometheus had used his foresight to buy up an entire floor of apartments, starting when the building was built in the sixties. He funded it through shady means of knowing the upcoming results of sports betting and big investments. We were still in the Upper East Side, near where the others had lived, but a couple blocks away from the East River rather than by Central Park. East 74th Street and 1st Avenue was still a prime locale, so I wondered how many millions Prometheus had at present and how much he'd accumulated over the years.

My friends were excited to have a free place of our own. The brick building was okay, but the apartment for the three of us hadn't been updated since the nineties, and some of the others—like the one for the freedom goddess—were updated.

I swallowed my resentment. I wished Dad were here, but she was more important to everyone. I just didn't want to admit that.

My buddies were celebrating the free new "digs," but I couldn't celebrate anything. Even though we had three unfurnished bedrooms we could camp out in separately, Himerus had said something about safety in numbers. We were all too wound up to sleep anyway.

The truth was, they didn't want to leave *me* alone. My dad died, and after all of that, things were a blur, but I remember Mom, Asclepius, and me helping the Titans, who murdered Zeus. Or maybe they didn't? Things were unclear, but I'm pretty sure Hera and Hermes ran off with his head as the Titans burned his body. Zeus, my "grandfather," was only a head. That was something I turned my mind away from because of the mere mental image of it.

By pushing Zeus out of my mind, Dad came to the forefront. I had killed him, technically. He made me do it, but I listened, and I got him killed. He chose to die to save his friends instead of staying here with me, with us. I envied the devotion he gave them and hated him for leaving me after we had finally become closer than ever. All that eclipsed that anger and jealousy was guilt, grief, and a foreboding feeling of what the future held without him in it.

"This is stupid," I mumbled. "Go to your rooms. We're not kids in Olympus, scared of the dark, anymore."

"Aios, I'm kind of scared about you getting hit with Apollo-depth powers." Himerus followed it up with a whistle. A pillow hit him. "What?"

Anteros scolded him. "Real nice. You could try to have some sympathy and class."

"Your family are the feelers, not mine."

"Guys, stop. I'm fine." My voice was thin, betraying my emotional state.

"You're not," Anteros said. "Which is normal. None of us are fine, and we're not his sons. I know you don't want to talk about it, but at least let us help you sort out these powers coming. Honestly, though, if you want to talk about it, I'll listen." I appreciated the subtle present tense of my dad since Callie had this belief that she could bring him back.

"By the gods, you're such a wussy Atlas." Himerus mocked Anteros.

I could hardly formulate the words to break it up. I was touched by my friends' concern, and I understood them both. Anteros was the one to talk to when I needed it, and Himerus would uplift me with his brashness. He was picking on his brother in hopes I'd get a laugh out of it, or at least distracted.

To divert them away from all subjects I said, "What about my brother and my mom?"

They both laughed. I groaned. I actually didn't really care that much. My mom and Asclepius weren't actually related. It was just weird that we shared a dad and that dad had been with her. No, it was definitely weird by modern standards, but not ancient godly Greek ways, I suppose.

This led onto an onslaught of crude jokes about one's lineage and my potential future brother-nephews and sister-nieces. Yes, I asked for the teasing because I wanted to lighten the heaviness in my heart. The laughter soon fell, the comments became brief, and then I feigned sleep. They went silent and were breathing deeply soon enough.

I wouldn't sleep, and not by choice. The heaviness in my heart led to heaviness in my body, like something was encroaching my space, then inside of me. I kept looking at the stove's clock. Hours went by, and sleep did not come. The feeling kept pressing me and squeezing me from the inside out, soon becoming suffocating, and I knew what it was: Dad's powers.

I took a deep breath. I was part of my father, and here his power was coming, trying to link back to what it recognized. It was all I had left of him, and I had to take it on. Another deep breath, and the pain and pressure became too much.

I screamed out as the pain became too much to bear. Then, I was pretty sure I lost consciousness, because everything suddenly stopped.

"Wake up!" I heard a shout, but my eyes were heavy.

My face was smacked, which made my eyes fly open. I heard pounding on the door, but it was so bright, I could hardly see the figures rushing into the room. Athena's gray eyes were in front of me. "Pull it in, the energy."

"Huh, who put on the lights?" I mumbled, still groggy.

"You did! Pull it in!" Someone shouted.

I was doing this?

Another set of eyes was in front of me, Callie's. Her hands touched my face, and I felt a strange uncontrollable feeling like I was being sucked into her eyes. My thoughts felt as if they were not my own, as if someone was rifling through them. When a strong thought was forced to the forefront of my mind, I realized exactly what to do.

I sat up. Callie and Athena backed away. The room was bright like the sun was shining, only I was the sun. And the sun was coming in through the curtain on full throttle as if it were noon on the equator. I pulled that string Callie had dived into my mind to retrieve. I pulled my newfound power in with great effort, and then it became dark both outside and inside. I kept holding it not knowing what to do, but instinct took over, and I envisioned it being enclosed in my heart. I probably could've picked my foot since it probably didn't matter where, but this was Dad's power, and it belonged there.

I took a deep breath, and the dozen immortals around me sighed in relief. A couple begrudged me, but my mother came to my side and touched my cheek soothingly. She was so overbearing, but I needed her right now.

"Thank you," I told Callie.

Callie smiled as she tugged the half-asleep Archer toward the door.

"Did you do that?" he asked her, flabbergasted.

Athena watched her go, her face concerned, Prometheus bracing Athena's shoulders.

"She just read my mind, that's all. She found a thread of strong power, and then I realized how to pull it in. Dad's power. It was like she pulled out his instructions for me to focus on." I explained the best I could.

Athena's face seemed even more puzzled, and she hurried from the room. I guess it was unnerving what Callie could do. If Zeus couldn't control her, and she broke his power over us, and now she could dive into our minds and meddle— even though she merely guided me—could anyone control her? I had this itch to find out, to uncover more about her, and I knew where it came from. Again, it was Dad's powers, seeking the truth. Getting his powers was hard enough, but now I realized the awful truth: my father would haunt me forever inside my own body and mind. The grief would crash upon me every single day.

I got a call the next morning. Dad's landlord was looking for rent. Apparently, knowing he was going to die and assuming it was this battle, he never paid ahead. We had forty-eight hours to move his stuff. My friends volunteered to help me and secured a truck. Busy would be good for me, but I wasn't sure what to do with Dad's stuff, and I was irritated that my mom and half-brother didn't stay to help me. She has been an overbearing mother, but at times like this, I could've used more of that.

The landlord wanted money when I got there, but Himerus intimidated him into giving us the deposit money back instead. Loved that guy's negotiation skills. We looked around at all of my dad's things. An empty coffee cup was still resting on the counter, books strewn on the table, his laptop closed on his desk. It was as if he'd walk right back in at any moment. Even though we had been in Iceland, we'd returned there before the Battle at Liberty.

"We'll start with the fridge." Anteros said. Of course, they would. All they did was eat.

I tried to warn them. "Some of it—"

"Eww." Anteros shut the door.

"—is probably rotten. We didn't have time to clean it out before or after Iceland," I finished.

Himerus grabbed a trash bag. "I'll start with the fridge then. You raid the pantry, as I'm sure there's something in there to eat." They got started as I surveyed the apartment.

"What should I do with all this stuff?" I was speaking to myself, but Anteros answered.

"We don't have a lot of furniture, so we could borrow it until he's, like, *back*. The rest, put in storage?"

"Don't need to rent storage. There's apparently an apartment for him. I mean, a couple extra ones. Remember? We could've opted to all live alone. Let's use one of the rooms to store stuff for now and see what we can use in the meantime."

It was settled, and the idea of Dad needing his stuff again one day gave me a glimmer of hope. I drew a deep breath, grabbed a few boxes and packing tape, and went into his bedroom, starting with his clothes.

I had packed the last box of things and labeled the box "bedroom," and heard knocking as I taped it shut. Looking around, the bare mattress and empty closet sent a wave of nausea over me. Trying to distract myself, I checked on the sun. I was off by a few minutes, so I moved it a tad in the sky. I was doing well, considering I had been unconsciously moving it all morning—on day one.

"Can I help you?" Himerus asked someone.

"Is um…Aios here?"

I recognized that voice. Eagerly, I hurried into the living room. "Linda?"

There she stood, pretty as ever, giving me a small smile, its delicate warmth shining upon me. As she surveyed me, her smile fell, my eagerness lower than she anticipated. Perhaps she could see the grief etched in my face or in my solemn gaze. I was excited to see her, but I dreaded breaking the news to her about my dad. Mortals didn't know that Lucien Veras was an alias. I couldn't report him dead without a body, and if he returned like Callie insisted she could pull off…well, that would create a lot of problems.

I opened the door farther to let Linda enter. She glanced at Himerus, who had answered the door, but then her gaze flickered to Anteros. Her eyes went wide. I forgot she had never met him. He looked spot-on like Archer but with slightly longer hair that was straight, with roots growing in mostly dirty blond and the tips a brighter blond from when they had dyed it to give him an exact doppelganger look. The likeness was so obvious that she noticed.

"This is Antony and Russ." I pointed them out but had to explain further to put her at ease. "Archer's half brothers from different sides of the family."

"Nice to meet you guys." Then she looked around. "Why are you packing up Lucien's things? Is he moving?"

We froze, and Himerus said something about grabbing lunch, and he and Anteros rushed out past her. *Gee, thanks.* I was alone with Linda, left to the task to tell her something devastating.

"Aios?"

"My…my brother's gone. Lucien's um…" I could not say it: dead. "In the Middle East, getting treatment for um…I don't know what, actually. He's been private about it. He's not well. He could die." I added the last part impulsively because what if Callie failed? They hadn't even left yet.

Linda sank onto the couch, upset, obviously, but asked, "Are you okay?" Then she cringed. "Sorry, no. You're not okay about it. Why would you be? I just…" She stopped trying to talk and just peered up at me with those dark eyes.

"It's okay. No one knows what to say because there is nothing anyone can say in a moment like this that would make a difference. We can just hope for the best, a miracle." At least my words were honest now. I needed Callie to pull off a miracle. I sat down next to Linda, covering my face before running my hands down it. I hated not sharing all of myself and my world with her. I could not mess

LISA BORNE GRAVES

up though. I faced her. "The question right back at you. Are you okay? It's just, I know you cared for him deeply."

"Aios," she whispered. "I don't want to sound insensitive, but I'm more lamenting the struggles of a friend and worried about you."

I was lost. I had thought she had loved my father. I had been afraid to do more than be friendly and flirty last time I was in town, thinking she wasn't over my dad. "Me?"

"I want you to be okay." Then she bit her lip, nervous. "You were gone so long. I missed you."

I wanted to kiss her and also wanted to jump for joy. She was admitting feelings for me. "I missed you too." I dared to take up her hand in mine. "I never intended to be gone so long."

She squeezed my hand back. "Are you here to stay?"

"Yes, no." What could I tell her when I had no idea where my life was headed? The truth thrummed in me like a pulse, wanting to come out. "I actually don't know. A bunch of us are renting rooms in an apartment building down the street, so probably. Living day-by-day at the moment." It wasn't like I could tell her about Zeus, the battle, and the fear of his return.

"I understand." She was disappointed.

My confidence about her liking me grew from that response. "I want to stay." I told her softly, leaning my shoulder into hers in hopes she would turn, and I could try to snag a kiss.

Archer's brothers entered with sandwiches from the deli across the street. Himerus grinned wickedly, surely in promise to make fun of me later. Anteros, as always, said the wrong thing. "You expect us to do all this while you get to flirt? Get packing, Aios."

I could just punch him, but my face flared up instead.

"Can I help?" Linda stood.

Himerus gave Anteros a glare for saying anything. I ignored their stares and said sure because, frankly, I wanted to spend time with her.

The other two ate their sandwiches while Linda and I packed up Dad's book collection. I was going to soak up every moment with this girl. Food didn't even matter anymore, only her.

11

CHAPTER 3

Archer

Callie. I would do anything for her. After almost losing my wife, I would take on Zeus myself. I had. But for Lucien, I'd do the same. I missed him beyond what words could express. Callie was my heart. Without a heart, the god of love cannot exist. Lucien? His absence felt like a severed limb. I could not imagine a world without him. Even though he was gone, it was not real—impossible. He was my brother, more than that, like one of my parents. It is impossible to describe the love we have for one of the most important people in our lives and give it justice. If I could have him back, I'd endure anything it would take.

I believed Callie could do it. I wanted to and truly did. I had to know he'd be with us again. I wasn't a fan of the Orpheus plan. Orpheus had been involved with Jason and the Argonauts, but Callie referred to his wife, Eurydice, who had been struck by a viper and taken by Thanatos shortly after she married Orpheus. He tried bargaining with Hades to get her back, and succeeded somewhat through his music, making Hades and Persephone weep over his grief, but Orpheus lost Eurydice at the mouth of the exit of the Underworld by looking back to behold her a moment too soon, the only rule he had to follow. It was a tragic story, and I did not understand how Callie thought this would work for us this time. If anything, Hades was less likely to be persuaded to give Lucien back. To lead the soul you wish to look at the most, over deadly rivers and other dangers—not to check, not to make sure… It was a temptation I did not wish to test. If we failed, it would destroy the others. I wished Callie and I had done it privately, snuck off. Then, if it didn't work out, only our two hearts would rebreak. Then again, in the Underworld, there were worse things than breaking hearts.

"You don't want to go?" Callie asked as we ate breakfast.

The rest of the family had been up and about this morning, unpacking boxes and making themselves at home in their new apartments, but Callie and I both slept late again. We unpacked enough boxes to make breakfast, and Dad had done a big food run for the staples of a kitchen, enough for basic cooking.

I put my fork down. "I never said that. I'm simply wary, nervous. Aren't you?"

She nodded as she bit into her buttered toast.

"And that's not fair, you reading my mind. *Quid pro quo.*" She kept reading my mind instead of talking things out, which left me in the lurch, unable to do so.

"I'm thinking about the apartment."

The apartment was amazing, with vibrant yellow walls in the living area, hardwood floors, and granite and stainless steel in the kitchen and breakfast bar. More importantly, it was safe. Everyone was on the same floor, and our apartment was at the back, furthest from the elevator.

She continued after a pause and a sigh, "It's amazing, but…" She didn't need to finish. At the expense of Lucien's life, everything, no matter how beautiful, was marred.

I nodded and clasped her free hand in mine. "I love you and will do anything for you, Callie. Now more than ever, but…"

Her voice was muffled by her mouthful of food as she prompted me to continue, "What?"

I sighed. I had almost mentioned how my parents would be affected if this went wrong and we died. Callie no longer had parents. I had to tread lightly and rephrase my thoughts before mentioning something like that, which might upset her. "How would our family bear it if this went horrifically wrong, and you and I ended up there for eternity? Athena, Prometheus, Ma, Dad, my brothers—"

"I know you have a lot more to lose than I do." She stared down at her toast as if losing her appetite.

Damn it. I tried so hard to steer the conversation into safe waters, but Callie still knew what I had been thinking. She had been through a lot, but she was uncharacteristically moody today. I couldn't blame her. I felt so many emotions warring inside me, but the overwhelming one was to protect her, care for her. "I didn't mean it like that. I know you're hurting from many things, but you know you are not alone. I have also dealt with grief. We all have. Living forever—it tends to happen more than we wish. But, please, know that we are your family too. You married into it, sure, but look at the amount of them seeking to protect you."

"I only want my father."

That was it. That was the problem. In the back of her mind, she must desire to bring him back like Lucien. Not that it was a logical possibility at all. He had chosen cremation, and his mortal body had failed.

"Callie, he will be there, waiting for you. You speak of my closure—"

"Why are you telling me what I already know?" She was staring off, nibbling her toast.

"Because anything that you and I are unprepared for could jeopardize Lucien's return. Hades might do anything, bargain anything, even if it is a lie, to keep us there." I placed my fork down, ignoring my eggs, wanting to explain better. "He is not evil—overly kind if anything—but lonely, damaged. As is Persephone. I think it breaks him to see her hurt."

13

Callie's eyes met mine, and we stared at each other for a moment. She stood up, leaving her eggs untouched, and came over to me. She sat in my lap, her ebony eyes probing deep into mine. "Like us."

I swallowed hard. "Like we were before, when we were apart, yes."

Callie's confession was full of love, but it also meant she was unhappy. When we reunited and married, she was happy. Her father died, and she still seemed to rally a bit, but Zeus's attack… How long had she been down? She was my heart; when it hurt, I did.

"Of course, Archer. I'm happy now, just too much going on in my head to show it enough. I'm sorry." She kissed me, so I made the most of that kiss, pulling her close and cradling her face. Pure love poured into me from her lips and coursed through me. With her love, I could accomplish anything.

Callie pulled away before I could take the kiss as far as I had wanted, the bedroom. I opened my mouth to tell her I loved her, but she placed her finger over my lips, grinning. With the happiness of love shining in her dark eyes, she said, "I know." She pointed to her head, then mine.

I frowned. "Reading my mind takes the fun out of being spontaneous and romantic."

"Oh, no. On my end, it is a much deeper connection." The coy look she gave me roused more than my curiosity.

"That is *definitely* unfair. You're going to have to speak your thoughts out loud to me. *All* the time."

Callie bit her lip, which made me kiss her, and all thoughts of the Underworld left me. All I could think about was what could be on my wife's mind at the moment. It pained me not to know, but I invented fantasies of my own as I followed her into our bedroom. I'd follow her anywhere. Somewhere in the deep recesses of my mind, that terrified me.

That evening, Athena and Prometheus came over with pizzas for a "planning party." That's what Prometheus had called it, trying to make it sound chipper. Sure, he was in a good mood, knowing some of the future ahead of us and having lopped off Zeus's head. I'm sure that satisfied some of the injustices he had faced at Zeus's hands in the past—but probably not all.

Callie and I took the sofa across from the dining room chairs where Athena and Prometheus sat, all of us exhausted. After Callie and I spent most of the morning in the bedroom, we unpacked most of our things all day, which had distracted me from our upcoming mission and Callie from her sorrows.

Athena's posture was stiff as always, but there was a sense of relaxation in her, despite what had just happened. Prometheus did that for her. As the god of love, I still couldn't believe I had never picked up on what was between them. Forbidden love, just like Callie's and mine.

"The plan—" I began, but my wife would not let me speak.

"I've told you all I can, Archer. We need to discuss the after part, how to get Lucien's soul into his body."

"I'd be more comfortable knowing all the details. What if something unexpected makes me mess up your plan?"

Prometheus sighed, clasping his hands together, as he met my gaze. "If she says she cannot tell you, you must trust her. Knowing could possibly be what ruins everything."

Damn it. I was over being told that. Didn't they realize I'd be more likely to worry myself into mucking up the plan?

"What happens after we get out?" Callie directed her attention to Prometheus. She was inches away from me, leaning forward. It felt like she was closing me off, closing me out. It was their plan, no place for me.

Athena answered instead. "It hasn't been done before, but my hypothesis is that he will only be a spirit in our world, free from Hades's control. Prometheus and I will be there, with Apollo—I mean, with his body, carefully prepping. I'm hoping we will be able to link the soul back to the body. If we can't make it work, we send for Aios."

"Hope?" Callie sighed and looked at me. Her warm brown eyes were full of concern.

I knew exactly what she was thinking about. Aios was far from stable. In his grief and onslaught of Lucien's powers, he was hardly able to function with daily tasks. Would he be able to try to save his father when his entire happiness and future rode on it? He had been soft and protected at Olympus before this. Did fighting a war and losing his father make him stronger, or was he broken from it? I didn't want to chance it, not with Callie. She'd see it as overprotective if I admitted that, but almost losing her and myself—more than once—was terrifying. I could not regret our immortal marriage. I would not live in a world without her, but I feared for her life daily now that it was entwined with mine.

Athena shook her head. "I will figure it out. You don't worry about the *how*, but just on your success."

My head darted over to Prometheus, who I swore I saw wink at my wife, espying it out of the corner of my eye. I gave him a glare, and his steady gaze met mine and refused to show emotion. He was hiding things from Athena too. He and Callie were doing that irritating conversation in their heads by reading each other's minds. I didn't like this. Heading into the Underworld half-blind, trusting two seers who would not divulge…

I sighed.

"What is it now?" Callie lashed out, giving me a pert look.

Something was changing with her, and it scared me. I liked her newfound confidence, but knowing she was immortal seemed to take it further, not egotistical exactly, but harsh with me and some others lately—easily annoyed. I could sense the love inside her for me, but her outward mood did not quite match that. She was unhappy. Yes, her father died, and Zeus was likely going to be back trying to kill us. But way too soon, the honeymoon felt over. I didn't know how to repair it. She was hiding something from me again. I thought we both had agreed to banish secrets between us in Iceland, but here she was doing it again. I would get answers and fix things, but she needed to focus on getting Lucien back; losing him was a weight upon us and a wedge between us. He died for Callie and me. I completely understood how our happiness felt tainted by his sacrifice. Bringing anything up now could jeopardize the mission. I'd back off for now, but once Lucien was among us, we'd have a full-transparency chat and hopefully a renewal of our unhindered love.

"Well?" she prompted as if I was the one in the wrong.

It rubbed me the wrong way. I'm not some toxic male, but she was treating me like shit lately. Acting like I was awful, then seducing me within the same day. I couldn't let it go. "Nothing. I just don't need to be Lucien to see the two of you hiding things for the *greater good*."

Prometheus wrinkled his nose at my choice of words, but I purposely chose them to trigger Athena's logic. He sneered at me. "Your father would know all about that."

I tensed. He knew well that my father had been on the Allies' side of WWII. "So would your fiancée."

Prometheus twitched and almost stood up, barely able to restrain himself.

Athena's gaze measured each of us in turn. "What is it with you two?" She pointed to him and me, not him and Callie. So, I was alone. She was all for blind obedience for the "best result." Great.

Prometheus's arms tightened on the chair's arm. "I don't trust him."

My fists tightened, my father's instinct to protect myself kicking in. "Well, I don't like walking into a possible suicide mission without the info you both have stored in your heads."

Callie was the one who stood up, walked away from us, and went into the kitchen. She grabbed another slice of pizza but did not sit down. It was clear she was done with us acting like children.

Athena sighed, a signal she'd announce a verdict. "We will do this. We leave tomorrow. After we have him back, everyone will spit out their issues, and we'll work it out. We have to be a family, stick together, and trust each other, or Zeus will win. We are like a chain—"

"If one link breaks, we all fall." I recited one of her many cliché lessons, but it hit home.

I was ready to get this over with and work on my marriage. After I banished my ghosts. That, indeed, was another painful thing I was not looking forward to.

CHAPTER 4

The news hit me hard. The text glaring at me from my phone sucked the breath out of me. My knees almost gave out. Polly's concerned voice rang in my throbbing ears. "Mom?"

Breathe, just breathe. I sucked in, trying to hide all emotion from my features.

I hated him. I had loved him more, but now I hated him with every fiber in my being. How dare he leave this realm? How dare he not make peace with me first? He'd had no idea about Polly. None.

I met Polly's gaze, looking straight into those honest green eyes that popped against her tawny skin. *His eyes.*

My stomach dropped, bile rising. Overwhelming guilt. I thought I had time. I had kept Polly to myself, protecting her. The deadbeat would have, at some point, swept in and taken my daughter—the result of our on-again-off-again love affair—away from me. Or worse. The Greeks might kill her. He was supposed to live forever, and when Polly was grown, she could've made her own decision whether or not to seek him out. Even then, he would have likely broken her heart with tons of attention followed by tenfold neglect.

That was the experience of everyone who had been "loved" by Apollo.

I looked back at the text from Artemis, praying to Shai, my people's god of fate, that I had read it wrong.

Akila, Apollo is dead. Hope that gives you closure.

It did the opposite, actually. How could I explain this to Polly without her getting furious, hating me, running away? *Sorry, my little sunshine, your father died without ever knowing about you.*

"Hang on," I muttered to Polly, typing quickly while pacing.

"I hate when you do that."

"What?" I asked, still staring at the screen, needing more detail from Artemis. Out of the blue, she'd texted me after years of no contact. Artemis was the only Greek who knew about my on-and-off relationship with her brother, but she had no clue about Polly. I made sure not to run into any Greeks; they might figure out who she was. Some cultures were not always permitted to marry gods outside of their own, and the Greeks were one of them. A child from two cultures? It was forbidden. Polly must stay hidden, a secret until she could defend herself.

Polly rolled her eyes, and finally answered me: "Move that way, all super fast. I hate it." Her tone was preteen cattiness or jealousy. At twelve, Polly had not yet come into her godly powers. She wanted to grow up to have these superhuman powers. She did not listen to the burden of what came with them. I wished I could fast-forward to Polly being an adult. Baby and kid years were a delight. But tweens were a trying age. I was dreading teenhood.

"It's important," I told Polly, frowning at the next message I received from Artemis.

He's a traitor and sacrificed his soul to save some wretched girl.

I had no love for Zeus or the Greeks, but the words stunned me. *Girl? Not goddess? Not demigod? Just "girl."* Why would Apollo die for a mortal? Truth? Love? A jealous pang filled me, quickly followed by self-loathing. How could I still love him after a thirteen-year break? Just because he was dead? Because of Polly? I was smarter than that. No, it was a desperate pang for truth and balance. I typed another message, this time slower so my daughter wouldn't get grumpy again.

The phone *ping*ed again. **Eros's wife that Zeus wants dead. I tire of this conversation. Goodbye.**

Once a bitch, always a bitch. I would get nothing more from her. Artemis was probably happy her brother was dead. No wonder Apollo was terrible with relationships. The only family he had was downright awful to him from what he had described. Artemis's texts were proof that his family lacked the warmth that made us gods more human.

I'd get answers from someone else. I texted him and waited. This had to be undone. Somehow, I had to make Apollo alive again. I walked out onto the balcony, smelling the salt air and staring at the beautiful beach where the waves lapped the sand. Things were in discord. It was off, the balance. The world was wrong without Apollo in it—despite my conflicting feelings on the matter.

My phone rang. I answered.

His deep voice came on the line. "Akila. You heard, I take it. I was going to tell you but should've known *she* would've taken the pleasure of giving you pain." He sighed. I imagined he was running a hand through his black hair, but I did not know how he wore it now to complete the image properly. "She sure has been a pain in my ass lately."

Greek moon goddess Artemis and Egyptian moon god Thoth always had butt heads, unlike Apollo, my Greek counterpart of truth and justice, and me. We had joyous unions—albeit short-lived—repeatedly over a long life. My body warmed at the memories. By the gods of my homeland, Apollo had been an excellent lover. Thoth and I had been very different when together. It was an ordered union that later broke, one forged of duty. Thoth had always loved another, and so had I. We had no passion, not like when the Sun set me afire with his warm gaze and touch. That flame was forever gone now.

My throat tightened. I had to clear it to speak. "It cannot be." Desperately, I wanted Thoth, my ex, my best friend and confidante, to soothe me by telling me it was misinformation.

"It is, I'm afraid."

I shook my head, not that he could see but more for myself. "I can stop it."

"He is dead. There is nothing you can do. I know part of you loves him, but Ma'at," —he used my given name so tenderly, I almost started weeping— "he is in their Hades."

"But he has not moved on. I weigh the balance for our people, their hearts. In their sector, he would go to Elysium and be gone forever."

"As it should be. I'm sorry, but preventing his afterlife will trap him there. His soul is gone. You'd create a zombie if his body is even intact. It has been tried before. You do remember, don't you? Is that what you want for your daughter?"

I cringed at the memory of reanimated mummies, bodies without souls. He was right, but I couldn't shake the thought of delaying the inevitable. "I agree with you, but Thoth, something in me is demanding a need for balance. Something is wrong, off. It is not my emotions. I haven't tried to process it. It must be delayed."

He huffed out a defeated breath, never having the courage to argue with me. "It sounds like you made up your mind, so why call me?"

"Because I'm going to do it. And I was hoping you'd prevent an Egyptian-Greek war."

"Why me? I'm not a war god, Akila."

"You're my only champion."

He sighed again, and I thought he had hung up after that with the looming silence stretching between us, but the tell-tale beep of a severed connection never came. Then he spoke: "You're not thinking straight. Hades would never let such a powerful soul escape his entourage. He will be there for a long time—if not forever. If your concern is Polly, she will have time to see him."

I weighed his words. My daughter would see Apollo in soul form, the wispy image of who Apollo once had been. Polly deserved more. She deserved everything I had robbed her of thus far. "Not good enough."

His voice was full of dread. "What are you going to do?"

"I don't know, but I'll go to the Greeks, talk to them."

"They are split. Zeus against the warmonger."

"Artemis said as much."

"If you are doing this, get a new phone. Artemis is on the wrong side for your goal. She wanted nothing more than to kill her brother and her nephews. She despises him and his children as she does with anyone connected to him." *Including Polly if Artemis knew.* It did not have to be said. It was a silent warning.

"Noted. I will send you my new number once I get rid of this phone."

There was silence again before he spoke: "Best not." When I didn't respond, he continued, "If you want the Greeks, they're in New York. I don't want to know more. I can't be involved. There is something about that girl they are protecting. She is…different. I've heard rumors that she is also a goddess of questionable heritage."

What a spineless coward. He could not feel the imbalance, the torment when things were not just right. It was beyond a nagging feeling. It was my essence, my life, the reason for existence. I must restore balance. Thoth had loved me and I him, a love formed of respect, habit, and duty. He would hide things for me, like Polly from the rest of our people, but he would never act. Not even for me. And not for another like Polly. How many of these "questionable" gods or goddesses were out there?

"I understand," I muttered and hung up. Then I chucked my phone off the balcony, far into the sea, about a thousand yards away. I was given these powers for a reason, so I'd use them. I could not raise the dead, but I could prevent the afterlife. That might give me time to figure out how to bring Apollo back one day. I didn't know how it could be accomplished. The past was not pretty in any attempts to resurrect mummified remains. I would do my best to help the Greeks find a way.

I went inside to break the news to Polly—not of her father's death, but about our move to New York. I'd figure out how to tell Polly after I found out what the Greeks were up to. I had a feeling they would not let him go so easily either. I just hoped they were ready to accept Polly and help protect her. Maybe I would finally get my answer about how Polly came into existence, how Zeus lost his control over his people's fecundity as the control freak was prone to do.

CHAPTER 5

I was in Hades, not literally yet, although that was the plan. Over a week ago, Lucien had died, and then there was this prophecy of Archer attacking me, which was absolutely out of character for him. He was such a gentle person toward me (all love and tenderness), I couldn't fully believe it. Yet I had seen him in war, saw him cut down his own family members to protect me. I saw him light Death on fire to save me.

My moment of Tartarus had everything to do with a situation I feared. I needed to get to the store, but with mortals growing sick and our concerns about Zeus's people being out there, we secluded ourselves as much as many mortals. That's fine, but not if you wanted to order a top secret item on a group list when Ares or Prometheus went out for the store run. I had been sly, and I tried to project my thoughts into the latter's mind. He didn't act like he heard them though. Prometheus and my mind reading abilities came in handy, but neither Archer nor Athena appreciated being left out. So, my being discreet might have failed. I tried to be patient until the guys returned from their run.

When Prometheus came home, though, he handed Archer our grocery bags, and as soon as his back was turned, Prometheus slipped a small rectangular box into my hand. I hid it behind my back and gave him a significant look; I hoped Prometheus heard my grateful thoughts about his discretion.

As soon as I entered our apartment behind Archer, he was unloading groceries onto the counter way too quickly, but now I could fully keep up with him. It only took months, but I was finally used to immortal speed. When I first tried it, I was a bit clumsy (or more like a hot mess), but now I was used to it.

"What do you want for dinner?" Archer looked up at me. His brow furrowed. "What's wrong?"

"Nothing."

He gave me that knowing gaze that he knew something was up (and I better fess up).

"Let me think about it." I went into our bedroom, then our bathroom and locked the door behind me. I was not thinking at all about dinner. In fact, if I had to eat right now, I might puke from nerves. I turned the fan on because immortal ears could hear though walls, but not over a fan. I stared at the slender box Prometheus had given me: a pregnancy test.

I knew the results already but was in denial. I was three weeks late, but immortals weren't regular I was told, but I had been like clockwork each month since I was fourteen. My boobs hurt, and I had weird cramps. On top of that, my hips felt off, making me clumsy, particularly when using my immortal speed. This all straight-up matched what sex ed had taught me and what the internet confirmed.

I waited the longest three minutes of my life.

Positive. My heart sank, and I stifled a cry. I should've been happy, but I was far from it. Why? The timing was terrible. I was supposed to enter the Underworld and bring my friend back from the dead. Archer was overprotective to the point it put a strain on our marriage. What would he become if I told him about the baby? He'd never let me go and rescue Lucien, and if we waited longer, the opportunity to bring him back, as himself, would dwindle. Archer would go with someone else and perhaps botch it up or get stuck there. It had to be me. I felt and knew that. Archer would stop me, and that dreadful prophecy-dream of him hurting me made me trust him less.

I took a deep breath. How could I believe for a second he'd hurt me at all? I clung to what the oracle had said. Things aren't always what they seem, and to use my inner eye. Still, a niggling voice in the back of my mind would not let it go.

I stuffed the test inside the box and hid it behind my unused feminine products. No guy or guy-god would look there.

Then I took a deep breath, painted the look all was well on my face, and headed out to discuss spaghetti and meatballs.

Little did I know, Archer was cooking for five, only five turned into six. His brothers were leeches, and where they went, Aios went, and apparently Linda was here too. I hugged her, and I felt so weird. Linda was me only a year and a half ago—mortal, ignorant of gods, normal. Well, I was never normal but had thought I was; at least she had mortal going for her.

The problem is, I had just gotten used to not hiding things, so now doing so in front of her felt strange. The way the gods around me "mortalled," acted like humans, with ease as we ate was incredible; only the knucklehead brothers kept slipping in jokes that were over Linda's head and made Aios unnerved and Archer angry. They'd had thousands of years to grow up, but I guess some people never do.

I gave them angry looks, and they stopped. Funny that. I was a newbie to the family, but they were intimidated by me. (I could learn to love that.)

Once they were gone, I tried to occupy my mind by loading the dishwasher.

Archer sat at the breakfast bar. "So, when are we going to talk about it?"

I froze, almost dropping a glass. We had a bond, but he could not know, could he? "About what?"

He gave me a *come on* look. "When do we leave?"

"Oh, for a second there, I thought you were asking me about paint colors again." He had been animated earlier about painting the walls when it was the last concern of mine and not what we needed to focus on.

He scoffed. "Don't you hate this plain cream?" He looked at the walls, annoyed. "You're distracting me."

"Tomorrow night." It came out of my mouth before I knew it.

He took a ragged sigh. "We've talked over the plan a dozen times with Athena, not that anything ever goes as planned for us. Look, I get why you won't tell me all the details, that maybe me acting on the fly will be a good thing. I know I worry too much. I'm trying to remember you're not this fragile mortal I had thought you were." He smiled, and for the first time in days since the prophecy, I felt the love he had for me emanating from him onto me and my love for him reciprocating.

I smiled back, thinking how silly I was for doubting him from that vision. I could not believe that of the man who loved me with every shred of his being—and being the embodiment of love, that meant a lot. I would get through this Hades trip, and when Lucien was alive and safe with us, I'd tell Archer about the baby and grill Prometheus about my vision. I just needed to focus on one thing at a time. Otherwise, when my mind dabbled on more, my throat tightened, and my heart raced. I took three deep breaths and cast worries from me. I could push the worry away, but not the guilt.

Athena arranged covert missions across the world like my mother-in-law had planned Archer's and my wedding: with stealth and precision. The fact Athena could not use Zeus's skies made it impressive. With three wind gods under her command, the next morning, we found ourselves in Jordan by the Dead Sea. We weren't far from the entrance to the Underworld, Lot's Cave, but Archer and I wouldn't be knocking on his front door, instead sneaking in the back, which made me nervous since he didn't disclose the details. Not that I could pressure him about details, because he'd push me to explain how we'd spring Lucien, and my visions had Archer working best on instinct rather than plans. We had to trust each other.

Athena had a warehouse rented with a ton of machines, and there was a large box that reminded me of a massive coffin (cringe). My stomach plummeted in realization—Lucien was in there, frozen. I placed my hand on the box. (I'm coming, my friend.) Knowing he was there, awaiting his soul's return, made this risky mission feel necessary. The anxiety and fear drifted away, replaced by determination and focus. I would get our friend back.

Early in the morning, before sunrise, we left Athena and Prometheus, who were carefully thawing Lucien's body. Already on the edge of civilization, we walked until the road gave way to gravel, then sand. Aside from the few scattered warehouses, the city spread out far behind us, with sand, mountains, and little to no vegetation in front of us.

Archer gripped my hand as he looked around. Not a person was in sight. Then he ran, tugging me until I caught up, letting him guide me up the mountain. Black rock gave way to more of a reddish-brown as we hit a peak. Archer stopped to take in our surroundings.

He pointed. "Lot's Cave, the entrance is over that way."

"You said we're not knocking on his front door though."

He shook his head. "Like I said, there are two other entrances, one for souls, which is too dangerous. The other is Persephone's entrance. Not many of us know about it, but she told me once." His cheeks turned pink.

I raised my brows. "Because she liked you."

"Not like that."

I stared him down.

He rolled his eyes. "Not like that when she told me. She wanted friends to visit. For a while, Hades was not keen on me seeing her."

"I wonder why," I teased.

He fumbled over his words. "She…she…uh, kind of liked me when we were kids, okay? We grew up together. It was only natural, but I never returned her feelings. Still, Hades had been a little possessive of her and who she was allowed to see in the beginning of their marriage. But she has been faithful to him and loves him. I never visited through this door. I'm going off a memory of thousands-of-years-old directions."

I grinned. "I just like seeing you squirm." I laughed and pulled him in for a kiss.

He pulled away quickly, looking at the sun starting to peek its rays above the horizon. "Let's hurry in case I can't find it at first."

I followed him down into a ravine, and we followed a winding natural path that looked like it had been carved by a long-ago dried up stream. It curved northward, according to his compass, almost directly behind where Archer had pointed to the "front" entrance. He stopped at a smooth-looking part of the mountain.

He just stood there, staring.

I whispered (not sure why, with no one around), "What are we doing?"

"Hold on," he said. The sun started to rise, the rays peeking over the cliff behind us, reminding me of Lucien's abilities. Archer sighed. "Almost missed it. Aios is still not used to this. The sun is rising too quickly. Athena did get the okay for us to enter this territory, so it's no god of theirs speeding it up." He walked along the wall, scanning where certain rays hit the surface. Then he stopped again.

I wanted to defend Aios since he was only eager to get his dad back, but he should've known better that any slip in detail could ruin the plan.

I took two steps to be by Archer's side and stared at the area of rock he was looking at. The sun's rays crossed over us upon the rock face. Golden letters appeared—in Greek of course—and I tried to translate, but it was ancient Greek. I didn't understand the first word before it vanished.

"What did it say?"

"Persephone's Gate. Enter at your own peril." He sighed and looked at me, as if to ask if I wanted to back out of it. He didn't dare voice it, because we both knew we had to do this no matter what.

I took up his hand in mine in affirmation that we would do this and do it together.

He pulled me in with one arm and kissed me hard. "I trust you. I'll follow your commands, but Callie, you must heed my warnings. There are dangerous things down here."

I nodded. He was right. I had to trust his advice as he promised to trust my council.

With a wary gaze, he placed his hand onto the wall. One moment, his hand was flat against a small hand-sized cavity in the stone; the next moment, inky blackness spread out from under his palm, like paper soaking up ink, until a huge archway stood before us. Archer's hand fell through the dark rock that was now apparently air.

I pushed my hand through (creepy cool, no, amazing).

Archer smiled at me despite the fact we were about to enter Hades. He loved it when I marveled over new godly things. "You remember the rules?"

I nodded. *No eating or drinking. Do not touch the water. Do not go near the soul gate. Don't talk to the dead without Hades's permission.* We had gone over it several times and the possible consequences, which was pretty much getting stuck there. If that happened, my baby would most likely never be born. Of course, I would never be stupid enough to break them.

He led the way and stopped a few steps inside. It was pitch black after the wall was back up. I touched it. "Will it open again?"

"At sunrise."

"We have to stay here all night?"

"Twenty-four hours, yes. Unless Hades opens it for us."

(*Not likely, if we were stealing a soul*, was left unsaid.)

I swallowed hard. That was a long time for me not to eat. I was not quite at the ravenous or morning sick stage yet, but I rarely went five or six hours without eating something. I would simply gorge myself later. We had gone over all of this, but remembering I could not eat made me hungry already.

After our eyes adjusted to the dark, we made our way down a rocky tunnel, taking our time because the ground was uneven, and I stumbled twice. Soon we came into a cavern that glowed with unearthly soft light as if the moon was the source. It was ghastly, depressing, but simultaneously beautiful. To our left, on the other side of two wide black rivers, stood many people—or shall I say souls—awaiting a boat. If my mythology was correct, they awaited the boatman Charon, who took the souls across the river to the Underworld. Two men and a woman were holding a clipboard and wore badges, looking very official. Fog drifted all around, making this feel so surreal. Archer put his finger to his lips to make sure I was quiet. We did not want to draw their attention. I didn't think they'd notice us anyway. The line was so long. Not that I knew how long it normally was, but my guess was the gap between death gods had caused a lag, and the epidemic was adding to their workload. When I saw a family of four, with young kids, I turned away, unable to bear it (or the guilt for bringing my unborn child into this place).

We walked past the line unobserved, the souls not even noticing us. That's when I realized we bypassed security.

Archer sighed and whispered, "Step one, success."

"Were they the three judges you were talking about?"

"Yes, they decide if the mortals go to Elysium or Tartarus."

"Mortals, so where would Lucien be?"

"He could be in the Fields of Mourning, where those who die cannot pass on without closure, usually from unrequited love, but after my brother was made to filter that better, I think it's more of a holding ground for those with unfinished business, ones who cannot move on until they come to terms with things. Lucien could be there. Or in the Asphodel Meadows, which is more likely."

"What are those?"

"We are not ever allowed to see it, so I don't know, but I'm pretty sure it's for those who have done evil and good, so they cannot be admitted anywhere. They cannot reach Elysium, but they also do not deserve Tartarus."

"Are they stuck, like forever?"

Archer shrugged. "Hades has many ghostly servants. I'm guessing they can reach Elysium after years of service? But...I think Hades keeps his precious collection of souls—mainly the gods—in his palace as his companions."

Twisted, but I felt bad for him—trapped with few companions, doing a job no one wanted. I hoped this would work, not just for Lucien's and our sakes but also for Hades's and Persephone's. "So...we will have to go through him?"

Archer nodded. "There is no way around that. You do not steal souls from Hades."

I hated to point out the obvious. "But that's exactly what we are doing."

"We are tricking him. It might seem similar to you, but to us gods, it is seen as more ethical. The person duped is to blame for not being wise enough, whereas stealing while they are unaware places blame on the thief."

Gods were weird (seriously).

Archer continued, "We will need to trick him, lie to him, and you promised me a foolproof bargaining chip, although you won't tell me what. He will not want to give Lucien up, such a precious soul for his collection." (So creepily twisted.)

"I'm sure it will work." I was asking Archer for a huge level of trust, and he was giving me that, which made me feel guilty about hiding the baby from him. At the same time, the vision of him attacking me terrified me, constantly being thrown forth to the forefront of my mind. After all, I confided in the only person I trusted wholly: Prometheus. He assured me nothing would happen to Philo as long as I abided by the rules. He agreed Archer knowing could ruin the mission, and he corroborated the vision about Archer's attack. It explained his snarky behavior toward Archer lately as being protective of me, but he insisted things aren't always as they seem. He could not believe the vision but could not explain it either. The prophecy was a poor excuse I was using to convince myself I was justified in omitting important things from my husband, but now was not the time. Regrets were for later.

We trudged on. I pulled out my phone and noted we had walked twenty minutes already, so we needed to gauge our time properly to get to the door by sunrise. There was no service underground, of course, as our journey slowly trekked downward.

After a few more minutes of walking, we came across a river. Aside from the lulling sounds of the water slapping along the banks, dogs were barking. They sounded far away as their echoes reverberated into the cavern at a low volume.

We crossed the river on a rickety wooden bridge. I was freaking out, not remembering which river was which or what they would do if I fell in. How could I forget? Then we crossed another. I felt awful, angry, and oppressed, wanting to lash out but knowing it was ridiculous. It was as if something was in the steam rising off the river. When we crossed the third river, of molten lava that spat out little geysers of steam and fire, I remembered them: Lethe, Styx, and this fiery Phlegethon. The Styx was hatred, and Archer had said falling into the Phlegethon—which looked obviously painful—would take you to Tartarus. I couldn't remember what the Lethe did.

Once we cleared the sweltering molten river, we found ourselves in a massive field that was full of long gray meadow grass and luminescent white flowers. I thought it might be the Asphodel Meadows, but not a soul was in sight. What dominated the field was a massive stately house of white stone that had a beautiful unearthly glow. It had a white picket fence around it with a gate, which was currently open. The barking I had heard earlier was much louder.

Archer stopped, took up my hand, and protectively pulled me into his arms. "Don't move."

I couldn't have if I wanted to. I was frozen in shock. Archer didn't seem afraid, his gorgeous face pensive and patient. That made me feel a bit better (very small bit). But the dog barking became deafening, and I heard snarls and snapping jaws. That was when I finally noticed them. The darkness moved ever so slightly in the swirling smokey forms of dogs. (Shadow dogs? Ghost dogs?). I was too freaked out to ask questions.

The forms encircled us, and we were trapped. Archer still did not seem fazed at all.

Then a female voice commanded "Halt!" That's when I saw the hooded form in front of us, dressed in all black, hard to discern from the darkness around her. She threw her hood back, revealing a pale, beautiful oval face with dark hair and eyes.

The dogs vanished or slunk back to somewhere—all I could tell was they were suddenly gone.

"Persephone." Archer bowed his head.

She gave him such a warm smile that I wanted to smack it off her face. "Eros."

Had Archer had told me the truth that he had only been with Psyche? Because the way Persephone's eyes roamed over him felt a bit invasive.

"This is my wife, Callie." Point to Archer, what a good husband. Jealousy dissipated (halfway).

Persephone's eyes darted to me, and then her features lit up. Okay, she actually seemed genuinely nice. She inspected me with an equally warm regard as she had for Archer. I didn't expect such a warm and friendly person in such a place. "My darling Pluto will be so happy to have visitors." It took me a second to remember Hades had been referred to as Pluto in ancient times. "Come, come."

Archer kissed my brow to reassure me things were fine, and I was safe, but I felt far from it as we followed her through the gate toward the house. The doors opened on their own, it seemed, until I saw the wispy ghosts opening them for us on the inside. A chill crept down my spine as I peered at the opaque outlines of what had been gods if Archer was right about Hades's staff.

We entered a foyer and then a parlor lit by antique-looking gas lamps. The floors consisted of black stone; if it didn't shine, I would feel as if I were walking on a void of darkness. The glimmer of the floor came from the white stone walls and ceiling that again illuminated our way. Still, it was so dark, I could hardly see.

Archer peered at me imploringly as he cocked his head toward Persephone, who led the way.

I gave him a confused look.

He tapped his temple and looked at her, then me pointedly.

(Oh! I got it.) I nodded as Persephone prattled on about the house and Hades's plans to add some light to the pool for her out back so it didn't appear like swimming in ink. I shut her voice out and pushed myself into her mind. It was way too easy, no barrier, her mind an open book. She was not simplistic in nature, but she simply never bothered to hide anything from anyone. She was a rarity, one of those honest and open people who don't bother with falsities. Or, she had not encountered a mind reader down here often enough to bother blocking her thoughts. She concentrated her mind on her speech, but when she went quiet as another door opened, her mind fixated briefly on her loneliness, her desire to have a baby, one she could not have with her husband in the Underworld. She would bear no other man's child.

The way her mind had "worded" (if in your brain, it's not actually words, right?) made me think he could not produce kids. I hoped it only meant because he was stuck down here, or both of them, where everything was dead. It made sense that life could not be created or be born where death reigned. The info drastically helped my bargaining chip.

I felt empathy with the Queen of the Dead, but I had to focus on being sneaky to get Lucien back. Archer squeezed my hand as another door opened for us. I gazed at Archer instead of the ghost servants. I gave him a smile and a wink. His shoulders seemed to relax. Good. I needed him on-point to distract them while I robbed minds of thoughts to use against them to get our way. I would not feel guilty. Lucien deserved his life back.

In the next room, Persephone halted once inside. The ghosts stopped us by stepping in front. There was a glow to the woman in front of me. Her face was forlorn and bored. She shimmered full of light.

I'm so tired. I launched a thousand ships, and for that, I have opened fifty times as many doors. When can I rest? I pray to you, Hades. Give me my rest.

I heard her thoughts. A ghost? A thousand ships must be Helen. This must be Hades's collection. My stomach soured. Where was Lucien?

"Darling?" Persephone chirped.

"Yes dear?" a voice asked inside. "Why are you smiling so widely?"

"We have visitors." Her excitement made me realize Archer was right. They weren't just lacking company down here. They were starving for it.

"Visitors?" Hades's tone was sharp, his chair scraping back, and then he was in the doorway suddenly. His concern dropped, and his face lit up. "Eros!" He grabbed Archer roughly by the shoulders into his arms, giving him a bear hug.

When he pulled back and inspected me, I finally got a good look at him. A splatter of unruly dark hair that reminded me of Lucien's, skin almost as pale as the white marble walls, were on a form that was tall and broad shouldered—Ares's height but less muscular. The strangest part was his eyes. They were…reflective (cat-like). I tried not to react to them, but it was hard not to stare. Now, I understood Prometheus's package that filled up most of my backpack.

"You," Hades purred. "The girl whom Eros would not do without, that started a war." He clapped his hands and then spread them wide. "The Battle of Liberty Island was the most fun I've had in ages, eons, really." He laughed and took up my hands in his, spreading them wide, and he made me twirl around. "Ah, forgive me for not seeing the amount of beauty I should to start a war. My wife, here, is all I can dream beauty could be. You are a close second, my dear." He let my hand go and winked.

Persephone rolled her eyes and whacked Hades in the shoulder, but she could not help but smile. "Don't let Aphrodite hear that."

Hades laughed, but then when it fell, he examined me again, meeting my gaze. "But…I admit there's something about you. A zing in your touch. Why is all of Olympia torn over you living or dying?" The "zing" he had given me felt of oppression, like a caged animal. He was on the brink of losing himself and his mind, being down here with the dead for so long.

Archer tensed. Hades's gaze darted over to him. He placed his hand on Archer's chest. "Protective, great-nephew? I understand. When one is poisoned by your arrow, they are hooked for life." Then he laughed thunderously, which echoed throughout the stone building (jovial-eerie). Then his face fell to a serious look.

31

THE IMMORTAL TRANSCRIPTS: GLIMMER

"What kind of goddess are you? And why does my god-for-nothing brother want you dead?"

CHAPTER 6

Archer

They were the last questions I wanted Callie to answer. Thankfully, she didn't, but she looked to me to answer. I had no idea what to say, and the silence stretched out between all of us. My great-uncle looked back and forth between us, his suspicion growing.

"Hades," Persephone chastised. "Could we at least entertain them before you give them the third degree?"

Hades crossed his arms, scrutinizing Callie. I tensed, feeling protective of my wife.

"Eros, relax." Hades grabbed my shoulder and shook it as if to force me to; his motion did the opposite. "This is a friendly visit. I am not *Zeus*," he hissed.

Would he be, though, after he learned what my wife could do for him? I sighed. There was no way around it, but I wasn't about to call her my freedom fighter in front of them. I could not bear to see the agony or rage Hades would go through if Callie couldn't free him as she had for Poseidon. This had to work—only we were basing things on an assumption and her and Prometheus's visions that I must trust although they refused to give me details.

Callie fidgeted. "I kind of don't know. I'm figuring it out. I'm kind of a mutt of three godly lines."

The duo of death froze, inspecting her anew.

Persephone pouted. "Athena had not said. I saw her in August."

I pulled Callie to my side in a loving embrace. "Athena had not figured it out until she found Prometheus. Lots of secrets none of us were privy to until recently."

Hades smiled. "My wife is right. Let's gather company and talk over a feast. It sounds like a story that needs time to tell. As always, there are certain times here to come and go, so you should enjoy yourselves while you're stuck." His reflective eyes gleamed. He longed for our company too much to let us go before sunrise.

I felt bad for him, yet it felt like a threat—he was in control, in power, and alluding to the fact he could keep us here. Only, could he? If Callie could breach the border—not that we were trusting that alone, in case she could not—he could not stop us.

"As you wish," I conceded. "At some point, not now, we need to make our peace."

Hades nodded. "I thought as much. Why else would anyone come here? We'll get to that later." Good, we had our cover set, and he would not be suspicious with our sudden visit not long after Lucien's death. The reality of our cover needing to happen crashed upon me, making my stomach sink, my throat go dry. My daughter, Hedone. I'd see her and have to let her go. Callie, her father.

I took a deep breath. I had to be strong for her, more so for Lucien. We had to save him.

Hades whispered something to a spirit, and it glided away. Then he motioned us to follow him. We went down a few hallways, my mind recalling the place as I saw it. I hadn't been here since the death of my brothers and sister many mortal-length lifetimes ago. We went out a door into a large courtyard jam-packed full of flowers, bushes, and ivy growing up the walls. The only clear space was a large table in the middle.

Persephone beamed. "My garden."

Callie told her it was beautiful. How pretty it would be in daylight, but in this dark place, devoid of atmosphere, they were beautifully eerie.

We sat at the close end of the table, Hades at the head, Callie and I across from Persephone, who was on his right.

Hades instantly got down to business. "My servant is retrieving the others. I will not deny them the joy of company, although Hypnos probably won't want to see you."

"Yeah, obviously." I had killed his brother Thanatos to save Callie.

"But before they get here, please tell me about your triple-godly wife, Eros."

I looked at Callie. Hades was a bit old-fashioned. No wonder. He was stuck down here while the world progressed around him. "My wife can speak for herself."

Taking my comment in stride, he focused on Callie.

"Well, I'm Greek, Norse, and Titan."

Hades slapped the table hard and laughed loudly. He had trouble stopping, which was creeping me out because I wasn't sure what was so funny. "My meticulous, controlling brother couldn't keep you all leashed in and marrying each other forever, could he? Sorry, it's not funny, really, but knowing my big brother messed up so bad is invigorating."

Persephone's brow wrinkled. "I'm confused. Who are your ancestors?"

Hades cocked his head, tapping his chin in thought. "I get the Greek-Titan connection, but Norse?"

"I don't. Zeus banned intermarriage."

Hades took his wife's hands in his. "The forever children you care for? One of them belonged to Prometheus and Athena. The other daughters who lived to almost adulthood moved on, but the littlest, she wanted her mother."

Callie shivered next to me, likely unnerved by the idea of spirit children stuck in the Underworld, allowing Persephone the children she could not have and them the parents they had died without. I rubbed Callie's arms, pretending I believed her to be cold.

Persephone frowned. "The maiden goddess? She never told me. What she must've gone through."

I nodded. "We were all duped."

Hades pressed on, "Norse?"

I admitted begrudgingly, "Apparently, that's where Psyche came from."

"She's Psyche's descendant? Oh, the irony." Hades laughed again and gasped "sorry" several times before he reigned it in.

I was trying to tamp down that Ares temper I had inherited. I had to play nice, even if he thought my love life was a joke.

"What are you goddess of, then?" Persephone asked.

"Err," Callie looked at me. Yeah, the freedom card was not what we should lead with.

"She can foresee some events, read minds, and some other things we are still unsure about." There. Not lying to them, just holding the bargaining chip close in case it wouldn't work.

"Read minds?" Persephone laughed, then eagerly asked, "Read mine."

Callie seemed bothered by the request, but then she stared at Persephone in concentration. "I already did. I know what you want foremost, and I think I might be able to help you with that." She spoke in coded language, so it was something private. I hated not knowing Callie's plans or thoughts, but I trusted her with my life.

Persephone laughed lightly. "That, I must admit, is as vague as an oracle. If you're referring to my desire to see the end of Zeus, the man who oppresses my husband, then you are spot on, but that is easy to guess."

"Wow, Persephone. When did you become so morbid?" I commented.

She laughed again, beaming like the sun shining in spring. I always liked how happy she was, exuberant, but a moment ago, she was cutthroat, not that I don't blame her.

Hades's gaze upon his wife almost shattered my heart. It was of remorse. It clicked together in my head. She had gotten this alter-ego due to staying with the god she loved, which brought her spirits down and enraged her to see his suffering. She was different from our youth when she tried to tag along with me.

"If I have my way, there will be no need for you to be morbid," Callie said. Again, it was coded. This time for me. If they were free, up out of this dark prison, they could be happy. Then again, my wife might be referring to some future event that made Zeus powerless or dead. I hated not knowing and, for the first time, wished I could read my wife's mind.

"That. That is something I long to hear about, but others approach." Hades clicked his fingers, and food was upon the table, all my favorites—divine smelling *paidákia* making my mouth water, and *loukoúmia* pulling at my sweet tooth. As he said, a few joined us down the table.

Lena walked in on the arm of Hypnos, both glaring daggers at me. My gaze instinctively shot away from Hypnos's droopy eyes. His face, his voice, everything about him made us sleepy. I looked down at my plate, but that was worse than hatred in my face. The temptation was strong, and my stomach rumbled.

"Archer," Lena greeted with a sneer. Her gaze shifted to Callie. She inspected her, and her face set into a steadfast glower, not greeting my wife at all.

Persephone rolled her eyes. Her kind nature would not do such a thing unless it was well deserved. Lena had been a grave mistake on my part. She should've never been made immortal. I would trust my wife's discretion for the last god-made punishment, of my "companion," if I was forced to fulfill the contract. She had chosen a great Death, far surpassing my sullen mistake, Lena. Sure, no one would love being in the Underworld, but she had the freedom to leave as Proteus's daughter.

Callie looked down at her plate to avoid the judgmental stares, making the same mistake I had. Her plate had a slice of pizza, a NY strip, glazed in what smelled like garlic-herb butter, a hefty portion of baklava, and a deli pickle wedge. Pickles? She picked up the pickle slice, her eyes intently focused on it. I elbowed her gently, and she shook her head and dropped it. Her gaze met mine as confused as I was.

"Do you like pickles?" I whispered. How did I not know this? I had never seen her eat one. In fact, I distinctly remember her offering me hers when we went to a deli early on in our relationship.

"No," she said. It felt like the truth wrapped in a lie. I did not know my wife anymore. Once we got through this, saved Lucien, there would be a reckoning. I'd get answers.

Her eyes darted to mine, worry etched upon her face. She could read my mind, how stupid of me. I pulled her in and kissed her temple to ease her anxiety. She needed to focus.

When I looked away, Hades was staring at my wife anew, his eyes meeting hers, and he winked. What in Hades—literally—was going on? She stared at her plate, her face paling. Then she stared at her hands that rested in her lap.

"Tell us about the war, Eros," Morpheus asked as he tucked into his plate.

Hypnos, his father, shot him a dirty look.

"What?" Morpheus shrugged. "A war could mean that maybe we get out of here. Dunno, see sunlight?"

"We are gods of sleep and dreams, Son, what would sunlight give us but less power?"

"Dunno. I'd like to see the sun once to know I don't like it at least."

His brothers nodded. Hypnos growled. Lena pushed her food around the plate, not eating. She was unhappy, and I felt bad for it, but why didn't she leave now and then?

"Now, this war. I was told Zeus got away, that he's *a head*." Hades made a poor joke. The whole table laughed, so Callie and I joined in.

"Please, tell us about the war. I'm raging to join," Styx stabbed a sausage on her plate with a too-large knife for dinner, and shoved the food into her mouth, cutting her lip and not even noticing. I was worried about in what way she would join. If Zeus swore on something to her, would she slaughter us with said knife?

Hesitantly, I told them about the war, and Callie joined in, telling them about her visions about how Lucien valiantly accepted his death. I finished up with the end of the battle.

"Literally, a head? That is all he is?" Eris, goddess of discord and jealousy spat out. Her dark eyes locked on mine before I yanked my gaze away, trying not to twitch from the sharp dagger of mental pain she threw my way. I blocked the images of Callie in other men's arms—Lucien's of course—because all she needed to plant was a seed of doubt, and your mind would take it over.

"Yes," I answered, wondering if freeing the Underworld in any way was prudent. We needed Hades, but what price would we pay for that? What price would mortals?

"Hera and Hermes. Escaped with his head," I explained.

Persephone scoffed. "Hardly a threat then."

I sighed. "I'm afraid that it isn't true, Persephone. My father is skilled in the knowledge of regrowing body parts, so he believes Zeus can grow his entire body back. With an unknown amount of ambrosia at his disposal, he could be back much sooner than we would estimate."

Hades put his fork down, seemingly annoyed. "Is that what you're here for, boy? To ask me again for help?"

"No," I said quickly. "We came to say our goodbyes."

He picked up his fork and pointed it at Callie. "Her? Yes. I understand that. She lost her father. But why, after thousands of years, are you finally going to take away my precious friends, Psyche and Hedone? You never cared—"

"I could not face it." My voice caught awkwardly in my throat, and I tried to swallow the lump forming. "Finding love again has made me look to the future, and I need to banish the past." I meant it, taking up Callie's hand and squeezing it.

"And we need to see Lucien," Callie said. "Say goodbye to him."

Hades's jaw tightened.

I squeezed her hand to be quiet. We had to tread lightly. I took over to spare her Hades's wrath. "He sacrificed himself for us. It must be done to let him pass on."

Hades's stormy eyes glared into mine. "What if we do not want him to pass on?"

"The sunshine has been a magnificent help to me. Although my Pluto can't bear the light, I cannot let him go." Persephone pouted.

How selfish. How absolutely disgusting of her to say such things. I stood before I realized my action. Callie peered up at me, frightened but nodding she would stand by me no matter what.

"I cannot sit here and pretend what you said was okay, Kora." I used her childhood nickname, which made her peer down to her hands in self-admonishment. "Apollo is my best friend, more than that. He is my uncle, my confidante, my family. I will not let him suffer some fate of being a lightbulb for your garden for eternity."

Hades stood, anger rippling through him.

Damn it, my love for my friend was about to mess this majorly up. I couldn't backpedal now. If we failed, Lucien deserved much better than this.

Persephone stared at her plate, her empathy winning—I hoped. I did not like admonishing such a kind goddess, but since her taste of revenge upon Zeus, she seemed different. I hoped my wife could free the two of them. They needed freedom more than anyone else. They didn't deserve this fate. Before Callie, it never entered my mind that my great-uncles could be free.

"Sit down and *eat*, winged one, before I lose my temper," Hades ground out, his eyes dark, reflective, like fires behind his pupils burned with a million dreams of vengeance.

"I cannot. I want to say my goodbyes, and we will not eat. We do not plan on staying long, and eating would prohibit us from leaving. We have a war to fight up there. I want closure in case the worst should happen to us in that war. This is why we are here. If you will not give my dearest friend in the world the permission to pass on, I cannot stop you, but it is our right to ask for our own closure and for you to fulfill that." I had to remind him of his own rules.

Persephone tugged his hand to get him to sit down. Growling, he took the advice of his wife and waved his hand, making our plates disappear, but not the others.

Callie sighed with relief.

I sat and kissed her temple, whispering, "I will get us a feast fit for the gods after we leave."

She smirked and rolled her eyes at my lame joke.

"You'll wait until we've finished dining, I hope?" Hades said, his tone softening. "These things are best done without an audience."

I nodded, the lump forming my throat. I could not do this, but I had to. Not just to get to Lucien, but...I had to let my daughter go. I had to let her be at peace. It was something I had thought about for more than five-hundred years, that bothered me, that I knew I had to do. Every time, my strength faltered, and my rage at my ex for putting our child in danger and getting her killed had stopped me. How can a father say goodbye forever to the last shred of his baby girl in the world, his only child he ever had? Love was not built to lose it. This would break me.

CHAPTER 7

I clutched Archer's hand tightly in mine—too tightly—but he reciprocated. His jaw was set. He did not look at me as we followed Hades, and his Adam's apple kept bobbing. He was a ball of nerves and emotions as much as I was. How was I supposed to say goodbye to my father? I already had in the worst way, seeing him die (literally Death taking his soul). Now, because he had unfinished business, I had to set him free. It was too soon. The wounds were raw. Yet I wonder how hard it would be for my husband. Surely old healed wounds would bleed much worse when reopened.

I squeezed his hand. He peered over at me, a sad smile toying on his lips. I had given him comfort in our mutual understanding, and his smile bolstered me. I took a deep breath, rolled my neck, and mentally told myself I was a goddess who could overcome anything.

Hades stopped and turned into a room that was not much more than a small carved cave of obsidian rock that gleamed only from a dim light in the corner.

"One at a time or together?" Hades asked, his tone gentle and eyes soft. For the god of the Underworld and dealing with death, I thought he'd be desensitized to grief. Instead, he seemed to understand and feel what I felt acutely. I might've read his mind to get that nugget, but knowing he genuinely cared about the souls he looked after and those who lost them was comforting.

Archer sighed out a ragged breath, his hand still in mine. "Together. Her father, Psyche, and my daughter."

I nodded. He should make his peace while I made mine, and then we should face Lucien. I slipped out my phone to check the time. We still had over twenty hours to waste if we waited for sunrise.

"As you wish." Hades's voice was merely a whisper.

Dim light appeared in front of us. Three small orbs elongated and brightened into beings. My father's form from when he had been healthy, stood in front of me, devoid of color but made up of pulsing light. He was the very image I remembered of my father. He had been fit, no grays, so much younger, when he took me to Mt. Olympus. The start of all this.

"Dad." I could hardly breathe the word out, but he heard me.

"Callista." His voice was full of strength and joy. I pushed away the thoughts of the brittle weakness it had the last time I'd heard it, what the disease had done to it and the rest of his body. I would remember him like this, not the man drained of life by Zeus's torture.

I reached out to touch this healthy version of my father, longing to see that he was real, but my hand went through him, momentarily dispelling the image before it recollected.

He spoke because I could not. "I could not move on. I had to know how you were doing. I was afraid the news, what I hid from you, could hurt you. That was not my intention. I just wanted to protect you."

I shook my head. "I wasn't ready to hear it. I had to see it, experience it with my own eyes." Tears started forming, and I cursed them for blurring my sight. I wanted to drink up this memory of him, for it would be my last. "I'm good, Dad, great actually. You brought me…home."

He sighed, his image flickering and almost going out. "Dad, wait!"

He illuminated again. "I'm so glad. It was all I ever wanted for you when I started to learn what you were. You have your family now. They will protect you. Promise me, we will never meet again, or at least until the end of the world since you will flourish forever."

"I'll never see you again," I forced myself to say, to placate him, to promise, but it broke my heart to say it aloud.

He winked. "I hope not." He started to flicker again. I needed to let him go. "Callie?"

"Yes, Dad?"

"You were my greatest discovery. Ten of Athena's shields could never compare to what you were in my life. I love you, always."

Before he blinked out forever, I raced to repeat him. "Love you, Daddy, always."

He smiled and closed his eyes. "Ellen," was merely a whisper on the breeze as he faded away completely to meet my mother.

I wanted to fall to pieces, but I gazed over to my husband, who was running his fingers through a brilliant specter of a young woman. His eyes were brimming like mine.

"Páppa, I love you," she whispered as she faded away. Hedone.

Archer stared at the ground, ignoring the other spirit. I took up his hand in mine, lacing my fingers through his, hoping to bolster him to face Psyche, although I myself was intimidated (like who wants to ever meet *the* ex?).

His eyes met mine, and he pulled me in, his forehead resting on mine. His eyes bore into mine. *Give me strength, Callie. I can bear no more.*

On my tiptoes, I whispered on his lips, "The hardest part is over," then kissed him.

Someone cleared their throat. It wasn't Hades, who remained behind us, staring at the ground, his face solemn, but an impatient spirit who had her arms crossed and her glare set on Archer.

"Psyche," Archer greeted, his voice devoid of emotion.

"Don't let me interrupt you. Is this our new piece?" Her eyes scrutinized me up and down, finding whatever faults she could fathom. Great. She was one of *those* exes.

Archer went in hardheaded. "My wife, immortally."

Psyche's eyes were wide, and she unfurled her arms, but her fists were clenched. (So, the conceited and jealous type—*I don't want him, but how dare he commit more to another.*)

"What possible unfinished business do you and I have, Psyche? I have forgiven you for getting our daughter killed. What more can you ask of me?" His voice was cutting, and Psyche's stance faltered, her anger giving way to despair. I felt bad for her at that moment, the truth not allowing her to keep up her false front. She had put her daughter in harm's way and gotten her killed.

When Psyche did not speak, he continued, "I want to start afresh. I should have come sooner for Hedone, but you? I don't understand why you are still here."

Psyche met his gaze. "I had a child with a mortal—"

"His descendant is right here," Archer pointed at me.

Psyche threw up her hands flippantly. "Never letting me finish a sentence. Oh, you haven't changed a bit." Her eyes darted to me. "Does he do this to you too?"

Archer's jaw clenched, trying not to rise at her bait. I ignored her and squeezed his hand, hoping my presence would give him patience.

"As I said," Psyche's catty tone continued. "I had a child, and he had the line you found. But he had an indiscretion, a child outside his marriage."

Archer's brow wrinkled. "Why does that matter? Callie is not here only because of you. How is this child different from any other demigod?"

She huffed out, showing her short temper at his important and kindly made question. I was starting to see their divorce hadn't been solely because they weren't suited for each other, but that Archer's description of her had been kinder than the specter in front of us. My curiosity getting the best of me, I pushed into her mind, since I had read Helen-spirit's prior, and immediately wished I hadn't.

Psyche had been one of those miserable people in life that leeched onto others to bring them down. She was full of hate and envy, her thoughts about Archer terrible and untrue. I could not imagine my husband being *a selfish brute* who *only cared about himself*. Other insults like Mama's boy and being a terrible lover were bashing around in her mind; although he and his mother were pretty close (I'll give her that one) she was way off about the other. In between, she thought amazing things about herself, how she deserved better, how she could control and manipulate Archer—no, everyone she met. I left her mind the moment she started mentally insulting me. She was way off, not even knowing anything about me. Sociopath came to mind.

She glared at me. "Hide your thoughts better, second choice. Yours are almost as unkind as mine."

Archer's confusion shot over to me.

I shrugged. "What? She's not a nice person," I muttered. "Her thoughts are way worse."

Psyche looked as if she'd attack me in a full out catfight if she had a body to do so.

Hades coughed, but there was a tinge of laughter he was trying to hide. *Yes, Callie, I will not miss Psyche's company*, his mind told me.

"To answer questions, you imbeciles, my descendants somewhere down the line crossed with Apollo's."

"Apollo's?" Archer repeated.

"Are you deaf?"

"Look," I stepped forward, having enough of her rudeness toward my husband. "You might've treated him one way in life, and he did not object, but you sure as hell aren't going to treat *my* husband that way in death."

Psyche went quiet and rigid, shock slipping over her features. "She's good for you," she told Archer. "She has a spine. Nothing less from my stock." It was her way of creating peace (with conceit). She started to flicker, the sign they were closing their business and moving on.

"Get to the point." I was done with her. At least she helped our moods, making Archer and I go from crying to annoyed in minutes.

"One of this family is a powerful seer, an oracle. Death is coming for Apollo's current oracle as we speak. This descendant of mine will likely gain the Delphi line. Don't let Zeus find out about her. Not for my sake, but for all of yours as well. She is the same as your wife, a blended-line demigod."

Now was not the time to point out I was a goddess, although it would be the final insult for her to know I'd live forever—another thing she took for granted and had lost. I couldn't (although I desperately wanted to) because it was catty, and I was raised better than that.

"I promise that someone in my family will see to it if I cannot," Archer responded.

Psyche flickered, but I still could see her less-than-impressed sneer. "Shirking off a promise to your *first* love?"

I took a deep breath, knowing it was me she was trying to irritate.

Archer shifted his weight, a clear indication he was losing patience. "There's a war going on, Psyche. Zeus wants us dead. I cannot promise what I might not be able to deliver. But we will tell my family, and someone will find and watch over her. That I promise. I'm not shirking but sharing the duty."

"You and your family, thick as thieves. How does that serve you, now?"

"I tire of this, Psyche. I was never a fan of your games."

"I tire of this as well," Hades muttered. Then his voice became more commanding. "He promised what he could. What more peace do you need, woman?"

Psyche stared at her hands, her shoulders slumped. Her posture and mood entirely changed, and I finally understood her as her thoughts became clear to me. She wasn't allowed to move on to the right place if she didn't swallow her pride.

"I…" She took a deep breath. "I'm sorry, Eros. I'm so sorry for my foolishness. For not realizing how what I thought had been boring was actually steadfastness, that I didn't understand unconditional love. I abused your kindness. I got our daughter killed."

Archer held her gaze. His thoughts vibrated with the rage of Ares, the compassion of his deep love, and he felt so much pity. "I forgive you, Psyche. Go in peace, and care for my daughter in Elysium."

"I will," she whispered as she vanished in flickers as my father had.

I leaned into the arms of Archer, who let out a ragged breath. We did not move for a moment, staring at the dark stone, unable to process what we had just gone through. I felt drained (mentally and physically).

"I had a room prepared for you. Would you like to retire?" Hades asked kindly.

We needed Lucien. We had to get him and get out of here, but I was exhausted. Could we get out without sunrise was the question. I felt the impulse to try, to get this over with. "I want—"

"Yes please." Archer gently squeezed my arm as if to insist he'd lead these next moments.

I wanted to protest, but Hades nodded and led the way. I gave Archer a wide-eyed *What are you doing?* stare.

He tapped his head, so I pushed into his mind. *No matter how strong your powers might be, can we leave before dawn, before Persephone's gate opens? We need rest, my love, strength.*

LISA BORNE GRAVES

I hadn't thought of that. The problem with visions was that time was indiscernible. I would trust him and wait. Because if we could not get out... and because we both just went through grief all over again. It was enough. Stealing Lucien's soul from the god of the Underworld would have to wait. I was terrified about what I planned to do. I didn't know what gods to pray to for help.

CHAPTER 8

Akila

I finished unpacking the last few items. Polly refused to help, sulking on the couch about the move. Why? Who knew? She said silly things about friends and such, but her schooling had always been online, and we rarely intermingled with mortals. She'd learn soon enough—within this century—mortals would die, and the only people you could rely on were other gods. Having been a mother for the first time long ago, I did not bother with a lecture. She must learn this on her own.

These mortals milled about the city like nothing was wrong. Sickness was coming for them like a shadow stretching around the world—if it wasn't here already. Like the many plagues I had witnessed, my daughter had never seen something like this. Polly was safe. I was safe. Many more could be, if could get Apollo on this side of the Earth. The world needed its healer gods. I could not explain my feelings. So many regrets threw my thoughts, my feelings, into disarray. I needed balance; I *was* balance.

Polly was also safer here in New York, masked by the Greek "scent." No one in my family knew of her existence, except Thoth. I hadn't returned home to Egypt since Polly was born, just in case. My problem was how my family would react and how I could explain it. I didn't know how it occurred in the first place. My false security that Apollo's father prevented such things was how I ended up with Polly. But how I adored her for being that special keepsake of her parents' love.

Yes, it was a good decision to come here for the duration of my daughter's young adulthood, masked from my people but, more importantly, Zeus. He might pick up on his granddaughter. That's what this was all about. A goddess he was scared of. I searched for the truth but could not find it—about anything Greek. How lies, omittances, and falsity would triumph in the Greek sector until Apollo's eldest could bear the weight of all those powers.

The world was not ready. When truth dies, so does civilization.

I needed to act quickly to save Apollo if it could be done. Had he been Egyptian, I would've forced Anubis's hand to save him. The god who led souls to Duat, our Underworld, was a good friend since I weighed souls' worth for him and Osiris, who ruled over them in the afterlife. Instead, I would have to deal with Hades. I needed the Greeks to get to him, though, which meant explaining Polly.

I would believe it was possible to save him until it was not. So was the theory of Polly's life. Greek gods and Egyptian gods could not mate, so it had been said...until her. I would believe in the unbelievable.

Polly slammed her books down one by one on her desk in the other room. I ignored her preteen moods, normally, but right now, the girl's melancholy reminded me of her father's: soul-crushing poetry and a propensity to be drawn to those in need of healing. I wanted to heal my child's superficial grief about living in New York, but bringing her father back was the only thing I could think of. It was time to treat her like an adult so she would trust me in this move. It was time to let Polly grow up—or begin to—treat her as a teammate rather than I being the dictator.

"Polly!" I called. "Come here." I left the kitchen of the two-bedroom apartment that had cost a fortune to rent. With the epidemic, work looked like an unlikely possibility to offset it. I'd have to find an online job.

She stomped over the hardwood floors and plopped on the couch with all the drama a twelve-year-old diva could cook up. "*What?*"

I pressed down my annoyance at her tone and called upon my patience. "I need to tell you now why we are here. It's going to be difficult to deal with, but I think you're old enough now to know."

Her face lit up with excitement. She leaned forward. "Is it about my dad?"

I was shocked at her change in mood and how she guessed it. "What makes you say that?"

"You never tell me about him. You've told me about my immortality, who you are, your family—who I can't see. I just thought the move was because of him and maybe you were letting me meet him."

"Then, why are you so mad about the move?"

"Because, if I'm going to live forever, I want to spend as much time with my friends as I can. What, when I'm like thirty, it'll start getting noticeable I don't look that age, won't it? I'm not stupid. Like you pretending to be my sister now. It's because you're too young-looking to pass as my mother. I'll likely never see my friends again."

I took a deep breath. "That is true. This is something you'll have to get used to."

"Why now? See, Mom, I expected this, but not until others would question your age. You're good with hair, makeup. You could probably age up until mortals get wrinkles. Why now if not about my father?"

I sat down next to her. "Yes. It is about your father. As you know, he was a god. A Greek god—something not accepted because it isn't supposed to happen. He and I loved each other very much, but being from different places, it could not be. So now, I've brought you to his people, Polly. I hope for protection and acceptance from them, but I hope for much more—"

"Where is my dad? You said 'his people.' Where is he?"

There was nothing I could say to my own child but the truth. Any other answer would make her resent me later in life. "He died."

"You said he was a god."

"Gods can die. I've told you this before."

"You…you waited until he was dead for me to meet his family? Why?"

"Your protection. We've been through this. You haven't even met my family. I hope the Greeks can help us. I hope, maybe, I can help them. Gods put off a 'scent,' for lack of a better word. As you grow into your powers, you'll be sensed by others—both Greek and Egyptian—so I had to make a choice soon. Since the Greeks are divided and we've lost your father, I thought it best you could meet his family, be protected by the sector that protects another being like you."

Polly bit her nails. I suppressed the urge to tell her to stop. It had been a habit of mine in childhood that I had outgrown at some point in my long years. I was raising my daughter opposite my upbringing or even that of my first daughter's. These times were so vastly different.

"So, they cloak me, and you cloak them?" I was so proud of her quick turn of mind, her focus on facts and truths rather than the reactionary emotions most preteens get.

How much to tell her though? "Good deduction."

The light praise was worth her smile.

"I want to speak with the Greeks to see if there is a chance—do not get excited about this, because it rarely has worked and might not be possible—but I want your father back, alive. Too late, I've realized protecting you deprived him of you, and you of him. I have many regrets and do not need your censure for this. I feel the pain of my poor decisions acutely right now."

Instead of lashing out for my massive mistake of keeping daughter and father from each other, she surprised me by touching my cheek. "Mom, I have no anger. I have plans. Can we meet the Greeks tomorrow?"

I nodded, so confused about what my daughter was and how she was suddenly the adult in our dynamic. My child definitely cooked up an impromptu plan, one I was not ready for.

LISA BORNE GRAVES

I felt ridiculous and in danger. I was standing outside of the first doorway from the elevator on the top floor of our building. The whole floor was owned by the same person, vacant until recently, according to the doorman. It was a big deal since some were purchased a hundred years ago and rented out until slowly the owner started not renewing leases. Apartments were left vacant and paid for, for over ten years. A bunch of young people lived up there, some old couples complained. Moved in overnight.

Dressed as a Girl Scout, although I hardly knew what they were, as I'd rarely graced America in modern times, my daughter knocked on the door with a wagon full of cookies we bought from a local food store in bulk this morning. This was her idea, and I had no better way to break the ice, so I complied, even when Polly "borrowed" a girl's uniform that was on display to explain how the kids weren't there to sell them because of the approaching epidemic. I was definitely making her drop it off at the nearest Girl Scout Office after this ruse with the Greeks.

The first door she knocked on, a middle-aged man answered. I tried to hide my confusion, but he seemed an observant type. Perhaps a demigod? He didn't look Greek, but that rarely mattered when you could mix among any culture of mortals.

"Hi. I'm Polly of Girl Scout Troop 341. Would you like to buy some Girl Scout Cookies?" My daughter was an admirable liar for the product of two truth gods.

The man leaned out the door and looked down the hallway. I followed his gaze to see a door pop open. They had overheard us.

My spine tingled with worry.

"Yes," the man said nervously. "Perhaps, you wait here, and I will talk to my friends, get an order for you ready. Hang on. He went inside and came back out his keys, shutting his door behind him. "Where's your form?"

"I don't have one." Polly shrugged. "My sister is just helping me sell the extras we ordered."

"Ah. I'm surprised the doorman let you in with the no-soliciting rules, but we are glad. We love cookies. I know everyone on this floor too. I'm sure they'll take all of those off your hands."

My daughter squealed with delight. I was seriously thinking about sending her to drama school for this level of acting talent she was showcasing.

I was happy to have this guide to meet her family, but his no soliciting comment made me worry. "We live on the fourth floor. Recently moved in. Please don't call down. I promised her sales and went to the top, hoping to bother only a floor or two before I cut her off."

49

"No worries. It's fine. I'm Raphael Ortega. Pleased to meet any neighbor of mine."

I followed him past a doorway, toward the god who had his head at the door, inspecting us with a curious expression.

"Are they not home?" Polly asked, pointing to the door we were skipping.

The mortal laughed. "Aren't you an entrepreneur? Good eyes."

I was starting to like this mortal, Raphael.

Raphael sighed. "No one lives there, sadly. It's rented for storage at the moment until the owner's family decides what to do with it." The man seemed down about it. He knew Lucien; he must. This was his place or where they kept his things. I wanted to blurt out a million questions, but the wrong comment at a fragile "invasion" of their territory could ruin everything. I trusted my daughter more than myself at this point.

Polly sighed. "Was he a friend? You sound sad." My daughter was becoming a con artist, which was destroying my moral code. I'd let it go, for Apollo, for my wrongs of hiding the truth from him.

Raphael smiled at her. "I knew him, but not well. Does that matter? When you meet someone and they pass away, it hurts."

My eyes teared up, and I looked away. I could not keep myself poised, in character for my child. I longed to hear his voice, his touch, his songs and words. I was failing her.

Raphael took up my arm. "Are you okay?" His face was full of concern.

I wiped my eyes, steadying myself.

"I lost someone recently. I'm sorry."

Raphael let go of me and offered me his arm like a gentleman. "My friend was important to everyone on this floor. We are in mourning. Cookies might be a comfort."

"Cookies?" the man still gawking at us said. "Over here first!"

Polly hurried to the door.

Having Raphael's full attention and with Polly occupied, I pressed for more information. "What was your friend's name?"

"Lucien," Raphael said quietly.

Light. Of course, we gods went for meaning in every choice of name. After a while, it became a fun challenge to reinvent ourselves.

There were two gods in the next room, whom Polly was taking money from and handing over boxes. A lot of boxes, twenty of them. One god appeared kind, and the other leered at my body. Neither looked like Apollo.

I was halfway to making my money back on this ruse.

The next door, a strikingly beautiful woman opened the door, her face full of tension. It was too soon, yet I wanted to help them not need to grieve, but how to bring it up? Her eyes lit up at the cookies, and she called over her shoulder. "Chase! Girl Scout Cookies! Come."

Before I realized what was happening, the door was thrown open, and the god had his hands on my throat, pinning me against the wall across from the doorway. He had no care to hide his immortal strength. He knew what I was.

Polly screamed, "Mom!" and leaped upon his back. If he hurt her...

"Who are you, and what do you want, Immortal?"

Raphael gasped. The pretty goddess started screeching for him to desist, and she gently peeled my daughter off her husband's back and pushed her toward the mortal, clearly a servant of the gods. He flung a protective arm out in front of her, his eyes worried. A good, honest man full of truth and kindness. Polly was safe.

I turned my attention to the god glaring in my face, holding me immobile with his unbelievable strength. God of war. I could feel it. He must be... "Ares," I pleaded.

His hand faltered. His wife's hands, Aphrodite's, peeled his fingers off my throat. Their family tree I had studied came back. Polly's half-uncle and aunt. I could find help here, but was my daughter's Greek blood enough? "I come in peace."

"Please. I'm sorry. Come in. He will not harm you. I promise. *Right*, Chase?" Her tone commanded.

His hands released me. "Sorry," he murmured. "We have to be careful, and I don't trust many others." He looked over at Polly. "I'm sorry, so sorry. Are you okay?"

Polly was shaken, but she nodded. She held Raphael's arm as we entered. I felt both scared and relieved.

The door closed behind me. I stayed near it. "We have something in common, then. I do not trust you, war god, especially after that." I rubbed my neck.

His lips twitched as if he wanted to smile at my comment. Tall, broad shouldered, with brown hair in a ponytail, he was a formidable form. His eyes were a buttery hazel, but their intensity was off-putting.

His wife was beautiful by American standards; slender yet busty, blonde-haired and blue-eyed. "Have a seat, I guess?" She fidgeted and then sat down. "You came here for a reason, I assume?"

Raphael led Polly to the couch and sat down with her, murmuring, "I'm sorry. I just thought they were selling cookies."

The door opened, making me jump, and I sat rigidly on the arm of the sofa next to my daughter. Two more gods came in. "Everything all right?" The gods from the hallway with the huge cookie appetite entered, a box in hand, already eating them. The one was clearly related to Aphrodite. I didn't recall her entire love entourage, but Lucien spoke of Eros often. I wondered if this was him, and if Lucien had ever told him about me.

"Everything is fine," Aphrodite replied. "It's fine, Raphael. She has a child with her. No mother would endanger her child by attacking other gods—not a good one at least." The last part was muttered. Her absentminded touch to her abdomen revealed she was pregnant, so it wasn't an insult toward me.

Ares crossed his arms, inspecting me. "Fair play, but you haven't answered my questions. Who are you, and what do you want?"

I took a deep breath. "I am Ma'at, and this is my daughter, Apollinaria, but we go by Akila and Polly."

It took a second for it to click. Then they all stared at Polly, which made her uncomfortably look down at her hands. The name was obvious. Everyone turned their attention to Ares—seemingly in charge at the moment—whose face softened, just a fraction, as he gazed upon Polly. Aphrodite's eyes went wide.

Ares came over and gently tilted Polly's face up to get a good look at her. "She has my brother's eyes." Then he went and sat down across from us with his wife. "I see my brother kept secrets from his own family."

Aphrodite frowned. "And one of his best friends."

Guilt flooded me. I had to give them the entire truth. "He didn't know. I never…" my emotions were getting the best of me, but I pressed the pain out of my wavering voice. "Only one god knows about Polly. The rest of my family still doesn't. I had to protect her. I thought to seek him out when her powers started, in case she took after him rather than me. You see, I never heard of children from two cultures. I thought it wasn't possible. Then I heard about this goddess you are protecting, the war, and then…Apollo's death."

Ares tilted his head. "So, you came here instead of your people, for what? Protection?"

I nodded. "To protect Polly, yes. There is something I wanted to do, and as your wife pointed out, I cannot put my daughter in danger. I want to strike a deal with Anubis and Osiris to see if they will negotiate with Hades to free Lucien's soul. It's a moot point, though, if his…remains are gone." My heart was pounding in anticipation and dread of their answer.

Ares exchanged a look with his wife, and then that intense gaze was back on me. Her face gave me no indication of her feelings. "Who did you hear all this from?" she asked.

Why wouldn't they just tell me! "What?"

Her face now seemed sympathetic toward my anxiety. "He is preserved. Now, which Greek leaked the information that he died?"

They were suspicious. I didn't blame them. The Greek sector was in pieces, and surely both sides were in desperate need of allies and what a spy could do for them.

"I am a goddess of truth, among other things. I'm choosing to be transparent with you. I was once friends with Artemis. She discovered her brother's and my relationship by happenstance, the second time—there were many." I was having a hard time framing this for my daughter's ears. Artemis had caught us in medias res by storming into his bedroom unannounced. Befriending her was how I was able to keep the relationship secret.

Ares's jaw tightened. "She is an enemy of ours."

I nodded. "I know. She seemed too happy in her texts about her brother's death and thought—because she doesn't know Polly exists—I'd find closure in it. I am not on her side. I'm on his side, so yours."

"If she didn't know about this child, who does, the one god you say?" Ares asked.

"My ex-husband, Thoth. He also knew about the death. News travels fast, I'm afraid. He has helped me keep this secret, supported me, but he doesn't want involvement in this other than protecting my secret. You are asking good questions, but I have one for you: how many goddesses like Polly and this girl you are protecting are there?"

Ares shrugged. "We know rough dates of when they could've been born if they are Greek descendants, and we know how. There is no way to easily trace them to know."

I appreciated him explaining it, but his vague answers spoke of distrust.

I pressed for an alliance. "Obviously, we can ask each other a million questions, but I need to know if you'll let me help get Apollo back. I would have to involve Anubis and Osiris, our gods of death."

Ares sighed, battling over a decision, his eyes probing mine. "We are already on it. I don't trust you yet for particulars, but we are in the middle of a mission to get him back. If we fail, it's your turn, and we'll support you, but we feel confident."

A huge weight lifted off my shoulders, and Polly perked up. "My dad is coming back?"

Ares shifted uncomfortably, his eyes flickering from her to me, unsure of what to say. "We hope so, sweetheart. If we fail, your mother can try. We won't give up. Of that, I assure you," he diplomatically said. Then to me he said, "Would you like to stay? We have so many questions as you must too?"

THE IMMORTAL TRANSCRIPTS: GLIMMER

A god of war offering me an olive branch? Strange indeed.

Polly bounced on the couch, excited. "Can you tell me about my dad?"

"Of course." Aphrodite smiled at Polly. "First, I need some cookies."

"I'm in," one of the other gods said while he pilfered the pantry, pulling out other snacks.

"Same." The other was in the refrigerator and grabbing cups.

Before I knew it, I was reminiscing about Apollo with Greeks over chips, cookies, and beverages. I didn't know if this odd situation was a good one, but I knew doing nothing would be worse. Hope sprang inside me, and for the first time since I had heard about his death, I felt I might see him once again. I wasn't sure how I'd feel when I saw him. Obviously joy and relief for Polly's sake, but Apollo and my relationship had been fiery in both good and bad ways. Not understanding one's own heart was an awful flaw. I would need to tread lightly.

CHAPTER 9

Archer

In our room, Callie slept. She was exhausted. I was too since it was so dark, I'd hardly slept the night before from anxiety, and my body and brain wanted to sleep after such emotional exchanges. It was only early evening, according to my phone. I was a live wire of nerves considering what we would do the next morning. The fact Callie was out cold worried me. The fevers were gone. She was healthy and immortal. Freya's irritating stabbing act had proved that in Iceland. So why was she sleeping as if Hypnos induced it?

I set an alarm and lay down with her, trying to relax, and I, too, drifted off. I woke up at some point from hunger pangs. I dug my phone out of my pocket: five AM—a half hour before my alarm. Sunrise was in less than two hours. I gently woke Callie.

She shot up as if having a bad dream, then pulled me close when she realized where she was and who she was with. We held each other and barely spoke. She didn't want to share her plan and absentmindedly kept touching the backpack she had brought. What miracle was inside to help us? I didn't know, nor did I pry. If she and Prometheus insisted my ignorance was necessary in this situation, I would trust them—well, her to be honest. Callie was my soulmate. She would never do anything to hurt me. This was the level of trust I had never had with Psyche. Just being in the room with her spirit and Callie by my side showed me how I had erred in my youth, chosen someone so wrong, unworthy of the amount of love I could give. Callie basked in it and grew stronger.

Her fingers weaved between mine. "I love you." Why was there a darkness in her eyes as she said that?

"Is something wrong?"

Callie shook her but then nodded. "I don't know."

"Talk to me," I pleaded, pulling her face to meet mine as I attempted to kiss her sadness away.

"After. I promise." Her dark, glistening eyes almost broke me.

"I'll make you swear that on the Styx so you have to," I teased.

She laughed and shoved me playfully. I was dying to know what was troubling her but knew better. Nothing could distract us from saving Lucien.

55

Except her kisses did exactly that. Reciprocated by mine. And then we were past the point of stopping, with zero cares about anything but being in each other's arms.

We dressed with much lighter hearts and pure love between us. I should've been nervous as we sought out Hades to say "goodbye" to Lucien, but I was fluttering in the sensations of love. We were now cutting the time to dawn close, though.

When I saw Hades approaching us at the end of the hall, his face stern, the confidence of love's wings started to dissipate. "What's the plan?" I said in a muttered whisper that even immortal ears would not pick up from the end of the hall. "We can't look at him."

"You're Orpheus's lyre." She slipped her hand into my pocket in a playful gesture, but she gripped my phone.

Ah, we were going to reenact the "myth." As Hades approached, I slipped my phone out as if to check the time and slipped my thumb onto the Music app to have it on the ready.

"My, you two look refreshed," Hades greeted.

"I slept well, thanks," Callie said.

"We have to go, Uncle, but we wanted to say our goodbyes to Apollo as we had requested."

Hades crossed his arms. "You wait for dawn, when he is strongest? What are you up to, little love god?"

"Nothing. I thought not to trouble you as Persephone's Gate will be open for a little while. I figured you're busy and didn't want to make you have to open the border for us."

Hades's eyes narrowed on us.

"He's being kind. It's my fault." Callie looked down to her feet, her face somber. "I could not say goodbye to another loved one after my father." Callie looked up, meeting Hades's suspicious glare with brimming eyes.

I pulled her protectively to me. He frowned, sympathy in his eyes. How hard was this for him, day in and day out? Watching the dead suffer until they moved on—some never doing so.

"I understand." He sighed. "Lucien is important down here. He's brought joy to my wife, the likes I have not seen in ages. Obviously, a nature goddess needs her sunlight. I cannot part with him, not yet. You can say your peace, but I will stop you if you let him move on."

"No," Callie said. The stubborn tone told me she would not yield to whatever Hades might propose. What was she up to? She was almost crying. If we didn't want him to pass on, and she was acting like she did...damn it, she was good. She was conning him. My wife did clever things that were sexy like this—had to shut these thoughts down, stay focused.

Callie continued her act. "I cannot let my friend be used down here for your comfort. If what we say brings him peace, you must let him go."

Hades's demeanor changed, as did the atmosphere around us. The torches down the hall dimmed, and darkness filled the air like a blanket of fog. "Who are you to command me, girl?" His face was full of barely contained fury.

Instinct made me step in front of Callie to protect her before thoughts of how to diffuse the situation occurred to me. "Uncle. We are not the enemy. Zeus is. Apollo died so we could live, so Callie could live. She is the key to bringing him down. She had to live, and so Apollo died. We must thank him."

His jaw clenched as he inspected me. He grunted and turned, walking down the hallway. We followed. I slipped the phone out of my pocket and selected a playlist, keeping it paused. I slipped it back in my pocket.

He stopped at one point to look over his shoulder slightly. "Goddess of what? What are those 'other things,' great-nephew?"

Thinking of my friend we were about to save, truth came to my lips; there was no point in hiding it, and the bargaining chip might be the very thing that distracted him. "Freedom."

He turned and beheld Callie, his dark eyes wide, his face slack. "Your…your uncle awaits, Eros." He pointed into a doorway, his hand shaking, his gaze distractedly upon my wife.

I knew we could not behold Lucien, yet he was inside a room, a cell for the lack of a better word—not with bars because where would a spirit be able to go without a living being leading the way? I had to coax him out.

I slipped out the phone, thinking of a crude joke between us, and deftly found and clicked on the Elton John track "Don't Let the Sun Go Down on Me." As the music played, I heard the voice within, "Archer?"

Hades's gaze flew to me, his hands outstretched as if to say he wanted to stop me and to keep Callie there to ask her what this freedom might mean. "Look upon your friend, *Archer.*"

The music was a dead giveaway. The jig was up. I called Callie's name and tossed the phone toward her as I tackled my uncle to the ground. I heard the music take flight, and she shouted, "Do you remember, Lucien? Remember?"

I jumped up, running at immortal speed to catch up to her, scraping a wall before I dared to open my eyes. "Lucien!"

"You said, 'Follow me.' I know. I'm here. This song, though?" He responded as if he were real, a body, my best friend right behind me.

THE IMMORTAL TRANSCRIPTS: GLIMMER

I itched to turn and hug him, to know he was there and not dead, but I wasn't stupid enough to give into impulses. "It worked, no?"

"Fair play, Archer, but Hades is hot on our heels, so maybe speed it up a bit. Um…what are we doing exactly?"

Hades bellowed. "You two are no Orpheus!"

"Correct. Orpheus failed. We will not." Callie said, picking up the pace, running through the halls and out into the front meadow. The dogs were already barking in the distance. Gods, she was brave.

We made it down into the tunnel toward the bridges when a dark shadow landed in front of us, and Hades materialized. "How in Mother Gaia do you expect to get past me? I *am* darkness, and down here, you'll find there is much of it. I have humored you long enough. I helped you with your grief, but this—this petty attempt of theft—is beyond my patience."

"Not theft," I corrected. "Trickery."

"How, you ask? Bargaining chips." Then Callie walked right by him, and so I followed. Hades made empty threats as he hurried after us. He ordered Lucien back to the palace, but the music kept him enraptured, his presence casting our shadows in front of us from his soul's faint light. Just as Orpheus had played his lyre in an attempt to resurrect his wife, my phone was doing the job.

When we reached the first bridge over the Phlegethon River, Hades was in front of us again, this time, full of rage. He grabbed Callie by the throat. I went to help her, but something pressed into my stomach. She was handing me my phone so Hades couldn't destroy it. Then I heard the last few notes of the song playing out. I hoped the second-long lag between songs, on my Cheer-Up-Lucien playlist I made a few years back, would not affect our escape. "Here Comes the Sun," by the Beatles, came on. My phone in the safety of my pocket for the moment, I grabbed Hades's throat. The river below of bubbling magma would kill a god, instantly.

In a strained voice, Hades said, "I'm open to bargaining, freedom goddess—whatever that entails—in my home, not in the middle of a soul-heist. You take my hospitality and throw it into my face? If you insist on taking my sun god, I want a soul in exchange." He had said 'soul-heist,' so Lucien was still with us, and there was a chance we could get out.

"Tread lightly, Hades. Her soul is connected to mine. You are no better than Zeus if you kill us. In fact, you'll play right into his pocket." I squeezed his neck to get his attention. Neither my hand on his throat or his on Callie's would kill either, but the hold was a statement, a stalemate at the moment.

Hades laughed loudly and let go of Callie. "Oh, Poseidon's trident!" He leaned over laughing, and I let him go, thinking this might be a good time to run for it. His next words froze me in my place: "He doesn't know?"

Callie's face paled, and her eyes grew big as she gazed at me in horror. My stomach sank. What didn't I know? What was he talking about? She glared at Hades with contempt.

"Never." She answered some mental question of Hades that I was not privy to, then kicked him and ran, yanking my shirt to get me going. We crossed the bridge, and I focused on my shadow. It told me Lucien was still following us.

Then, not far on the bank, Hades was in front of us again. "This is a tiresome game. Give me the soul, Callie, and I'll let all three of you go."

Now, I was super confused. It sucked when your wife could read minds, and you weren't privy to the info.

"Whose soul?" I demanded. There were four in the equation if he wanted a soul and was letting three go.

Hades grinned as if to laugh, and then his face fell. "I think it's only right he knows what he sacrifices to save his friend." His hand reached out and touched Callie's lower abdomen.

That's all it took. Everything clicked into place, and I snapped. *Philo.* I lost track of what I did or what was going on. My pulse was in my ears, my immortal heart beating more rapidly than it normally did. Callie's arm clutched in my hand, I pulled her to run for it. *Oww.* My hand was broken. Had I pulverized my great-uncle out of a protective instinct?

Before the third bridge, Callie yanked me to a halt.

"How could you?" I spat out.

Her eyes met mine. "Hate me later. Focus, or we all could get stuck here." Then she kissed me quickly and the love from that bloomed inside of me, dissipating my anger and hurt. The fear for her, for my child, for Lucien, was still there. I would have to be the soul if it came to sacrificing one. Surely Hades had the power to sever an immortal marriage to let her and my child live?

"Stop those thoughts. We're all getting out of here."

"Not so fast." A voice rang out. Persephone. Across the bridge in front of us.

If we could get past her, we could get out. We could hide among souls, cause confusion, or do a number of things, but here we were trapped—her in front, Hades bringing up the rear.

Persephone's voice broke. "How dare you, Eros? You were my friend."

"Kora," I used her childhood nickname. "I've always loved you like a sister, but I need my wife alive and out of here. I need my friend back too."

"Three souls entered, Eros. Three souls leave. My husband and I are torn between the options of a baby or the sunshine."

"I'm not some toy for you to play with, Persephone," Lucien said. I had to remind myself not to turn toward his voice. "I understand now, Callie," Lucien said. "What you tried to tell me in Iceland. I had to die, and you would save me."

"Any ideas?" Callie muttered to him.

"Yeah." I heard a smile in Lucien's voice at the same time I heard Hades's footsteps approach behind us. "This is the playlist Archer made me after a heartbreak a decade or so ago, but we updated it, remember, in Germany? Put on the last song, Archer."

I remember his depression after he had come back from a few personal years in Italy, before Germany, but I didn't recall heartbreak in our conversations. Still, I already had the song playing before it registered. Fall Out Boy: "Light Em Up."

I looked at Callie, whose eyes probed mine. *Squint.* I turned my head away and closed my eyes almost shut as Lucien's soul unleashed the power of the sun. Hades's reflective eyes could not handle it, and he screamed out in pain. I rushed forward, knocking Persephone out of the way to cross the bridge. The smell of burning wood filled the air, and I opened my eyes to see the bridge on fire. Literally. Fire was death. I grabbed Callie, who was too close to the flames, and shoved her in front of me. Single file was slower but safer. I would not let her die, my child—no. I could not afford to think about him.

When we made it to the bank, a crashing and splashing noise behind us almost made me turn. "Lucien?"

"I'm here. Hades fell in the Lethe."

"Eros!" Persephone's voice screeched, far from her normally kind tone. I heard wings flapping. All of Hades, including the Furies likely, were coming.

"Callie."

"No," she said as I pushed the phone into her hands. "Not without you."

Traveling as a trio was not helping us, and we were so close to getting out. If I could delay them… I did not want to say the words, but I needed her to leave. "I said goodbye to my only child today. If you let my next child die, I will never forgive you."

Regret laced through me as her face screwed up in agony. She was going to cry. Part of me wanted to console her, but the smarter part of me knew it had to be done. She turned away.

"Hurry," I ordered. Looking away so Lucien could pass by left me vulnerable to Persephone's attack, but I could not mess this up now that we had gotten so far with his soul. "I'll meet up with you!" I called so she would keep her head on straight. This was no noble sacrifice. I was going to live to see my kid be born into the world, damn it.

"What happened? What is going on?" Hades asked, crawling up the bank. The Lethe had robbed his memory. How long would it last on a god?

Persephone tackled me at the same time Hades jovially greeted me. The furies were fluttering overhead like terrifying bats, but with Hades senseless, they had no certain target. Persephone wrestled me. "You will not leave with that child. It is mine!"

I flipped us over and pinned her down, headbutting her. Holy Hades that hurt! Ridiculously. It did stun her though. "*My* child. Not yours. That's not on the table. But my wife can do something so much more for you."

I was thrown off Persephone and landed on the bank of the river, my face inches from the forgetting waters. I flew up in the air, away from the river but not high enough for Hades's trio of Furies to attack me.

"What is the meaning of this?" Hades demanded. He hadn't liked how I defended myself against his wife, and in his confusion, he thought I had been the attacker.

"My wife freed Poseidon." I threw it out there for confusion's sake and made my escape via air. When I turned a corner, there was a faint light around the next. I landed and closed my eyes. "Lucien?"

"Keep your eyes closed," he hissed. "Move, quickly."

I raced down the cavern, stumbling but not falling, until the light seemed less bright behind my lids, and Lucien sighed with relief before telling me I was clear.

Callie was in front of me still, her back to me since she could not gaze upon Lucien behind us. "I can't see it, Archer. Is this the right cavern?"

Who knew? But it was a dead end. I glanced at the completely smooth stone wall. It had to be the gate. I came up beside her as we approached it.

"Maybe I'm not… Greek enough," she whispered.

That was an exceptional point we had not thought about. Athena had proven via DNA that Callie hardly was related to her, by proxy Callie's and my DNAs were the same percentile as strangers. This was a Greek Underworld, not Norse like a shred of her ancestry, and definitely created to keep Titans in, which was the majority of her ancestry in genetic terms.

I reached my hand out to open the wall. Too late. A dark winged one had descended from above me, blocking my way by breaking my hand to stop me. I backed up, holding it as it healed.

The Erinyes, or Furies, punishers of sinners, were standing between us and success. And, by the gods, the worst offense one can commit is sinning against one of our own. I had offended a couple gods during this escape. Add in the fact I had murdered one prior to save my wife's life, I might not leave here alive if Hades let them have their way.

I looked to Callie, hoping she had some miracle to get us out of this, but the fear in her eyes told me I ought to pray to any, all, of my compassionate comrades.

CHAPTER 10

So close. We had been oh-so close to getting out of Hades (with Lucien in tote) that my stomach sank, and all I wanted to do was curl up into a ball and cry. Pathetic as it sounded, my excitement and anticipation of getting Lucien back skidded to a halt, and dread and fear came over me as fast as a flash (or more like being unexpectedly doused with ice water). Furies.

They had dark wings—literally, not Archer's metaphorical ones—which was a dead giveaway. They appeared like a wall of fog rolling down in front of us, of smoke and darkness. Black hair, clothing, and wings, they were hard to make out at first. But the sword gleamed in the pale light Lucien cast from behind us, making me duck in time not to lose my head.

"Whoa, whoa, whoa!" Archer shouted, hands up in surrender.

They hesitated, floating above us. That was when I noticed their sharp elfin features, not of beauty, but the angles of their chiseled faces spoke cruelty. Their eyes were as dark as the shadows around us, and their smiles were vampiric, with pointy teeth that probably could shred through even godly skin. The worst was their clothes, which I had first thought drifted in some wind. But there was no wind down here, and their clothes slithered. Snakes, my biggest fear (so in my personal brand of Tartarus).

"What offense have we committed to be attacked this way?" He crossed his arms, but I knew from his racing thoughts he was faking his ease. Inside, his mind was churning for ways out, things to say, hoping I had something I could do. I didn't. I had not foreseen this. I depended too much on that power, not common sense and the knowledge Dad had instilled in me.

The furies (or Erinyes, officially) had been on our side at the Battle of Liberty Island—the flying gods I had seen—but not so much now. The mythology came back to me: Alecto, Megaera, Tisiphone. It didn't help. What could I do? How to impart this helplessness to Archer without the Erinyes knowing?

"Stealing souls," one hissed (literally).

The bile in my stomach bubbled. They were actually snake-like.

"Well." Archer mused. "There is only one soul behind us, unless I have an uninvited tagalong. He's walking on his own, so no one has *stolen* him."

Of course, the music was about to end, and my breath caught until the next song came on.

I saw what Archer was doing. Using logic to stall them. Without an idea of how to escape, I joined in. "Goddesses of retribution and vengeance, no? What offense have we committed when the soul in question is still in the Underworld?" My voice shook with fear, which earned me three sly smiles from them. Oh, how their thoughts thrived on my fear.

"Go out," the same one in the middle spoke again. "Be our guest. We shall be right behind you."

The one on her right laughed.

"Good work, ladies." Persephone applauded from behind us.

"Let us go, Persephone," I called. Now, she and Hades, I could deal with. These three in front of me, just no.

"I don't think you're in the position to call the shots, dear," Hades's voice said smoothly. He clearly had his memory back. *That* was what the Lethe did. Wiped memories, the vapors so strong, they momentarily wiped mine each time I crossed it. I heard him approaching. "You might have my one brother frightened, my other in your pocket for somehow freeing him, but you don't have me, *Callista*. No one controls me."

He was eyeing me suspiciously as he came in front of us. His formidable form with three freaky flying women covered in snakes was an intimidating picture.

I took a deep breath and took a page out of my husband's book, faking the confidence I severely lacked. "Except Zeus."

Hades bristled and strode toward me, grabbing me by my jaw, his fingers pressing into my face as he growled. His green eyes, pale and feline, glared into me to the very depths of my soul (eww, a bit invasive).

I threw one hand out to the side as my other attempted to pry my jaw free. "Archer, don't. Go, take him. You have the music."

With a calmer voice than I could ever muster, he simply retorted, "Absolutely not. I go where you go."

"Then be still," I ordered.

"You two have about thirty seconds before I sic the Erinyes upon you and let Chaos reign." Hades did not take his eyes off me for a second.

"I have an offer you can't refuse," I told him.

Hades dropped me so quickly, I lost my footing and fell onto my butt. He doubled over in laughter. I was confused. Was he losing his mind?

"I made him an offer—" Hades tried to say in a weird strained voice, but could not stop laughing. Persephone started laughing as well, still standing behind us. Blocking us in.

Archer was not joining in their laughter but helping me up and protectively pushing me slightly back. I noticed his hand was in front of my midsection. Philo. He would protect us, no matter what, and I had taken that selflessness and hid something so monumental from him. He would not forgive me.

Hades attempted the quote again but didn't finish. He quickly lost his mirth the moment he realized we did not laugh along. "Come on, *The Godfather*?"

"Kind of hard to laugh at the moment, Uncle," Archer muttered.

"I don't get it."

"Don't get it? The movie, silly girl," Hades was now staring at me as if I spouted new heads like a hydra.

I shrugged. "Never saw it."

"I'm in the Underworld, and I've seen it." He scoffed, "Kids these days."

How did he watch movies? Was there electricity? An Underworld movie theater? (Focus, Callie!) Why was I wondering about stupid details when we needed to get out of here? "As I said, I have an offer." I went for the more dramatic reveal because he seemed like the type to appreciate it, and I was tired of being laughed at for not seeing an old-person movie. "I will offer you what is in this bag for Lucien's soul."

"Do you think me stupid?"

"Absolutely not, quite the opposite, which is why you can look first." I held out the bag, his eyes scrutinizing me. I wasn't sure if there was some godly weapon that could kill him in a bag, maybe some kind of fire bomb, but I was no Zeus. I did not want a god harmed, not after what we had to do to Thanatos for my survival. All I knew was it was a message, the bargaining chip from Prometheus—one he knew would work, or so he said.

Hades hesitated, opening it slowly, peering in. I watched in anticipation as his face went through varying emotions in a godly speed. From confusion, to pain, to wonder, and then his hand reached in and touched something, his face transforming to hope. The one emotion I clung to myself in desperate times, the one human emotion every living being (immortal and mortal alike) needed to survive.

Hades's gaze shot up to meet mine. I nodded, answering the questions in his head, the main one of disbelief if this was real, an actual possibility.

"What is it?" Persephone demanded, not liking the shock on her husband's face. When he didn't answer, she pressed, "Eros?"

"We didn't pack the bag. I didn't ask. This entire trip had to have me blind so I could not mess this up. My wife sees the future. Prometheus helped her plan. I trust her implicitly." The way he looked at me, eyes full of love tinged with hurt, almost broke me. I had kept a secret, broken his faith in me—in us—and here he was, still steadfast and trusting me. It had to be done. If we succeeded, I could not regret a thing.

Persephone gave up watching our backs and hurried around to her husband, looking in the bag. She pulled out each item and dropped each back in with the frustration of someone who does not understand: an umbrella, sunblock, sunglasses. Then, when she pulled out the baby shoes, tied together by their laces, she stopped, and her hands shook. "Is this some sick joke?" She met my gaze, her eyes cutting but filling with tears.

"She said she freed Poseidon," Hades murmured.

"I can give you freedom, Hades. Persephone too, without being forced to return to the Underworld, no longer bound by Zeus's border and pomegranate seeds. I cannot promise—not fully knowing the issue—but if freed, perhaps a future child could be born."

"How?" Persephone stared at me, her hands clutching the shoelaces so tightly, her knuckles turned white.

Archer looked up at the Erinyes. "Can you call off the guards? It's not a way I would want all the Underworld to know. It must be contained—to just you two."

Hades thanked his guards and dismissed them, which upset them greatly. They flew off, hissing and wailing, likely to go back to torturing mortal sinners.

"I have a barrier of my own to keep dangers within. I have spent my entire existence trying to undo Zeus's, to no avail. Slipping my soul out into the shadows was easy, but the Helm of Darkness was my greatest creation, for it let me out in person. Since my brother destroyed it, I've had to leave my body behind when I slip through. Thousands of years, and you're trying to tell me a teenager figured this out?"

(Rude!) I wanted to get defensive, but I was so close to getting Lucien back. I swallowed my pride. "I didn't figure anything out. I just exist."

Archer explained quickly what that entailed.

"So, once we leave, we can come and go as we please?" Hades's voice was skeptical but laced with an underlying hope.

"That is what happened to Poseidon," I responded.

Hades grinned. His smile lit up his face. It was genuine this time, which made me feel bad for him. The terrible jokes, the jolly personality—it was all forced to keep himself positive, to keep his wife happy. But right now, he was actually happy. "I'd like to see Poseidon." Tears started forming. "I forget what he looks like. What many gods look like who have not visited."

Persephone shook her head, the baby shoes in her hands. "It won't work. I know it."

"Let's find out?" Archer offered.

I pointed to the bag. "Better prepare. It's dawn."

Hades stared at the wall, his back turned. "I remember the sun. I remember the last day I saw it. It burned inside of me forever with the lie my brother had told me." He turned to look at me. "Zeus said once I had everything under control, he'd lift the barrier. He never did."

My stomach went sour. How horrid was this god of gods? Of course, I hated him for hating me, for trying to kill me, killing my parents, but this was worse than death. To torture your own flesh and blood for eternity? Zeus was no god. He was a devil.

Hades put up a shaking hand on the wall. Nothing happened. I took a step forward, slipping my hand in his. It shook in mine, from fright, excitement, a dare to hope. Then he tried again, and the wall dissipated in front of us, letting light in. I pulled my hand away, and it closed. He placed his hand again, but it did not open. He looked at me, eyes full of warring emotions.

"You will go blind." I pointed out the obvious.

He fumbled with the bag, slipping the sunglasses on, slipping the bag onto his shoulder.

"If I get you free, you'll let Lucien go too."

"I swear." His eyes met mine. "It has never been done, and I do not know what will happen. Is his body still viable?"

"Right here. Not that you've noticed," Lucien said drolly. He must be losing his mind, awaiting a fate much more drastic than Hades, yet he joked. My friend would live again.

"Yes," Archer supplied. "Athena and her cryogenics."

"Hmm. I will have to think about how to reattach the soul, but I promise I will give it my best effort once I'm free. To be honest, I can hardly wait. Can we do this?" He put up his umbrella in haste.

I nodded, wanting out of here as much as he did. I could not imagine him going back on his word once I gave him this gift. I took up his hand and then Persephone's. Archer fell in behind me.

Hades pressed his hand on the wall, marveling as it disappeared and the sunny desert and rock scenery came into view, the morning air bitingly chilly as I pulled in a nervous breath. At first, he could not move. Persephone broke away from me and ran out, so I moved forward, pulling Hades gently by the hand. Once we were outside, he spun around and let go of my hand. I could not turn back, not knowing if Lucien was out or not. I felt Archer's hand on the small of my back. "You did it, my freedom fighter," he breathed upon my neck, kissing it gently.

"Is Lucien out?"

"Yes, yes, and looking at him won't matter now. Turn that dreadful music off." Hades said impatiently.

Archer turned his phone off, pulling me into a side hug.

"Let me see if I can get back in and out. Persephone?" Instead of enjoying his freedom, there was a whole back and forth inside and outside to assure the barrier was permanently broken. Once it was clear that he was free but could still care for all the souls of the dead when needed, he whooped loudly.

It echoed throughout, bouncing off the rocks. Then he fell to his knees, weeping loudly. Persephone rushed over to console him.

I could not imagine what he was going through. I wanted to weep with him, my emotions everywhere. I turned. Lucien stood in the sunlight, a barely visible outline of his form but quite detailed. He was staring at his hands. "I'm free but not alive?"

Archer was standing with him, his back to me. "We have your body. We're going to bring you back."

"I can't believe you two came for me." He placed his hand on Archer's shoulder, but it swept through Archer, making his smile fade.

We had succeeded, only halfway. "Lucien."

He grinned again. "Well, the freedom goddess has proven herself useful yet again. Who will speak of Orpheus when Callista outdid him?" He almost hugged me, but his arms dropped, realizing he could not touch us in this ghostly form.

I heard Hades murmur to Persephone, "Plan us an extravagant day, my love. The Dead Sea, the museum, the places you have told me so much about in Jordan that I have never seen—everything modern. But first, we will help them with Lucien. It is only right. This girl has given me a new life, and Lucien died so that she could live. The Fates weave a mysterious web with their strings, and I will not interfere with their power when it brings me such blessings."

She squealed and took up his hands, pure joy upon her face. "I'm going to take you everywhere, my love. Show you all the places in the pictures I brought you."

It was adorable, but my stomach was not having any of it. I leaned on the nearest boulder and vomited. Archer was beside me in a flash, pulling my hair back away from the spillage. I wanted to tell him to leave me alone.

"You need food."

I heaved violently, but nothing came out.

"And water. Come. Lucien, follow us." Archer scooped me up in his arms despite my protests and floated over the terrain by defying gravity at a godly speed until we had to slow down in civilization. I watched Lucien follow us, being sure I did not lose sight of him. Hades and Persephone hurried, both brimming with joy but concerned about my and Lucien's states. We only encountered one mortal in this sparsely populated area. The fact he did a double take at me in Archer's arms and not at the spirit beside told me mortals could not see him. Then again, paranormal things have been claimed before, so maybe only most couldn't.

As soon as we entered, Athena went all Mom on me (Hello, save the ghost). "What is wrong with her?"

I retched, and a bit of foamy bile came out.

Archer placed me down on one of the cots Athena had set up, not knowing how long we'd stay. His hand touched my abdomen gently. "She's pregnant." The way he said it made my heart take flight. Pride and happiness, unconditional love. Too soon, his hand left my abdomen, and his tone changed. "Which she hid from me and risked our child's life." (Truth cut like a knife.)

"Archer," I pleaded.

He was up, away from me, his hands behind his head, walking away. He was distressed, choosing space over anger.

Athena threw her hands up, face incredulous. "What were you thinking?"

I had thought anger would assuage my guilt, but this was worse. Tears pouring from being hurt by two people who loved me in the span of a minute, I screamed at them, "This!" while pointing at Lucien. "Both of you would have never let me go save him if you'd known. Only *I* could get him back. I had to go."

Prometheus headed over. "Thena. You are needed. Archer, you should get some air. All of this is a lot to deal with. I'll look after Callie, make sure she is well. We have a hospital set up here. I won't let anything happen."

Without even looking at me, Archer stormed out of the building, the door slamming shut, echoing throughout the warehouse.

Prometheus brought me a bottle of water and some crackers and squatted down. "Small sips, small bites." He winked.

I wanted to hit him. "I brought back one friend, but it will cost me my husband." It suddenly felt not worth it. We needed Lucien, but was he worth destroying Archer and my relationship?

"Shh," Prometheus said, making me take a sip by holding the water bottle to my lips. "It'll be okay. Lucien was needed. You'll see." He brushed the hair out of my face, his dark eyes full of concern and empathy.

He reminded me of Dad, just the littlest bit. "He can't forgive me for this. His only other child died. He just let her go. He *literally* can stay mad at me for centuries."

"No regrets, Callie. What we must bear and do weighs heavily upon us, but no regrets. Be strong." He squeezed my shoulders. "I must help over here, if only to keep Athena calm. Eat, drink, and here's a bucket if needed. Let me know if you need me." Then he was off.

I obeyed and slowly got half a water bottle down and six crackers as I watched them prepare Lucien's corpse. His soul was silently looking at his body, pain and confusion rippling across his face. What must he be going through?

Prometheus's insistence on no regrets did not soothe me. I had not seen the result of this after we freed him. I was now in the unknown. Seeing Lucien's tortured face after remonstrations from loved ones? I had many regrets that were ongoing.

CHAPTER 11

Aios

I saw Linda or texted her every day. Himerus had told me I was supposed to ignore her for three days before I'd respond, but I just couldn't wait beyond a couple hours after she helped me move. Anteros's opinion on my conduct was worse. He claimed I was using Linda to fill up the void Dad left in my heart and that she was doing the same. I punched him, even though I think he was right in a way—a beautiful distraction. After that, he admitted she didn't have unrequited love for my father. That would've killed me. She had seemed as interested in me as I was as her. I knew she cared, and I wasn't using her. She just so happened to walk into my life again when I most needed her. I mean, there were far worse distractions than a beautiful and interesting girl. There was only one problem. She asked too many questions, which made it difficult for me to keep up the mortal façade while trying to control these powers, all while we awaited news about the Underworld trip. My nerves were on edge, but I allowed my best friends to convince me that seeing her would distract me from my worries. Plus, I was worried this virus thing would keep her from me. What if going out with her tonight was the last time for a while?

We went to a late movie because of our spur-of-the-moment plan, then went to a breakfast place—we as in all four of us. This was ridiculous. I needed my dad back for girl advice. I couldn't make a move on Linda. Even though I had been embarrassed to ask him anything specific since he had dated her, I needed some kind of guidance that my numbskull friends didn't know because they were actually crap with girls, especially for members of the *love* entourage.

As we made our way out to the street to walk home, my buddies sped up, joking around, leaving us falling behind. They were giving me space.

"Come back to my place?" I asked, gently tugging her hands.

She gave me that cute, smitten look I adored, and tugged back to get me closer. Looking up at me, she said, "I've got to tell my mom where I'm headed." She rolled her eyes. "She got weird after I moved onto campus and then pulled me home after my first semester. I only agreed because my best friend, who was also my roommate, turned on me completely."

"Why? You're the nicest person I've ever met."

She got bashful and roped her arm in mine, likely because the annoying duo were making jokes—not about us—but it still probably made her self-conscious.

"My best friend was Emily. When Callie arrived at our high school, Emily got nasty. I knew I shouldn't continue being friends with her, but the way she spread so much hatred so fast…" She sighed. "It was jealousy. Straight up. Not because Callie's pretty. I mean, I think she is. The thing is, I feel guilty because she's so nice, and she went through so much with her father dying. I was bad to her for a little while. It eats me up, Aios." Those dark eyes peered up at me, and my heart lurched when I saw they were full of tears.

"Please don't cry. Callie would hate it. I agree she is nice, which is why she'd chastise you if she were here. She is your friend. She always will be because you are a good person. All that matters is what we learn from our mistakes, not that we made them."

She leaned into me, her head downcast, so I dared to kiss the top of her head. Linda didn't react at first. Then she pulled out her phone and broke away from me. "I'm calling my mom. Don't mock me. She doesn't control me, but I worry she'll stay up thinking something happened to me."

I took up her hand. "Hey, I get it. You should always check in to be safe."

After her call, we went into the apartment. Anteros and Himerus hit the Xbox instantly. Linda looked at me uncomfortably.

"I'm going to ask you to go down the hall to the spare apartment we use as Lucien's storage, but not in a weird way. Just to get away from *them*."

She nodded vigorously.

Once we entered, she looked around. "You have an apartment for just stuff of his?"

I nodded. "This whole floor is people you know. We're friends or family, renting off the owner, who knows us."

"My mom—she's a real estate agent—said these apartments were 'collected.' Over a century, they were bought." Her gaze challenged me. She was sharp.

"I don't know about that. The owner I do know. He's from a wealthy family and said things were passed down." How proud my dad would be of me spinning truths for my own purpose. I needed to shift the subject off any suspicions though. "Now, my parents are musicians. Although I haven't unpacked my…brother's guitars yet, I can and play for you—if you want."

She was up and excited. "Let's do that."

"Really?" I shrugged off her interest, weirded out that my father might've played for her before me. I had to stop this comparison issue I was having, because I liked her a lot, and he had cared more about Callie back then. I took a deep breath. I was not mad at him or Callie or anyone else. I was mad at myself for these feelings.

"Where did you say Callie and Archer were?"

This was a vast change in subject. I opened a box, this one being huge, as I thought over my answer. "I hadn't."

"That's me asking you where they are, silly. I wanted to see her, and *everyone* in your little group seems to live here." She tossed a towel at me that she was unpacking. I sure hope my friends hadn't packed anything incriminating for mortal eyes in the boxes.

"Oh, wow." I gasped seeing the three guitar cases stacked upright in the box surrounded by a comforter to keep them upright. This was my dad's sacred collection; ones he had never let me play. I pulled each one out.

"Lucien's guitars?" Linda's face was solemn. Would it always be that way between us? Feelings for each other but a wedge of the past stopping us from being together?

I nodded. "Did he ever play for you?"

"No, but he had spoken about playing and music a lot. I could tell he loved it."

"I'm not as good as my…brother, but I can play a tune." I was being modest, of course, because Dad had taught me everything when I was little, and some of the Muses continued my musical education after he'd split.

A small smile played upon her lips.

I placed a case down and opened it, removing Lucien's Martin Sunburst. Perfection. My father wasn't around to be overprotective of his instruments. If he came back? Well, he'd never know. What harm was there?

I strummed it once and felt transformed by the sound, launching into a medley, seamlessly combining my favorite tunes. Lost in my own world, my phone buzzed, distracting me. I opened my eyes to see Linda staring at me with admiration and awe.

"You are a-*maze*-ing."

My face flared up, showcasing my embarrassment.

"At the guitar, I mean," Linda blurted out.

How my friends and father would tease me at this moment. I married people for gods' and goddesses' sake, but I couldn't suavely take a compliment or even flirt back. "Er. Thanks."

My phone buzzed again. Not knowing what else to say to Linda, I snatched it up and saw the texts from Anteros: **Archer called.** and **Hello? Stop flirting with the mortal and call me. Important!**

"I have to make a call. Be right back." I hurried into a bedroom and shut the door to not be overheard. If this was the everyday stress Archer went through, kudos for him sticking with whom he had believed to be mortal. This would be work, and it would have to end eventually. I didn't want to think about that.

Anteros answered immediately, yelling at me. Himerus was in the background, making lewd suggestions about what I was up to with Linda to prevent me from answering.

"Tell me!" I shouted to shut Anteros up. My heart beat wildly in my chest. My dad, was he alive? I still had his powers. My stomach turned sour.

"He's alive, but—"

"I don't care. He's alive!" I didn't care if Linda overheard me. She'd find out when Dad returned that he wasn't dead.

"Listen, Aios, there's a problem. You need to go out there. Meet up with Archer and crew. Zephyrus is picking you up in like five minutes—well, a couple minutes ago, he said that. Get rid of the mortal before she sees him appear out of thin air."

Crap. I had to hurry. I hung up and went into the living room. "You got to go." I said, not realizing how rude I was being until it was said. "I mean I have to go, so you need to go."

Her brow wrinkled, and her eyes were hurt. "What's wrong?" She wasn't getting up off the couch yet.

How could I get rid of her? "The call was about Lucien. He might...he's alive." The truth came out of me. To be honest, it wasn't the power I'd inherited from my father doing it. I simply didn't want to lie to Linda.

Her eyes went wide, and her lip trembled. "How? What?"

Finally, I just pulled her up by her arm. "I need to fly abroad, like as soon as possible, and see how he is. There's a problem, but I'm not sure what it is. I need to go."

"Oh, sorry," she finally snapped to it. "I'll go. Um... Can I call you while you're abroad?"

"I don't know the plans yet. I'll call you."

I had the door open and stood in the doorway, with her in the hall. *Please go. Just go.*

She looked up at me with those gorgeous doe eyes. "I won't see you for some time, I think."

"Huh?"

"Don't you watch the news? There's an epidemic, so I don't even know if you'll be able to travel. There are talks about lockdowns."

The epidemic. It hadn't occurred to me that anyone I cared about would be in danger, because the ichor in our blood burns off illnesses, but Linda was mortal. I swallowed hard. "Stay safe, Linda. I don't know how long I'll be or if I'll be able to travel back, as you say. I'll call you, promise."

As soon as she turned away, I closed the door, wishing I had kissed her, but there was no time. I'd see her when I returned. I'd be sure to finally make a move then. I was getting to a breaking point, and it wasn't Himerus's powers fueling my libido but my own.

A few seconds later, Zephyrus appeared in a whirlwind, scattering some of Dad's lighter belongings. Many things crossed my mind, but my excitement to see my father and fear for Linda's life warred with each other. In the forefront, though, was this "problem" no one explained about my dad. Not knowing any god coming back from the dead before, I was worried he'd be a zombie or something worse.

Zephyrus took us in his wind to Jordan in an instant. How I would love to see Linda's face if I could explain his power to her. We were in a warehouse. The only people inside were Athena and Prometheus. But then I saw him lying there, hooked up to machines that were clearly life support assistance. My father's body was technically alive, but he wasn't present. We did not truly have him back yet. My heart sank.

"Aios," Athena spoke first. She was worrying her top lip. "We need your help."

My help? What was I to do?

Prometheus came over. His tanned face was grim. "Hades cannot reattach your father's soul. It seems to be a one-way street." He sighed. "There are other gods we could contact, but I'd rather you have a try first. Involving any others could get problematic."

"I don't know…" My mind whirled. "I join souls. How can I join a soul to something else like a body?"

Athena's shoulders slumped. "You're our best chance."

"Safest chance," Prometheus amended.

Athena gave him a look.

Archer returned and not alone. Persephone entered, followed by a man I had never met, dressed in a dramatic black robe, his hair matching, as well as sunglasses. He closed an umbrella. "Hymenaios, I take it? Hades," he offered his hand, "Your great-uncle."

I shook his pale hand in awe, but my eyes darted behind him to the wispy form of my father as if carved out of fog. "Dad?"

"Aios," he beamed, his image brightening.

Tears prickled my eyes. "Dad." We had his soul, Hades free, and there was only one last step that I had to somehow perform.

Archer put his hand on my shoulder. "I didn't want you here or for you to even see him until he was back—fully back. But we needed you."

I nodded, just now noting I didn't see Callie.

Archer squeezed my shoulder. "You had never linked an immortal couple to another soul before until you saved our lives. I have faith that you can do this too."

Dad smiled at me. "I'm so sorry I made you do that. Callie's life has a worth much greater than mine. One day, you'll understand and forgive me."

I did understand, and yet the pain inside me at being abandoned for what I had thought was forever, as I had been abandoned as a child, still echoed through me. Now was not the time to hash out my emotional grievances. I needed my father alive in body as well. Only then would we have lifetimes for him to make up for the things he'd done and made me do. I wanted to hug him but knew, without him being in material form, it might shatter my fragile hold over my anxiety.

They caught me up on the logistics; the story of their success at bringing his soul back and freeing Hades could wait. Athena had Dad's body revived and on life support. The thought was, with the ichor flowing and heart beating, he was alive, but just not in there. How to get his soul to stay in his body was the problem. Hades who, just like Death, could pull souls out of bodies, could not reattach them. For Persephone, her assistance in life and death did not extend to human beings or gods—she had tried, though without success.

Too excited to wait, I insisted we make an attempt. Dad's soul lay down on top of his body, his face cringing as he entered. I closed my eyes and picked up his hand, surprised by the warmth. I focused on the "hot zone" as I called it, the pull of energy I felt in tune with at the base of the skull, the medulla oblongata. If one were to stick or weld a soul back into the body, that was the port of entry. I hoped. It was the place death pulled it from.

I tried. And failed. Multiple times, my confidence dwindling. Each time, my father's spirit sat back up, outside of his body, shaking his head. We took a break while chatting about possibilities. My father's spirit simply stared at his body, watching the rhythmic rise and fall of his chest. I wanted to comfort him, but what to say?

"Dad, we'll figure it out."

He smiled slyly at me. "God of truth. I know you don't believe that, but thanks, kid."

"You are not giving up. Either of you," a feeble voice rang out.

I turned to see Callie lying on a cot, her face pale. I was surprised Archer was not by her side, doting on her because she looked ill. "Uh, what happened?"

"She's pregnant," Archer murmured. Again, he didn't seem happy as he normally would be. "She's probably sick from going into the Underworld."

"Eros of Olympus, you say that one more time, I'll send you to the Underworld." Persephone crossed her arms but looked too sweet to be formidable. "I already told you, it's not the Underworld. It's just morning sickness."

Archer sighed and went over to her and said something quietly to her.

"I'm fine," she said, getting up, pushing his hands away when he tried to help her.

They were more than frictional. Archer hadn't known. Ouch. I couldn't empathize with his anger at the moment, because my father was back because she took that risk.

"Aios, you'll do it. I've seen him alive in the future. I just didn't get to see how."

"What was Orpheus's plan?" Athena asked with that faraway look in her eyes, retreating into her mind, where she usually came out with an amazing answer. "Did you ever find out what he had planned to do with her soul?"

Hades ran his hand through his hair. "Of course, I looked into it and got every morsel of information he had before I allowed him to move on and be reunited in the afterlife with his wife. I had pitied him. I thought his plan was pure madness." He sighed and started pacing. It was strange seeing someone indoors wearing sunglasses, like a celebrity desiring freedom from others. "Orpheus was depending on Gaia to help."

Athena pinched the bridge of her nose. "She's dead now."

"Stating the obvious, my love," Prometheus said, his tone kind, despite the light censure of the comment.

"Yes, yes. I know. She's not needed. I have created life." She pointed to my dad's body. "I need you to bind the soul. Callie is right. It is you. It has to be you."

No pressure, with everyone looking at me. "I have tried everything. I have nothing else to try, except a Castor—"

"No." The spirit of my father sliced his arms through the air. "No."

"You'd be alive, Dad."

"And never see you again." The idea hit me hard. Dad and I had gotten close toward the end of his life. To not see him again? It would be like he was still dead to me. But he would have half a life.

"Moot point," Hades said, the frustration in his voice growing. I was sure he wanted to see the world but was stuck failing like I was at what we should do best, dealing with souls. "We have an extra soul, not down one. He's out of Hades. I don't think—and this is a guess—that going back and passing on is an option either. We tried everything, but to ask the one god who knows more about this than any of us."

Athena shook her head. "We can't trust him."

Hades shrugged. "He's the only hope. Otherwise, Lucien remains stuck permanently in spirit form."

"Who?" I asked.

"Do it. Get Callie out of here in case he's in Zeus's pocket. It's the only way," Persephone piped in.

"Who?" I repeated, getting agitated.

Hades sighed. "There's one problem. It's not his turn."

Tired of being ignored, I lashed out. "*Who?*"

They all looked at me, and Hades and Athena both said simultaneously, "Pollux."

"How can he help?" Dad asked the very thought on my mind.

Persephone sighed. "To put it plainly for sake of time, Pollux is able to tether his soul to his brother to give him a half-life and is able to untether it. We think it's the only reason it actually worked for them. That and the twin thing. He's in the Underworld, so we'd need Castor and him to temporarily switch places."

No one spoke, so I did. "What are we waiting for, then? Get him."

"You need to know it's going to be tempting. Your father has an immortal body and a soul. Pollux might want a full life, all year long, let his brother have his body."

"But my dad's body wouldn't be Pollux."

"It hasn't happened before. But I imagine the brain and the soul would fight, and we have no idea if he would be your father or Pollux. But he's our only hope. We have to chance it," Hades said.

I turned to gaze at my dad's soul, hating seeing him in this form. "How do you feel about that?"

He shrugged. "I'm dead, kid. Anything else is a step above it. And I have faith that Pollux will do right by us. We had been friends. He hasn't picked sides in this war with Zeus."

Hades nodded. "You can believe he'll be on ours," Hades said, his sunglasses hiding his full expression, making me unsure of his mood. "If not, I can always make him. I control whether souls move on. He wants his brother's to remain here, and yet, sometimes, Castor thinks about moving on—quite more often than his brother knows."

"Let's hope it doesn't come to threats," Athena said. "We don't want him heading to Zeus's side. Bribery first."

With the decision made, Hades and Persephone left to seek Castor—who likely would have a heart attack when Hades showed up above ground. They would sort it all out and return with Pollux.

While we waited, Archer and Callie fought. This time, it was because she refused to leave until she saw Lucien alive in his own body. They both had valid points. She came in handy with inexplicable powers at times, but she was risking her and her baby's life by being seen by someone not on a side.

Waiting felt like forever.

Finally, Zephyrus appeared with Castor or Pollux—they were identical so… Then Persephone and Hades entered through the door.

"Ask and I shall deliver," Hades clapped his hands, rubbing them together, way too excited about what felt like a risky experiment with my dad's soul in the balance.

"Pollux," Prometheus greeted.

"Prometheus," he said back.

Hades tried to put us at ease. "I've promised him he could experiment with his brother's soul on a god if one perchance dies in all these wars. Zeus has made some of his demigod kids immortal recently, Athena has said."

She looked away guiltily, likely wishing she had not said that.

I cringed. Hades was sacrificing a new god. Likely, he'd kill one for Pollux. It made me sick because no one deserved that, but I wanted my dad back, and the new god would be the enemy, someone trying to kill us. I still felt bad, but remembering my aunts and how they didn't care whether I lived or died, how they tried to kill me, made me less empathetic; they'd do the same—if not more— without thought. I could not afford to be gracious and forgiving. I needed my dad.

"It can be done," Athena said quietly. "Arrange for Iris to take the demigod's body to my cabin in Iceland for preservation. They have to die a particular way."

"I will have Death take the soul," Hades nodded.

Pollux and Hades shook on it. Chills shot down my spine. Chase had said we needed allies, and Castor and Pollux would be two more.

Athena nodded and straightened her shoulders as if to get rid of her emotions. "Let us bring Apollo back, and then I will help Castor in Iceland."

And then things started. Pollux approached my father's spirit. "I appreciate you letting me experiment. I can make no promises that I will succeed."

My father nodded, then walked through his body, trying to lay back inside himself as he had before when I had failed—so many times.

Pollux placed his hand on the back of my father's head by the brain stem and closed his eyes as if that allowed him to see inside. He concentrated, his brow furrowing and then relaxing twice before he opened his eyes and looked over his shoulder at me. "Come. I have him there, but it's not as easy as swapping Castor's. I just need a little binding push."

I walked over, feeling sick. This wasn't going to work. I had failed my father already, and I would fail him again. I took a deep breath.

"Hope, Aios. Have hope," Callie chimed in.

"Ah, the reason for all this. The freedom goddess," Pollux inspected her. "One goddess altering our entire existence."

"And?" Athena defensively pressed.

He shrugged. "Things have been the same for thousands of years. Change will be good. Hades above ground, perhaps my brother can be too."

"Can we?" I asked anxiously. "How do I...?"

"Bind the soul as you do with an immortal marriage or how you soul-shared my brother to me. I do this for you, Aios, because you saved my brother in the only way we could."

That gave me some confidence, and as he held my father's soul in place, I whispered all the words of soul-sharing, knowing some ways might not work.

But then Pollux spoke. "Stop. I think...it's tethered. Nothing else can be done." He smiled at me, and my heart did a flip.

Dad didn't move.

Athena took him off the life support. She carefully, but quickly, pulled out the breathing tube. Checking his pulse and giving us reassuring nods, we waited in silence. Then Dad took a deep breath as if he had been holding it. His hand went to his chest to confirm his heart.

He blinked a couple times and then sat up. He looked at everyone and the room, his expression confused. When his gaze met mine, my stomach lurched. Zero recognition crossed his features.

"Where am I?" He peered at his hands. "Who am I?"

Bile rose up in my throat as realization hit. His mind was a blank slate.

My gods!

What have we done?

CHAPTER 12

As soon as Callie and I returned home, Ma and Dad were at the door, asking a million questions. I briefed them with Lucien's condition, and how the others were staying behind to try to find a way to restore his memory. With Mnemosyne on Zeus's side, because he let the Titan have day passes out of prison in exchange for her memory altering services, we could not trust her yet. Mortals' memories needing to be "erased" so often after gods slipped up, she was practically free most of the time. She did not trust a rebellion yet, even though the braver Titans had been freed to join us at the last battle. The only other hope was Dionysus, but he was only good with madness.

As if Ma sensed something was amiss between Callie and me, she hastened their departure despite Dad seemingly wanting to talk more.

Then we were alone. I knew we had to hash out our issues. The sooner, the better. She started to walk away from me, so I grabbed her arm. From the incredulous look on her face, I was using my immortal strength. I lessened my grip, but the anger pulsed through me. White hot rage boiled inside of me, ready to explode, and my stomach turned sour. I had no idea which emotion would win, but the rage and hurt warred inside of me. Still, underneath it all was love. "How could you hide my child from me?"

"Don't shout at me!"

I hadn't raised my voice at her. Terse and short with her, yes. Every emotion boiled over, but I let the pain overtake the anger. Fighting would not get us over this obstacle between us. "Callie, why?"

Her posture softened at my change in tone, and her guilty eyes darted away. "Because if I told you, you wouldn't let me come. Only you and I together could get Lucien back."

Not good enough. I let her go so that my boiling anger wouldn't use immortal strength. "Damn it, Callie! You took my child into the underworld without asking me, without telling me. What if he—"

"Philo."

Then it hit me. I was going to have a child, a son. I felt my lips tug into a smile. *Wait.* "Don't distract me. Is he still alive?" I tentatively reached out to touch her lower abdomen, which still looked flat. I half expected her to bat my hand away.

81

"Yes," she said quietly. "If I didn't eat, drink, or give birth down there, I knew he'd be fine. As you can see, we are far from the last one happening."

I let my hand drop. "Hades wanted our child's soul. What if he had taken him?"

"I had something better to offer him. It wouldn't have come to that. A live child or the soul of an unborn one? One that is theirs and not someone else's? They would pick their deepest desire."

"No, Callie. Not good enough. Stop hiding things from me. Stop taking risks. Just because you're immortal does not mean you can't die, that our child wouldn't die."

"I know that. But Lucien died for us!"

I sighed, sitting down, rubbing my hands down my face, knowing full well deciding between protecting my child and bringing back my best friend of millennia would've been an impossible choice. It must've taken all her mental strength to go forward with it.

I tried to remain calm. "Do you realize what would happen to me if you died in the Underworld?"

"Yes, the immortal marriage you forced me into would take your life too."

Forced. The word stung, only because I had been trying to protect her. She would've never agreed. In hindsight, the comparison felt just, but that was only including the two of us. This went further.

"As you saw, Callie, we remember in the Underworld. You would have taken my heart and my child from me. I cannot exist without you, even in Elysium. I lost a child before. I just said goodbye to her. Do you realize that Love cannot deal well with losing it?" I could not go through that again. Nothing filled the crack in my heart that Hedone's death had caused.

Her face softened. She touched my cheek. "I'm sorry, Archer. I can't imagine what you went through except that I lost my father too, more recently."

I gazed up at her to see her eyes full of tears. I had a bad feeling about what she'd say next. My stomach sank.

"Archer, you're too overprotective. You can't watch over me all of the time. In fact, I think I want to stay at Athena's—just for a few days. Be by myself to think about things, let you think as well."

It was a verbal slap in the face. "What?" I could form no other words.

"I'm not leaving you. I just need some room to breathe." Only, it felt very much like she was breaking up with me. Her eyes no longer shined with adoration. She still loved me. I could feel it, but a comfortable love, not like the fervent intense love I had for her. Every time I beheld her, I felt more alive than I had all those years I had spent alone, unknowingly waiting for her.

I wanted to voice all that, but anger and hurt overruled my heart. How could she? It didn't make sense. If I was overprotective and smothering her in attention and affection, it was something we would talk about. I could back off a bit—if she'd stop putting our and our son's lives on the line. There was something else wrong. I wished Lucien was more with it, and here, so he could ferret though her lies and tell me what was really going on.

"Don't do this." They were empty words because I knew she had already decided this, maybe even before our trip. She had been acting strangely toward me.

She looked away with tears in her eyes. "I don't want to hurt you."

"Hurt me? You're destroying me. I love you, Callie, with everything that I am. I would do anything for you. We are at war, my whole family divided because of our love, and now you just want to throw it all away? I've given you everything I possibly could. For you to say that's not enough—"

"I didn't. No. I just need time!"

"It feels like you're ending us, Callie. With my baby in your belly, you're going to destroy our family. What's next? A divorce?"

We should've waited. She was so young, and had we known we could have forever, maybe we wouldn't have married so hastily. I rarely fell in love, and so when it happened after so long, it was hard to wait. I had married Psyche too soon as well; she had been immature, making me regret having married her at all, if it hadn't been for Hedone. Was I repeating the same mistakes again?

I would show Callie. I wouldn't let the Fates determine history would repeat. I would fight for Callie, win her over again and again if I had to. We were bound forever, and we had that time. Space might be a good idea…for now.

After a moment of silence between us that spoke volumes, she sat down next to me, pressing herself against me, wrapping her arms around me, head under my chin, trying to get me to hold her. "No, Archer, I love you."

The long pause before denying we were headed to a serious separation stung, so my arms remained limp at my sides, unable to pull her close. Then she backed away slightly, those dark eyes peering up to meet mine. I could feel her love as if it was a tangible bond between us. When she leaned up for her lips to reach mine, I made the most of the kiss, hoping this was not going to be our last, pouring all my love into it.

Too soon, she pulled away.

"You love me, and I love you. We're having a baby together. I just don't understand."

She sighed. "You wouldn't."

"What is that supposed to mean?"

"It means if Prometheus and I can't make sense of it, there is no way anyone else could."

I was lost, and paranoid why she'd talk to someone else about our relationship. "You're talking to him about *us*?"

"No, yes. It's complicated."

"Then explain it to me, Callie. Don't shut me out. Don't hide things from me. That is half our problem right now." I wanted to say *all* because I wouldn't be over protective if she wasn't so rash and hiding dangers from me, but I was trying to make this work between us. There were two of us, so I had to take half the blame. Then my mind clicked onto another possibility. Did she crave distance to hide something else from me? "Does something bad happen and you foresaw it?"

Her eyes darted away, and she pushed out of my arms with a sharp inhalation of breath. She stood staring at me, her hands balled up, trembling.

I stood up at an immortal speed and took a step closer, entreating in a gentle tone, "Tell me."

She flinched when I got close as if I was about to hit her? How could she ever think that? Why would she?

She took a step back. "It's you. You hurt me, Archer—in the future, I mean. I…I think you might try to, or might be successful. I foresaw you attacking me with a rage I have never seen before."

It felt like Zelus, the ice daemon, had just attacked me again. My blood ran that cold. I stood there, mouth agape and confused, for I didn't know how long.

Finally, she spoke. "I wouldn't believe it possible—"

"It's not."

"—but I saw it."

"How could you even believe it for a moment? I'd never lay a finger on you. Have I ever physically hurt you or made you think I ever would? Come on. With you carrying my child? I'd never hurt him or you. Never."

"It was a prophecy given to me in a dream, like Lucien used to have."

Weird and irrational. Why was she seeing prophecies, and why was she trusting one implicitly? Lucien would never trust one or believe I'd hurt him. The more she talked, the more she wounded me. "I trusted you with my life in the Underworld, followed your lead, and did as you said. That is how much I trusted you. And what do you give back? Zero trust in me. You believe a snippet of a prophecy without context over me? And you lied to me? If your heart cannot trust in me… Yeah, maybe we do need a break."

"Archer." Her voice faltered. Good. She was feeling just like I was. "You want us safe, and that is what I'm trying to do." She rested her hands on her belly.

"Well, you believe I'm the threat, so far away from me is where you should go." It was childish, but I wanted to emotionally wound her as she had me. I started to walk away.

"Where are you going?"

"Out."

"Where?"

"Out of this apartment." I was aware of how childish I was being, but I had to get away from her. I was too upset at what she had done and what she believed I was capable of. The lack of trust on her side of our relationship while she was the one hiding so much was astoundingly hypocritical. I loved my wife, but I no longer could trust her either. I needed space too.

Late that night, when I got home from my brothers' apartment, I was prepared to sleep on the couch. But Callie was gone and her suitcase with her. So sleeping across the hall from me at night wasn't enough space? She had to make sure she wouldn't come back into our apartment for days, a week? Why else would she pack up necessities unless she wanted to avoid me at all costs? I knew one thing. We'd have our space, but I wasn't waiting nine months to prove her prophecy was ridiculous. She would miss me, and I would miss her. Something would bring us back together. I just hoped I could figure out what that something was soon.

CHAPTER 13

Callie

I was shocked Archer didn't fight me on my decision to leave. To be honest, I thought he'd fight for me. Wasn't the god of love supposed to keep it at all costs? As I placed my case in Athena and Prometheus's guest room, doubts crept in. The myth of Cupid and Psyche came to mind. When she broke his trust, he fled from her, abandoned her—pregnant, if I recalled the myth correctly. Would he do the same to me? No. He would stay. If anything was clear, he wanted this child (maybe without being with me though?). He would never abandon his child. Philo. I touched my stomach, wondering about the miracle that was growing there. Was Archer right to worry? What if Philo was damaged from the Underworld? I had risked our child's life. I understood his anger after I really thought about it. But the guilt I had felt over Lucien dying to save me, the limited timeframe to save him…

Now the guilt transferred from Lucien to the baby. No matter how I rewrote the scenarios I could've chosen, I'd lose someone. Archer would forgive me (right?); it wasn't permanent.

A soft tapping announced someone at the door on the second day. I had spent all day alone, reading a pregnancy book, and was contemplating video chatting with Linda for some social interaction, but there were too many things to hide from her. I had hurt enough people hiding things lately.

Part of me hoped it was Archer, but that idea was dashed when Aroha's voice called to me through the door. "Callie? Would you like to join us for dinner?"

I wanted to say no, but the mention of food gave me a simultaneous hunger pang and nausea. I had to eat for Philo. But was my mother-in-law up to some matchmaking scheme? Or revenge for upsetting her son? Would the Aphrodite side of her personality attempt to give me impossible tasks as she had Psyche? I pushed the thoughts from my mind. Aroha was the only true friend I had. I could not share these troubles with Linda. Yeah, things were going to be weird right now, but I had no desire to cook myself something. I opened the door.

She studied me and shook her head, disappointed. That was worse than berating me. "Why didn't you tell me?" Her eyes stared at my non-existent belly as she patted her hand on her own.

"I was scared you'd all stop me from bringing Lucien back."

She bit her lip, truly thinking it over. "I would've warned you what could happen, and, more importantly, how to protect yourself. Your power to free us of Zeus's control is the only reason you still have your child. I would've helped you, not stopped you. Part of all of us died with Lucien." (More guilt.)

She yanked me into a tight hug. "Congratulations. We'll be doing this together. I can't thank you enough."

"Thank me?" I didn't expect Aroha to be kind after I wounded her precious son's heart. He obviously told her that I was pregnant (likely painting me in a bad light).

Aroha touched her lower abdomen, full of happiness. "Zeus controlled us in every way—even when we could have children. Your freeing abilities are the reason we are having a child after so long."

I nodded, not sure what to say. Two thoughts filled my mind as I let her lead me by the hand out of the room and down the hall: when would Zeus heal and come for me again? And how to digest the power I had over other gods without consciously doing it? I wasn't used to compliments, her thanking me? It felt undeserved (I merely existed).

When we entered the apartment, I heard male voices—one belonging to Archer. I froze. Aroha tugged me along, rolling her eyes. "Stop being so immature."

"Said by someone who is thousands of years old to a nineteen-year-old."

"By the gods, I love you and your snark, Callie. Don't change." She laughed lightly, then met my gaze. "He's not staying. It's not some setup. It was his idea for us to feed you, and him, but he decided to just pack up some food to take to the apartment."

(Where he'd eat alone.)

I sighed. "He can stay. I'll grab the plate and leave" (and be alone). It was depressing. My parents were dead, but he didn't deserve me to usurp his.

Archer was suddenly in front of me. Why was I still not one-hundred percent used to their fast moving or my own fast movements? (Like seriously, I fought in an immortal war for crying out loud.)

"Callie." His voice was devoid of emotion, so I couldn't gauge how to react. His blue eyes inspected me, trying to read my mood. How I longed to see their luminescent glow when he beheld me in utter devotion. "We had a fight. We want time and space, but tonight—you have to be as hungry as I am. Surely, we can eat in peace?" He was calm, collected, and it made me feel like things were fine but over between us. Archer was normally a ball of emotions, unable to hide his feelings from me. Tonight, he was shut off.

Holding back the tumultuous emotions that rattled around in me, I nodded. "Do I smell bacon?" (Where did that come from?)

Despite our issues, there was a twinkle in his eyes, loving the idea of my sudden change in topics and craving for whatever Chase was cooking in the kitchen. "*Koto-bacon*." Archer's lips turned up into that adorable smile. "Chicken thighs wrapped in bacon. Everything Dad cooks has bacon in it."

"Good man," was all I said as I stormed the kitchen with my first (okay, second) pregnancy craving (had to count the pickle situation in the Underworld).

"Hey," Chase greeted a wide smile. "Gotta say, becoming *Pappoús* and *Bampás* at the same time has me excited."

"It's suddenly domesticated him." Aroha grinned as she swept her hand toward the table that had an array of foods already set out. There was lamb, beef, the beloved *koto-bacon*, and various fruits, cheeses, breads, and veggies. I eyed up the juicy buttered corn, but then my gaze darted to the deli pickles.

Aroha continued, "He's watching cooking shows while he works out."

A treadmill sat in the corner of the apartment. Typical of my father-in-law. Full of energy and needing to spend it. At least it wasn't focused on war. The proposed lockdown was going to be hard on him.

Unable to care about manners, I grabbed a skewer off the plate beside the stove and bit into the steaming meat, burning my tongue but not caring since it was instantly healing (so weird).

Chase's eyes left the grilling pan he was tending and watched me inhale the entire skewer of meat. "I have more bacon if—"

Mouth full, I incoherently half shouted, "Yes."

His eyes crinkled in amusement as he got out more bacon.

Arms wrapped around me from behind, and Archer pressed against me. Held up in front of me was another skewer. "Feed our baby," Archer whispered in my ear, making goosebumps raise on my neck as he kissed that spot under my ear where it met my jaw.

I took the skewer, confused. He was mad at me but doting on me. For Philo. After the baby was born, would he ditch me? I really hoped hormones were what was making me this insecure. My depressing thoughts seemed uncontrollable.

"Callie, here. Archer told us about your underworld platter. Pickle?" Aroha tempted me.

The idea was appetizing. I put my skewer down and took a pickle from her. I had it in my mouth and took a bite in superspeed, so the smell of the vinegar had a delayed arrival. Instantly, I gagged. I spit out the piece of pickle, onto their floor, and then ran to their bathroom. No time to shut the door, they heard me hurl the little food I ate into the toilet.

Archer was right there, beside me, pulling my hair back.

"Shut the door!" I managed to get out before I threw up again.

He kicked it shut.

I wiped my mouth. "I meant with you out there." I made the mistake of meeting his concerned gaze.

"Never." He kissed my forehead.

I glared at him but looked away as my stomach turned on me. I dry heaved.

He left me alone. I heard Aroha whining about her stomach bothering her and the bacon sizzling on the stove. It smelled so good, but my stomach was angry.

Archer was back, the door closed again. On a small plate, he had a lemon sliced in four wedges. I looked at him oddly.

"Bite into one. Try it. If it doesn't work, we can try crackers or dairy. Whatever it takes, we'll find what settles your stomach. I wager you're a lemon girl." He had a wry grin on his face, but his eyes were still crinkled in worry.

"Lemons?" I gave well warranted side-eyes. Lemons were acidic, so if my stomach was in turmoil, how would that help? I should have something basic. Milk. Eww, the idea felt hideous.

"Trust me." It was a torturous phrase. I hadn't trusted him enough to tell him the truth before. I had to now. What was the harm? Another round of dry heaves?

Against all instincts, I bit into the lemon, trying to salvage this relationship in hopes my visions were completely wrong. How could a man—I mean, a god of love—ever hurt me when he cared this much?

The citrus was harshly sour in my mouth and made my mouth pucker up. Surprisingly, my stomach settled. He was a genius! (wait a minute...) He had done this before.

"No?" he fretted. My face was likely grimacing.

I schooled my features and coolly asked, "So that worked for *her* too?"

His brow furrowed in confusion, then it went blank. He stood up. "I learned it from Lucien. She...I didn't know Psyche was pregnant until later, so I wasn't around for the start. But I have seen my mother go through it."

I created a distance between us, leaning back against the wall. I put another lemon in my mouth, hoping my reference to Psyche would vanish. My stomach settled more. I didn't understand why or how lemons worked, but they did. "Archer—"

"Let's go to dinner and, if you can eat, eat. Seems like the baby wants protein. Eat what you can."

That was it. I had opened my mouth about the past and angered him. Dinner was awful. The food was good, but Archer and I were no good company. I was able to eat meat, bread, and branched out to corn without a problem this time

89

around, thanks to the lemons. I sucked on a slice at the end to make sure my full stomach stayed calm.

Aroha and Chase attempted to keep lively conversation going, so much so, I felt bad for them. Aroha ended up doing most of the talking, telling us all about the new arrivals, an Egyptian goddess, who apparently had a past with Lucien, and a secret child. It was just too bad Lucien came back without his memory, something I hadn't foreseen. I hoped that meant it would come back.

Finally, I left. Archer did not follow me.

I lay down in bed, alone, feeling desperately sad. I wanted Archer, but he and I just kept upsetting each other. I understood how he cared about me enough to make peace, but it was not lasting due to me putting my foot in my mouth, as always. (Wish Dad was here to remind me that it always got me in trouble.)

I could not sleep, thinking of Archer and all the good times we had. Considering we had gone through hell together (Hades literally), the good times were the loving moments behind closed doors. And those risqué memories made me feel flushed. I tossed and turned, unable to stop my thoughts. White-hot desire pulsed in me when I simply thought of his lips, his body, so perfect as if sculpted from marble.

I put on a robe and left the apartment, rage now taking over. Why were my emotions so wild? (Hormones, ugh.) I pounded on the door across from my in-laws. The jerk I wanted to kill answered the door, groggy. Was it that late? Archer's brothers stayed up late gaming most nights.

"You all right?" Himerus blinked a few times.

"Stop meddling for your brother."

Himerus shook his head in a very Chase-like move of confusion. Then his gaze locked onto mine in understanding. He laughed. "I did nothing, but if you two really aren't together, and you're feeling, you know, I could—"

"NO!" I shouted and stormed off. If he hadn't tried to put Archer and I together by instilling me with lust, then…hormones. (Scream.)

I stood outside Archer's door, hesitating. I shouldn't go in, but I *needed* to. I tried the knob, and the door opened. He either trusted the doorman not to let anyone onto our floor or hoped I would come back.

Nothing mattered right now. I needed to feel everything, including him. I raced in and threw myself into the bed beside him. Archer sat up in bed, shocked by the interruption in his sleep. *Need.*

I threw a leg over his lap to straddle him and kissed him. As if nothing had just happened, a fight didn't exist, his lips claimed mine, and his arms pulled me in. I continued to kiss him. There were no words. We were both angry and upset with each other, but there was that something between us no obstacle could crush: love.

LISA BORNE GRAVES

In all ways, love, love, love. We gave in to the feelings we longed for, forgetting about everything else.

For a short while.

When the early morning light poked through the window, I snuck out, regretting how he'd be even more confused now. I had to figure out what my vision meant and how to trust him and get him to trust me again.

CHAPTER 14

I felt so alone in Jordan.

Callie and Archer had left immediately because she was sick, and they were in a fight. I had seen Archer mad in the past, particularly at his brothers, but this cold shoulder he was giving her and the terse one-word answers were pretty telling.

Hades and Persephone were gleefully on holiday since he was finally free. There was no point in them staying to try to help us. Lucien didn't remember them anyway. Prometheus told us to be patient, that his memory would somehow come back, but the fact Prometheus didn't know exactly how or when that would happen meant this wasn't his foresight speaking but his wishful thinking.

No one was helpful, except Athena, who kept trying to explain things to my father. "You are Apollo, god of truth, the sun, poetry, medicine."

"Yes," my father said impatiently. "You told me this. I don't feel the powers. I don't know what I'm supposed to do."

"I still have them," I muttered, noting the time and starting the sunset.

I was depressed, and no wonder. I had gone through the beginning stages of grief, postponed by the hope he would be resurrected by Callie. I should be happy. My dad was back. But this wasn't my father. The relationship we had just built up over the past year and a half was gone. Having him alive and a blank slate felt selfish. I was happy he was alive, but it wasn't the same. If his memory never returned, would it be better for him to have remained dead?

I had another thought, and it was time to voice it. "What about Callie and Archer?" I hoped his death had undone my work, how he had made me perform soul-share to Callie, giving her his soul so she could live. I was unable to follow the connection anymore but wanted to see if he still felt attached to Callie in some way.

Lucien looked so open and unaffected, not like the experienced and hardened man I had looked up to. Was this what he had been like as a youth? I had never felt more like him until this moment.

"What about them?" He was lost.

"Are you still in love with her? Do you feel connected to her?"

His brow wrinkled. "No. She's beautiful by any standard, but she's my best friend's wife—at least you've told me he was my best friend. Why? Should I have some sort of feelings for her?"

"The old you wouldn't have hesitated to steal a wife; let's put it that way." Prometheus chuckled.

I didn't find it funny. "If he wants to be a better person this time around, then let him."

Prometheus rolled his eyes. Of course. He'd expect my dad to revert to who he was once this "miracle" happened to restore his memory.

"Please stop talking about me in front of me," Dad complained.

"Sorry, Dad. Maybe if we took you home to New York?"

"His old apartment is gone. It'll still be a new place to him," Athena mused, still talking about him in third person. "And he died for his best friend and his wife. There was some feeling there. Let us not forget how many forms of love there are."

Prometheus and I exchanged a look, mine surprised and his vindicated. Athena talking of love was not an everyday occurrence for the rational creature. His influence was clear.

I sighed, not wanting to stay here. I wanted to be back in New York, to talk to Linda, to see my friends. Most importantly, I wanted Dad somewhere that felt safer, surrounded by faces he might somehow remember. "Your things though will be familiar: furniture, pictures, clothing. Maybe something will trigger your memory."

He placed his hand upon mine and squeezed it. "I appreciate you trying to help me, Son, but I can tell you're exhausted. Whatever you think is best."

There it was: "Son." I had a glimmer of hope that his Iceland-adopted moniker for me was a shred of memory of who he was returning to me. I didn't say anything, though; he didn't need the pressure.

I had hoped Athena and Prometheus would return to New York with us, but there were discussions of allies, to see who was with or against us. Well, from her. But Prometheus said something about a ceremony and extended honeymoon. Trust Athena to package her wedding with ally visits. Maybe there was no romantic hope for her after all.

What it meant was Dad was fully my burden to bear. I couldn't tell my mom or my brothers, share the responsibility. Athena insisted we must keep his resurrection a secret—as well as Hades and Persephone's freedom. I understood. Blindsiding Zeus with three powerful gods would be a spectacular tactic. Still, it added to the stress. How would I explain Lucien's state to Linda or even tell him who she had been to him and who she was to me now. Things were about to get weird, but I had promised to call her tonight, and if we were headed back via a wind god, I couldn't call her from my apartment all of a sudden. "I'm going to video call someone. She uh…her name is Linda. Do you remember her?"

"No, should I?"

"Friend of Callie's who knows nothing about what we are. You uh… dated her briefly."

"But not now?"

"No."

"Because I loved this Callie girl?"

"Yeah." I smiled. "You're getting it all as if you remember—at least the logic of your life."

He grinned. "Some things you say are like memories I just can't grasp, but familiar."

I didn't dare hope it was the beginning of something just to have it dashed away.

"Should I talk to her?"

"No." I said too quickly.

Dad gave me a thoughtful side-eye. He smiled. "Oooh, you like her? Hey wait, did I care about that? My son and my ex?"

Now was not the time to bring up how his son, my half-brother, Asclepius was dating his ex, who was my Mom, Euterpe. Even thinking about it was so confusing and weird, so I reminded myself that they were not blood related. Pushing them from my mind, I answered, "No. Linda was just a mortal cover, a dating life to fit in with the mortals. At least, I think. Regardless, she liked you, hated you, then sort-of friends, you died, and I told her you were alive but there was an issue."

"Yeah, I'll leave you to it. That's a lot for someone to handle and me not remembering her will probably be worse for the mortal." Then he stood up, tousling my hair, before he left the room. Another familiar gesture.

Linda would have to wait a minute. "Dad? Why did you do that?"

"What?" He leaned in the doorway, reminding me of another posture he tended to do.

I smiled. "You messed my hair up. That's like your trademark 'dad' move."

He looked at his hands. "Instincts? Maybe behaviors are returning to me unconsciously." He smiled. "Maybe it'll keep happening. Will you keep telling me when I act like me? It makes this ignorance less daunting."

I nodded.

"With this girl, whatever truths you can tell her will create a bond. You have gone through a lot, Aios. The least amount of lying as possible will simplify your life."

I didn't have the heart to tell him his great advice was something he hadn't lived by since Callie had freed him of always telling the truth. I hoped more than anything that just a sliver of his former self didn't come back—the selfishness, the disregard of loved ones, his inability to express his feelings…

Then I felt like crap about it as he left the room in a good mood, closing the door. I was the selfish one for wishing that upon him. I wanted him back, flaws and all. I missed my dad, his face not enough to fill the void the pain of his death had left. I still felt traumatized for how he had forced me to do it myself. There would be time for healing once I had him back. Right now, he needed me.

After the call, it dawned on me how much I'd missed Linda, more than I thought I would. The talk uplifted me. She made me feel positive about Lucien's amnesia, that he would remember in time and that all would be okay. Well, after she was highly suspicious. Archer had used the excuse of why he hadn't returned when the mortal high school had believed him dead. I had to spin truths to make Archer the one lying, by saying his family wouldn't let him be with her but eventually relented, that he didn't really have amnesia and that Callie knew the truth. I heavily pointed out that Lucien had been pronounced dead, put into a coma, and that we had no hope of him waking. When I carried the power of truth, it made telling it easier but in a way that was crafty. I almost felt bad having the skill. Hopefully, it was only on loan and my dad would take it back.

I longed to go back to New York, but I wasn't sure if my father was ready for it.

Over the next few days, Dad started acting more himself, the personality returning, gestures, and certain expressions he often used, but no memories came back, nothing he could recall. I was stuck with his powers, which meant work, work, work—so trying to help him remember in a place foreign to me was difficult. I missed Linda. Our daily video chats I snuck in when Dad was sleeping—he did that a lot—were not satisfying. Each of us had nothing to talk about with me not being able to tell her much of where I was or what was going on. She was bored because her mother was making her stick to the house because of the virus—the now pandemic.

I made the executive decision and prepared for the return home. It was uneventful—thank the gods, excluding the ones on my shit list like my aunts who tried to kill me and my grandma who would turn on her own son.

It was good I hadn't truly believed other, on-our-side, family members would miraculously restore my dad's memory in New York because they didn't. From their expressions, they were all torn about him being back while in this state too. Don't get me wrong. Everyone was happy to see him. Aroha and Archer tried desperately to share information of their past with him. It worked to reestablish their friendships, but even they grew melancholy around him when he couldn't remember big things they had gone through together. Aroha's hormones weren't helping her. She got weepy often, about him, about Archer and Callie's fight—even good things like having a baby and a grandkid around the same time.

Chase was much kinder to Dad than he had ever been in previous centuries, maybe—I hoped—trying to be a real brother to my dad. I also sensed he was hiding something. Dad's truth power was too strong in me. I cornered him while Aroha was regaling Dad with a story about his antics in Germany. Despite their humor, she was tearing up.

"What are you hiding?"

Chase went wide-eyed and then huffed out a breath. He leaned back against the counter, examining me, making me feel as if I were the one being interrogated. "Truth powers, huh? What do you know about your father's time off the grid?"

I wanted to tell him I was the one asking the questions, but he stumped me with the subject change, and the mystery behind his question intrigued me. "I was never close to him until recently, and a few spells of time in my youth."

Chase nodded in thought. "Archer and Aroha said he'd part ways with them now and then."

I frowned. "Which is normal and expected when you spend so much time together, no?"

He nodded. "I agree, but they only remember each time on his return depression or anger—like he really needed the two of them to get him out of a rut. The last time, Archer said it was so bad, he made a playlist of silly songs about the sun. He played it for him to get him out of the Underworld."

I stared at him. Why was he telling me this? What did he want me to see?

"Aios, what troubles your father more than anything else?"

"Women." It came out without thought, but it was the truth. The god unlucky in love. "Chase, what's this about?"

My tone must've been frazzled, for he touched my shoulder, comforting me. "Forget it. You have a lot going on. It's not anything that can be fully solved until he gets his memory back. I believe something happened that last spell of time he was away from us. I just want to get the facts straight. We're about to enter a mortal lockdown. If the world waits, so shall we."

I didn't like it, but I didn't want another problem on my table, another thing Dad could not remember. Call it cowardice, but I dropped it.

I'm glad I did. Dad settled in pretty well since everyone treated him as they had before. Still, my anxiety increased. Living with him, there were so many questions, nonstop. How could I fill in his thousands of years when I only spent a few years here and there with him?

Today, a few days after our return to Manhattan, was another day of questions.

"Where are we going?" he asked as we got in the elevator. I swore I had told him the night before, but maybe I had gotten all mixed up with so many questions. Panic filled me momentarily that he was losing memories. I mean, how many gods are frozen and resurrected? Maybe some wires got loose in his brain, or it was degenerating. I wished Athena would come back.

"Out, for food. It's my turn, and I need your help to carry it all. Here." I handed him a mask. It was his first outing. I was nervous he'd say something wrong.

"You said we could not die from the mortal illnesses, so why wear a mask?"

"Because we'll fit in better. You cannot tell anyone about who you are. It's called 'mortalling.' We pretend to be like them. If you don't and slip up and say you're Apollo, or even say 'mortal' like you just did in front of them, they will lock you up and—"

"I know, my asshole of a father, who I can't even remember, will try to kill me or you—again." Could he say it more like a petulant child?

"No memory, none at all of him?" I tried for the umpteenth time, hoping like before when he had heard the thunder and shuddered, remembering his dad for just a moment. I longed for another inkling to come through and give me hope.

He shook his head and sighed. "What I hate is how much that disappoints them all and you. I want you to know something, though, but I do have a question first."

"Go for it."

"Was I bad at expressing how I felt? Or is my brain destroyed from my death? I feel things, but the words don't come." Well, he was worried too, but admitting he sucked at feelings was absolutely true. Maybe he was okay after all.

Then my mind turned to what feelings he was lingering on. "If you tell me it's about Archer's wife, I swear I'll scream. I enjoyed a break from that hopeless heartache." It was muttered under my breath. The elevator slowed down. Someone was getting on in a moment. We had to end the conversation.

"No. She is nice and pretty, but she is my best friend's wife, and they have been great to me. I don't remember Archer, but the stories he tells me about our past together feel familiar. It's like being shown a memory, and then it becomes one, maybe distorted, I'm unsure. I feel a connection to him. I know he is my friend. But Callie, no. I don't remember her much."

It made sense. No matter how intense his feelings had been, she was a blip in the memory of an extensive life. "Don't worry about it. We'll talk later."

"I feel like I was bad at it. Talking about my feelings. If I'm back from the dead, should I not try to improve myself? When I look in the mirror and then at you, I feel pride. I love you. I want to see my other sons."

I wanted to say it was a bad idea before he had some more memory, but the elevator doors *ping*ed open. I could not help but smile at his admittance though. He wanted to learn how to express his feelings better. Perhaps this would be his rebirth?

A dark-skinned young woman with striking blue eyes and an adolescent girl were outside. The elder saw us and froze, her mouth open. Recognition crossed her face when she beheld my father. Crap! Who was she? The doors started to close, but my dad leaned over for the open-door button, pressing it a few times.

When he drew his arm back, he went rigid. His eyes bore into the woman's. "Ma'at?"

The woman gasped. The child glanced at her, concerned, and then at my father. Her eyes darted to me. The young girl had slightly lighter skin than her companion, but not by much. And strikingly familiar, openly honest, green eyes—my eyes, both my brother's eyes, *Dad's* eyes. Such a vibrant green hue is not common among mortals. Confusion and theories swirled in my brain. Chase's comment about something happening the last time Dad had been away…

I looked back to my father. His face was still in shock, but I could tell the gears were turning. He did not move, and my confusion grew. Was he remembering something? Did he know this woman? I was scared to interrupt if it was a memory coming back.

The woman gripped the girl's hand tightly, territorially, and the girl became concerned. "Mom?"

That was a tell-tale sign. If that was her mother, the woman was immortal like us, unageing. The pair looked less than ten years apart. This was a goddess, and the name finally clicked as my father repeated it again, his voice surer.

He looked away from her to the floor, his eyes darting around, trying to figure something out. The door was yet again closing. I sensed this was important, that my father was truly remembering. I threw my arm out and stopped the door from closing. It reopened.

"Please," I begged the woman. "He has amnesia but knows you somehow. Don't go. You might be able to help."

She walked into the elevator, hesitant, but her eyes never left my father, nor did she let go of the girl's hand. The doors closed.

"Lucien, what do you remember?" I called him by his alias because this woman was definitely not an Olympian. I had to be careful.

"Ma'at, love, during the Ptolemaic Dynasty." His eyes met mine, terrified.

Clearly, from the name and her calm nature at hearing about herself from ages ago, she was the actual Egyptian goddess.

I was confused but not as much as him. I had to help my dad. "That was a long time ago. Just take a minute, and formulate your thoughts."

The woman looked at the girl and then at me. She was nervous.

"Hi. I'm sorry. I'm Aios, Hymenaios originally." I offered my hand. Did she know most of the Greeks like we studied others, just in case we ran into them? Each god's family tree was a lot to remember, and I was afraid to call him dad in front of her.

She gave me a nervous smile. "I go by Akila right now. I met Chase. He told me to wait before…"

"We were heading to get groceries. Perhaps a detour to somewhere else we can talk in private?"

"Central Park," she said.

Her daughter's eyes lit up. I saw myself in her a bit. This was my half sister; I could swear it. I didn't dare say a word in front of her. It was clear she didn't know this was her father and half brother in the elevator. I was dying to know what was going on and how it was possible. We were never to get involved with the others. If we did, there would never be a child. It wasn't possible.

Except that had been under Zeus's control, and Callie was alive before this girl's birth. And the whole Prometheus and Athena romance, their children killed. Now, I understood part of her fright. This wasn't just forbidden love, but a forbidden child to boot. This might be bad, another target on our hands.

The elevator slowed. I put on my mask and nudged my dad to do the same. Akila and her daughter did the same. The doors opened, and two mortals entered. I glanced at my father. His eyes were bemused, still dancing about as if reading a mental book. I prayed to Mnemosyne, who likely would not answer my prayer, to restore his mind. He remembered an Egyptian goddess. It was too much to hope that she could help us. Her being here was too much of a coincidence as well, but she knew Chase. Why hadn't I pressed him for more info?

"How long have you lived in the building?" I ventured a safe question in front of others.

Akila met my gaze. She looked at my father, her breath coming quickly, moving her mask. She was upset. I didn't want to provoke her, but I was a ball of nerves and emotions as well. I had lost my father, then was given hope only to see him return an empty vessel. One she sparked alive, somehow.

She lovingly put her arm around the girl, pulling her away from the mortals. "A few weeks. This is Polly."

Way too coincidental of a name not to be my sister. My mind could not wrap around this. She was young and powerless like most of us were in childhood, vulnerable against gods who might want to harm her.

The girl turned around to look at me, sparing a glance at my father, whose eyes were wide as he met her gaze. "Polly is short for Apollinaria. Some of my old friends thought it's weird, but I think it is rather beautiful."

"That's enough," the mother scolded as the elderly man in front of us turned and gazed at us about the name that was strange to him.

To me, it was affirmation. To my father—I wasn't sure what his broken mind was doing, but the shock on his face was piecing it together.

Finally, we arrived on the ground floor. "I agree with you. It is pretty," I told the girl and gave her a wink. I tried to ignore the motherly-seeming middle-aged mortal whose eyes gave me an indulgent smile as if a kind teen was a rarity. Ageism. If she only knew how old I was.

Once we hit the pavement outside, Polly's mother told her not to discuss certain things in front of strangers. Compared to normal times, there were a tenth of the people who'd normally walked the streets.

"They're not strangers, Mother. Don't you feel it?"

Akila's brow scrunched up in bemusement. "What?"

"The warmth."

"I feel it," Dad said, his voice hardly a whisper through the mask. He looked at Akila. "You and I were together? Is she mine?"

Akila looked affronted.

I jumped in before this got heated. "No memory. The price of being raised from the dead."

"She is *mine*, and will never be yours," Akila hissed.

"Let us find a private area in the park, please," I begged her. "He had changed before his death. He was a good person. He would never try to take her from you if that is your concern. Things in the Greek sector are not going well, so we'd never want to endanger you or Polly."

She seemed hesitant and then said, "I heard. I came here for Polly's protection, so she could meet family. I came to try to help you get him back, and then was told you all had it in hand. Then I was rudely told to stay away."

I clenched my jaw and shook my head. "Chase didn't want to admit to you that Lucien came back with no memory. We are at war, and your kind have stayed out so far. We cannot fully trust you, even though Polly draws us closer together as allies."

The goddess looked like she was about to scream or cry. "I hate him, but I wanted him alive."

"Hate me?" Dad asked. "Why would you hate me?"

"Mom?" The girl asked, confused. "Is he my father?"

Akila sighed, glancing at both of them intermittently. "Yes." She glared daggers at Dad.

He stared back like a wounded puppy. "I don't understand."

"You were terrible with women, Dad." I offered.

"So, that means…you're my brother?" The girl's eyes lit up.

Shoot, I had slipped up.

"Half," her mother said in a clipped tone. I wondered if she was not a fan of my mother. I had heard tales of my mom's artful revenge antics.

"All you need to know is that he is back without his memory. It's been familiar to him after we explain things, but you are the only person he has recognized without prompting."

Akila's eyes went wide, and she took in his confused face. "You mean he really lost his memory?" Finally, sympathy came through. "I cannot promise a solution, Aios, since I don't have memory skills, but perhaps he is seeing truth in Truth? My wisdom? Or perhaps my need for balance is trying to heal him? I don't know."

Dad hit my shoulder gently. "Aios, can we stop doing that?"

"Huh?"

"Talking about me as if I'm not here, again. I'm flesh and blood, and I have a brain. My memory is faulty, not my wits."

"Sorry, Dad. Really. It is just hard when you can't remember."

"Well, *you* can't remember one simple request," he muttered, pulling off his mask in frustration, slipping a band onto his wrist.

I sighed, but Akila's eyes squinted with her hidden smile. "I think more of you is back than they realize."

My Dad's mouth twitched, and then he grinned. "Is it? I sure want to remember my past with you." His tone was flirtatious. Awkward.

Akila gave me a high-browed-*see?* look.

Somehow, Dad was coming back, and I'd be lying to myself if it wasn't because of this woman. The *how* was looming in my mind as an unanswerable question. Dad didn't remember, and the Egyptian was not forthcoming. Chase knew something, but how to get all the pieces together?

CHAPTER 15

The most beautiful being I had ever beheld stood in front of me. Her tawny skin, voluminous dark hair, with those vibrant pale blue eyes under thick black lashes and expressive brows made me not want to wake up from this dream. But it was real, right? As plain as day, those startling blues, in the warm tones of her face, were staring through me—like matching portals of truth—into the depths of my soul. I could never forget a woman this perfect. So familiar. Only, how *did* I remember? Her name came from some hidden depth of my mind to my mouth, "Ma'at?"

Ma'at, or she had introduced herself as Akila this time around, was as beautiful as she was the day she tackled me over a territorial dispute. Of course, I was unable to lie back then, and my first words were stupidly asking her how she was so gorgeous.

Ever since I "woke up" and understood my existence again, I had been lost and only going along with what my friends and family told me. It was clear Aios was my son; he looked like me, and there was a deep connection there I could feel. But this was not the déjà vu feeling I had talking to Aios; it was a real memory.

The way the blue-eyed beauty glared at me told me I had not treated her right, but lies danced around her mood. She still cared about me in some capacity. Did I care about her? I tried to remember more of her than her gorgeous face, elegant neck, but only lustful moments of making love to her and tender moments in her arms came to mind. *Hardly helpful, brain.* I drew a blank to anything else, as if only snippets were breaking free from wherever they were walled up in my reanimated brain.

The more I focused on remembering, the more the pressure in my head built until it was painful. I stumbled onto a bench and sat down. My ears rang, breaths came quickly, and I couldn't hear the concerned words of the gods around me. My heart raced fast. Clutching my head, I closed my eyes. My heart pounded and pounded, the only sound and sensation I could feel—

Akila sucked in a worried breath. "Your heart."

It felt like it might burst.

Her hands gently touched my shoulders, imparting soothing energy into me, slowing my pulse down in tandem with some other eerie feeling, much like an assault on my neurological system.

Images shot forth at amazing speeds, reminding me of Chaos's reign; only, these weren't all of time–just my past. The strange thing was that I knew who and what they all were: memories. *Euterpe, Aios, Zeus, Maia, Artemis, my other boys, Archer, Aroha, Chase, Callie…*

After it stopped, I took a few deep breaths, my head aching as if someone had hit me upside it with a sledgehammer. "I remember."

"What?" Aios's face was etched in fear and excitement.

I met his gaze, my eyes squinting with pain. "Everything."

Aios's mouth dropped. When he recovered asked, "How?"

"I am balance?" Akila shrugged. "I don't know how, except—"

"You bring order without knowing it." Then to Aios, I explained, "She's kind of like Callie in how Ma'at's power is not always a controllable one. The fact she exists brings balance to unequivocal situations."

"I just poured my power into you to ease your anxiety, that's all." Akila looked annoyed to be compared to Callie.

"Well, memories came with it."

She crossed her arms. "Is that why you kept coming back and leaving? You wanted my balance to help you with justice?"

By the beard of Zeus, I could not deal with this right now. Why were women so difficult? Two could play her blame game. "I think you know very well why we both came back but hardly appropriate conversation in front of the kids, dear."

Her mouth dropped, and her brows narrowed in irritation, but the suppressed smile of my son told me I was more myself than ever in that one loaded comment. Akila was not impressed, and I couldn't even look at the other younger being by Aios's side. I could not process her yet after being bombarded with my long lifespan.

"Look, Akila, I just had thousands of years of memories jammed into my head in under a minute. I can't deal with any of this." Having enough of her attitude and feeling weak and confused, I was off the bench. I ignored my son's entreaties to take it easy and walked off at a brisk pace. I ached to run at an immortal speed, but some mortals were milling about on such a nice day, not interacting and remaining at a social distance in their little clusters.

I kept walking out of the park. They didn't follow that quickly, giving me space, but I heard them behind me. I crossed the street and down an alley. Free from mortal gazes, I ran through interconnected alleyways at immortal speed until a dead end stopped me. Apparently, I could not recall all the streets accurately or had not been paying attention.

A daughter? A half-Egyptian, half-Greek daughter, likely born only because of Callie's existence and Zeus's loss of control over our fertility. *Polly*. My mind was fully restored, but she was not in any memories I could recall. Truth power had come back to me, its power overwhelmingly and clearly guiding me to the answer: Akila never told me I had a daughter, that she had gotten pregnant even. I'd never met Polly. I traced time backward. New York, Germany, Australia—Italy with Ma'at. A secret and blissful two-year liaison with her when Aroha and Archer went off to some Caribbean island with her mortal millionaire husband at the time. That was ten—no thirteen years ago. Ma'at had conceived. She never thought to tell me? Never asked me to stay?

I was angry with her, feeling betrayed. Yet I owed it to the child—because of her mother hiding us from each other—to pull my shit together and be a good father the remaining years of her childhood. I only got okay at the dad thing recently. What was I supposed to do with a kid? A girl especially?

A voice broke me from my reveries. "You sure scare easily." Polly stood, hand on hip, her green eyes judging, lips curled in amusement. She was a miniature combo of us, with my eyes, plenty of Akila's sass, and both our dark, untamable hair.

Then again, I hadn't been the sweetest kid either, but it had been more of rebellion and angst to be free of Olympus, and an overbearing hard-ass father, a stepmother who hated me, and a mother who loved other children more than me.

"You try getting your entire existence of thousands of years downloaded to your brain and your powers back in one go." The joke did not take flight due to my grumpy tone. I felt the sun's arc in the back of my mind and adjusted it in the sky—a few minutes behind schedule—and injustices were fluttering all about the city. I took a deep breath to prevent my anxiety from making my heart almost burst again. The powers that had felt like second nature were hard work right now.

"Well, how about you try being told you're moving to another country because your dad you never met died—oh, hey, wait, he's alive now." Her sarcasm matched my own and a toss of her hair threw in some extra sass. She was adorable. Fatherly pride started blooming in my chest, making the anxiety quell.

I approached her, not sure what to say next. "Sorry, kid. I never knew about you."

"Yeah, Mom fucked that all that up, didn't she?"

"Hey! Language." My paternal instincts reacted before I even thought about it. Hearing a kid swear? I'd normally laugh at hearing it, but this was *my* kid.

Polly measured me up, pursing her lips, scrutinizing whether I was an authority figure worth listening to. The brazen front she had maintained started to crumble, and the lost little girl underneath was surfacing. "Sorry. Don't tell my mom, please."

I smiled. "I won't. It'll be our secret."

She gave me a mischievous smile, one very much like my own.

"Your mother, she…uh, probably had her reasons." I had no clue what those were, but I had to tread carefully, or Ma'at— "Akila" I had to get used to—might disappear with my daughter.

Polly huffed, making me smile. I ruffled her hair, and she scowled, fixing it. Ah, she believed she was all grown up already, not a kid—*that* stage.

"I don't pretend to know why your mother never told me. We parted on decent terms. Your mother and I weren't supposed to be together, so…" I wasn't sure how else to explain it. It was the truth, but other truths were not for a twelve-year-old's ears. I tamped down those steamy memories of Akila, although my mind wanted to go there again.

"I was some dirty secret."

"No, never that." I placed my hand on her shoulder, guiding her through the alleys, figuring her mother was frantically looking for her. A kid could take off running in Central Park, but her mother chasing after her probably would've caused a scene. "Because our relationship was forbidden, so were you, and so you are still. You'll have to ask your mother, but my guess is she was just protecting you, but things are different now. There is another goddess like you whose bloodline crossed godly cultures. There could be more. I think—"

"There you are," an exasperated and cross Akila approached with my son awkwardly trailing. She drew Polly away from me and protectively draped her arms around her daughter, who was only a head shorter than her tall stature. "Don't ever run off like that again. This city is huge and filled with strangers."

Polly shrank away from her mother's scolding voice and pushed herself under my arm. My chest inexplicably tightened for some reason. My arm tightened around her, the instinct to protect what was mine flaring.

Akila glared at me. "What lies did you tell her about me?"

"I defended you, for some inexplicable reason. My guess is she doesn't like you yelling at her for starters."

"You are going to tell me how to parent now? That's a laugh. She was going after *you*, worried about *you*."

Of course, it was all my fault to her. Damn woman. "Seriously? You blame my parenting faults after hiding my child from me so I couldn't even try to be a parent to her? That's rich." This was the problem between us. Hot one minute, at each other's throats the next.

Aios cleared his throat. "Perhaps we should take this back to the apartment."

"Yeah, mine," she asserted.

Polly asked curiously, "Can't we see his?"

Akila's jaw set.

"Or mine, little sister?" Aios offered. Perfect, a neutral setting.

Akila's glare moved to him.

"What? Neutral ground, or so I thought." Aios supplied, his hands up in surrender.

We walked in silence, Polly glued to my side, her arm around my back, my hand draped over her shoulder. The thing was, it didn't feel weird to me. Maybe I could do this dad thing better this time around.

The thought was fleeting when I saw the bubbling tension building in Akila's features, her shoulders tense. The kid would be the easy part of all this. Akila would be a formidable force that I wasn't sure how to tame. The old me would seduce her, but there was a kid in the mix who could get hurt. I had no idea how to proceed or even how I felt. What did I want when it came to Akila?

Akila's nasty attitude continued, and I could hardly handle regular thoughts by the time we got back to the building. On my son's good sense, we parted ways—they went back to the park for Polly, and we went food shopping. I had made Akila promise she would stay in the building and talk about things once I came to terms with my memories. I was glad. I was ecstatic to have a daughter, but my head ached as if swollen by information.

When we returned to the building and exited the elevator, Archer was out in the hallway, leaning on the door at the end of it as if he had been knocking on it. He peered over at me, his face distraught, but then his eyes opened wide. He stood up straight.

He eagerly asked, "Lucien?" Could he see that I was back? My eyes prickled. How I loved my best friend, the rock in my life. He'd know exactly how I should deal with Akila.

"The one and only." I pointed at myself, a gesture he knew well that I had done when I was a cocky god in my first millennium that he loved to bring up and tease me about.

He rushed to me, and I met him halfway, giving him a hug and slamming his back. I backed away and saw the worry still in his eyes.

"You okay?" I asked.

"Yeah, Callie and I are having some issues."

"Well, you sort out my woman issue, and I'll sort out yours. Deal?"

"You've been back from the dead for like five minutes, and you already have issues with a woman. You're definitely really back." He grinned, his mood improved at my expense.

I normally would have a witty retort, but it was too good to see the people I remembered, as if I had been away from them for centuries like we had been every now and then—a reunion. I felt like all the Callie nonsense was behind us. I hoped. When I thought of her, I didn't feel the pangs of love, lust, or jealousy, but only seeing her would confirm that.

"Uh, Dad?" Aios called. He had his foot in the elevator, rapidly moving grocery bags into the hall as it tried to close on him—probably for the second time.

Archer and I helped him get the last few bags into the hall, but the commotion outside made a bored, cooped up god come out.

"What's all this noise? Need help?" Chase came out. Unlike Archer, he didn't realize I was restored. He bent to get some bags.

Aroha followed. "Which ones are ours?"

"Ma, Dad," Archer said to stop them. "He's back."

Chase's face slipped into shock before his smile came out. "Knew you'd get it back, brother."

"Brother?" I raised his brows. He rarely called me his brother.

He shrugged, and he hefted a ton of bags in one hand as if they were weightless. "New you, new me." He slammed the other hand on my back harder than a comfortable gesture, but he was Ares after all.

"Oh. My. Gods." Aroha was wiping her tears away and threw her arms around me, squeezing me way too tight.

"Okay, okay," I coaxed her to let go.

The boys came out next, Archer's brothers. Raphael came out behind us, and then the last door on the end next to my apartment opened. It had been explained as Athena and Prometheus's place, but Callie came out of it, the same door Archer had been leaning on. Girl trouble. They were in a fight. Archer looked away from her, grabbed a bunch of bags and brushed past her as she walked toward me, her eyes never leaving me.

"You are back? I mean, really back." Her lips quivered. She had ignored me, had barely come out of the room to talk to any of us, and said little to me since I had returned.

I nodded.

As I gazed into those brown eyes that used to light my soul afire, I felt nothing intense. I did not long for her touch or wish she were mine. She simply was Callie, my dear friend whom I'd helped through a hard time, whom I cared about saving more than my own existence. For her, for Archer. As her last words to me came back, I remembered: the baby.

She pulled me in for a hug. "Thank you. You saved us."

I let her go. "Thanks for saving me back. Best buds, for eternity." I held up a fist for her to fist bump me. She did, giggling.

Archer stood at the end of the hall, leaning against the wall, watching us. His face appeared confused. As god of love, he'd know my heart and what type of innocuous love I had for his wife now. The one perk of dying had spared me from loving the freedom goddess. Perhaps death had freed me in a way, given me a second chance with everyone to be a better god.

Archer nodded and smiled as if he understood the inner workings of my mind. I grinned back. All would be right between me and Archer now.

"Let's get these groceries away before things spoil, and we all meet up at Lucien's to hear how in Hades he got his mind back," Chase said to get us to disperse.

I gave him a look that could kill. My trip to Hades was no joking matter.

"What?" Chase grinned wickedly. "Too soon, brother?" He gave me a wink.

I was to expect *that* kind of brotherly love. I hoped we didn't return to the Hellenistic age when him beating me to pulp to assert his dominance was where we'd resume our brotherhood.

I entered my apartment and looked around. Everything felt familiar when, only an hour ago, I had no memory of my furniture, clothes, or knickknacks. I recalled how Aroha picked out the couch for me.

I went to my guitars on the wall, itching to play. Only yesterday, I'd sat holding my dreadnought guitar, trying to pluck notes without any memory or skill. I had sucked and given up.

I grabbed down my Martin Sunburst as Aios put the groceries away. I strummed it. It felt right and natural in my hands, but the tuning was off.

A possessive anger at my most prized possession being tampered with rose up in me. "Who touched my Sunburst?"

Aios's eyes went wide, showing his guilt.

I was up and after him. "You little…"

Aios dropped the can and was running down the hall away from me, him pleading that he was only trying to impress a girl and me swearing and scolding him in various languages.

He knew never to touch that one guitar. Everyone knew.

Chase stood in his doorway, grinning as if to say he was happy I was back.

So was I.

CHAPTER 16

Lucien was back (for real), which majorly shifted Archer's mood. It was good to see Archer do something other than be mad, sulk, or beg me to come home. On an our-friend-is-restored high, he invited me over for dinner. He cooked, being much better than me. (Hey, I was learning, and he had thousands of years' experience.) Archer was civil, and this felt like a huge olive branch being offered. I sat at the breakfast bar as he cooked so we could talk. I waited for him to bring Lucien up so we could apologize to each other and I could land him with an I-told-you-so. Only, he spoke about what food I was able to eat. With the menu worked out, he started cooking, rejecting my offer to help. (Pregnant, not helpless, but I let it go.)

It was weird sitting in my own house, feeling like a guest. We had to fix this, but Archer had been my first boyfriend, love, everything. I had little experience with fights and make ups. It showed. We were silent.

Awkwardly, I finally brought it up: "It is good to see Lucien back, like truly back."

Archer looked at me over his shoulder as he mashed up the ground beef for our tacos. Then, a beat later, as if he had thought his words through first, he turned. "I am glad we did what you said we should. Even after he was back and not himself, I was glad we took that risk. I thought he and I could become friends all over again if his memory never returned. The fact it came back after seeing the Egyptian goddess? Incredible. It just shows the power of love. It restored him. I'm so going to rub that in his face for always telling me my power was useless and nothing but trouble."

He stirred around the meat and said, "I'm saying, you were right. It was what had to be done." Turning again, his blues met my gaze, love in them (as always), but his mouth was grim.

"But?"

His brows rose in surprise. "Reading my mind?"

I shook my head. "I try not to do it often around you and others. It feels rude, and it still takes effort. I'm afraid practicing it too much might make it too easy after years and years. Like, what if I can't turn it off, and I hear everyone all the time?"

He nodded. "I think we'd all appreciate a shred of privacy, being that we are all here together for the foreseeable future." Archer sighed, his gaze darting to the floor. "But…I'm still upset about what I had originally said. You didn't tell me you were pregnant. You let me walk in there blind, with so much at risk. Do you realize what could've happened?"

"Yes, we would've all died together, but you lied to me too, Archer. You didn't tell me what I was signing up for with immortal marriage. You didn't even let me know what I was vowing to."

He crossed his arms and cocked his head, not angry but irritated, as his voice snapped back, "We can't keep going through this. What is done is done. Had I known you were immortal, I might not have done it" —he must've seen the whiplash of pain across my face because that stung— "yet."

"*Ever*, you meant. You regret—"

"No!" He slammed down the spatula and was over to me in an immortal second, kissing me.

I made the most of it, hoping he'd let me sate my annoying hormones. I wrapped my arms around him, pressed myself up against him, and started to back my way to the couch. His hands cupped my bottom as he staggered after me, not ready for me to move so quickly. Immortal speed. I was still not used to it. I increased the speed of our kisses, trying to pull him down onto the couch with me. He did not follow. Panting, with need in his glowing eyes, it was clear he wanted me as much as I wanted him, but it wasn't enough. He had cut off our kissing session before it could become more.

Too soon, his eyes dimmed, and he caught his breath. "Dinner." He turned his back to me and went over to stir up the sizzling meat.

"Seriously?" My tone was more cutting than I'd anticipated.

Archer went rigid, but then relaxed and faced me, crossing his arms. "As much as I'm tempted—which is *a lot*—I won't let you use me, Callie."

This rebuff hurt worse than words, but what had I expected? We had hurt each other, and I was putting my needs over healing what was wrong between us, acting as if pleasure would simply fix this riff. I was dealing with a love god, not one of lust.

Still, I was embarrassed he was right. I was frustrated in multiple ways. I scoffed to not lose face but could not meet his gaze. Using him was exactly what I was trying to do. I hadn't trusted him with the mission. I still didn't with that prophetic dream looming over us. Then, I expected him to please my raging hormones, do what I say, even if it might end in our deaths.

He gave me a leveled gaze. "I mean it. Listen, before you cut me off so pleasantly—" He smirked in that way that made my heart flutter. "—I was trying

111

to tell you that I don't regret it, our immortal marriage. I never will. Don't ever interpret my hurt as a lack of love for you. I love you more than any other being in existence."

"I'm sorry, I know." Then I started bawling. (Freakin' hormones!)

Archer sighed and pulled me into his arms, holding me up (holding me together). It was a comforting embrace, and I didn't want to pull away.

He rested his forehead on mine. "Stay, Callie. Come home. We cannot live like this. Have faith in me. Trust me. And I will trust you. We have to be open and honest with each other. I love you."

I pulled away and wiped my ridiculous tears away. "I love you too." I wanted to give in, especially when he looked at me with those glowing eyes, so full of adoration, only a tinge of pain left in them from my lies.

As if he could not control his own actions, he kissed me. I tried to make more of the kiss, distracting him, but he pulled away, his gaze reluctant. "Come home," he begged.

My hand touched my belly unconsciously. I could not risk Philo's life. In the vision, I hadn't been visibly pregnant. His attack would occur soon or after the baby was born, since I hadn't been showing. I couldn't imagine either. The length of my hair in the vision felt like it could be soon, but who knew what I would do with my hair after birth. Things weren't as they seemed, I had been told, so maybe the prophecy was wrong. Still, would it be safer to wait until I showed, until he was madly in love with the idea of his child, whom he'd never harm—irrefutable evidence he would hurt more than me if he laid a hand on me. "Not yet. I'm sorry."

He let go of me. "Not as sorry as I am. I rushed us, didn't I? You weren't ready. So young." His pitiful expression tore at my heart.

"No. Not that. I regret nothing. I will spend the rest of my life with you, Archer. I just need to stay away, but I can't."

He sighed and ran his hands down his face in frustration. Then his eyes narrowed on me, making me feel detested. "*That* is what I'll never understand, my love. You trust a vision over love."

"Archer I—"

"No. You can't even fathom how much this kills me. I *am* Love. Nothing overpowers that, not even some vague prophecy you're likely misreading."

"You'll never understand how my abilities work. I've foreseen things; they have happened. I will not let this one."

"This is different, a dream of yours, a nightmare."

"My dreams have been right."

"And sometimes a dream is just a dream. Damn it, Callie." He walked away toward the stove, ignoring me.

I wasn't sure what to say or do. He cut the peppers and onions and then diced them at an immortal pace, full of more slamming and huffs than needed (without cutting himself—impressive), but I wasn't about to leave with the scent of food promising me of a different type of pleasure.

A knock on the door cut through the building tension. He asked me to get it—like it was his house, not mine. I could not trust him, and I didn't deserve his trust. We were at an impasse.

Glad for the interruption, I opened the door. Lucien stood there, his mouth tugging into a grin. "My girl, my heroine." He pulled me into a tight hug, pushing his way inside. "Thank you."

I felt Archer's gaze and shrugged Lucien off, not wanting him to bring up the wedge between Archer and me. "It was nothing."

"Nothing?" Lucien's face crinkled. "I wouldn't exist anymore if it weren't for you two." His gaze flickered between Archer and me.

"And we wouldn't without what you did," Archer said quietly.

"Even though I told you not to do it." I scolded Lucien.

He smirked. "You knew I would. Archer is like my brother—well, more than my brother since I don't get on with any of my real brothers—er, Chase is a 'maybe' now. Archer's my best friend. Callie, ever since that sacrifice, I see you like a sister. A better one as well, but comparing you to mine is an easy win."

Archer nodded and tended to dinner. Lucien watched him, and knowing my husband so well, he then looked at me with questions in his eyes.

"Have a seat. Want something to drink?" I asked to cut through the uncomfortable silence.

Again, Lucien's eyes darted between us. His tone hesitant, he said, "I feel like I'm intruding."

"You're not. There's enough food for three of us or more, but don't tell my brothers. If they show up, we're screwed." Archer gave his friend a wry grin.

I felt like the intruder. As Lucien sat down at the breakfast bar, Archer handing him a glass of water, I snuck off to the bathroom. As I washed my hands after going, I thought about how I had hidden my pregnancy test from Archer in that very bathroom. Guilt flooded me. I could not take it back. Things felt hopeless between us. I dried my hands and opened the door to hear hushed voices.

Lucien's reached my ears first. "I thought Akila and I had some serious tension, but you two…" he made a huffing sound.

"Well—"

113

"I get it Archer. I'd kill for one of my boys—er, children—so not used to having a daughter." I could hear the smile in Lucien's voice, which brightened my mood. "But I think—"

"I know what you'll say, so don't. Of course, I'm likely adding my past grief about Hedone onto what could've happened to my unborn child. How could any being with a heart not compound about the loss of one child when another was at risk?"

The guilt grew. I stepped out of the bathroom but stopped, not turning the corner.

"Okay, okay, but she doesn't deserve to be chastised while she's pregnant. You guys need to—"

"There's more to it, Lucien. While you were…gone—for a lack of a better word—she had prophetic dreams."

Silence. I could imagine Lucien's confusion, and I feared what he might say. I also didn't want Archer to admit what I saw to Lucien, who might also not believe me. Of all people, Lucien would understand prophecies, but he was too close to Archer to be objective about this. I purposely walked heavy-footed like a mortal for their immortal ears to hear me coming, to cease their conversation.

"Dinner's almost ready," Archer said, tending to the stove, adding spices. "Maybe, you can help?" He raised his brows, trying hard to make things feel normal.

"I'll get the fixings," I said, heading into the kitchen.

"Callie, sit down. Please," Lucien said. His tone was what made me turn. His eyes were concerned.

I was going to protest until Archer ran his spare hand down my back and gave me a forced grin. I sat down as I heard Lucien chop the lettuce and tomatoes then set the table all in immortal speed.

We ate with little conversation. It was clear Lucien was only hanging on for the food and out of courtesy. After we finished, he helped Archer clean up—neither letting me lift a finger (sort of annoying but kind). Then Lucien raced out of there.

Silence built between us. Archer kept himself busy as I felt increasingly more awkward being there, but leaving would also be weird. Finally, gaining the courage, I spoke. "I should go."

The statement hung in the air like a question that everything hinged upon.

He turned to me, swallowing hard, his eyes fixed upon me. "I wish things were different. I want you to stay." Archer's tortured tone made my throat catch. "But you should go. I need you to go." As he approached me, his eyes burned with the opposite sentiment. He walked over to me, pulled me in, and rested his forehead on mine.

"I wish it were too. I love you. I'm just so scared. Maybe my vision won't happen, but I need to wait it out and see. For Philo's sake. Can't you understand how I want to protect him?"

He pulled away. "That I understand fully, Callie. What I don't get is how you can even believe for a second that I would ever physically hurt you or him." He turned away from me. "You can let yourself out."

He left me (speechless) standing there as our bedroom door slammed shut. I fled across the hall, locking the door, Philo and me in.

I needed to get out of this building. I could not breathe. I felt trapped.

The next day, that was exactly what I did.

I called Linda up, convincing her we should sneak out. She was all for it because rumors claimed we were going into a lockdown due to COVID. We decided to stick to the outdoors, Central Park, because her mother forbade her from leaving home, even to see Aios.

I knew the overprotectiveness in Archer would make him furious if I stepped foot out the door, so Linda and I both could get in trouble if we were found out. I decided to get myself some bodyguards. I might've exploited Aios's feelings for Linda (and wanting to make Linda happy), and Archer's brothers' restlessness caused them to agree.

I half expected us to not make it out of the building, half suspecting Archer kept tabs on me. That thought was unkind. As we met Linda outside the building, guilt filled me for my thoughts and for excluding Archer from the excursion. He'd be fine, though, once I returned. Maybe he'd be none the wiser.

CHAPTER 17

Archer

Knowing Callie was just across the hall was killing me. While I washed the dishes, she was all I could think about. I was ready to cave in to do whatever she needed me to just to get her home, but there was no fixing this. I couldn't make her trust me unless I waited this out. I'd keep my distance because being near her was painful in pride, lust, and heartache. She had used me for gratification, but last night, I had denied her. It was the hardest damn thing I'd had to do in my life—Love denying all forms of love combined. She would not use me for her wants and deny me mine. The only way she'd learn relationships were reciprocal, a fifty-fifty power dynamic, was if I drew that line. I had failed to do so with Psyche. I would not make that mistake again.

There was a knock at the door. I shut off the tap and dried my hands. The dishes could wait. With wild hope in my heart, I raced to the door, hoping it was Callie.

It was Lucien.

He raised his brows as if to ask if I had a minute. I opened the door further and walked back to the sink. He sat at the breakfast bar in a huff. It was my turn to raise my brows in inquiry.

"Goddesses." He ran his hands down his face in frustration, ending with a groan.

"You said it." I loaded a few dishes into the dishwasher.

"That bad? Doing dishes in mortal speed?"

"It wastes time." I closed the dishwasher and went into the fridge, grabbing out two of Dionysus's potent beers.

I slid one over to Lucien, and then he cracked a grin. "You remember how I used to crack these open with my teeth and when you tried it, you broke a tooth?"

"And you made fun of me for years about it." I snapped off the cap using my molars without incident to prove to him I had mastered how to do it properly.

He laughed. "Don't take it for granted, Archer. Memories. It was horrible not remembering any of you, losing all those layers of years that made us best friends."

I nodded, not able to imagine. "But you have it back now. You're alive. You have a daughter, but not the goddess or you'd be there, not here."

"She's impossible. She brought my memory back. How? It has to mean something."

"So, you're here hoping I know how and why this all happened? That is something only the Fates would know."

"Or did we defy them? Was I supposed to be dead forever?"

I froze. If Callie and I defied the Fates, would they be coming for us now? Was she something so powerful, too powerful to control, as Prometheus and Athena's other children had been? No. I couldn't believe that. It was too frightening.

I turned my attention to Lucien's problems. "You always underplayed the power of love. If you love Akila, if you did before you died, then love is how you got that memory back."

"She was the last person I thought of when I died. I regretted not making peace with her. I think it was my only regret—no, my *largest*. I regretted leaving all of you, but I had made peace with you. Not with her."

"These are things you should be telling her."

"She'll rip my head off if I even look at her. She's unhinged."

I smiled, shaking my head.

"What?" He hesitated taking a sip of his beer, giving me that puzzled expression he always did when he knew I understood women way better than him despite my limited relationships. He never understood love and how it made people behave in strange ways, influencing their actions and reactions, heightening their emotions.

"She loves you. That's where the rage is coming from. You abandoned her without warning."

His face tightened, eyes narrowed. "She hid my child from me!"

I put my arms out in a *chill out* motion. "Don't attack me. I know. You both did wrong. I'm simply explaining how *she* feels. You know how you feel."

He frowned and took a large swig, his face deep in thought. "You try applying that logic to your situation?"

"Callie and me?" I had thought about how she felt, and we even talked about it. "It's different."

"How so?"

I took a sip of my drink while trying to figure out how to explain it. "Our trust and faith in each other are broken. How can I mend that?"

"Start trusting her."

"Her vision is ludicrous. I'd never—"

"Prophecies are a fickle thing. I'm glad I haven't had one since I've been... 'back.' I'm hoping they are gone, to be honest. They are never what they seem. I believe she saw you hurt her. She's—"

I slammed the bottle onto the counter. "Aw, come on, Lucien!" Thankfully, it didn't shatter. Instead, the beer foamed up and overflowed. I ignored it, just glaring at him for such a thought.

"Hear me out. She hasn't been wrong yet. Instead of denying it, think how it could ever be possible. It can't be what she thinks it is, I agree. I can't imagine you laying a finger on her, but what can she really be seeing?"

I was confused. What could she be seeing if it wasn't me partaking in abuse. I had never laid a hand on Psyche, even when she hit me in one of her hissy fits, long after our love had faded. Never. I was the love god. Any violence I had ever partaken in had been trying to protect my loved ones. Yeah, part of that Ares's rage came out now and then, but never would I ever direct it toward Callie.

"Look, I don't have answers to what that could possibly be. Just trust her, believe her, be there for her. Then she'll eventually trust you."

I nodded. What else could I do? Callie and I were being stubborn, and neither of us was about to give in. Maybe it was time I did. She'd eventually see her prophecy was wrong.

Eager to change the subject, I moved on to another topic. "Now that you're back, there is something I have to tell you that I couldn't burden you with while you had no memory. Psyche had a last request I said I would perform."

"By the gods, knowing her, I'm afraid to ask."

"There are more godly lines that have crossed that we didn't know about. Somewhere along the line, your demigod stock crossed with Psyche's."

Lucien's eyes went wide.

"Not a Callie situation, so relax. The descendants are mortal. Still, Psyche said your oracle died and that one of these descendants will inherit the Delphi line, become your new oracle. She wants us to protect her."

"Did she give you a name?"

I shook my head.

Apollo sighed. "Well, at least I kept track of my mortal children. I'll just have to seek out the oracle by tracing the power. The only problem is, I don't feel that power anymore. I haven't had a prophecy since I came back."

"We'll figure it out. Finding out a way to stop Zeus is probably more important anyway."

There was a knock at the door, halting the conversation. Hope leaped into my heart. Callie?

Before I could answer it, the door opened, and Athena and Prometheus entered.

"You're back." I was so glad to see them. With Prometheus's understanding of prophecies and Athena's intellect, they would be able to help us.

Lucien swept Athena into a big bear hug. "I can't thank you enough."

She pushed him off, visibly uncomfortable. After all these years in her company, he knew better; getting in her personal space unnerved her.

She took it in stride, at least. "Enough of that. We'll catch up later. Where's Callie? I need to talk to her."

My stomach sank with unease. "At your place."

"Her stuff is, but no one has seen her today. Anteros, Himerus, and Aios aren't home either."

"Aios went out to see Linda," Lucien supplied.

Dread filled me. "The idiots took Callie with them." I glared at Lucien.

He put his hands up in mock surrender. "Don't shoot the messenger, here. I only know Aios met up with Linda, via a text. He said nothing about anyone else going."

Panic filled me. "It's dangerous out there—"

"You can't keep her a prisoner here, Archer."

I ignored Lucien's comment about my overprotectiveness. It was something I had to work on now that my wife was not a fragile mortal, but the thought of anything happening to her and Philo scared me halfway to Hades. Trying to stay calm, I closed my eyes, scanning for her.

I located her quickly. "They're in Central Park."

Athena took a deep breath of relief.

Vindication that I wasn't the only one worried flooded me. "Lucien, you wanna come?"

He shrugged. "So you don't look like an overprotective jerk? Sure." He finished his beer, but I was too anxious to bother with mine. Athena had said she needed to talk to Callie. I hoped that bit of info would make my wife come back to the building, to safety.

Once Lucien and I hit the street, I closed my eyes to reassure myself Callie was okay. That's when I saw something that terrified me.

My eyes shot open.

Lucien grabbed my shoulder, shaking it. "What? You look like you saw a ghost."

"I better not have." I just stood there immobile. My blood ran cold.

CHAPTER 18

Callie

The fresh air was invigorating. I pulled the mask down to expose my nose just to get some of the chilly fresh air in my lungs. I had been cooped up, hiding from Archer, the formerly-blank Lucien—just not wanting to deal with anyone or anything. I needed air, sun, and exercise. It felt liberating...for a moment.

The streets were bustling. It was as if everyone was trying to fit everything in before who knew what would happen or how long we'd be stuck in a lockdown. The crowd was making me claustrophobic, and the masks were unnerving because I couldn't see who was who. I was having massive regrets, but part of it was being on my Olympian family's enforced lockdown before the human lockdown. No one wanted me to go anywhere (especially Archer). Some goddess I was to need so much protection. Goddess of hiding should be my role.

Someone bumped me, making my heart jump into my throat. He had white hair and blue eyes, my mind going to Zeus before I realized this was an old man.

Humerus shoved the guy away a bit roughly for mortal strength. "Watch it."

The man hurried away, muttering about "today's youth."

I gave Himerus a warning look not to draw attention. He rolled his eyes at me like I was an uptight mom (good practice, I guess).

The park was much better. Sucking in the fresh air, I felt at peace again. People kept their distance to be able to unmask and do the same. We'd walked for six or so blocks to get to the park; it was nice to be out and getting exercise. We entered around the model boat pond area and headed out of the wooded area into the sun and found a somewhat less busy area. Many people had the same idea to get out on a sunny day.

Linda opened her bag, pulled out a blanket, and threw it out, Aios helping her. She sat down on it, her hopeful eyes staring up at him. The blanket could seat two or three of us.

Aios smiled but hesitated, looking at me. "Go ahead, Callie." He offered me his hand to help me sit. I appreciated it, being off balance lately with my center of gravity changing. Linda frowned and looked between Aios and me, jumping to ridiculously insecure assumptions (definitely still the jealous type).

I thanked Aios and gave him a severe look, nodding at Linda.

He was confused until he took in her expression. "Callie should sit, you know, being in her condition."

(Oh crap.)

Linda's brow wrinkled. "What's wrong?" Her jealousy slipped away into concern. "Not a fever again, is it?"

"Err." Aios shuffled his feet, making a *sorry* grimace at me.

"Good one, Ass," Anteros muttered, standing still and looking around, nonchalantly scoping out behind us. Himerus had his back to us, watching the front. I was out in the open and still felt imprisoned. It wasn't the boys' fault. It was Zeus's, who still had power over us because we were scared of him.

Aios shrugged. "Sorry, but she'd find out soon enough."

I wasn't sure why I hadn't told Linda about Philo, but with everything going on with Archer and me (she knew about that at least, sort of, as a petty argument), I kind of forgot to include her.

"Find out what? What's going on? I've always felt like your friends were in some club I'm not allowed in."

(Double crap.)

Aios looked away, guilt in his eyes, his jaw tightening. Oh, the many secrets he had to keep from her.

I felt like I was looking at Archer and me not all that long ago—me in the dark. I now knew how dependent I'd been when I was with Archer and how weak when he had left me. I remembered this park, Archer and I, before we were forced apart, when he told me the truth in the only way he could at the time: *"What if I told you I could never tell you everything about me, Callie? Would you still want to be with me? What if knowing these things would put you in danger? Could you live without knowing them?"* He'd wanted to protect me from his world, and I dove right into it. I did not stay in the dark as he'd asked. Just like Psyche, who'd gotten their child killed—his only child, until now. I could see how raw and lasting his grief was from losing them. Again, I was following in her footsteps, in his head at least. If Dad were here, he'd lecture me about not letting history repeat itself. He would tell me to trust Archer. He would tell me my prophecy could not be true, because he left this world knowing my husband would die for me, not hurt me.

I was starting to understand how strong Archer's power was. Love was stronger than anything, and I believed even more in him now. I had to give him the benefit of the doubt. I would believe in Archer and go home to him. I would fight the prophecy with him. I didn't care what Lucien told me about the Fates and prophecies. I would beat them at their own game.

"Callie?" Linda asked. "You're staring off."

"Sorry." I shook my head. "I was just reminiscing. I once felt like you did, Linda, an outsider of the group. Now, not so much. All in good time, you know? Then you'll regret being around some of these guys so much."

Linda giggled, her lovestruck eyes darting to Aios. "I doubt it."

I smiled. It was time to at least come clean to her about what I could. "I told you Archer and I had a stupid fight, but I didn't tell you what it was about. I didn't tell him something because I was scared, and it was something really important. I guess I should've told you too. You see…I'm pregnant."

After her initial shock, she started shrieking, giggling, and smiling. Then she hugged me tightly, congratulating me. This was probably the reason I forgot—accidental avoidance of all full-on girly attention.

After I apologized and acted as if I wasn't telling people until the twelve-week mark (Next week? Time was flying), she was pretty cool about it and calm, asking me a lot of questions.

She was the first one who asked me the most important question the others had overlooked: "How do you feel about it? Becoming a mom, like now, I mean?"

I frowned, picking at a blade of grass. I shrugged. "Scared, not ready."

Anteros met my gaze, dare I say, with empathy? From the outside, he was a childish brother and buddy of Archer's. I took for granted he felt things as acutely as Archer did, but of unrequited or thwarted love (equal opposites).

I said the truth in a coded way to include Linda and the boys. "The timing is just bad. I wanted to feel settled, secure, first."

Linda tried to make me feel better, but I stared off again, thinking of Archer, wanting to go to him because, despite prophecies, with him was where I felt safest.

"You okay? Or do you wanna go home?" Anteros asked as if he were the mind reader, not me.

Himerus was scanning the area the entire time, not talking, making me nervous. We had only been out for a half hour, but I was ready to go.

I shivered from this sudden foreboding feeling. "Yeah, I think so."

"Cold?" Linda assumed. "I am too."

I nodded (not like I could explain the ichor regulating my temperature).

Aios suggested, "Get some coffee?" He wanted to extend his time with Linda.

"You two go. If Russ and Antony will take me back, I'd rather go home. I'm tired."

Anteros gave me a wry grin. He knew. Knew that I was going *home*, home to Archer. He held out his hands for me and helped me up, a small smile playing on his lips—so much like Archer's (as if mocking me).

Himerus turned, wide-eyed and way too fast. He was over to me, grabbing my shoulders, shoving me behind him. I stumbled back, almost losing my footing.

Hermes stood twenty feet from us under the shadow of a tree. Terror filled me. He was the one I feared more than Zeus, because he could take me away from those I loved and to those who might kill me. Zeus had faced a massive setback, but (apparently) his minions hadn't.

Aios and Himerus moved in blurs of immortal speed. Linda gasped, her eyes not keeping up.

A form landed right in front of me, his back to me, protecting me. Archer. I was so happy to see him, a lump formed in my throat. I swallowed hard and clung to him. Although staying alert, his body leaned into me ever so slightly. He squeezed the hand I had on his side slightly and thought for me to hear, *I'm here. All is forgiven* (or perhaps I was hoping those were his thoughts).

Himerus screamed out.

"Himerus?" Archer asked.

He answered with an intense growling and whipped his arm out. He held a bloodied, smoking knife. He had been stabbed (and apparently was badass enough to just pull the knife out).

Another knife was knocked astray by Himerus using his to deflect it.

Hermes vanished. Being outnumbered, he likely fled.

Archer asked again. "Brother?"

Himerus turned to us, looking very much like Ares going into war, in stance, stature, and anger levels. "I'm fine. We need to get out of here."

Anteros said, "We need to stick together. Safety in numbers."

"What the hell is going on?" Linda's eyes darted around at all of us, resting on mine, begging for answers I couldn't give her.

Himerus lunged with the knife. I almost thought he was going for me until I heard the clink of a knife being deflected.

I didn't see him, but Hermes was back.

So many things happened at once. Archer spun around to face me, his eyes wide, and he grabbed me roughly, spinning me around behind him. I held onto his waist to steady myself, to stay connected to him, and peeked around his shoulder. I saw a glimpse of Hermes throwing another knife. Linda was right there, stepping in front of us…my arms breaking away from Archer. I staggered backward.

Hermes's face loomed in front of me, his smug arrogance gone, but he had a determination in his eyes. He grabbed my arm.

No! I yanked my arm, trying to get away.

Linda was falling backward, a knife in her belly.

I froze.

Hermes's got a good grasp on me.

THE IMMORTAL TRANSCRIPTS: GLIMMER

My stomach plunged like I was on a roller coaster. Pressure. I couldn't breathe.

I realized what was going on. That's when my shock left me. Dread replaced it.

Fear. Guilt. Regrets.

CHAPTER 19

Once Lucien and I hit the street, I closed my eyes to reassure myself Callie was okay. That's when I saw something that terrified me.

My eyes shot open.

Lucien grabbed my shoulder, shaking it. "What? You look like you saw a ghost."

"I better not have." I just stood there immobile. My blood ran cold.

Lucien shook me out of it.

I could only utter one word: "Hermes."

Something primal in me snapped. I was running, zipping through mortals, knocking a bunch down until I took to the air in large jumps. I was sure Lucien was on the ground making his way there, but I had no time to worry about him. I had to close the distance between me and Callie. I could not let anything happen to her. Or Philo.

I prayed to any gods listening to help me get there in time. I was not going to lose my wife and child. Not again. This could not happen to me again.

Reaching Central Park, I took to the trees by the model boat pond, not caring if mortals were confused by a sudden flicker of something crossing the sky. Their eyes could not grasp it, and if they could, they'd think they were seeing things and excuse it away as they always have.

I stopped, clinging to a thick tree branch after I found the group.

Hermes stood in front of Callie.

Himerus between them. Damn it, I was proud of my brother.

Something that shined in the light left Hermes's hand. A knife. Flying at my brother.

I landed down between Callie and my brother—another line of defense if the knife bypassed him.

It did not. Himerus roared in pain.

Callie, on realizing it was me, clung to me.

I was grateful she was okay, but my concern was with Himerus. I squeezed her hand gently to let her know I was here for her, that I forgave her.

"Himerus?"

Instead of answering me, he took a deep breath and yanked the knife out of his side, growling through clenched teeth the entire time. The ichor sizzled on it, making what must've been a formidable sight from the front, so much so, Hermes went wide-eyed. Giving me a glare as if to say we were far from finished, he vanished.

"Brother?"

He turned panting, eyes animated, knife outstretched and ready. "I'm fine. We need to get out of here."

"We need to stick together. Safety in numbers." Anteros insisted.

"What the hell is going on?" Linda was there. *Great.* I hadn't noticed her.

Aios looked at her and then me, at a loss of what to do. The last thing we needed was another Callie situation on our hands, a mortal uncovering our secret, the very thing that had started the tear in the Olympian family. Looked like it was too late, from her expression. In fact, mortals nearby started to stare in confusion.

A knife flew toward me from the side. Himerus lunged forward and deflected it. As soon as I spotted Hermes, he was gone.

He was going for me or Callie because it would incapacitate us the same. She would not be wounded but feel the pain, like my poor Ma during every war my father managed to get mangled in. We had to protect Philo, at least.

Then a knife came flying at Callie from in front of us. I yanked her behind me, ready to be struck but hoping to knock it off course and hurt just a hand.

But the knife never hit.

I lowered my arm.

Linda stood in front of me. She turned, wide-eyed, mouth open in shock, her hands involuntarily moving toward…the knife embedded in her abdomen. She had intercepted it somehow. Before I could even reach out to catch the staggering girl, Hermes reappeared behind me, slamming me in the shoulders, toppling me into Linda. Someone caught her. I scrambled back up. Hermes had appeared almost on top of me to break me away from Callie—successfully.

He grasped her arm. She struggled, almost yanking free. Then they were gone.

I sank to my knees, ignoring the distress about Linda behind me. My stomach lurched. Terror filled me, and a scream built up inside. Before it surfaced, Callie was suddenly back in front of me, stumbling back into my arms, crying. I caught her.

Hermes had one of his throwing knives embedded in his side.

Himerus was on top of him in an instant, stabbing him repeatedly with his knife.

With a look of torn anger and agony, Hermes vanished, leaving Himerus huffing over the ground, knife hovering in the air.

Hermes would not be back.

I assessed Callie. "Are you okay?" I checked her body, her arms, her face, cradling it in my hands.

The love was absent from her eyes. "I'm fine. I can defend myself, Archer." She pushed away from me. What was with her front? Her voice was thin and higher pitched, heavily distressed. She had narrowly escaped abduction by stabbing a god. Had I ruined the woman I fell in love with from exposing her to my world? Was she that desensitized?

She avoided my gaze. Cold. Unfeeling. Anger. That was the only energy I could feel emanating from her, no love. How could she be mad at me still? I didn't dare ask about Philo and set her off. I withheld the admonishment for going out without telling me, or even my Dad or Athena, who would be best at protecting us. She must be feeling the acute sting of the unspoken I-told-you-so that hung between us.

My attention was diverted to the mortal who was dying because she tried to save Callie and me. I could hardly take in what was happening.

Mortals were gawking and staring. We had to get out of here immediately.

I was torn about what I had just witnessed and what would happen here on out. I had a sinking feeling that Callie and I just crossed some kind of precipice—not exactly sure what kind. Part of me innately knew that nothing would ever be the same between us again.

My chest ached as if I had just lost her for good.

CHAPTER 20

Archer had gotten to Central Park before me. I'd arrived in time to see Hermes throw a dagger at Callie, and Archer move to try to intercept it. Anteros and Himerus had rushed from either side, trying to help, but Linda had only been a step away.

She'd known what she was doing. She'd purposely stepped and leaned in front of Archer and Callie, her hands up to protect her face and chest. The knife had flown just too low to strike her defense. It embedded itself in her stomach cavity, right under her folded left elbow.

It all happened before I could reach them. All in a split mortal second. My immortal legs were not fast enough.

Linda fell into Aios, blood blooming on her shirt as he caught her. He half reclined her on the ground.

Mortals were looking. Tons of them.

"Hospital?" Himerus said. He had a huge hole in his shirt but appeared fine. He must've been wounded moments ago.

"She's not going to make it." Anteros pressed his hand against the wound to stem the blood flow.

Archer was busy trying to check over Callie, who was being nasty. My guess was she was irritated that his over protectiveness was vindicated for once.

Aios's gaze met mine, and I saw the unadulterated fear in them. He was in love with this mortal. She was dying right before his eyes. I was the god of medicine, of healing. Could I save her? I had not used those powers since I'd returned. Would they work or be gone like the prophecies? I was thankful for not knowing the future after previously knowing of my own demise. But healing was something I had loved to do.

I met Linda's horrified stare, and a montage of memories bombarded me as they did every time I saw someone after Akila had brought my memory back. *Kissing, talking, a watch, breaking her heart*—my eyes pulled away as I instinctively scanned her. Stab wound to the abdomen, internal bleeding, punctured intestines. She wouldn't make it. But my son needed her. I had to prevent his pain. He was no womanizer like me. He fell for this mortal girl, probably the first one in his entire existence, and she was dying. Then, like riding a bike, the solution came back to me.

"Hold her still," I ordered my son.

At immortal speed, I withdrew the knife; I poured my healing energy into her, fusing the stomach lining back together, stitching her muscles back together, sealing her skin closed. She screamed out in pain before she lost consciousness. It was all I could do, but there was blood everywhere. So much blood loss. Something about this girl's blood was off, different. I homed in, searching the blood on the ground, and noticed the abnormality in its cells.

Sirens were ringing, coming closer. Someone had called the police or an ambulance. Nothing that just happened could be explained to mortals, particularly the missing wound on Linda. We had to escape.

"Archer. Take Callie back. Call Hebe."

His eyes were wild. "What?"

I didn't blame him. My dad's people just tried to kidnap his wife, and his aunt Hebe lived with Zeus. Who knew what state my father was in at the moment? "There was a deal in your punishment, remember? You can make one more demigod immortal."

Aios was struggling to reign in his emotions. "She not—"

We were wasting time. "It's in her blood that is all over my hands. Are we going to argue about this or try to save her? I only stopped the bleeding. Demigod or not, she gets injured like a mortal. Let's get back to my apartment." It was the only way I could imagine saving her life.

Himerus took Linda from the worried Aios. She woke up for a moment to cry out in pain, and Aios apologized to her before Himerus—the fastest of us—zipped away, leaving a couple mortals gasping. While they were distracted, we all followed via less observable routes.

Bursting into my apartment, Himerus had Linda already on my couch. She was pale and lifeless looking.

"Are we really going to do this?" Himerus asked, biting his lip. "If she is a demigod, like you say, is she one of us? If she's not, don't we need permission?"

I shook my head. "I don't think she is ours, but we cannot let her die." Quietly—even though he could still hear me—I added, "He can't go through losing someone he loves again."

Anteros nodded, placing a hand on his friend's shoulder. Himerus sighed and then nodded.

Archer, Callie, Chase, and Aroha all raced in.

Archer clung to Callie, who was oddly quiet, but who could blame her? Hermes had almost kidnapped her.

Archer spoke quietly, his face full of regret. "Hebe will be here shortly. She will know where we live."

"Archer, they found Callie. They already know where we live." Aroha pointed out. She went to Linda and touched her forehead, smoothing her bangs out of her eyes despite her being unconscious. She definitely had her maternal vibe in high gear ever since she warmed up to Callie. That and being pregnant got her all motherly.

I checked Linda over. Mild internal bleeding, but enough to make her blood pressure drop a little. This was going to be risky. I was going to need something more than ambrosia to keep her alive.

There was a knock on the door. Aios, desperate to save the girl who stole his heart, yanked it open. In walked Hebe and Eurus, the only wind god in Zeus's pocket.

"You said it was urgent?" Hebe asked in her soft, high-pitched voice. "Oh, no!" She was over to the girl, pulling her up to a sitting position. How Zeus ever created such an innocent and sweet one of us was beyond me.

Linda's eyes flew open, and she screamed in pain.

"Drink. It will dull the pain, heal you."

"What?" A confused Linda tried to swat her away but was too weak. "Aios."

"I'm here. Right here, sweetheart. Drink. Please. I need you to live." I could see how torn he was about her choice. Die or live forever. She had to know the truth.

I snapped my fingers in front of her face to snag her focus. "Linda, I healed you the best I could, but you could die if you do not drink. If you do drink, you could live forever."

Linda seemed lost, and her eyes started to roll into her head.

Aios grabbed her shoulders, bracing her. "Please, Linda. Don't leave me. I need you...forever." The last word was a whisper on his breath that I was unsure a mortal could even hear.

Linda blinked rapidly and met his gaze. Hebe held the vial up to her lips. Linda nodded and allowed Hebe to feed it to her. She swallowed it, and we all let out a held breath, worried she'd slip away before she could drink.

Her eyes went drowsy, and she slumped over into Hebe's arms. Hebe gently eased her down with care. Aios clutched her hand.

Chase quietly asked his sister, "Will she live through the change?"

"I don't know. Apollo fixed the injury, but the blood loss... I can only say, 'Hope for the best.' We did all we could do."

Chase closed his eyes, rapidly moving them as if reading the back of his eyelids. Then they snapped open, and he cursed.

Aroha, concerned, asked, "What?"

"Hebe, go. *Others* are here." He kissed her forehead and pushed her toward Eurus. They vanished in a whirlwind of dust and wind, knocking things about and off my end tables.

"Others?" My stomach dropped. Were they here for Polly, to take her and Akila away from me? "Egyptians?"

Chase shook his head, his face turning to stare at Linda. No one said a word for a moment. We knew who it meant.

I thought aloud, "Linda had told me her father was from China. He had left when her mother was pregnant, and she never met him." Her godly father was here, but which one was he?

"Oh, no." Aroha moaned. "Where is Athena when you need her? Chase, you cannot fight the others. Peace, please."

Where were Prometheus and Athena? We had seen them less than a half hour ago.

Chase gave Aroha an incredulous look. "Don't worry about me. I'm in defensive mode. I won't attack. You better watch Lucien's tongue if he makes his views known about that virus."

Aroha moaned. "Right, China was the origin." Then she turned and had her finger in my face. "Now is not a time to mention anything about this mortal epidemic, Lucien."

"Pandemic," I muttered to correct her.

She gave me a glare.

I should've been thinking about the pandemic, but trying to regain who I was, grasp what I could do, and figure out how to do it again, consumed my time—not to mention a long-lost daughter, a severely bitter ex, and a son who was dealing with trauma for a second time.

There was no knock.

The door was kicked open, slamming into my wall with such force, the wood split, and the doorknob smashed through the drywall. Archer and Anteros pulled the expecting Callie and Aroha into the back of my living room. My son threw himself over Linda to protect her. I rushed to the door to stop the intruder. Chase beat me there.

An Asian god stood in the doorway, calm, staring at us, taking in the scene, his dark-brown eyes measuring us up, but the lack of fear upon his features—and oddly a lack of aggression considering the grand entrance—made me hesitate to attack. He was of medium height and build, but broad-shouldered, his dark hair cropped short. Without his classic long beard and mustache, it took me a moment to recognize him.

Chase bravely took a step closer. "Jade, what do you want?"

I was often frustrated and disliked my older half brother, but here, his audacity and bravery were commendable. This meant something huge: the Jade Emperor, the god of the Chinese gods. My heart sank. He was in charge of their underworld, heavens, and gods, of it all in his domain. He was more powerful than Zeus—a Zeus and Hades combo.

"You Greeks." The emperor's eyes narrowed into a glare as he met all of our gazes in turn. "So much trouble as of late."

"Could say the same for your Pestilence," Chase countered back in reference to the Wen Shen, a group of deities responsible for illnesses and plagues upon wrongdoers.

Aroha huffed at him for mentioning the pandemic, which drew his attention to the protected women at the back. And she had thought I'd be the ignoramus to bring it up.

The Jade Emperor's glare softened. "I mean no harm unless you force my hand, war god. We all have our insubordination going on at the moment. Do you intend on as much harm as my Wen Shen? What son dares to defy his father?" To him, family was the most important thing. It was something we Greeks understood with pride, but for the first time, I realized my father had destroyed that part of our culture. Throughout this Callie ordeal, I had blamed Archer, Callie, and his parents on top of Zeus, but truly, it was all Zeus. Callie could not control who or what she was, while Archer should be allowed to love whom he wanted—especially since it was so rare for him—and parents protect their children no matter how old they are. Zeus, however, never changed with time: a dictator for millennia.

Chase shifted his weight. "Sons who know right from wrong, a son who is protecting his daughter-in-law, who has done nothing wrong but exist. My father wants to kill a goddess merely because he did not create her and has no control over her. Another son," —he pointed at me— "who risked his life saving his child who was ordered to be killed for doing his job. The one there, my father's own grandson, the one who loves this girl here on the couch. We all are on the just side, a defending side."

It was touching that my half brother was speaking of me as some war hero, but I was now worried about said son and the other little girl of mine downstairs. "Why did you come?" I asked to distract them from the topic.

The emperor pointed in Linda and my son's direction, but his intimidating gaze stayed on me. "Apollo. I did not like that you hurt her. And if your spawn does so, he has me to answer to."

"I don't understand. Who is she to you?" I asked, although I already knew the answer.

The emperor stared me down. "My daughter."

Silence filled the room as the emperor stared at me, and I could not look away in defeat. Just my luck. I messed with not just any demigod but a god of gods' daughter. I had meddled with his daughter, but at least I had not taken it too far. When it came to godly behavior, I had been a chaste saint with Linda. Things were clicking into place through my resurfaced memories. I had been so distracted by Callie back then that I hadn't noticed why I'd chosen Linda of all mortals or why I had been drawn to her. Demigod stock does that.

Archer broke the tension-filled silence. "We're trying to make her immortal, save her. She is my wife's best friend."

The emperor crossed his arms. "Very well. If my daughter dies, it is on your heads. If she lives—"

"You will sign a treaty with us against Zeus." Chase wasn't just brazen. He was stupid. Half of us gasped at his audacity.

The emperor grinned. "As much as I dislike your father and disagree with his ways, what's in it for me? If I risk the lives of my family, my reputation, my lands, and my own life, what do I get in return?"

I was stunned that the emperor didn't immediately rip Chase's head off. "That depends on what you want. Why don't we have a discussion over dinner?"

"Dinner." The emperor smiled broadly, his arms uncrossing as he stepped into the room, his wide-stance narrowing and relaxing. "Dinner sounds great. The restaurants will all close down soon for lockdown. Perhaps Apollo should join us to discuss how to stop this illness."

I froze, meeting Chase's gaze. How could I fix a global problem that no other healing god had yet while Linda needed my care? I hoped he could read me well.

"Let us discuss terms first before we ask for my brother's services. No? He must stay here to care for your daughter." Chase gave me a pointed stare that commanded me to not mess up, to make sure she lived—or else. As if I didn't already know so much hinged on her survival.

The emperor agreed, and they left as friends cracking jokes.

The door closed behind them, the splintered wood making it difficult to close at the top of the doorframe. Chase had taken any threat to our safety out of the room. There was a collective sigh.

"Dad?" Aios said, his voice strained. "Her pulse is going a mile a minute."

"Blood loss." Came out of my mouth before I even thought about it. "Aroha, call Dionysus. Some nectar can buy time, but more importantly…" I looked around. Aios would not leave Linda's side. Himerus was the strongest one left in the room, and Chase would kill me if I sent Aroha anywhere dangerous while being pregnant. From the look of Archer doting on Callie, he would never stray far. That left one god at my disposal.

"Anteros, I need you to break into a hospital. I need everything for a blood transfusion. We'll text you a list."

He smiled a wry grin, excited for a mission, and he was out the window immediately. "Aios, I'll rattle off a list and you send each to Anteros with pictures to help him. Himerus, you're on guard duty. Archer, you're in charge when I leave."

His brow wrinkled. "Where are you going?"

"To get some sun. I'll need to recharge at some point."

They all followed my commands.

"What can I do?" Callie asked, her voice gravelly.

"Food. I'll need all the energy I can get once I come back." She uncharacteristically rolled her eyes and went into my kitchen to rummage around. After we'd just saved her life and her friend's life hung in the balance, she was being a bit ungracious. Now was not the time to think about her superficial issues.

I pushed my son aside to pour my healing energy into Linda, feeling her rapid pulse barely slow under my power. We needed nectar, blood, and IV fluids. I rattled off my list, and Aios frantically texted Anteros after researching pics and sending.

There was some nervous conversation, but I focused on my task.

Dionysus arrived, drunk of course, and was singing about being a hero as he pushed me aside and used a medicine syringe to suck up some of the nectar from a bottle and then went to drip it into Linda's mouth. He hiccupped, making his arm jump and poke Linda in the nose.

With a growl I had never heard come from my son, Aios snatched it from Dionysus and took over. The nectar helped her heartbeat slow down, but we were not in the clear.

Anteros burst into the room, making all of us jump, except Himerus, who had been scanning nearby for immortals and knew who it was.

With the fresh supplies, I set up. I washed down with antibacterial soap next to Callie, who cooked. She was quiet, passive. I wondered about her behavior. First, using a prophecy as a divide between her and Archer, getting nasty with him, and now not concerned over her only mortal friend. What was with her? Pregnancy was no excuse to become so hateful to all. If her hormones were causing this, something might be wrong. I wanted to scan her, but my son's worry over Linda's increasing fever drew me over. I'd talk to Callie later as I had with Archer.

I put on gloves and got the IV splice into her inner arm quickly, having Aroha fasten the blood bag and fluid bag onto her makeshift IV pole, an upside down hanger hooked on a coat rack.

"Dad, her temp feels too high," Aios fretted.

I touched Linda's head, which was flaring up, a high temperature but not too bad. Not like Callie's worst days had been. I lowered it and watched the blood flow into her through the IV line. It would slow her transition into immortality down, but speeding it up with blood loss and her shaky blood pressure might kill her. It had to be a balanced practice. Balance. That made me think of Akila and a certain possibility that could turn this situation around.

We waited. I kept my hands on her, pouring in as much power as I could, hoping the backup plan I had would work—just in case I wasn't powerful enough.

The others talked quietly, trying to pass time. Aroha worried about her husband. Callie brought me food. Beef tacos. Good one-hand food. The food only did so much. I needed the sun to recharge me, but I could not leave her. I let my energy run low. So low, I had to pull away.

I fell to the ground, which made Aroha gasp and pull me up to sitting. "You need the sun."

I nodded.

Archer pulled me up. "I'm in charge now. Go recharge, then sleep a little. You've been at this for hours. Keep your phone on full volume. We'll call if anything changes."

I bent down and checked Linda's vitals. Her heartbeat was steady and strong, the nectar healing her further, but the mortal blood running through her IV would dilute her godly-forming cells for some time. She would remain in a coma or crash on us. There was nothing else to do but wait for the godly cells to change the human ones over time.

Two rounds in the sun for an hour and one nap later, Linda was still in the same condition. I needed to enact my backup plan, but it had to wait until morning.

Chase returned, after giving the emperor the proper attention his culture expected for such big business deals and flourished the written treaty—written on a napkin. The entire deal banked not just on me saving Linda, but also me helping them try to end the pandemic. Thanks, Chase, no pressure.

I went to bed, unable to do anything but tell Aios to feed her drops of nectar every hour until the sun rose. I passed out fully clothed, with no energy left to shower.

CHAPTER 21

There was a knock at the door. Dread and anticipation warred inside me, wanting it to be but also fearing it was Lucien. Ever since I somehow restored his memory and he found out he had a daughter, he was trying to insert himself back in my life. I was scared of what that might mean, my defenses up to protect me from his womanizing ways that always ended in heartbreak.

At first, he'd given me space for a few days. His family celebrated his memory restoration. Even though Aphrodite invited me, I only brought Polly there the next day since she wouldn't stop pestering me about seeing her dad. After that, I limited their time together, always at my place. I could not lose my daughter.

I opened the door on the second knock before Polly woke up and came out of her room.

It was Lucien. It was early, but I supposed he would wake up with the sun if he chose to. Instead of looking on guard for my nasty greeting because—gods of my homeland only knew why—my temper was high around him all the time. He looked disheveled—no, *destroyed*.

His hair was a mess, and his shirt was covered in dried blood, the sleeve rolled up but also covered in maroon-brown evidence. His eyes were wild and exhausted. His hands were shaking. I had never seen him like this before, not wholly in control. His cocky arrogance usually bolstered him through everything—or so I had thought.

"What the hell happened?"

"Can I come in?"

"No, not like that. I don't want Polly to see this...blood? What is going on Lucien?"

He shook his head at me. "You can't keep her sheltered, Akila. That could get her killed. Someone almost died today. Well, they would have if I hadn't expended all my energy healing her."

"Don't tell me how to raise my daughter."

"*Our* daughter." He sighed. "All you care about is keeping control of her, isn't it? I just told you someone died, might have died. Only Hades knows if she'll make it. I did all I could."

Guilt washed over me. "Sorry. Just let Polly stay innocent just a tad longer. Let's go to your place." I penned a note that I was helping Lucien with something and left it on the table. I pushed him out of the doorway and rushed after him, closing it.

"I don't think we should leave her alone."

I gave him a death glare, texting as we went to the elevator. "I'm telling Raphael to go babysit. Hopefully, I'll be back before she wakes anyway…I hope. Is that good enough for you?"

He raised his brows. "Yeah, I'm good with it. He took on Death with a baseball bat to save Callie."

This made me like Raphael even more. "And lived? Impressive."

Lucien's gaze darted to me, trying to read my mood. "Well, Archer killed Death and got us in this war as a result."

"You don't support it?"

He groaned, frustrated. "I didn't say that. I died for Callie, for Archer, because he bound himself immortally to her. He is my best friend, a brother. And she—"

"You loved her."

He nodded. "Something about the freedom she gave me enticed me. That love died with my sacrifice. I don't love her now, but I will support them. How can I not? I have a daughter like her. What if Callie was Polly? You would—"

"Don't presume to understand anything I would or would not do for my daughter."

His mouth dropped, but he recuperated as the elevator door opened, and dodged out of the way against the wall to hide his bloodied appearance. An elderly man wearing a mask and laden with grocery bags stood inside.

"Forgot my mask," I managed to get out. "I'll wait for the next one." Once the doors closed, I started walking. "Forget dealing with mortals. You said you needed me. Let's take the stairs."

We headed to the end of the hall and entered the stairwell. I turned around on him, and he bumped into me. I backed up a step, not wanting him that close to me. One kiss from him had done damage to my heart many times. "What do you need? What happened?"

"Linda—you haven't met her. She's my mortal ex-girlfriend—well, my son likes her now—a façade relationship, for me I mean."

"Just stop and take your time. Gather your thoughts." I did not want to think about his mortal playthings.

"It's not what you think."

"What do I think? And does it matter what I think?"

"You think I slept with her. I didn't, even though she had wanted to. I've changed, Akila. I *do* care what you think of me."

I started walking before he could turn my resolve to putty with his honey-breathed words or poetry. I would not let him seduce me.

He followed, still talking as we climbed case after case, somewhere in between immortal and mortal pace. He told me about Hermes's attempted kidnapping of Callie, and how Linda had been gravely wounded. He saved her for his son, only to find out she was a demigod of the Chinese sector, her father being…

"The Jade Emperor." I turned, and he bumped into me.

Being a step behind me, he was right on my level, his eyes meeting mine, his lips so close to mine. He stood transfixed, silent. How easy it would be to lean forward…

I pulled away and kept walking.

"Yes," he said in a thick voice.

I could not help but smile in discovering the attraction was not one-sided.

"What do you need from me?" I stopped. We were at their floor.

"Well, I could answer that many ways, but you remember that first time when we realized what your balance could do for us in the bedroom—"

I cut him off with a slap. It had been reactionary. I hadn't even intended to hit him for the reference. But the fact my body warmed at the memory of how my powers could recharge his passion… It dawned on me how scared I was to get involved with him again. It was too much. To love Apollo was like staring into the sun.

When I saw the upset look on his face—not insulted or amused—regret overtook the warmth in me, like an icy blanket of self-loathing was draped over my shoulders. "I'm sorry. I…"

"You've made your feelings about me quite clear."

I could not tell him he was wrong, that I didn't know my feelings and that I was scared. It would give him hope we'd get back together, leverage over me. "I didn't mean to react so hastily."

"Can I explain, or will that cause a full-on brawl?" He walked past me. Instead of going out the door toward his apartment, he climbed the last stairwell that led to the rooftop gardens and sunbeds.

"Where are we going?"

He opened the door at the top to the outside, not answering my question because the answer was in front of me.

I walked out into the sunlight. "You're exhausted. You need to recharge."

The wind whipped around, and it was much too cold for any mortals to be outside to enjoy the area. The bushes were just starting to blossom green buds, and the ivy-covered arbors toward the front of the building were vibrantly green.

"The girl is immortal now. The only way to truly save her. I've had the Jade Emperor breathing down my neck with a death threat if she didn't make it. It's been a rough twenty-four hours. I need her fully healed and healthy pronto. So yes, a recharge. I was hoping you could find a balance to the energy to speed up the process. Before you slap me again, listen. I was hoping you'd be able to do it with a simple touch, not, you know, that kind of connection we had before."

It was kind of cute how he nervously rambled over referring to our steamy nights that had lasted hours because my abilities inadvertently recharged his prowess. Then, admittedly, sometimes it was on purpose.

"I think I can do that."

He grabbed up my hand and kissed my knuckles. "Thank you Ma'at." He used my real name. "Dare I ask another favor?"

"What?"

"After I heal the girl more, can I see my daughter?"

I nodded. "Change your clothes first."

He noticed his bloodied clothes and dropped my hand. "Sorry, point taken."

I touched his chest, feeling the erratic beating of his heart. Slow for an immortal, almost slow for a mortal. He turned his face up to the sky, letting the sun spill onto his bronze flesh. Eyes closed, he basked in his light. So beautiful to look at.

I tore my eyes away and stared at his chest, my area of focus, for I could not concentrate on much else, but even as his pec tightened under my palm at my touch, I knew none of this would feel innocent between us.

I closed my eyes and felt the energy around us. The sun was mighty powerful, and he was weak—so weak, I grew worried. I poured my balancing power into his heart, and the pace picked up a notch.

In seconds, like a sieve, the sun's energy was pouring into him. His heart beat in tandem with mine, then picked up its pace more.

I yanked away before I hurt him.

He opened his eyes, looking very different already. Strong, glowing, gorgeous, and well rested. His eyes crinkled before the smile spread across his face. "Thank you, Akila. That was…" He leaned in, affected as much as I had been through the power exchange. Too personal, too close, the powers flowing between us like a mini seduction.

THE IMMORTAL TRANSCRIPTS: GLIMMER

His lips came toward mine. I yearned to give in. At the last second, I turned my face away for him to get my cheek. Still, he kissed it. Then he smiled against my cheek before he pulled away. His hands did not leave my shoulders.

I had to get him off me. "Don't you have a girl to save?"

His hands recoiled; then I met his gaze again. Pain flickered in them. I had hurt him. "Thanks again. I'll see you later."

He left. I let out a huff. I'd be prepared. I would combat his seduction techniques with every little bitterness and pain he had caused me in the past. He would not break my heart again.

I could not, would not, let that happen. Polly needed me stable, needed me to have a platonic relationship with her father until she was an adult. I could not let silly fantasies into my head, ones only created because I thought I had lost all chances to tell him everything. When I had thought him dead, I could feel regret. Now, he was alive, I couldn't let myself dare to hope.

140

CHAPTER 22

I was beyond exhausted. Every emotion I had undergone was spent. I could not lose Linda. Dad was right. After losing him, I could not bear for it to happen again. Even though he was alive, the grief was still lingering, leaving a healing scar.

Linda was stable but sleeping. Dad said, if she didn't wake up soon, we might need to take her to a hospital. I knew that meant a coma. We were on hour twenty-four, and I hadn't slept in a day and a half.

"She'll be okay," Anteros said for the fifth time.

"And you know that because…?"

My comment gave him whiplash. I never lashed out at him.

"Well," he fumbled for a way to reassure me. "Archer said—"

"I don't care what he said."

"Aios." Himerus's tone exposed that rising Ares's temper. "He said this was normal. She'll wake up."

I rubbed my eyes. "He also said this was not normal."

Himerus scrunched up his face as he often did to think. "Do either of you find it weird Callie isn't here? Linda is her best friend—well, the only friend outside of us. Even Thena and Prometheus came by after they got back from meeting with Poseidon."

They had missed the entire attack. Some foreseeing god he was to not warn us about an attempted kidnapping. I regretted the thought instantly. Pettiness was not in my nature as the god of marriage, but seeing my loved ones die or dying lit some temper in me I was not aware I ever had.

"What about her mom? Why isn't she here?" Anteros asked.

"Linda's father is telling her everything. He is coming back here today to take her home. What will he do to us if she's still in a coma?" Great. Now there was more anxiety on my plate.

"I'm texting your dad. He has to be able to wake her up."

I didn't respond. I wanted him here, dependent upon him time and time again. That had been taken away briefly. I had been burdened with his powers. When his memory returned, I was freed. His responsibilities were not something I wanted or could shoulder. For some reason, neither of us had prophecies. Callie professed she suddenly did. I could not make sense of my world anymore.

THE IMMORTAL TRANSCRIPTS: GLIMMER

Dad had come three times so far to check. Archer twice. Callie never. Himerus was right. Something was up with Callie, and it wasn't only hormones or her fight with Archer. She should be here, worried about Linda as I was. "What *is* with Callie?"

Anteros ran his hand through his hair and stood up. They were on our other sofa, waiting it out with me, refusing to sleep as well. "Hasn't said a word to me since the kidnapping. Her mood was like a light switch. One moment, she was pining after Archer, and the next, ready to rip him to pieces."

I had Linda's head cradled in my lap as she slept. Her fever was gone, but she simply would not wake up.

Himerus frowned. "She's talked to me. Asked me something weird."

"What?" I was glad for the distraction.

"If I'd protect her from Archer if he tried to hurt her."

Now, I was the one with whiplash. "Him, hurt her? Or the baby? I'd never believe it."

"Yeah, she had a 'prophecy' about it." Anteros sneered. "She's a good girl and all that, and I can see how great Archer and her were together, but ever since they…well, your father's sacrifice and bringing him back. They're not the same. Archer has been more than understanding because she's pregnant, but to actually believe the prophecy is true? That cuts deep."

"I don't want to pick sides." I had to be diplomatic. They were soulmates. I wouldn't have seen such a clear connection between them when I immortally married them if they weren't. "She'll see the truth eventually. They have time." I peered down at Linda. Would we? Would we have time to be together, or was this simply a prolonged ending? If she woke—no, *when* she woke—I would make us official. Sure, we both knew we were technically dating, but I had never really asked. I was afraid to take things further, to make promises I could not keep. I was stuck going where my family went—for now. Maybe, just maybe, if I let things get serious with Linda, she would come with me, or we would strike out on our own. I wouldn't have to hide who I was from her anymore.

My dreams were dispelled by the real world when Himerus spoke next. "She, Callie, she…she was acting like she wasn't pregnant."

"Huh?" Was all I could ask because I had no idea how someone acts or doesn't act like they're with child.

"She asked me to come around for a beer to talk about an emergency plan if Archer hurt her."

Anteros and I looked at each other, our faces matching the shock. It sounded almost as if she was trying to get him alone. But why? She never showed interest in him before. She only had eyes for Archer, even in their anger. Today, though, she ignored everyone else. Even Prometheus said she had shut him out and wouldn't even telepathically talk to him.

Before I could contemplate it further, there was a knock. Himerus hopped up and let my dad in.

He sighed, disappointed at seeing her asleep still. "Let's try to wake her."

"If you could before, why didn't you?" My question came out harsher than I had intended.

He gave me a measured look. "Because she needed rest, and I had no power left, but I'm not eager to be on the wrong side of the Jade Emperor. I already am since I can't do the impossible to stop a deadly virus taking the mortal world by storm." Dad was tired, unshaven, but had at least showered and changed to get rid of the blood, Linda's blood. Himerus and I had changed as soon as we could shuck off of our bloody clothes and trash them.

Guilt tortured me these past hours. If Linda hadn't been there… No. I could not regret this. She would wake up, and we would have eternity together.

Dad rummaged under the sink until he found the ammonia we used to clean the floors. He came over and opened it. I grew wary. What was he doing?

He opened it and held it near Linda's nose.

"What does that do?" Himerus asked.

"Aside from smell terrible?" Dad looked at him. "The gas aggravates the lungs, forcing her to inhale. More oxygen gets to the brain, stimulating it. Then she wakes—in theory."

"Like smelling salts," Anteros realized.

Dad nodded.

Linda's nostrils started flaring, irritated at the smell. She breathed in deeply a couple times. My heart started racing with hope. I met Dad's gaze, and he gave me a small smile. He stood up, taking the cleaner away and closing it. Then he placed his hands on her temples and closed his eyes in that way he does when he concentrates on healing.

Linda stirred. Her eyes fluttered open.

"You're awake," I gasped.

She flinched. Her eyes darted around, confusion in her features. I had been so worried about her waking that I hadn't prepared anything to say to her. How could I break it to her that she had been dying, and we saved her by giving her immortality? How much did she remember?

"Aios?"

"I'm here."

She gazed up at me, blinking a few times until a smile formed on her lips.

143

Overcome with emotion, I leaned down and kissed her. I heard my father say something about leaving us alone but paid them no heed. Her lips pressed against mine.

I broke the kiss to make sure she was okay.

We were now alone, the door closing behind the three of them, who'd left at immortal speed. Not that she noticed. Linda was staring deep into my eyes.

"I love you," came out of my mouth. Thank the gods she was immortal, or I would've bound her to me for that honest slip up.

Her response was to sit up at immortal speed and then hold her head, closing her eyes.

"Are you okay?"

"Dizzy. I moved…fast."

I took up her hand. "Linda, what do you remember?"

"Remember?"

"The last thing before waking up?"

Her brow wrinkled. "Where am I?"

"My dad's place."

"Your dad?" Her gaze darted around the room. "This looks like Lucien's place."

All in Mother Gaia, how stupid could I be? It's not like it was a secret or would remain to be one in a few minutes, but knowing Lucien was my father was the last bit of evidence of immortality I had wanted to share with her.

"Uhhh…"

There was no backtracking. None at all. I was scared of her reaction. I wanted the others back, to be honest. To get them to come back meant I had to unload the truth.

"Aios?" Her bottom lip trembled.

"I'm trying to think of where to start. I love you, Linda, know that."

Her face softened. "I love you too."

I stole a kiss that led to another and another. Part of me hoped she would let us get lost in our feelings, but she pushed me away, eyes wide, and gasping for breath. "I remember a knife heading toward Callie, then pain. The worst part was the pain on your face. Then…" She hesitated. "Lots of people talking, rushing around, then nothing. What happened to me?"

I backed away from her reluctantly and took up her hand. "Linda, I'm going to tell you the truth, and there is no way to downplay this. You also won't believe it, but let me say it all before you interrupt."

"You're scaring me." She drew her legs in toward her body for comfort. I saw it as a barrier between us I had to get rid of. The truth would let her relax…eventually.

I let out a breath. "You would've died. We had a way to save your life. It was to make you immortal. We took that opportunity."

She stared at me blankly.

"All of us are immortal—even Callie."

She studied me. "Like vampires?" Her face was serious. She must've seen or suspected enough to know there was something off about us.

In one deep breath, I said, "My real name is Hymenaios. I was born in the Hellenistic era. Lucien is actually my father, and his name is Apollo."

At the mention of his name, recognition took. Of course, as a lesser god, the average person would not know my name. Everyone knew Apollo.

"I don't believe you, but I know something is way off with all of you and what I remember happening, and oh my god, why is my mouth moving faster than normal?" She touched her lips to stop them.

"Being a goddess has its perks. One is quick movements and reflexes. Obviously, the other is immortality."

She put up her hand. "Stop." She took a deep breath. I could tell she felt different. She knew it.

"What do you need me to do? Linda, please. I don't know what to say."

"Immortal. I will live forever?"

"Yes."

Her eyes searched mine. "I want to believe you, but this is insane. I want to talk to Callie."

Then she started to cry. This was going horribly. Not knowing what else to do, she needed a demonstration. I sighed and stood up. I called Callie. It went to her voicemail. I hung up. I stormed out, angry, upset, feeling kind of rejected.

My dad was outside with Himerus and Anteros. They looked at me.

I shrugged. "She's not taking it well, wants Callie. Maybe even Archer, or you, or Dad could help?"

Dad rubbed his hand down his neck. "I think you need to deal with this on your own. I'll talk to her father, alert him she's awake, and smooth things out. He'll help explain a lot to her. Anteros and Himerus, go find Archer and Callie. She'll feel better with them around. Their place might be a nice neutral zone for Linda."

My friends left. Dad pulled me in for a half hug, then touched my cheek. "You do not need me. You want me around, but there is no need. I'll be dealing with Akila."

145

I laughed. I wanted to make him help me, but I knew it was a situation I had to deal with head-on. He was giving the situation distance as her ex and my father. Gods, my life was twisted.

I went back in. Linda was standing and watching her hands as she moved them fast.

I closed the door behind me. "Sorry." Then I realized what I had to do. I needed to go into teaching mode. I grabbed a paring knife off the block. "Immortal means this." I sliced my palm.

She gasped. Then she watched it close up, her eyes making a study of it. I loved that about her, her thirst for knowledge. My mind was already planning an introduction to Athena. Linda would love what she knew, and Athena would adore a new pupil—she always did.

I took up Linda's hand and, with a smidgen of worry she wasn't immortal, sliced her hand. She yanked it away with a hiss of breath. She opened her palm and watched as the wound closed. Her eyes met mine. And then, she attacked me.

She tackled me onto the couch, her lips moving quickly against mine as if immortal speed were nothing new to her. I was baffled by her split-second reaction, and her hands weaving through my hair, making me almost lose my mind, just added to my confusion. This was not the timid mortal girl I had been dating. This was a confident goddess in my arms.

I pulled away, my eyes dancing across her gorgeous face. "I never officially asked you, but will you be my girl?"

She smiled. "I already am."

I pulled her close, kissing her back.

Kisses and words of love were all she wanted. The question and answer session would wait. There was time to catch her up to speed, explain everything to her. Sure, my family history was extensive, but we had time now. Lots of time.

We were together, alive, and I was happier than I could ever be. The god of marriage, always the officiator, never the groom, was finally getting his well-earned chance for happiness.

CHAPTER 23

Archer

Things were a mess, but I loved Callie, damn it. I had to make this work for her, for the baby. And the attempted kidnapping made me realize our problems with trust were not a sliver as important as the love in my heart for my wife. Love was my existence, my purpose, and almost losing the person who embodied that for me was too much.

We had prevented her kidnapping by quick thinking, but she was mad about me coming after her pre-lockdown excursion. She claimed I had a territorial outburst, which contrasted her feelings that day of anxiety, desperation, shock, horror, and there was a desperate pleading for help. Her relief when I arrived, her clinging onto me in mutual understanding…nothing made sense. I knew how she felt because we were tied by our immortal bond, to sense each other's needs and feelings. If she died, so would I. How could she not expect me to go to her when she was in distress?

When I found her, she was different, annoyed, and kept saying she was fine. What scared me was her lack of concern for Linda, who'd almost died. Callie's face was expressionless, cold. She closed herself off from me, and she felt…nothing. It was as if she had detached herself from all of us the moment she'd come back.

This wasn't the Callie I'd fallen in love with. That Callie had been good friends with Linda and would've wanted to save anyone—even that vile Emily from high school, who'd jealously verbally attacked Callie often. My wife was a kind and loving person—a bit headstrong, and her powers had blindsided me at first—but something had changed lately. Sure, our fight, her morning sickness, and her hormones made her lash out more, but that would all pass. In a small blip of time when one could live forever, this fight would be nothing. I couldn't care less about her moods while she was bringing our child into the world. But three days ago, something had shifted in me, in her, in us—I don't know. The fact she didn't talk to me at all or respond to my texts since the incident was a big red flag. She didn't even visit Linda after she woke up—immortal. Linda was her best friend. Athena said Callie came out for food, gave one-word answers, and stayed in their guest room almost all day and night.

The largest red flag arrived this morning under my door. It was a letter addressed to me, asking for a divorce—typed up and printed out. Who does that?

THE IMMORTAL TRANSCRIPTS: GLIMMER

I was going to head over there immediately to demand answers, but I heard Ma squealing outside my door, besotted by something. I opened the door to see Prometheus in a suit and Athena in a plain white dress, so subtle and informal that, had I not seen the small bouquet in her hands, I would have never realized they were on their way to get married.

I smiled, unable to help myself. I might be struggling with my marriage, but to see true love in front of me always put me in a good mood.

Athena scowled at me. "Shut up, love god."

"What did I say?"

"You don't need to say it. I see it in your eyes."

I offered my hand to her, knowing her dislike for hugs. "Hardly fair, justice goddess."

She took my hand in hers and grasped it. "Your power is unfair. It makes reasonable people weak."

I nodded. "I concede that, Athena. You're right. But it is a fair trade, is it not?"

She gave me a measured look.

To appease her, I added, "In moderation."

A small smile tugged on her lips, and the war goddess actually blushed. "I suppose so."

"Congratulations."

"Thanks."

Prometheus next shook my hand, but then squeezed it, not letting go.

Athena started talking to Dad.

"Congratulations," I told Prometheus, wondering about his death grip on my hand.

"She's...something is off." He shook his head. "I should stay." We both knew he was referring to Callie.

I shook my head at him. "You need to go. Get married before they shut down everything. It means a lot to her, even though she pretends it doesn't."

Prometheus smiled at me—for once—before he gazed at Athena adoringly.

"Look," I said, "I agree with you. I was on my way to see her, or so I thought. I'll check on her in a bit and get some answers."

Prometheus looked torn as he joined Athena. It made me anxious as I slipped back into my apartment. The foreseeing god not knowing what was going on or would happen? I knew Callie clouded his vision at times, but that had been the very reason they had stayed away until recently—and allies, according to Athena.

When the foresight god could not explain, that was telling. Of what? That was the issue.

I showered, dressed, and went back out into the hallway after the excitement had died down. Callie was alone, and I was going to get answers.

As I knocked on the door, I heard someone crying out.

Instinctively, in case Callie was being attacked, I twisted the knob to find the door unlocked. I pushed it open. What kind of cries they were was now clear. My stomach clenched. I stopped breathing. I dreaded what I would see once I walked further into the apartment. Feet heavy, stomach bile rising, I walked in and turned the corner toward the guest room Callie was staying in.

The door was wide open. Flesh showing, kissing, moaning, movements under the covers. Himerus. Callie. Together.

Before I could fully comprehend what it meant when my wife was nude in the arms of my brother, she turned to look over her shoulder and smiled at me. The expression was evil. Twisted. Terrifying.

My head spun. My pulse throbbed erratically, and I leaned on the doorframe to steady myself. This was not Callie.

My brother cursed, and shoved "Callie" away, his lust clearing the moment he saw me and realized what he was doing. Not my Callie but a sick twisted version. To get the woman I loved back, I had to stay in control of my emotions. I turned away, hesitating in the doorframe. Turning slightly, I managed to mutter, "We need to talk." I held up the note she had left.

She slipped out of bed with no shame and slipped on an oversized T-shirt. The back of her figure exposed, I saw two dots on her lower back right over her butt. I had to yank my eyes away before she'd see the surprised expression on my face. Callie didn't have the dimples of Venus on her lower back.

I hurried from the room and sat, shooting off a 9-1-1 text to the rest of my family. Despite faking such a cool demeanor about the situation, I was a rattling live-wire on the inside. Where was my wife?

The imposter looked at me oddly and sat at the table.

"You too, *brother*." I stopped Himerus from trying to sneak out the door. I was furious with him. He believed this creature was Callie, his brother's wife, and yet he let her seduce him. The note, the doors left open—it was becoming clear this was a setup, but why and what for?

Himerus sat across from me, on the other side from fake Callie, his gaze glued to the table, his head down. Good, at least he wasn't in love with her or professing they'd run off together or some nonsense like that.

Ma rushed in, with Dad right on her heels, "Archer, I got your text. What—"

The looks on all our faces and the tension in the air were a dead giveaway of what was wrong. Anteros came in a moment later, as well as Lucien.

There was no turning back now. I pulled the folded evidence out of my pocket and threw it onto the table. "I received a letter."

Ma picked it up, confused about her features. "Typed? Divorce? Who types up a divorce letter?" Her glare set on Callie, the first unkind look Ma gave her in ages.

This thing that looked like Callie sneered at her. My wife never sneered.

My father snatched it from Ma and read it. He eyed Callie, who crossed her arms, rolled her eyes, and huffed. Not a Callie move either. Dad's eyes narrowed on her.

I explained, "The door was unlocked, bedroom door wide open, and I find these two going at it."

"Fighting?" Anteros asked.

"No." I glowered at him, refusing to be more specific.

"Oh," he said, realizing. "I just didn't think he'd be that dumb." He glared at Himerus. "How stupid are you, man?"

"God of lust, here. It's kind of hard for me to deny a hot girl when she's all over me. I kept trying to stop her, but she was literally attacking me!"

My dad scoffed at him and shook his head. Himerus looked ready to cry as he stared down at his hands. All he had ever wanted was our Dad's and my approval, and now he'd lost it in one stupid move.

"I'm sorry. She called me and begged me to come over. She was crying and said she was scared of Archer. When I got here, she was chatty and kept giving me nectar whiskey. And then she came onto me."

I expected my dad to push him further, demand answers, but Ma's venomous voice challenged first, "What do you have to say for yourself, Callie?"

Everyone stood on edge. When Ma was pissed, she was a force to be reckoned with. When you messed with her son, she had often been likened to the Furies exacting their divine retribution.

The imposter grunted in a very non-Callie way and stood up. She walked over to the fridge. "I don't have to explain myself to any of you."

"You kind of do," Dad hedged, his brow wrinkled as he examined her. I wanted him to see it, to assure me I hadn't lost my mind, to tell me this wasn't my wife. "We fought a war to protect you."

"Um, remember. I died for you, Callie." Lucien frowned, examining her, his eyes flittering all over her in confusion. Was he detecting lies?

The bottle of beer she had in her hand almost slipped to the ground in shock, and she turned from us. More evidence. She didn't know Lucien was resurrected? She turned around, looking smug, as she twisted the cap off and started chugging it. Definitely not Callie. This imposter didn't know Callie was pregnant and that she didn't really drink or even like it before her pregnancy.

This creature put the half-finished beer down on the counter. "But you are very much alive now, so no harm done. Look, I don't love Archer anymore. I want a divorce, and I want to have fun." She giggled, "Himerus was lots of fun."

I was up, making her flinch as I crossed the room. I was done with this mockery of my Callie, how these false memories of her would be ingrained in my brain, although they were not truly her. When I was uncomfortably close to her, she backed into the wall.

"Don't besmirch my wife through such lies. Tell me where she is, and I might let you live."

"No, Archer—" my Dad started.

"Dad, this is probably that little vision Callie was convinced where I would hurt her. We all know I never would, and I never will. This is not Callie."

The imposter shouted out, "He's crazy!"

Ma was over, trying to pull me away. "Archer, really. Sit down. Talk us through what is going on in your head, but please don't hurt her. You love her."

This poisoned version of Callie tried to get around me, and I grabbed her to stop her, but as she squirmed to get away, the only part I could get ahold of was her throat. I could not make sense of the cacophony of voices behind me, but arms were trying to pry me off her. I held on, steadfast, but slipped my hands down to pin her shoulders against the wall. I could not bear to hurt her, even though she was not Callie.

"Don't hurt me, Archer. You love me." Now that her voice was distraught, I could easily hear how the timbre of her voice was off, as well as her reaction. Callie would've used those moves she'd mastered in Iceland to protect herself, the ones Dad taught her; she'd kick my ass if I ever laid a finger on her.

I tuned out the imposter's words.

"Everyone, stop!" Lucien shouted. "He's right. There are lies all around her: her words, her voice even, her face and body—all fake."

Ma, losing her patience, shouted, "What?"

Done with waiting and needing real answers, I shoved her into the wall hard, making the shapeshifter grimace. "Tell me where my wife is, *Lena*."

"I am your wife. Archer, please." It hurt seeing Callie like this, and I could never kill Lena when she resembled Callie in any way.

Dad groaned behind me. "The shapeshifter we created, Proteus's daughter."

"I'm going to throttle you until you show them who you really are and tell me where my wife is. And if you don't do both, I'll kill you. You know I've done it before and will do it again." It was a lie that I hoped Lucien wouldn't call me out on because I couldn't do it when she looked like Callie. I didn't know if I had it in me to murder anyone else after I had Death. That was different. He had been hunting Callie down to reap her soul.

"Allow me to interrogate her, Archer." Dad touched my shoulder gently. "You don't need the memory of hurting someone who looks like her."

He was right. It was killing me to detain her against a wall.

I nodded and let her go. I turned. I heard a tussle behind me like she was naively thinking she could get past the god of war. When the others collectively gasped, I finally turned around, and saw the final seconds of Lena becoming herself, holding on to the arm of my father, who had her in a choke hold. Her human instincts to breathe were still kicking in, making her panic.

Dad let go. She coughed and slipped down to the ground in a ball.

"Where is my wife?" I demanded.

"Zeus has her." She coughed a couple times. "I was planted in her place when you all believed you had saved her."

It hit me hard. That was the moment the imposter with all the wrong reactions entered the scene. I had traced Callie through our connection though, so she had to have been right there close by, needing our help. I growled. "I could just kick myself! We severely underestimated Hermes. He's one of the best tricksters on the planet. The open attack was a ploy to switch her for Callie so we would not follow or retaliate. They've had her for days!"

"What are their plans?" Ma leaned down and pulled Lena up by her hair. Lena clawed at Ma before Anteros interceded and shoved Lena down onto the couch.

I closed my eyes, scanning for my wife; the other half of my soul would show up in my powers like a beacon. I breezed past mortals who were seeking love, hoping to help them more one day, and found her. "She's in Fiji."

"Then we will get her back," Dad said.

Lena got up. "You can't just storm into Zeus's resort in Fiji."

"Oh, yes, I can." Dad got that war gleam in his eye.

I nodded. Anything for Callie.

Dad shifted his weight, and I knew what was coming next. "Let's plan elsewhere. Lucien, you and Aroha detain and question her here. She's a prisoner until we decide what to do with her later." He was entering his war general strategy mode. What would follow would be uninterrupted orders until he was confident of a foolproof success.

"Me?" Ma seemed pleased to have a role.

Chase gave her a lopsided grin. "I wouldn't want to be cross-examined by you, not when someone messes with your kid, so you're the best, along with Lucien seeing the truth."

Lucien shoved Lena into a chair and then gave me a quizzical look. "Archer, how'd you know it wasn't Callie?" Of course, as always, Lucien was looking for the truth foremost.

Not wanting to reveal Lena's failings in case she got away, was freed, or wanted to attempt it again, I opted to be vague but wanted to instill guilt in her for not knowing one huge clue. "I know my wife. Callie is pregnant. *She* didn't know that." I stabbed the air with my finger in Lena's direction.

Her eyes went wide.

"So *now* you feel guilty?" I chastised her. "My child and my wife could be killed, and you are partly to blame. I hope it hangs over you forever."

Dad was in his war-monger mode, ignoring the side conversation completely. "Anteros, Archer, come with me. We're going to make some big plans."

"And me?" Himerus asked, glumly, eyes looking up at us under hooded, puppy-dog eyes.

I wanted to punch him for the betrayal he had been prepared to make with his brother's wife. The only luck on his side that I wouldn't hold a grudge forever was that it hadn't actually been my wife.

"You?" Dad gave him a disappointed look, which—coming from him—was worse than his indomitable rage. "Stay here as a guard. If she tries to leave, destroy her."

"With pleasure," he returned, quietly, staring down, unable to look at me as I left.

CHAPTER 24

I came to.

In the back of my mind, I realized I had not fallen asleep. I had that heavy-headed, groggy feel one gets when waking after fainting or being ill. Had I been knocked out? Being a goddess (still so weird), it couldn't have been a knockout, could it? I've never seen a god being knocked unconscious, and I watched part of a war.

Memories bubbled to the surface: being grabbed, squeezed through darkness, appearing in another part of Central Park. Something had covered my mouth and nose. The scent of chemicals. I had lost consciousness as my wrists were yanked behind me, the feeling of them being bound. I had been taken.

I moved my arms. They were no longer tied up. I opened my eyes a fraction (ouch!). I closed them.

Philo. Had they hurt him? The chemicals? I moved my hand to my lower abdomen. People say the mother's body protects the baby. I had to do whatever it took to keep it that way.

I needed to figure out where I was (Step 1). Then I could plan an escape (Step 2—an infinitely more difficult task than Step 1).

I sighed and opened my eyes a fraction, allowing them to adjust to the bright light before I opened them a bit more, then fully.

Agony sliced through my head. I didn't dare move to cause more pain. I was on my side, in front of me, a wall that had tribal mosaic wallpaper. The pattern's lines rippled right before my eyes as if they were jumping off the wall—stretching, elongating, and shrinking back up. (What the hell?)

I closed my eyes to stop it because it made me sick. My stomach was queasy. If I knew what being drunk felt like, I would be able to confirm that this out-of-it feeling was just like that.

I could hear the faint sound of waves. I could swear there were voices in the waves. These hallucination vibes were scaring me.

Where was I? (Dumb question.) There was only one place I would be if I were kidnapped. Zeus lived in Fiji. *If* he had lived. I still couldn't believe Chase, who insisted body parts could grow back, and if he were right, how could a god grow an entire body back? My twisted imagination thought of Zeus's head sitting on a throne talking. Eww. He probably didn't even have a voice box, for starters; I shut the thought down.

I rolled onto my back, ignoring the pain and queasiness. Surely, the ichor in my blood should burn off whatever this chemical was that had knocked me out (soon, please, ichor).

There was a TV on the wall across the room, two doors, and a balcony sliding door. There wasn't a piece of furniture, aside from this bed in the room, nor decorations on the wall. It was a prison (with freaky dancing wallpaper).

I pushed myself to sitting, and the room spun. I took deep breaths, trying to quell the nausea. I pushed up to standing. The room teetered before righting itself. I took a few more deep breaths. This was definitely what being drunk must feel like (not a fan).

I tried the closest door. An en suite with a large tub, sink, and toilet. The only window was tiny and composed of glass boxes. I gave up there after my cursory glance told me that nothing could be made into a weapon, for it was bare, not even a towel, shower rod, or curtain present.

I returned to the room and shut the door.

I went to the balcony door, knowing already it would be locked. I tapped on it—plexiglass. Maybe I could pry it open? And go where? Drop all those stories down and shatter my body? Even if I had the godly instant-healing abilities, did my baby? It might be safer to play along, stay put until I could learn more.

I went to the main door, but it had no handle. I tried gripping the gap in the door with my nails to see if I could pull it open, but it was clearly locked (note to self: immortal nails bend backward and hurt like crazy too).

Next, the central air intake vent was screwed into the wall and my poor hurting nails were not strong enough to budge a screw. It was definitely a prison, but at least not a dungeon of torture I'd imagine someone like Zeus to have. Running water and a comfortable bed was a tiny consolation. Food would be ideal.

According to what Archer and his brothers had said when we had been momentarily stranded on Montserrat, immortals could last a while without food. Only, I wasn't sure what toll that would take on me, particularly if Philo took the nutrition he needed from me as mortal babies do from their mothers. And if I was stuck here for a long period of time, I would start showing.

Unsure how to pass the time, and knowing I needed to preserve my energy, I lay back down and closed my eyes, waiting (who knew what for). I thought of Dad, and it panged me he'd never meet Philo or any of my children. Before I let the tears come and let my hormones overtake me, I shifted to what Dad would do in this situation. Play it safe. Observe. Learn. Use knowledge against them later. Reveal nothing. Hatch an escape plan.

I planned while I rested. At some point, I must've drifted to sleep, because a hand was shaking me awake. A soft, child-like voice asked, "Callie?"

I opened my eyes to see a young girl, only not quite. Her age was indiscernible, somewhere between fourteen to twenty, but her eyes told me instantly who she was. They were hazel and vibrant, like her brother Chase's. His were full of raging emotions, but hers were open and wide with innocence. Archer's aunt, Hebe, goddess of youth, the cupbearer, who was offering me a drink.

I was parched and wanted to snatch it from her but stopped. Was it poisoned?

She cocked her head, confused about my hesitation.

I pushed myself into her mind. She was genuinely confused, and her thoughts were of concern for me, what distress and injuries they might've inflicted upon me when they captured me, and if that entailed hitting me upside the head. No sinister thoughts of poison. Not one bad thought about anything. Innocent to the core (and highly naive).

"What is it?" I asked.

"Nectar. I thought you'd need it...for the baby."

I scrambled up, away from her, frightened, pressing myself in a sitting position against the headboard.

She frowned. "You don't trust me? Did my brother, my nephew warn you against me?" She appeared hurt.

Had I not read her mind, I might think her kindness was an act. "No, but I was taken. I'm a prisoner."

"I'm the cupbearer. I have never harmed another being. It is not my nature."

This sounded right, but I couldn't trust anyone. As she held the cup up, I felt very much like Snow White being offered an apple. I shook my head.

She sighed. "I understand. Let me put you at ease. I will swear on the Styx that this is just nectar..." she leaned closer to whisper, "and a tiny bit of ambrosia, for the babe." She leaned even closer to reach my ear. Almost inaudible to my immortal ears she said, "No one knows but me that you are with child. A cupbearer power. I protect the innocent and young brides. You're both."

For some reason, I easily believed her. The mythology my father had told me as bedtime stories, having me help him type up his book—he had prepared me for these moments, thanks to Prometheus's warnings.

As she pulled away, she offered the cup up again. "Hera will also know when she sees you. I do not know my mother's mind. I do not know why you are here."

Hera, the mother goddess. Her ties to Zeus would make her want my death. Her goddess role would make her want to protect my child. Which part of her would win?

"Not drinking will make the baby vulnerable. Please. If you don't drink it now, I'm not sure when I can bring you a drink again."

"You're not supposed to be here?" I assumed.

She shook her head.

"Why risk it? Why do this?"

"I love Ares. I love Eros. I love you and my great-niece or nephew. I know nothing but platonic love for all creatures alive."

"Let me out of here."

"I cannot do that. I'm sorry. I'm no fighter and only protect. An escape will let others hurt you."

"If they want to hurt me, and they likely will while I'm imprisoned, why wouldn't you help me. Are you afraid?"

"No. I love them too. I love *all* creatures." She stared off, thinking, with a wistful expression. "When the cyclopes and satyrs still existed, even them."

I thought there was no such thing as being too nice, but here it was (and both of them had existed, for real? Whaaaa...). I took a deep breath for patience and focus. "Can you tell Cha—Ares I am here at least?"

"I lament that I didn't know you were here until today. I could not warn my brother when I saw him."

Fear crept over me. "How long have I been here?"

"I think three days."

Three days, and no one came for me? Why?

Hebe turned her head as if hearing something I didn't. "I must go."

I tore the glass from her hand. "Swear on the Styx."

"I swear on the Styx the contents in the glass you are holding are nectar, ambrosia, and some ginger to calm your stomach, and will not hurt you or your unborn child."

I wasn't sure what the Styx pact fully was or how it worked, but I was pretty sure something terrible would happen to her if she lied in this situation. I chugged the drink, tasting its sweetest with that hint of ginger.

Before I could thank her, the cup was yanked out of my hand, and she was gone, the door clicking shut behind her.

I scooted down and closed my eyes as I heard footsteps coming. Not one second later, the door unlocked, and someone entered. I pretended to sleep.

I focused on keeping my breathing deep and even as I listened. Too many steps for one person entering, but a couple of them (or maybe three?).

"What did you do to her?" a female asked.

THE IMMORTAL TRANSCRIPTS: GLIMMER

"She's fine. He said he'd knocked her out, handled her with care," another female voice scoffed. "Really, Hera. Do you actually care? She's here for her execution. Let her stay in her oblivion for a few days."

I had to withhold a flinch (crap, crap, crappity, crap). At least I knew one was Hera. Who was the snotty one?

"No, she is not. She is a bargaining chip to get some semblance of peace here. *Your* father almost died in his quest to kill her. Threat after threat, her family defends her—Norse and Titan included. You are delusional if you think we can simply ignore the repercussions of what an assassination might bring."

There was a catty snort. "I merely follow my orders, unlike you."

"Begone, then. I don't trust you in here. You are stripped of privileges in the maximum-security wing. You are not to see the prisoner or any we capture who come for her."

As much as I wished Archer would not be reckless and come for me, I had deep regrets about things. If he were captured, we at least could make peace and then fight for survival together. We were one, so if I died, so would he. We should be together, but I had pushed him away because of a prophecy that likely wasn't true. It had steered me away from him to get captured.

"But—"

"Who do you think is in charge until Zeus heals? Oh, let me guess. He made you some silly promise you could be in charge if you did the deed. Killed her? He made the same promise to Hermes, to others, and even to me. I am the only one with the logic to stop another, more deadly, war. We lost a muse and—"

"Some loss." The voice said before she laughed.

"Artemis," Hera hissed.

My blood ran cold. This was the goddess who was ready to let her nephew die for marrying Archer to me. This was the sister who glorified in the death of her brother, according to the Egyptian goddess Akila. Artemis was insane (perhaps clinically).

"Seriously, such useless powers. One goddess could carry the whole bulk of it. Muses are like a collective cat: nine lives. Oh well, we're down to eight. My bad, seven of them since Euterpe ran away like a coward for the spawn of her own ex."

"Get out, I said!" Hera lost it.

So did I—of my concentration to stay asleep. I jerked up with a start to see Artemis scowl at me before she left the room at immortal speed. With Hera's shouting, my reaction was instinctively on point. I could not pretend to sleep through that. With that realization, it was time to act. I put on a surprised act, freaking out about where I was and what was going on (not hard to do when you're mega anxious).

Surprisingly, Hera soothed me. She was kind, placating. Told me she would let me out to get some food.

Then she gave me a candid look and spoke. "I've heard you can read our minds." Then she tilted her head. *Do it*, she mouthed. Her eyes darted up behind her. There was a small black dot over her head, embedded at the top of the wall where the molding met the ceiling. Was it a camera? It would be filming the back of her head.

She was helping me?

I drew myself back toward the headboard, continuing the act of being scared. I pressed my mind out, trying to push into hers. I met her gaze and got the connection. *I know you are with child. You know who I am and what I represent. I will keep you safe in my rooms if you'll come with me.*

I wasn't sure how to answer her, but out of this room gave me more opportunity to escape. Safety felt paramount. I thought back to what she last said out loud. Reading minds.

"I am hungry," I said.

She gave me a slight smile, took up my hands, and pulled me up.

She walked me right out the door, throwing my hand down, as she stormed ahead of me. Hera glanced back, giving me a trust-me glance. She was acting too. Her bold walk and righted shoulders spoke power.

Ahead of us, Hebe popped out of a room not far from mine. She carried empty IV bags.

Spying Hera, then me behind her out of my room, she froze. "Mother, what is the plan now?"

"Keeping this one alive to stop a war as I instructed you earlier."

I saw the door close, a prison, like mine. The IV bags. Zeus. Under protection in a locked room.

I have no idea why, but on impulse, I wanted to face him. He was likely half alive. Maybe I could do this, end it all. How powerful could he be in this short period of time after he had been decapitated and his body burned?

I darted into the room and shut the door. Fear did not stop me. I was done with Zeus and this. I could not live with him looming over me with my child in tote. We could not run any longer. I hoped Hera and Hebe were stronger than Artemis and whatever forces Zeus had left.

I moved into the room to see a form on the bed with multiple IVs in the patient. I crept closer, quietly, taking in the white hair and beard. He was sleeping. Face gaunt, eyes sunken, I recognized him at once: Zeus.

The body under the sheet was thin, the arms that rested on top of the covers were merely skin and bones, veins under the skin visible. He reminded me of an alien or a lizard (how else could he grow a body back?). The silvery liquid in the IV bags must be ambrosia. The myths had said gods blood was silver, but we bled red. Ambrosia mistaken for blood. Chase had been right. Zeus was growing his body back. The fact he had limbs and a torso already, over a month after his beheading, was a good indication of how soon he would be able to attack me. I now feared for Philo's life even more. If I got away from here, escaped, it wouldn't end (unless…I killed him, right now).

I crept closer to the bed, examining the complex IV system. They were in his arms and hands, spliced, so eight lines ran to IV bags. The skin had grown over the needles, which made me almost retch. A small price to pay to grow a body but it was something I'd never get over. I wondered if I disconnected them if he'd die, but likely not. Archer had shown me the only real way to die when he saved me from Thanatos, lit Death on fire.

Then Zeus's eyes opened.

I couldn't take another step.

The gray-blue orbs of cold hatred peered over at me as he slowly turned his head.

My heart slammed in my chest. He looked weak, and I was strong.

I froze in inaction. I was not as ruthless as him, not as cruel.

An eerie grin spread across his lips. "Come to kill me, Callista?" His voice was raspy and soft. He was far from the intimidating god of gods whom I had met before.

"No," I found myself saying. I pitied him. I should hate him for everything he had done to my parents, me, my loved ones, but instead, I felt bad.

He had pushed so hard to get rid of me that he became this, this shell of a being. This was where hate led him, and I would not lower myself to be like him. It felt like something Dad would tell me to do, forgive. He would be proud of me.

"I know why you hate me, but I feel bad for you. Letting hate destroy your family? Look at you. It's sad, pathetic. I don't want your power. I just want to live."

Hera and Hebe hustled in behind me.

"The Olympians need to be controlled. You do not know what they are capable of without being checked." He truly believed it or convinced himself of it because he was used to being in power.

"I have seen what they are like free from your oppression. I have seen love, respect, friendship, happiness, and belonging. They are happy. Still, you want to lord over and control them. You just don't get it. What you are telling yourself is a lie. You aren't scared of losing control; you're more terrified you are already redundant."

"That little power of yours is annoying." He sighed as if bored and looked away from me. "I'd like you to stop invading my thoughts."

I hadn't read his mind, but his assumption meant I had been right.

"Do away with me, then," He said. "Take your revenge and 'free' your family."

"I was raised better than that." I clenched my fists to hold back my anger. "You killed my parents: my father just for spite, my mother because you thought she was me. I would never do that to anyone."

"Thanatos would beg to differ if he could."

Archer had killed him, not me, but it was pointless to argue the issue further. "Attack and defense are different issues. We will do whatever we need to in order to survive. You had me kidnapped and held prisoner. After I get out of here, you will leave us alone, let me live my life in peace."

He laughed, making chills shoot down my spine. "And if I don't?"

"We were never attackers. You were. We only tried to survive. We had a defensive battle, if you recall. You crossed the line." I walked closer to him, hoping to unnerve him.

His breathing grew faster.

"If you do it again, I will sic my father-in-law, my grandparents, and your brothers on you." It was something that could easily be done. I was sure the suppressed brothers wanted their revenge after they settled down, enjoying their freedom.

Hera and Hebe gasped in tandem. So, Hades hadn't revealed himself on the surface to his brother yet (living his best life with his wife no doubt). He would one day, and Zeus was screwed when that day would come.

"My brothers, as in Hades too?" He eyes me suspiciously. "You lie."

"I sprang him too. I wouldn't be surprised if Hades comes for you once he knows you have me."

"There's a reason they haven't come for you. They might not realize you're gone for a long while if everything goes according to plan. You see, Archer created a demigod shapeshifter as a punishment for killing Thanatos, and as a shapeshifter, she pulls you off quite well. I'm sure she's warming your husband's bed right now."

My stomach dropped. I kept my face impassive. Surely, Archer would know it wasn't me. He would sense it, our connection gone. But we were in a fight, and if that shapeshifter knew, she might avoid him. No, no. Archer would not let more than a day pass before he'd check on me to see if I was able to eat. A sharp hunger pang struck me (ravenous).

"He'll know. I bet they're on their way right now." Lucien would know too, but I already let Hades out of the bag. Best let Lucien be a major distraction in the future if needed, since they had no idea we had brought him back to life.

161

"Is that true, Father?" a voice asked. "Hades is out?"

I whirled around. Hermes was in the room, behind me, to the left of Hera and Hebe, who waited to see what might happen next. Where had he come from? (duh, teleporting god).

Zeus tried to prop himself up but couldn't, his arms too feeble. "She lies. Don't believe her. Get rid of her. Kill her."

"Yes, Father." Hermes grabbed my arm, and I felt a squeezing sensation.

We appeared in my room. "Stay put. He can have you killed at any moment."

I raised my brow at him. "He just ordered you to kill me."

Hermes let go of my arm. "Is it true, what Hera said?"

"How would I know what she said?"

"You're...you're pregnant?" His eyes were wide.

That was why Hera and Hebe had taken a minute before they'd entered.

I didn't need to answer.

His eyes softened as they trailed down to my abdomen. I was not used to his face looking at me with anything other than sneering hatred (confusing). "You're Eleutheria." His eyes darted up and fixed over my shoulder as if lost in memories or thoughts.

"Yes, in a manner of speaking." I admitted to being the freedom goddess, hoping he would not hurt me, knowing there was a child, knowing I could break Zeus's hold over him if he chose to leave.

His eyes cut back to me, looking filmy as if he were upset about something (weird). Then he vanished.

I sighed, now wishing I hadn't let my curiosity get the best of me. I could've been in Hera's rooms, safe. Or was I better off not trusting her? Was being in this room where everyone knew I was located, that was being watched, safer? The thought of Artemis coming after me also made me wish I had Hera on my side.

Hermes was suddenly back, making me jump, his eyes as large as saucers. "He's not in the Underworld, Hades. He's gone."

"He's free," I told him.

Hermes looked at me in a new light, backed away from me, shaking his head as if he could not believe me. "You returned. After he made me..." He shuddered. "I thought there was no hope of..." He shook his head. Then he vanished again, leaving me alone and confused about what he was talking about.

I was alive because he refused to follow Zeus's orders. Perhaps, I could get him to help me. Or Hebe or Hera. What had he meant by how I "returned"? If I figured it out, maybe I could get out of here alive. Despite Hermes's vague words, they resonated with me. I was piecing together the past from Athena's accounts. If so, I had the largest bargaining chip, the same one I cashed in to free Hades and bring Lucien back. Perhaps Hermes and Hera needed their own type of freedom too.

CHAPTER 25

Fiji. Dad had wanted me to stay behind with Ma, but there was no way I was not going after my wife and unborn child. Ma sided with me because she wanted to go to control my father. She was worried he'd cause mass destruction if unchecked and, perhaps, more importantly, get them killed.

Zeph left Dad and me on the beach. I was itching to race into the resort to find my wife. I had to wait for Zeph to collect the rest of our crew. I closed my eyes, searching for that other half of me. Like a beacon drawing my heart to her presence, I found her in the main building, where Zeus resided. Of course, he'd keep her close.

"Well?" Dad asked.

"She's here, main building, top floor."

Chase cracked his neck. "*His* floor."

Athena and Prometheus were next, followed by Anteros and Ma pairing, and lastly, the most important duo, Heph and Belle. I felt a tiny bit of guilt about leaving Himerus behind, but I could not concentrate with him around. I still saw images of him with my wife, burned into my memory, even though it hadn't been her. I needed time to forgive him. Love could not hold grudges forever, but betrayal still stung.

At least he had company. Aios was hesitant to return to the home he now spurned, nor did he want to leave Linda. Lucien said he'd come, but Dad could tell he didn't want to leave his newfound daughter and son, so he tasked him with protecting the homestead and seeing that Lena was taken back to the Underworld for punishment that Hades would see to since he owed Callie his freedom—and that might be temporary if…

I could not let myself complete the thought.

"Ready?" Dad asked.

"Yeah, yeah, yeah, I didn't agree for you to be in charge." Athena crossed her arms.

Chase stared her down; she stared back at him.

This was insufferable. Trying to control my temper, I said, "My wife is imprisoned there. Does it matter?"

Prometheus gripped Athena's shoulder, trying to get her to loosen up. "Team Rescue headed by Belle. Team Beat the Tartarus out of Zeus's Guards headed by Heph."

Chase and Athena stared at him in shock.

He shrugged. "What? If you can't play nice, you don't get a choice."

"The kid is right. Let's go." Heph started lumbering toward the resort. "We're losing the element of surprise."

"Where are we going?" Chase demanded, following after him.

"Through the front door. Distract them."

Athena rushed after them. "Is that wise?"

I looked to Belle for guidance. "This way." She took off at immortal speed, and I raced after her. We stopped in the shade of the building, glued against the wall. Our rescue team was us two, Ma, and Anteros. We waited for Belle's instruction. She had lived in this Olympus location the longest. She knew every nook and cranny, which was why Athena had gotten her on board.

Belle pointed to a security camera at the corner of the building that was scanning, but we were just out of range. She pointed at me. I nodded.

I waited for it to start panning away from our area and defied gravity, "flying" as I called it. I went above the camera and then smashed it with my fist. I landed below, Belle and the others already rushing over to meet me. Belle put a code in the service door, and it clicked, unlocking.

We hurried in. Belle pushed forward and took us down a hallway with loud humming machines. The laundry. She took us into a room where there was a massive bin of dirty bedsheets and comforters. Above was a laundry chute.

"You first since you can fly," She told me. I had to climb into the soiled sheets—gross—to get the right angle. Hearing voices coming, they scrambled in after me. I floated up stories, hoping the noise below was them scrambling in and up the chute behind me and not being discovered. I could not wait for them. I had to find Callie.

The chute dead-ended. I flopped out of the chute's door onto the floor of a service room. A mortal woman stood there, her mouth wide. I raced out the door at an immortal speed. She'd think she was hallucinating until the others crawled out. I slowed to a walk and closed my eyes, homing in on Callie. Six doors down. Really, I should have waited for the others, but I couldn't. I had to see she was okay.

The door was locked. I grabbed the handle to snap it off, when gods poured into the hallway from both ends: my family and Belle on one, two Muses and Zelus on the other. I was tired of the zealous ice god. Wanting Callie to stay safe inside away from him, I let go of the handle.

"What?" I looked at the ice daemon. "You want another snapped neck?" Twice now. Was he going for a third?

He smiled, that eerie scar elongating it oddly to one side. "What, you want to almost die again? The only reason you live is if other gods help or die in your place, *love* god." It was meant as an insult, but I could never see it that way. Love was the strongest power; it overcame everything.

"Archer!" I heard Callie's muffled shout through the door. She pounded on the other side. I had to keep her and the baby away from Zelus. The idea of him hurting them sickened me.

"Zelus," Belle came up behind me. "I'd love to say it is a pleasure to see you, but it's not."

"You, a traitor, Belle?"

"Depends what side you are on. I always choose good over evil, love over hate. What is your excuse? Following orders mindlessly as always?"

He scowled at her. That's when she lurched slightly. He was attacking her with ice shards he could command mentally.

"Oh, no you don't." Anteros muttered, using his magnetic abilities to crash into Zelus and tackle him to the ground. The Muses, armed with short blades, went in for my brother. I flew at them, clotheslining both into the ground. Belle recovered and joined the fray. The Muses were disarmed, and it shifted to wrestling like children fighting over a toy. The door to the stairwell busted open, and Heph lumbered in. He grabbed a Muse, Terpsichore—who had Belle's left arm restrained in a half nelson—by her hair and threw her aside like a rag doll. His eyes burned with rage as he helped Belle to her feet. She clung to him. He scolded. "Rescue, dearest, not fight. Go get Callie."

He tossed the other muse, Erato, aside into the wall. I raced down the hall to Callie's door, which Ma was trying to bust open.

She was yanking on and twisting the handle with all her might. "It's unbreakable, Archer. Titanium or something even stronger I have never dealt with."

I tried too and felt the rigidity of the metal not turning or bending to my will.

"Heph!" Ma called.

He grunted at her. "Little busy right now, Dite. Let me thaw this thing out, and I'll be right with you."

Zelus backed up, although he still wore his intimidatingly eerie grin.

A fire-and-ice battle was kicking off.

The door was pointless. I rushed down the hall, up a flight of steps and kicked open the locked roof door. I floated down to her balcony, peering inside. Callie

166

was standing on the bed, Hera and Hermes in the room, looking as if they were trying to calm her—or attack her?

I kicked in the glass, the sensation jarringly painful. Plexiglass.

I grabbed the handle and yanked the door open with all my strength, the lock catches snapping off.

"I came for my wife."

Callie's eyes lit up with vibrancy. It was her, truly her, my wife.

Hermes moved before I could take a step inside, grabbing Hera's hand as he dove onto the bed and grabbed Callie's ankle.

They were gone.

I screamed in frustration, my heart pounding in my ears. It took me a moment to realize the pounding was not just within me but around me. My family.

There was no knob inside: a prison.

I went out the way I came and met up with my family in the hallway to find the Muses gone and Heph's hands around Zelus's throat. Zelus was fighting back, but his icicles did nothing to Heph who could burn them off easily.

"Ice can't burn." Zelus laughed until Heph choked the air out of him.

Heph growled. "Well, it has to melt at some point. Shall we experiment?"

Heph's hands were aglow with a temperature beyond my imagination—beyond the volcano that I almost threw myself in, beyond anything I could fathom. Just like that, Zelus's eyes bulged, and then he exploded. Like a water balloon bursting, water splashed everywhere.

"Ugh," was all Heph said about the water all down his front.

We all just stood there in shock. Zelus, a free Titan, or had been, didn't evoke Chaos.

Athena, Prometheus, and Dad busted through the door of the staircase.

Dad demanded, "Where is she?"

I was lost, witnessing a god explode.

Anteros recovered first. "Zelus. Boom. Water." Right, maybe he hadn't recovered.

"Zeus?" Ma asked.

"Somewhere on this floor," Athena went from door to door as if she could sense him.

"Hera and Hermes took her," I told Dad. Then I closed my eyes, looking for Callie.

Still in Fiji, still nearby, the beach.

I raced down the hall.

Dad intercepted me. "Not alone."

"You kill Zeus. I'm getting my wife."

THE IMMORTAL TRANSCRIPTS: GLIMMER

Prometheus kicked a door that also had an unbreakable handle. It did not budge. He cursed in an ancient tongue I couldn't understand. He leaned on the door. "I know you're in there. I know you are weak. You need to know something. I can get to you again. I will, and next time, you're mine," he growled.

Athena stared at him, worried. "Theus."

He glared at the floor. "Not now, Thena. Just..." He couldn't speak but held out his hand.

She stared at him a moment, and her crazy intelligence or knowledge of him caught on. "Callie is who we came for. Anything else was a bonus," Athena said. "Zelus dead is a victory. He's who almost killed Callie last battle."

I was done with waiting for Prometheus to let go of his revenge. "Prometheus. They leave with her, we lose her."

He sighed, and like that we all raced to the beach. I was getting my love back. Even if I had to fight my grandmother for her.

CHAPTER 26

There, on the beach, Hera and Hermes stood with me, while forms on the horizon grew bigger. They had brought me to this remote part of the beach to lead my family away from Zeus, to protect him, but they also refused to kill me. Because of my baby. Or did they like the idea of being free but were too scared?

I turned to face Hera. "What happens? When I have my baby, will you then kill me? Will you kill my child if he takes after me?"

Her stern eyes met mine. "You think I relish the idea of your death? You are freedom. When this ends one day, remember me. We are not free yet." *We*, as in Hermes and her, and likely anyone else in the Fijian stronghold.

It had to be said, so I went for it. "You could end this all by ending him."

"How do you kill the person you love most, even if you hate them? How do you destroy the man who gave you your children? What happens when there is no god of the gods? Anarchy?" Hera retorted. She gave me a sad look as if I were the naïve one.

I did not want to press her so close to my freedom, but she was so repressed and scared of her spouse, so much so, she would take the comfortable route. At least in this instance, she chose her instincts and morals to protect her great-grandchild and me from Zeus.

"Look," Hermes said, "we can't defy Zeus. Understand that. But I will not kill a child for him, not again. Know that, if you see us again one day, we are still the enemy. There is only so much defiance we can manage. In this case, Hera's power to protect your child outweighs Zeus's control. That is a tenuous protection."

I swallowed with difficulty. If he ran into me in the future, not pregnant, he might kill me.

The forms down the beach were getting bigger, running toward us. I could not quite make them out and was afraid to leave in case it was Zeus's people rather than my own.

"Tell Athena…" Hera hesitated.

I kept my eyes glued at the horizon, looking for recognition of the fast-moving forms.

"Tell her every time Freedom died, part of me did as well."

I didn't know what she meant, but I recognized a form flying above the others. Archer. I started running toward the crowd, breaking into my immortal pace, eager to meet the group, to see him, to have him hold me and tell me everything would be all right (wussy, I know, but I was exhausted and craving safety).

I heard a swoosh far behind me of my captors escaping. When the group saw me alone, they slowed down. Archer and I did not, and we collided. We tumbled and rolled in the sand, me ending up on top of him. We stared at each other in wonder for a moment before he spoke.

"Callie." His voice was laced with love, agony, and relief.

"Archer."

He leaned up and kissed me with a sigh that told me our fight was over, forgiveness of my omissions gone, and trust restored. My absence had left him shaken.

He devoured my lips. I tried to ignore everyone else—Chase's annoyance at missing revenge upon Zeus, a confused Aroha, the rational Athena, told-you-so tones of Prometheus—my family.

Archer let his head fall back in the sand to gaze at me, his hands framing my face in his palms, ever so gently. "I refuse to fight with you ever again. You will always be right." (Every girl's dream, right? Or not.)

"No. That would be a horrible idea. How about we discuss things like rational adults without bickering? You needed space, Archer. What I did was wrong."

"It ended up getting us Lucien back, though, and I was wrong to be so controlling, so overprotective. I have to remember that you aren't this fragile mortal I had believed you were when we first met. You are a multicultural goddess, more powerful than I am. You can fight your own battles, even when with child." He kissed me again, and when he pulled away, his expression was soft as was his voice. "I thought I might lose you. And the baby." Then his brows raised in questioning, his one hand sliding between us to my abdomen.

"He's okay. He's fine. I can sense his mind, his soul, not words but sensations, moods."

"I can't sense him." Archer's concern grew.

"Philo is pure happiness at your touch. Are gods normally able to sense unborn children?" I didn't dare bring up Hedone and whether he sensed her while Psyche was pregnant. For once, we were happy again, not fighting.

He shook his head. "Only those who deal with childbirth can, but I dunno. I had thought with Hedone that I could feel her energy. Everything was a pleasurable experience. I felt that before she was born, but it was much stronger after. Athena would know. I think she said something about powers forming in utero can sometimes give off vibes."

Athena. I pushed up off the ground to see my family look away as if they hadn't been watching Archer and me reunite. All except Aroha (of course), who had happy tears in her eyes and stared directly at me as if I were this puppy she couldn't live without. She yanked me into a soft embrace, crying and muttering things I could hardly understand. Then there was a crushing hug around us both with a grunt (Chase), followed by Archer to my back, the four of us in an awkward group hug.

It broke me down into tears (damn hormones). Everything I had just gone through, and they had come for me, ready to fight and die to save me: my family. Chase and Aroha could never replace my father or the void in my heart of my forgotten mother, but they were a second parental unit I would always have, and I would never see them otherwise (despite their eternal youthful faces).

When the circle broke, I pulled Athena and Prometheus into half hugs on each side of me, the former cringing before softening in my arm. They were the grandparents I never had, the wise and worldly ones I would go to for advice.

I remembered Hera's message and thought about how important it might be, an olive branch she was offering with my release. I whispered. "Hera said, every time Freedom died, part of her did too."

Athena's grip tightened, and then she let go completely, walking off.

Prometheus drew away, his hand on my shoulder, his dark eyes meeting mine. "Thank you." Then he was down the beach after Athena, who needed some time away from us to deal with the mental scars of her grief.

My brother-in-law, whom I had overlooked, Anteros asked, "Why did they just let you go like that? What in Hades? Are they stupid?"

I smiled at him, the annoying brother I never knew I had been missing. But where was his sidekick? "Where's Himerus?"

Anteros let out a long whistle, and Archer's jaw tightened. (Oh no, what happened?)

Then something much more important flashed into my mind. "Linda? She saw things. She was stabbed. Is she okay?"

They all looked at each other in turn, no one speaking. The tension was killing me.

Finally, Chase stepped up. "A lot has happened while you were gone, but I want to get us out of here, and you to safety, first. My mother has acted out of kindness. I'm not sure she's in control or will extend that kindness to us all, particularly after the Zelus explosion."

THE IMMORTAL TRANSCRIPTS: GLIMMER

I was curious but still groggy from being drugged for days, so I didn't even want to know. I looked to Archer and leaned into him as Zeph, Iris, and another wind god with a gray beard showed up who had helped us in the Battle of Liberty Island—Boreas.

Archer wrapped his arms around me. "There's a lot to explain when we get home. Linda is fine. You'll see. Himerus is a whole long story, but he won't be coming to our home for any holidays for a decade at least. I will forgive him one day. Love does not hold grudges; that's Anteros's line of work."

His cryptic comment confused me, but hearing my friend was alive was enough. Archer held me upright as Zeph took us home and left us in our apartment alone. A place we hadn't been together much since we had returned from Hades.

Archer placed me on the couch. "What do you need?"

"Sleep—no food first, a bath, food, you."

He chuckled and kissed my forehead and was gone in a flash. I heard water turn on, the fridge open, some noises on the counter. Then I was scooped up as I almost drifted off to sleep. Groggy, I was undressed by my husband, whose eyes devoured my flesh as it was uncovered, but he behaved, only kissing my lips, before sneaking pecks on my neck and shoulder. He helped me climb into the bath, his hand touching my lower back as if examining my butt (hmm, that was a new fixation). Then he was gone in a flash.

I wanted to call him back, needing him by my side. I was afraid we'd be parted again, anxiety building. I sat down in the tub, trying to let the hot water burn away my stress. I squeezed bubble bath into the water and sighed, the water starting to cover my legs. Immortal bath preparation doesn't make water flow any faster. My stomach growled, making me want to abandon my bath for food, until Archer showed up, tray in hand.

"Oh my god, you read my mind." The tray wasn't even on the side of the bathtub when I snatched a piece of bread and bit into it.

"Well, I'm no Callista Ambrose, but all gods know a pregnant one must have sustenance."

I laughed at his comment, still weirded out I was a goddess. I scanned the tray: cheese, almonds, grapes, bread, ham, and baby carrots. A lemon slice on the side. I met his gaze, and he grinned.

He shrugged. "In case. I'm glad you're hungry though."

My heart panged at his level of focus on my comfort, remembering sour was my tummy settler.

"Which reminds me." He was gone and back in a second with a bottle.

I looked at him oddly, remembering our honeymoon in the Plaza and my disgust for champagne—just as he had inadvertently saved me from the champagne toast to us winning the war against Zeus. Tendrils of guilt enveloped me.

"Pure nectar. You and my son need it."

"Hebe gave me some, but I was unconscious for days, so…" No wonder I was starving (literally).

"Of course, my aunt would look after you. There's not a mean bone in her body."

"Why doesn't she leave?"

Archer looked down at the bottle in his hands. "She did, for a long time actually, but Heracles—her husband, whom Zeus had made immortal—was slain again. She returned home, and despite her outward bubbly, youthful exuberance, she mourns inside."

"That's sad." I didn't like the story much. "Again? He was poisoned by centaur blood…but became immortal."

"I forget how much you know, sorry."

"How much my father primed me because of Prometheus, you mean."

"Callie, give yourself credit. You sense more than you were taught. You see way more as well."

"And my gifts scare you?" The question had hung over me for ages, and I hadn't had the courage to ask it. After my abduction, I had the confidence to express all my feelings and thoughts to the man I loved. I had taken his—our—immortality for granted. We could die, be parted, or break up. I had to express everything to him and him to me to make this relationship work. I had found Lucien's obsession with truth irritating, but he was right. It was time for full transparency with my loved ones.

"Not anymore." His conviction convinced me his words were true. We simply stared at each other in understanding. We would have our petty arguments as all couples do, but we would no longer hide anything.

Archer cleared his throat. "Centaurs, they're extinct now, among other beasts."

I tucked in, trying combos of flavors. Carrots with cheese, a slice of heated ham with an apple. Why were the combos so good?

"Heracles was killed for invading another immortal territory without permission, which almost caused a godly world war. In hindsight, I wonder if he was only made immortal as a pawn for a war Zeus had wanted. Athena squashed it, made peace."

What a sad story.

173

"Anyway, did you want something else to drink?"

The sweet taste of nectar made me thirsty. "Is there a risk of too much nectar?"

"No. If anything, you should have some every day for the baby."

I nodded. "Your mom drinks it for beauty."

He laughed. "For her vanity, you mean."

He poured us each a glass. "So, you ready to hear about Linda?"

"And Himerus?"

His jaw clenched. "And him. Also, there is Lena."

My jaw clenched. I was not going to like the tale about everything I had missed, especially one about a shapeshifter pretending to be me.

Linda's story I loved. My only mortal friend had been a demigod and was now immortal? She was with her mother right now, but she'd be back because of Hymenaios. (Not gonna lie, I was more excited by this "ship" than my love god husband was.)

I did not like the Lena-Himerus story. I was weirded out that my brother-in-law slept with a copy of my image; this would make life awkward with him living down the hallway, friction between brothers, and poor Chase and Anteros in the middle of it. I knew Archer would forgive him. He just needed time to get over such a betrayal. For his brother to allow his nature to override his moral code was something Archer likely wasn't a victim to.

Sadly, my mind fixated on Lena with jealousy (loads and loads). I stared at the food, my thoughts making my appetite leave me.

"What's wrong?" Archer asked. "Are you nauseous?"

I frowned. "No. Hopefully, I'm through that stage."

"So?"

I sighed. "I'm only saying this because I swore to myself that I would give you full transparency to my thoughts to compensate—no, sorry, wrong word—prevent any secrets between us."

Archer slipped his hand in mine and squeezed it. "I did the same." He smiled softly, his eyes drinking me up. How had I thought he'd ever hurt me?

"I was so wrong. You hurt her, not me. She was an imposter, and you were worried about me."

His smile fell. "There's nothing I wouldn't do for you." Although a romantic notion, his intense eyes made a chill shoot down my spine. He would kill for me. He already had.

But one thought kept bashing around my brain. "Were you intimate with her? I mean, it's okay because you didn't know. I just need to know." It was far from okay, but I could not blame him if he'd thought she was me.

He laughed and leaned over the side of the tub, kissing me. When he pulled away, his vibrant eyes were penetrating mine. "Please tell me these are just hormones and you trust me. I *see* love. I know it better than I know myself. It wasn't you. I knew that, despite not figuring it out quickly enough. The pregnancy, our fight—I had thought you were having a hard time and needed your space. I gave you—I mean, her—that." Archer picked up a piece of cheese, wrapping it around a carrot. He urged me to eat it.

I had been so wrapped up in our conversation that I had stopped eating. My appetite was far from satisfied.

Archer sighed as if not wanting to continue the story. "She hid away from me, and Athena and Prometheus, so she had to leave a note for the setup. When I saw her with my brother, I knew. Callie, you'd never do that to me. I *know* that. The cheating she tried to enact to likely have an excuse to get away before I figured her out was her mistake."

He sat back away from me, his face wary. "She tried pretending to be you before. When I was in Belize, before we knew her abilities, she pretended to be you. I did kiss her then, but immediately knew it wasn't you and made her leave my room." His head dipped back to stare up at the ceiling before he groaned and then gave me a leveled gaze. "I see that look in your eyes. We said transparency. That's what I'm giving you. Plus, it is why she kept her distance. She knew I would find her out."

"Why did they send her? Did they think she could pull it off?"

Archer shrugged. "Maybe. She resented my rejection of her, resented going to the Underworld. Pure revenge on me? Anyway, I think Zeus wanted a delay. Long enough to get you away and—"

"Have me killed."

He cringed.

I sighed, needing to tell him. "He ordered Hermes to do it, but he couldn't. Hera protected me from Artemis. They're falling apart."

"Let's hope they do and there will be no more war, no more hiding."

"So...you and Lena never..."

Archer shook his head. "I know you and the depth of your love. After the Underworld, you were torn. Lena had no love for me in any way. Obvious now, in hindsight, but I was hurting and not thinking clearly. She was never you, so no. I didn't touch her. Had I? I would've known immediately. There is only one of you, Callista of Olympus, Othrys, and Asgard. No one could ever replace you. I've waited thousands of years for you."

Instead of kissing him as I should, I started bawling like a big baby. Mentioning the three godly-line homesteads that all made my life possible, for him to say he waited for me all those years, it was too much. So much love. How could I have ever doubted him?

I felt arms around me, caresses, and sweet words. Before I knew it, I was half dried off, in bed, with him in my arms, and the sadness shifted to need. When his lips met mine, it was clear to me as if the fog of jealousy never existed: he loved me. He lived only for me and our love. He'd never stray, always committed. It was true love between us.

When I woke up from a nap, well satisfied and hormones calm, True Love brought me dinner in bed. I was famished and inhaled it.

I could get very used to a pampered life like this.

CHAPTER 27

My best friends were reunited—Archer and Callie. My son's girl was now immortal. She was an ex, which was weird, but my family was far from the norm, and my other kid was with my ex-wife—not his mother. My life was ridiculous.

Everyone seemed content knowing immediate threats were away. Weeks passed without hearing anything from Olympus. I had called my son, Asclepius, and he sent all his data and information about the virus itself and the vaccine formation. I had spent hours poring over the materials until my mind ached. I needed a break. My memory was back, but the niggling feeling throughout all my memories and thoughts was how alone I was. Everyone had someone they loved.

I needed some kind of comfort. An impulse arose. I wanted to see my fourth kid. I had a little girl, and I wanted to see her. All the times I'd tried, Akila made me so uncomfortable, I didn't stay long. It was time to put my foot down. Demand time with my kid. I could not press Akila about the attraction between us, because she would run from it, become combative again. I had to work on my relationship with my daughter, and then eventually, her mother might warm up to me. If all she wanted was co-parenting, I would have to settle for it. Foremost, it was all about being a good dad now.

With my shield at the ready, which was Aios, I took a deep breath as we approached the door. Akila was an on-and-off nightmare, so I wasn't looking forward to this confrontation, but I had every right to see Polly. Surely, the harridan wouldn't kill me in front of my kids, would she? We had that moment on the stairs and the roof when she helped me, and I felt that spark between us still. But after Linda was better, Akila had a guard up. It was impossible to even become friends after that. I didn't understand her at all.

Aios snickered. "You're so nervous."

"She's a force to be reckoned with," I defended.

The little swine was smirking, enjoying my agony. "You're the one who dated her. Repeatedly, from the sound of it."

"She was…different then, each time—shut up."

"I suspect most women are before you piss them off. You have a penchant for that."

"Ha, ha." I smacked the back of his head.

He laughed and smacked me back.

Akila opened the door, hearing our antics. Those strikingly blue eyes narrowed on me, her expressive dark brows terrifyingly sharp. "What do you want?"

"Hi to you too. I'd like to see my daughter."

"Oh, so after twelve years, you want to see her? She is my kid, not yours. We've gone over this."

By the beard of Zeus, she was maddening. "Yes, we have hashed this out—repeatedly. I never asked to see her because you never told me about her."

"Had you bothered to contact me, I would've told you."

"Really? You would have? I see lies and omissions. Why do you even bother to try with pretenses around me?"

Aios cleared his throat. "Perhaps we could come in and talk civilly?"

She eyed Aios, but her glare softened. Akila wasn't unhinged, just wanting to punish me, which thankfully did not spread toward my softhearted son. She opened the door wider with a sigh. "Your father is not capable, but I'm sure you are."

The sarcasm dripped off my voice as I entered and closed the door behind us. "Thanks."

Polly bounded into the room and rushed in for a hug. I kissed the top of her head, which was not a far reach down, only being a head shorter than me. How much time I had missed made my heart sink, but we could have eternity. I would not waste this second chance at life being a bad father. I would make time for my children, but first, I had to ensure their safety from my father.

She pulled away and gazed up at me. "Hi, Dad."

I could not help but grin widely, loving being called that. A little girl. I had never known she was something I had always wanted. I wondered about her powers, what they'd be, her hobbies, interests, if she loved poetry and music. There was so much to learn about her, and she had only graced this Earth for twelve years. My gaze darted over to her mother, who looked away quickly. Too late though. I saw the sappy joy in her eyes, seeing father and daughter together. So why was she so nasty to me? If she truly wanted me in Polly's life and my family's protection, why wasn't she trying to be kinder? Why did she act as if I were in the wrong? I'd have to ask Aroha or Archer again. Women still confused me. Thousands of years was not enough time to understand the complexities of the female brain.

"Will you stay for dinner?" Polly asked.

"We were actually going to invite you up to our floor," Aios told her. "Chase is making a feast."

She gave her half brother a hug too. Where the mother was cruel, the daughter was sweet: opposites.

I watched Akila's expression. Nervous, worried? Did she think so ill of us Greeks that we would take Polly from her? "No."

"But Mo-om." Polly whined, hand on hip. "I want to go."

"Akila," I pleaded, giving her my best shot at puppy-dog eyes. "Please. She will come to no harm."

"You don't make these decisions. You are not her parent."

"He is, though, Mom," Polly huffed.

I dropped the nice act and gave her a glare. "Because you won't let me be."

"I want him to be!" Polly shouted.

Akila's glare turned on our daughter. "Tough."

Polly's face screwed up in irritation. "I hate you!" Then she ran from the room into her bedroom, the door slamming.

I went to go after her, but Akila was in front of me, her hand smashing into my chest to stop me. "No."

"What in Hades is your problem, Akila! Why did you even come here if you won't let me see her?"

Aios sighed, went around us, and tapped on the door, saying something to Polly, but Akila spoke over him. "Because I thought you were dead. I was going to let her meet your family, hear stories about you, get to know the good parts of who you were. I thought they could help me keep her safe."

"So, you waited until I was dead?" The anger at her manipulative deception had built up. I wanted to scream at her. I knew enough of her temper that I had to suppress the urge. She was trying to make me mad, so I had to act in a different way than she expected.

I took a deep breath. "I would've helped you, Akila." My voice embarrassingly cracked with the emotions bubbling up in me. "Whatever you think of me, you know I would protect my child."

Akila's face screwed up in a combination of pain and rage. "I didn't want her meeting you, being disappointed by you, or worse. You hurt everyone you profess to love."

Ouch. Low blow. She would've never contacted me had I not died. An adult Polly one day would've sought me out, and I would've missed another kid's life. "Do you know how messed up that is? Do you realize you never gave me, still aren't giving me, a chance?"

"I gave you enough of them in the past!"

"Uh…" Aios awkwardly entered the room, with Polly behind him, tears down her face, her gaze on the floor.

Instinct made me want to hold her close and cheer her up.

"I'm taking her upstairs for a little bit…" he said, "…if that's okay. It's what she wants, and frankly, your bickering is upsetting her more. I think you need to talk about all this alone."

Akila was about to lash out at my kid, her mouth open in shock. I grew defensive. I gave her a look of warning—do not mess with my son.

"Figure this all out for all our sakes." Aios gave us a look of contempt. Here he was, being the only adult in the situation.

She sighed and waved her hand for them to go.

"I'll join you when I'm done dealing with…this." I waved my hand around, not sure how to describe the situation.

Akila scoffed. As the door closed, I truly examined her, this time not letting her beautifully fierce features distract me. Lies were all around her. What was she hiding from me?

"You're hiding more or lying. You know I sense it."

"What would I be lying about?" She countered, her anger still simmering, but there was more to her mood than that.

"I don't know, but I'll find out."

"Whatever." She walked away to her refrigerator and opened it. Trying to stay busy to avoid me. Now that both our shields were gone, she felt vulnerable.

"Why are you so angry at me? What have I done? We parted in peace last time, didn't we? You named our daughter after me. There had to be love in that choice or at least respect."

She huffed, taking ingredients out for the fridge to assert that she was making our daughter dinner, and the trip upstairs would be short-lived. I had to make this work somehow but didn't know what she wanted from me.

"You've done nothing, precisely the problem, as always. I'm not mad at you, Apollo. I hate you. I hate seeing you when I look at my daughter, the little quirks, those eyes. Every. Damn. Day. I hate you!" She turned, her eyes brimming, the hatred she spoke of being a complete lie.

The truth struck me like a bolt of my father's lightning. My heart started thumping wildly in my chest. I hesitated. What would I do about it? What did I want?

Risking her ripping my head off and hoping I was guessing right, I gave her a sympathetic stare as I walked closer, trapping her by the kitchen counter, getting way too close for her comfort. "I know that's a lie. You don't hate me at all, do you? In fact, it's quite the opposite, isn't it?"

She shoved me, but I stayed rooted on the spot. She cursed in Ancient Egyptian before switching back to English. "You are so smug, you arrogant…"

Then she slipped into another language but was speaking too fast to tell what she was saying. She pushed me again and again, her voice going higher pitch as she always had right before she'd start—

Sobbing. "You died! You selfish prick. You sacrificed yourself for your friends without even a goodbye. You didn't even think of me!"

I said nothing, because it was true. I'd said goodbye to my sons, my first love Euterpe, and my best friends. I gave some of my past loves a fleeting thought as I died, her most of all, lingering regrets as I had left the world. Now, I understood how I hurt her. She was in love with me, and I hadn't reconciled with her before or even said goodbye before I died. It would have given her closure. I knew I'd die too, and I'd forgotten those who might still love me. Had Callie not miraculously brought me back from the dead, I would've never met my daughter, leaving Akila a gaping hole of regret and without a father for her daughter. That thought was sobering, making me want to ease what pain I might've caused her.

Now, with a second chance to fix things, I felt a pang for something more. "Ma'at," I whispered her real name.

"Don't," she begged.

I wrapped her in my arms. Not knowing what to say, how to word my hurt or alleviate hers, I kissed her lips. Want boiled up inside me. More importantly, how comfortable her lips were on mine: home. The loneliness in my heart dissipated. I needed Ma'at, and she needed me.

She went rigid in my arms.

I pulled back and met her gaze. "If you are so hurt, as hurt as I feel knowing I died without knowing about my kid, it can only mean one thing." I left the words looming as those eyes, which contrasted so pleasingly with her tawny skin, tried to read my own.

"I…" She tore her gaze away from mine, unable to say it. "I thought I was content with you leaving. I didn't know about Polly when we decided to part ways. How often do we goddesses get with child?"

"Often it seems, since Callista Syches was born nineteen years ago, and considering two goddesses in this building are pregnant right now, I think coming into her powers fully has completely freed us from any restraints."

"Polly said the boys told her you loved her once."

"I did, but she was in love with Archer. Nothing happened between us. I think the truth, that she was freedom, was the allure. But something severed that in the Underworld. I don't feel anything for her anymore, just friendship. She's a best friend."

Akila nodded and stared at my chest as she spoke. "Your child growing inside me shifted my entire emotional plane when it came to you. It was different, and

181

when I gave birth to her, I saw you in her more and more every day. I just…" She struggled, pushing me gently as if she wanted me away, but the lack of effort kept me grounded. I would get her to tell me what the heck was going on in her mind. "It became more than our past of common interests and great chemistry in the bedroom."

The mention of that brought back memories of glorious escapades in her arms, and part of me wanted that again with her. I prodded her chin and met her timid gaze. Her mood shifted after seeing whatever shone in my eyes. Want, desire, temptation all rose to the surface, for her, for me. The tension grew between us as neither of us spoke. Like me, she might be afraid of what would come, what lines might be crossed—with a child affected by our mess. I needed to kiss her, but I wanted more answers. "But you did not contact me."

"How could I? I have had to hide from my own people all this time, keep Polly a secret, from Amun and, more importantly, Zeus. Our love was forbidden. What would happen to Polly if they found out?"

She might be dead, just like Athena's children had been killed, just as Zeus wished Callie was.

"Things are different now. Callie is from multiple god lines. If there are more out there…"

"This is why I came to the Greeks. This sector would protect Polly as they have this Callie goddess."

The topic of my daughter being in danger was not where I wanted this conversation to go. "Akila, still, you could have told me. Let me meet her."

"I couldn't!" She was getting agitated again, moody.

I was lost and angry. "Why?"

"Because I'd be stupid enough to stay with you and get caught. Apollo, I love you, and I hate you for that!"

Present tense *love*, not *loved*.

My lips crashed into hers with that admittance. I kissed her again and again, feeling so many different things. She turned to putty in my arms, kissing me back. I pulled her against me and deepened our kiss, pressing her back into the counter, not being able to get close enough. She slid up onto the counter, and I pressed in closer, her legs wrapping around me. I pulled away, trying to slow things down, to process a thought, but my mind was a mile a minute, deep into fantasies of how far this moment could go.

I kissed a trail down her neck as I toyed with the bottom of her shirt, itching to pull it up over her head to see more of the woman I remembered so vividly.

"Apollo." Her voice was torn.

"Lucien," I whispered, kissing her lips, "and Akila." I meant it as a clean slate, a start over, two different beings coming together without a past or families to worry about.

From the way she ripped my T-shirt literally off my body and kissed me, she agreed. I took full advantage of the situation and retaliated, drinking in the sight of her.

"Wait, stop," she said.

I moaned, frustrated, and rested my head on her bare shoulder, kissing it.

"Polly could come back. To see us like this, she'd get so confused before we sort any of this out."

"I can't think straight right now."

"Do you love me, Lucien? I know you can lie now, but please don't." So vulnerable, so beautiful, those lush lips.

Gods. How could I answer that question when my libido was in overdrive? "You know I do, in my own way, but I am hurt from all the lies. I cannot process anything while I feel this *need* for you."

"I'll make you love me." Her eyes burned with determined lust, but before I could utter my thought of, *Please do*, she yanked me in for a searing kiss.

I picked her up by her bottom as we kissed and stumbled into walls before I could locate the bedroom door that wasn't Polly's and kicked the door shut behind us. Akila slid down onto her own feet, reached behind me, and locked the door. When our gazes met, it was clear the truth goddess and the truth god would burn like the sun as one tonight.

CHAPTER 28

I woke up in Lucien's arms, facing him. He was fast asleep, looking as handsome as the day we met when I attacked him for encroaching on *my* truth territory. After he incapacitated me, I realized he had been right. We were a couple miles into a non-claimed territory at the time. To make it up to him, he insisted I must give him one kiss. Foolishly, I gave in; he was gorgeous, and I was divorced. *What harm?* naïve me had thought. Neither of us had expected such chemistry.

Last night had been the same. How I had missed him more than the other spells of times prior. It was having Polly, a link to the man forever, a longing to be with him one day as I watched her grow.

I could not bear to let Apollo go—Lucien. I couldn't lie to Polly either or pretend in front of everyone that nothing was going on between us. Lucien had texted Aios to keep Polly for a sleepover. For the first time in twelve years, I felt she was safe, with her half brother and his friends, playing video games, surrounded by Greeks, with their war god already wrapped around her finger. I should've trusted my own people, but I feared they would never let me keep Polly, or ever see Lucien again. I had wanted to tell them so many times. No more running away from my own feelings.

The front door opened, and I heard Polly talking to someone. I went rigid. The whole point of the sleepover was to avoid her finding out too soon. "Shit."

Lucien moaned.

I shook him. "Wake up."

Those green eyes shot open on alert. He heard Polly. Then he shrugged and pulled me closer, giving me a scorching kiss.

I pushed him away. "Get up. Get dressed. Get out of here. The fire escape." I didn't await a response but scrambled out of bed and threw on some pajamas. I turned to see him smiling in the bed, with no urgency about getting up, his chest exposed, his hair rumpled, and his waist barely covered, arms folded behind his head, watching me.

"What are you doing?"

He smirked that annoyingly seductive, cocky expression of his. "Enjoying the view."

"Mom?" Polly called.

My heart raced.

A male voice, Aios likely, was suggesting go back upstairs and have breakfast there because I might not be home. Polly was too clever for that lie in the middle of a pandemic. Where could we have gone? Maybe Aios thought we'd gone to Lucien's apartment. In hindsight, we should have, but last night wasn't a planned thing.

I gave Lucien a fake glare and threw his clothes at him hard, remembering how he had no shirt after I had shredded it. The torn evidence of our transgression on the floor in the kitchen, along with my shirt.

In godly speed, Lucien was dressed, except his shirt, digging through drawers until he found a larger T-shirt. His head cocked, and a smile spread across his face as he slipped it on. Ugh, of course it was his T-shirt. I had slept in it until his scent faded and then again later in my pregnancy when I was overly emotional. I hadn't worn it since but couldn't give it away—nostalgia's sake.

I rolled my eyes at him.

He unlocked the door, walking out like he owned the place. All the gods in the world combined, what was he doing? I had no choice but to follow, as he picked Polly up into a bear hug, spinning her away from Aios, who was holding our destroyed shirts behind his back, giving me a wide-eyed look. I snatched them and put them in the garbage can before Polly could see.

Lucien put her down, and she looked at me. "I'm sorry, Mom. Aios explained that you and Dad had things to talk about, and the only way to make you both happy was if I stayed out of the way and you duked it out."

"I didn't quite say it that way," Aios defended with a nervous laugh.

Polly surveyed me head to toe, and Lucien too. Her face wrinkled. "Did you two have a sleepover?"

Aios coughed uncomfortably.

My cheeks heated.

Lucien laughed. Was he truly enjoying how uncomfortable this made me? "Silly goose. No. I came over here and woke this sleepyhead up. We had to finish our conversation." His heated eyes burned into mine with promises that we were far from done in any way. Not a fling in his mind.

He made himself at home, digging in the pantry. My traitorous heart fluttered with excitement to restart a relationship, one that could possibly last, with the man I had never let myself truly love until I thought he was gone. We had another chance to make things right. How I wished there was no Zeus and a war that we all knew would come, with Polly's and Callie's lives hanging in the balance. Zeus was the only hiccup to a future of our dreams.

"Who wants pancakes?" Lucien asked.

Polly shouted that she did. He had a pan heating on the stove and the batter made in seconds, Polly laughing at how fast he moved. Funny that. She'd scold me for it, but this was her dad, who in her eyes, could do no wrong. I thought her becoming a daddy's girl would scare me, that it would take her away from me. Surprisingly, it didn't.

Aios gave me a bewildered look, feeling out of place or concerned about what was going on with me and his father—I wasn't sure.

"Stay, Aios. He's made enough batter to feed an army." I felt like the awkward stepmother to a grown child who didn't need me, while I was also insecure I'd be judged as lacking in comparison to his mother.

Lucien's son sat down at the table with Polly in this strange family dynamic. Not as collected as Lucien was, I offered to take over at the stove. Polly blabbered about the video game she played with the boys.

Lucien didn't let go of the spatula, his vibrant green eyes probing deep into mine. A soft smile danced on his lips as he said quietly, "Sit down, relax, Akila. Let me treat you like a queen."

"I can't. I'm not sure how to handle this, and you're doing...so well."

"The power to hide the truth is so addictive after thousands of years of blurting out everything. I quite like being deceptive at times. It's like a game to see when the truth wins. Like last night when you finally admitted how you felt."

"Stop," I hissed at him. I was afraid of Polly overhearing, reading too much into it, and when—*if*—things didn't work out, she'd be devastated.

He winked and handed me the spatula. I took it and flipped the pancake. His hand touched my hip, and he whispered in my ear. "If we are in this for the long haul, she'll find out eventually."

His lips brushed my ear in super speed, and then he was away from me at the table next to Polly, giving her noogies.

She whined about him messing up her hair.

I took a deep breath, trying to ease the tension in my body. This was too weird too fast, and the person I would've expected to panic his way out of responsibility and a family breakfast was orchestrating it. He was right in that he was no longer Apollo, who had been scared of being tied down. He was Lucien, who was vulnerable and craving to be loved. I had to give him a real chance to persuade me we could do this. I had to let my walls down, which was against my nature.

Lucien and Aios left after breakfast. Polly went to her room for her online schooling, leaving the door open a crack so I could hear she wasn't putting on a blank screen to game like some kids were likely doing during the lockdown. It was oppressive to be in this huge city without the ability to leave this 800 square-foot apartment. Unable to bear a moment inside any longer, I wrote a note for Polly.

I left the apartment, locking her in, and made my way to the stairs. I ran up flights of steps at an immortal pace, loving the feel of movement, of being myself. Near the top, I slowed before exiting the building onto the rooftop garden— thankfully, no mortals were enjoying the crisp spring morning sun.

I sat down, taking several deep breaths. I could not stand being cooped up. I let the sun glide over my skin, annoyed that I adored to bask in the warmth when I knew the man who controlled it.

"You sparkle in the sun, you know." *His* voice.

My eyes snapped open. "I came here to be alone, Lucien."

"I'll go if that's what you'd like. Saw you alone up here and thought it would be a good time to talk without Polly hearing us."

"She's doing her schooling, and this pandemic cooping us up is driving me crazy. Shouldn't you be dealing with this?"

"Not you too. Linda's father is breathing down my neck."

"The new immortal, your ex?"

He smirked, likely hearing the pathetic jealousy in my voice. I knew he had many physical relationships, so my jealousy was unfounded. I had broken it off last time. My feelings were everywhere at the moment and not at all logical. I suppressed further comments.

"She's actually Aios's girlfriend, I think. She will be, at least. My son has none of my charisma or experience. Their relationship is moving slower than a tortoise."

"You Greeks."

"Yep, pretty much. This whole pandemic thing is out of my grasp. I just got my powers back. Then there's someone who has highly distracted me in many ways."

I did not take his flirty bait to evade the conversation. "Have you tried to cure it?"

"It's not that easy. I have a son who is skilled far beyond me. He cannot crack it, but we are in contact, trying things. He is on the front line. I'm attempting to help the vaccine the mortals are trying to perfect. I'm not just sitting here watching mortals die."

187

THE IMMORTAL TRANSCRIPTS: GLIMMER

"I didn't mean it that way." I had been so defensive, closed off, and cruel to him. It was a wonder he would even try to love me. I just didn't know how to go about this, how to let him in when I was afraid he'd hurt me or, worse, Polly.

Lucien sat down next to me, leaning back, closing his eyes, basking in the sun with the beauty of the Grecian god he was. I longed to touch him, his lips, his jawline, every soft and sharp angle of him. "What do you want from me, Akila?"

"What do you want from me?"

He opened his eyes and gave me a scolding side-eye for answering a question with my own. "I thought I proved my interest last night, *twice*."

"Aside from your *interest*," I pressed, trying not to smile at his innuendo. I had to know. Although last night had been incredible, I wanted to know where this was headed. I wanted more from him, including silly pancakes and video game banter mornings.

He leaned in and kissed me. "I'm distracted again. When can we have a moment alone?"

I smacked him upside the head, gently, but enough to get my point across that we were already alone, and I wanted a serious talk. "That is yet to be seen."

He sighed and leaned back, soaking up the rays again. "I'll start with the easiest. I want to be a part of Polly's life, no matter what happens with us. I want to protect her from my father, and what about your people?"

"They don't know."

"Might be time to tell them, Akila."

"Why? I feel like they'll be as torn as your people about her existence."

"If the Egyptians join us against Zeus, with everyone else we have on board, we can truly stop Zeus, protect Polly, Callie, any others."

"Do you know something?"

"God of prophecies," —he shrugged— "but I haven't had one since I 'woke,' for lack of a better word, but deep down in my core, I believe the battle at Liberty was not the prophesied war. There will be another."

A chill shot down my spine. "I will talk to Thoth, then."

"You'll tell your ex about me, us, Polly? Do you trust him?"

"He knows about Polly already. He has been covering for my absence, protecting me. It was an arranged marriage, as I told you the first time we met, but Thoth and I are true friends. We have our daughter, Seshat, together. Just as you have your sons. How is Euterpe?" I gave him a side-eye for worrying about exes.

"Fair play. She's with my other son, like *together*, together."

That gave me whiplash, and he laughed lightly. "They're not blood related at all, but still...weird."

"You Greeks." I withheld my bubbling laughter, awaiting his response.

"Like your people can talk."

We burst out laughing at the repetition of our comments, how, in the past, most cultures used to turn a blind eye to inter-family marriages, and the odd pattern of his exes ending up with his sons. Strange coincidences or perhaps Lucien was only part of who those women needed in life, and his sons were different versions of him. Aios seemed a softer, kinder version of Lucien. To me, Lucien was stronger, raw, addictive. I wanted him. It was always someone like him I'd pursued but never quite him, not good enough, not him. I needed to figure this out once and for all. My frustration made me rash. "Lucien, I need to know. No playing around. What do you want?"

He gazed deeply into my eyes. "You."

"In what capacity?"

"In every capacity." The way he said those words felt like a vow. His beautiful green eyes, like emeralds, bore into mine like the intensity of the sun. He meant it this time. Never had he lied to me—he couldn't have during some of our flings. But the others? No, he had been open and honest. We both had been.

I grabbed him by the neck and pulled him in for the kiss I had been longing to give him since he came up to the rooftop. The truth of his words and expression crumbled my resolve. The all-consuming love I wanted to avoid was burning down the walls around my heart, letting him in.

He pulled away, cradling my face. "Woman, you might be the legendary goddess that made the Apollo settle down for good."

"For good?" It wasn't that I didn't trust him—well, I didn't, to be honest—but I didn't trust myself either. Each spell of time we had been together, one of us ended it because the fighting became too much. We were extremes. "How about we just take things a day at a time?"

He seemed to have changed after dying, as if parts of him were muted, or he realized them and desired to change. We had Polly. I would make it my goal to fight as little as possible, to embrace happiness until she was grown. If it felt temporary, a couple decades, I could easily agree to get my heart broken for my daughter's sake.

"I dunno, settling down has to happen at some point for me. Thousands of years of fleeting or failed relationships are starting to get to me." He shrugged, giving me that cute smirk that made my pulse speed up. "Maybe it could stick this time?"

Because of Polly, I was forever entangled with a man I loved to hate and hated to love. Who was I kidding? If Polly's life was openly accepted and she was safe, I would love to love him.

He stared at his hands. "I've been a deadbeat father for so long, with so much guilt. I'm kind of open to the idea of actually being there for a kid's entire life. Dunno, all these babies on the way…I kind of want one. I was mad at you for hiding Polly from me for so long because I missed another kid's childhood. For once, it wasn't my fault. I know, Akila, I'll get to see Polly grow up and be able to help her with her powers, and I already love the kid. I don't know what I'm saying. I just want more. I want it all."

I pulled him closer and kissed him, not trusting myself to refrain from saying yes to another child. I was not immune to this baby fever with the pregnant Olympians, but we could not rush this. "We should take things slow."

He quirked his brow. "You and me, slow? Since when was that our jam?"

"How about living together, marriage, then a baby?" I draped his arm around me.

He squeezed me gently. "Move in with me today. Marry me tomorrow—don't look at me that way, Akila. Aroha pulled a wedding off in twenty-four hours before." Then he stared up into the sky, his face drinking up the sun. "And the baby in nine months, of course."

"You're hopeless," I scoffed, although I found his flirty eagerness endearing.

"Quite the contrary. I'm full of hope."

"I can name something else you're full of," I muttered.

"You little—" He pinned me under him, a grin on his face before he devoured my lips.

Surrendering to him easily, I had to acknowledge he was right. Slow was not us. We burned hot like the sun. I let myself go, thinking of nothing but sensations I was feeling and hopes I had of our future together. I would let go of my anger and fear. I would love.

CHAPTER 29

Callie

All was quiet from Olympus. We heard nothing from Hera, Hebe, or Hermes, even after Chase sent some prodding texts to his sister. Nor were there threats from Zeus or Artemis. Months passed by quickly, the only thing marking time to me was my expanding waistline. There was no hiding my baby bump now.

At first, we were stuck indoors due to the pandemic, only leaving to get food or walking for fresh air and exercise. It had a snug atmosphere. It no longer felt like a prison. I learned the hard way that my husband's protective nature had been legit.

Spring gave way to summer, lockdown was partially lifted, and people returned to a new, albeit masked and socially distanced, normal. My morning sickness subsided, but I had awful ligament pain, my formerly slight abdomen stretching at a rate it did not like. Lucien often felt my discomfort and eased it when around—although most of his time was spent with Akila and Polly. It was good to see him happy.

Owning the entire floor had its perks. We left our doors open, so all of us mingled in different places or hallways, giving it a college dorm vibe, according to the gods. Not going to college (I'll get there eventually, Dad), I thought of it as a mansion we all lived in. We were one big, happy family. We were getting a glimpse into a future without Zeus controlling us. I wished I could ignore the niggling threat of him in the back of my brain.

Today, Prometheus was taking orders for grocery deliveries, and he had left the door open. I heard Linda in the hallway. A new goddess, in a blossoming relationship with Aios, meant she was in our building almost every day.

I pushed myself up using my hands, my stomach muscles useless. Pain stretched across my lower abdomen, making me wince.

Archer must've seen it on my face. He was by my side, pulling me up. "Are you okay?"

"Yeah." (Wow, my response didn't even convince me). "Pain again. Just the stretching ligaments." I took a deep breath and exhaled.

Archer's hand rubbed my belly, which made Philo push against his touch. Archer beamed as he had done every time since he first felt the baby move. He couldn't get enough of it. Or me. He leaned in and kissed me. I made more of it, trying to pull him back onto the couch.

"Hey, lovebirds." Lucien came in. I was so happy to see him finally find someone. *Lovebirds* used to be said in annoyance, and now it was only made in a caught-you type jest. "Linda's here."

"I heard her, but getting up is starting to become harder."

"I'll wager it's that gut of yours," Lucien teased.

Akila and Polly came in behind him. The former had her mouth open, aghast at Lucien's comment. She smacked his stomach pretty hard with her hand, earning an *ooph* from him.

"What? She knows I'm joking," Lucien complained.

Polly gave me an awkward side hug. "We're saying goodbye. Going to Egypt. I'm sooo excited."

"Egypt?" Archer was as surprised as I was.

Lucien shuffled nervously. He was anxious about going. "It is time to see if they will help us or side with Zeus. Chase is afraid the silence from Olympus is them gaining allies. Zeus is only getting stronger."

Akila gave him a look, and he returned it.

"More importantly," she corrected him, "We must present Polly to them. My family doesn't know about her. We are hoping that protecting her, as hopefully will be their nature, means by proxy you too, Callie."

"Of course, Polly and Callie are the most important part." Lucien rolled his eyes but smiled. "I was just talking to Chase and Athena for an hour. They rub off on you." He shrugged.

Akila smiled at him and him at her, their eyes locked in loving amusement.

I liked Akila for Lucien. She had sass, power, and fought for what she wanted without couching things in false kindness. She was raw. Lucien needed someone to love and butt heads with, someone to tell him when he was being stupid or when he was right. Akila represented balance, and that was the influence she was having on him.

"My dad discussing war? No way." Archer chuckled.

Lucien scratched his chin. "Yeah, the peace is leaving him, bit Ares-like these days. Just a tad."

Archer rubbed his hand down my belly again. "Yeah, he's like that when Ma is pregnant. Overprotective." He met my gaze and smirked. We both knew he was suppressing the same urge to protect me, but like Akila, I was putting my foot down more. It now was a cute little battle between Archer and me, a joke between us. He truly had improved, but the moment danger came, he'd likely revert back.

Looking down at his hand on my belly, I'd let him. I was learning the fierce protectiveness of a parent as Philo's existence crept nearer.

"We'll be back before the baby is born," Lucien said.

"You better. You promised to assist when you all dropped the bombshell I couldn't have a hospital birth."

Archer groaned, his hand slipping away. "We're not revisiting that argument, are we?"

I gave him a pert look. "No. I was surprised and a little scared when Aroha told me." (Scared to death, more like.)

Linda came in. "Wow, Callie, look at that baby bump! I swear he's twice the size since I last saw you." It was an exaggeration since she saw me a couple days ago.

Aios trailed in behind her.

Lucien and Akila hugged me and Archer, ready to leave for their trip. I watched them go, hoping Lucien stayed true to his word about the birth.

"How far along are you now?" Linda squealed.

"Thirty weeks."

Linda smiled wide, Aios adoringly watching her. They were so cute, reminding me of those first few months Archer and I were together. "Only ten more? Time flies."

"Or a tad sooner," I responded, thinking about those ligaments stretching so much more. I could not imagine my body expanding even further to accommodate the baby. It would be nice not to have the last two weeks at least.

"No visions or dreams that tell you when?" Aios finally tore his eyes away from Linda.

"Nothing about the actual birth, no. Lots of visions of him later though."

Linda sighed. "To know, to truly know what your baby will look like. That is a blessing."

"It is."

Linda smirked. "Please, sit down. I'll catch you up with gossip." (Gossip? Not a familiar term recently.)

I sat. She took a seat next to me. Her statement made the guys move to the kitchen to have their own conversation.

I put my feet up on the ottoman. They ached. "How is there possibly juicy gossip during a pandemic? I have nothing to catch you up on. Same old thing, every day."

"Same here, but it's better than the alternative. You know, almost dying and becoming immortal was pretty eventful."

"True." I laughed despite the subject content being pretty serious.

Linda smiled. "All summer, I've video chatted friends to stay busy. And guess who's together?"

"I have no idea where to start. Just tell me."

"Emily and Dan."

I gasped. Memories of their cruel treatment of me bubbled up. Emily had been so mean to me due to jealousy because of her crush on Archer. And I had fleetingly sort of dated Dan when Archer had been "dead." Dan's controlling attitude ended that quickly and nastily. There was only one thing to say to that: "Wow, they deserve each other."

Linda giggled as she launched into how they ended up getting together.

I peered over at Archer. Even though he was listening to Aios, he met my gaze and winked. What a passive-aggressive revenge he had performed as the god of love. And I loved him for it.

It was great seeing Linda. In fact, being able to tell her everything over these past few months was a burden lifted. She was a great friend, and that barrier of hiding things from her was gone. I always had Aroha, but she felt more like a mother in some ways. It was good just to have someone my age around, in actual years, not just looking like it.

"You hungry?" Archer asked.

"Um, *always*."

He smiled. "What do you want to eat?"

There was a knock at the door. We had only been alone for an hour after the others had left.

"Ugh, no, wait," I protested as he went for the door. "Chip time."

He shook his head with a laugh, called for them to come in, and went to the pantry to grab me a bag of chips. He handed the bag to me as Athena and Prometheus walked in. They looked…conflicted. There was no other way to describe the look of bliss on their faces and the worry lines around their eyes. (Maybe I was reading too much into people lately?)

"What's up?" Archer asked since they merely greeted us, as I inhaled chips and said nothing more.

Prometheus looked at Athena and then Archer and me in turn.

Archer sat on the arm of the couch next to me, resting his hand on my shoulder. We waited.

"We have an announcement. It is quite unexpected, which is saying something from me," Prometheus began, shifting nervously. "We haven't told anyone yet because I was hoping" —he grabbed the hand of Athena, whose eyes were darting around wildly in distress— "Callie might see more than me."

I stopped chomping on chips and stared at them. His words clicked. "You guys as well? Freedom goddess? More like I'm a fertility goddess." I scoffed.

Athena's face strained, and then she was off running into our bathroom.

"Morning sickness?" I raised my brows at Prometheus, hoping he'd go help her as Archer had comforted me.

He shook his head. "She's..." He ran his hands down his face in frustration. "Past trauma... Can you please help, Callie? I've tried to calm her for hours after the positive pregnancy test this morning. She's just—I don't know what to do. I'm sorry."

"Say no more," Archer said. "Sit down, try to relax. It's a good thing. Everything will be different this time."

"I can't see anything to know that, and she knows my reassurances are empty."

I huffed and pushed myself up. Archer was there helping me. I abandoned my chips, which Philo might not forgive me for until I returned to them, but my relative needed me.

What to do? I did not see her future nor Aroha's. I did not see their babies because I hadn't focused on them. That's when it dawned on me that every vision I foresaw involved me in some way, even if it were via Archer. It made me feel selfish.

I knocked on the door. I could hear Athena trying to breathe on the other side, hyperventilating if she had been a mortal. "Athena, please open up."

The door popped open, surprisingly. She let me in and closed it behind me. Her eyes were wild, and she was pacing in the few steps our powder room allowed—constantly. "I can't do this."

"You don't have a choice. But it won't happen again."

"Have you seen that? My...my baby. Will it live this time?"

Her desperation sprang tears to my eyes. I could not lie to her. "I have not seen, but neither have I seen Aroha's baby. I only see things about me. Maybe, maybe I could try to focus on how I relate to you to try to see something. I can't control the visions, but I'll try. Prometheus could go away from me and see maybe?"

The idea of his leaving was horrific to her. I was not used to seeing her so vulnerable, needing assurance, needing me to tell her everything would be fine. It had been the other way around since I met her.

195

I braced her shoulders. "Athena, use your brain. It will be okay because you will make it that way. I am alive. I give freedom to you to live the life you want. If you want this child, you will do everything in your power to stop Zeus, to keep me and your unborn child alive. You will succeed if you focus on a logical defensive plan."

She nodded. I opened the bathroom door and led her back out.

Prometheus pulled her into his arms, pleading with her not to run from him in soft whispers. *I should've shown her what I took a pic of today, but maybe now isn't the right time.*

An image that made me want to giggle seeped out of his mind. "Show it to her. It might cheer her up," I told Prometheus.

Archer moaned. "Ugh, will you two stop doing that?"

"What? Oh, did we talk in each other's heads again?" I really had no idea he hadn't said those thoughts aloud (oops).

Prometheus cracked a grin and slipped out his phone, showing a picture.

Archer was up and over to us. "What is it?"

We peered at the screen to see a picture of the Prometheus statue at Rockefeller Center, wearing a mask.

Athena led out something like a combination of a sob and laugh. Then she smiled, laughing wholeheartedly. We all shared in the joke, finding it ridiculously funny. (I really don't know why, but when you start laughing, it's hard to stop.)

Before the laughter could die down, Chase entered our apartment in a hurry, his face firm and eyes full of concern, Aroha trailing behind him. "It's time."

"For what?" Archer demanded.

"Zeus is coming for us. Hebe sent me a warning."

No one spoke for a moment. We all simply stared at one another in turn. (What could we say?)

"She did say he has an army, but not to hurt Mother or Hermes." Chase's brow wrinkled at that request.

"Any word from Lucien?" Prometheus asked. "It's been a couple hours. He has to either have formed an alliance or not with the Egyptians by now."

"I'll call him." Chase slipped out his phone. "He must tread lightly though. He'll need some time."

"No, Chase. You, Prometheus, and I must call upon our allies. Gather the troops. Let Archer call." Athena's fear over her unborn child was gone, and the warrior in her rose to the surface.

"Archer." Chase gave him a loaded stare. "Protect your mother while I'm gone."

He nodded.

They took off out the door at immortal speed, leaving a speechless Aroha with us.

"Is it a good idea to send our best fighters away right now?" I asked Archer.

He frowned at me. "What am I, chopped liver? Dad trained me and Himerus when we were young. If Zeus didn't have his lightning power, I could've bested him by the time I was sixteen."

"And you are so modest."

He smirked at me. "I'll text my brothers. Safety in numbers."

"I bet I could still best all you boys," Aroha scoffed, her pregnant belly belying that statement at the moment.

Archer's head cocked as he stared at her belly.

I elbowed him in the stomach. "I'm sure if we weren't growing important lives, you could. I think we should play it safe."

Aroha ran her hand down her belly, her mouth spreading into a smile.

"Anyway, I better start getting some food together. All those boys do is eat, and I will not let them eat my share." Cooking when a war was coming to our front door seemed a bit silly, but I was desperately hungry, and once Archer was fighting, I'd be too nervous to eat.

"I'll help you," Aroha offered.

Archer was texting at an immortal speed.

I could've made something simple like sandwiches, but I needed the distraction to settle my nerves. I had not foreseen anything about a war to even know the outcome. It was the first thing Archer's family asked upon arrival. Everything I had seen was Philo surviving. I hoped it was a sign of the outcome, only I did not see anyone else, aside from Archer, in the future. That scared me more than anything.

I missed Dad, but I had grown close to my Olympian family in my time in hiding and in our own world of this apartment building during the pandemic. The sting of losing Dad and Lucien felt all the fresher, even though the latter was among us again. I could not lose anyone else.

"Can't reach Lucien." Archer placed his phone on the counter.

"I'll keep trying." Aroha pulled out her phone, texting.

The foreboding feeling of loss was creeping up on me even more. Surely, the Egyptians wouldn't hurt Lucien. Akila would be sure of it. (Right?)

My mind drew a blank at what gods I could pray to at a time like this.

CHAPTER 30

I was nervous. I had just left the safety of my friends in Manhattan and let Iris take me to Egypt. I had no clue about the reception Polly or I would receive. Akila was safe with her people, but could she get the same for me and our child?

We walked into the lobby of the Nile Ritz-Carlton, in awe and freaking out about the fact I was in Cairo. I held fast on to Polly's hand, afraid if I let her go, an Egyptian wind god would steal her from me. "Are you sure this is the right course of action?"

Akila gave me a death stare. "For the fiftieth time, it is what must be done to get their fealty. They will never support Zeus, but they might not help unless I give them a reason."

"Dad." Polly yanked her hand out of mine, wringing it.

I must have squeezed it too hard. I muttered an apology.

"Pull yourself together, Lucien. I need you to read the truth off them as well. If you don't, I'll throw you into the river to get a limb nipped off by a crocodile." Hand on her hip, Akila was everything a goddess should be.

Transfixed by her annoyed stance, I couldn't help but say, "Gods of every culture, you are hot when you're pissed off."

"Eww. Your kid is right here." I received a well-deserved elbow in the ribs from my daughter.

I apologized to the kid, "It just came out, sorry."

Akila raised her expressive brows, which made those blues shine. All I could stare at were her eyes. "Thought you didn't have to blurt out the truth anymore." Distractedly, my gaze was pulled to her adorable and knowing smirk. If I let her fog up my mind, I might not make it through this meeting alive.

"I don't." I touched her chin, wanting to pull her closer, to pour my feelings into a kiss.

Polly pushed us apart. "What is wrong with you two? This is serious business, and yesterday you were arguing about leaving me behind because you were worried that I might get killed. Then you decided my other family had to meet me, so they'd care enough to protect me. Now you're wasting time making eye babies with each other."

Akila raised her brows. "Eye babies?"

"Whatever. You know what I mean." Polly rolled her eyes at us and half stomped to the front desk.

I laughed. "To be twelve again."

"Bet you were a nightmare as a teen?" Akila took up my hand in hers as we followed Polly.

"Yep. You?"

"The worst."

"Ah, something to look forward to," I joked.

Akila leaned into me. "She's right. No making eye babies. We need to focus."

"Agreed."

Polly turned to us. "We're in the Abdeen meeting room. This way." She was such a sassy little woman that it was delightful, like a bumbling puppy trying to impersonate adults.

We followed her. The doors were closed to the meeting room, and a man and woman stood outside of them.

"Thoth," Akila greeted the man. His eyes darted away from her and landed on me in scrutiny. It was her ex-husband.

I swallowed. It was her land, her people. I'd let Akila introduce me.

Akila tightly hugged the woman. "It's been too long."

She responded in Arabic, saying teasingly that it was Akila's fault.

Akila stuck to English. "I was busy."

In Arabic, the woman responded that her father had told her. This must be Seshat, Akila's other daughter. I smiled, remembering those sweet nights with Akila in Venice after us Greeks had long left the region—a neutral and romantic territory we'd liked to meet in. She told me many tales of her daughter with the great pride only a parent can exude.

The goddess inspected me. She told Akila she understood exactly why she was busy, with more than enough suggestion in her tone that had I not known the language, I would have grasped her meaning. Her appreciative eyes also were a dead giveaway.

Tired of her inspection, I said, "I can understand Arabic, by the way."

Seshat gave me a once over until Akila's reprimanding gaze forced her to look away.

Thoth looked none too pleased. He walked over to me. "Back from the dead?"

"Something like that."

"Not sure of how Osiris feels about that."

"Not his territory I escaped from, so why would he care? Plus, he's not one to talk now, is he?" It was a poor joke at Osiris's expense, but—as the god of their

199

underworld had been reassembled and reanimated like a prehistoric Frankenstein—he really could have no scruples to my soul being put back into my defrosted body.

The exchange actually made Thoth smile. As soon as he looked downward to the quiet and observant Polly, it disappeared into a grim expression. "This is the girl?"

"Yes." I looked over at Akila, hoping she would lead this whole situation. Seshat was staring at Polly too, like she was a specimen in a lab. I didn't like that one bit.

Seshat quietly said, "She is clearly both of you."

Akila scoffed. "That's usually what happens, no?"

"Not across cultures. How?" Seshat pressed.

"That's a long story I don't wish to repeat here and then inside to them," I urged them to drop it. Going through the private events of the Olympian sector was treason to Zeus, not that I cared, but I didn't really want to keep repeating it.

Thoth sighed. "I met you out here because it is best to discuss it without the child present."

No way was I leaving my kid standing in a hallway alone. "I'm not leaving her side."

"We will look after her. Get some food." Seshat smiled at Polly. "I have a sister."

Polly smiled up at her.

"I trust them both with my life," Akila assured me.

Still hesitant, I said, "Good, because if anything happens to her—"

"You'll what? Kill me?" Akila looked amused and offended simultaneously.

"Someone. I dunno. It was an instinctual expression."

"I'll help you kill that someone. Look at me, Lucien. I trust them."

I nodded as I watched Seshat and Thoth lead Polly away. Seshat said something to Polly that made her laugh. I took a deep breath and looked at Akila. She nodded.

We each opened a door and entered.

I wanted to shoot a prayer up to the Olympian goddess who protected children, but that was my demented sister, who would likely kill Polly. The thought made me sick with worry. Instead, I shot a prayer up to the Egyptian protector of children in the room, who could keep my daughter safe from my sister.

It was clear who Bes was when his gaze darted over to me, his brow wrinkled, while the rest of the room, stoically, intimidatingly stared at us with expressionless faces. Likely, he was floored that I was asking an other, rather than my family. Still, he nodded slightly, but his eyes moved over to Amun. In a way, he had been Zeus's equivalent—god of gods, god of sky but also the sun in his territory. From my understanding, this table of roughly twenty were the elected government of Egyptian immortals, that Amun had decided he no longer had to lord over everyone as my father still did. Proof Athena's dream of an immortal republic for us Olympians was possible.

I knew no other face. It was alarming to be in a room of strangers who were all as powerful as you. To make matters worse, there was a time and place in Egypt when they worshiped my son Asclepius for his medicine. I was not sure if the encroachment had been welcomed or an affront. I, as his father, could be blamed—for his existence or for not controlling him. It was something Akila and I had never discussed. There were so many things we needed to talk about.

I felt tense, until a feeling of ease permeated over me. Gods alive, I'd forgotten about Akila's ability. She was the goddess of harmony and vital to her people to keep a balance on things. I was the thing she'd just balanced. I felt more confident, and my anxiety slipped away.

"Welcome, weigher of the heart," Amun greeted, but no smile was on his face, clashing with the lighthearted greeting. The heart weigher was something else entirely that kind of weirded me out: Akila measured a soul's worth, whether it deserved eternity or to be devoured by Ammit.

"Sun god." I got no warm welcome, his tone as blank as his face. I had no idea what to expect, and it frightened me. Polly's life was tied to how this meeting would go, as well as those of Callie, Archer, and the rest of my loved ones.

"Ma'at, you have come with wild proclamations of an Egyptian-Greek child-god that you somehow birthed. Where is this child?"

"Amun. Thank you for the welcome. The child is with Thoth and Seshat. They thought it best that the discussion happened before meeting her."

"A girl?"

"Yes."

Next to him, a goddess asked, "How did you become pregnant?"

Akila looked at me for help, but I was lost. Surely, the gods didn't want me to give them basic anatomy lessons.

"Apollo and I met accidentally when I wandered into unclaimed territory, thinking it was mine. We became involved. This was not long after my divorce with Thoth. Every few centuries, he and I had reunions but knew that it could never be. Thirteen years ago, we had a rendezvous in Venice—"

"Former Greek territory," Amun interjected.

Akila nodded. "We parted ways, and I found out shortly after that I was with child. I did not tell him. I told no one. Later, I needed Thoth to help me hide her. I did not know how it happened. I could not give you, my family, an answer, so we hid. What changed was I'd heard about Apollo's death and deep regret for never telling him, wanting Polly—"

"Polly?" another god asked, likely because it sounded like an English name.

"Apollinaria." Hearing her say Polly's full name, the beauty of it made me lament the parrot-sounding nickname. Pride bloomed within me, and deep respect and love for Akila. She had named our daughter after me—something I knew already, but I felt the impact of the weight of her decision to do so. Our next child would have her name. I shook the thought. Not the time and place for my fantasies.

Akila continued, "I wanted her to meet that side of her family. To see if they could offer protection."

"But not us?" Amun asked, his brow raised.

"Thoth told me it was unwise, but I am here. To ask you now."

"But *how?*" the woman who had asked about the pregnancy pressed again. Then it clicked. I felt stupid for thinking too literally about how an unsanctioned pregnancy between gods occurred.

"I can explain…" But I stopped, trying to figure out a quick summation.

"Please do," another god teased.

I smiled at him. "It's a bit difficult to sum it up, but…" I took a deep breath and rushed out with the rest. "Zeus has lost his power to control that aspect of us Greeks, and many other powers of his. A girl was born nineteen years ago—a demigod we had thought. The new wife of Eros became a god, frankly through accidental science, recessive genes. She's Norse, Titan, and Greek descended."

There were murmurs of whispers and shock among them, but I pressed on, raising my voice, "Goddesses can get pregnant because she breaks the powers he had held over them. We have two pregnant goddesses now, having children for the first time in eons. My guess is that since this goddess was in Greece when Ma'at and I were together in Venice, the girl's limited power gave us just enough freedom from my father's control over my…over that situation."

Akila's eyes widened on me.

I gave her an apologetic look for not telling her prior. "I didn't realize till now. Archer told me about how she spent part of her childhood there, then recently, Prometheus said he told her father to leave the US when she was five. That was fourteen years ago." Akila and I had spent over two years together.

Callie had inadvertently given me my daughter.

"How? What is she goddess of? Fertility? If she's from a mixture of cultures, what would those powers even be?" I had no idea who asked the question, because my gaze was still on Akila.

LISA BORNE GRAVES

I turned to my left, the general area where the question came from. I knew my next statement was a make-or-break point, but Callie and Polly both needed protection. As the god of truth, I would give it to them: "Free will."

The entire room collectively gasped.

CHAPTER 31

Could Lucien be more melodramatic?

I found it endearing, especially when he sang and played, when his abundance of emotion would come through his music, making it feel alive. His songs were rendered as clear as people, with personalities, emotions, and purposes. I had no time to reminisce how hot he was when singing with his lyre, because the room erupted into chatters. Everyone started talking over each other and asking questions all at once.

I put my fingers in my mouth and whistled. The noise died down, and they all looked at me. "Maybe one question at a time."

The first came from Isis. "What are your child's powers?"

"She has not grown into her powers yet," I admitted.

"But it will likely be some of ours or both of ours. She won't be like the other goddess we are protecting, a free will. And free will does not equate to chaos, let me remind you. You have a great system of equality of gods here, created by Amun. We Greeks do not have that. We have a dictator, one who is waging war to cling onto his power. He sent death for this goddess, tried to kill one of my sons, his own son, many of us," Lucien explained.

He did not go further into how Zeus succeeded when Lucien sacrificed himself for his friends. I was about to add that, to make him look good, to get my family to like him, but it would involve the whole complex coming back from the dead and soul explanation. That would lead to a myriad of tangential questions away from the chief concern: our daughter.

"Can you assure us your daughter is not the same type of free will goddess?" My father, Ra, of all people, asked.

Why was he asking when he was our sun god? What did it matter to his roles? He had stepped down as our leader a long time ago, allowing Amun to rule before our democracy was established.

"Yes. She will not be. This other goddess, Callista, is the descendant of gods of the soul, foresight, and justice. This combination of powers created a seer, mind reader, and liberator of oppressive power. Since these powers were in different concentrations, I think it would be difficult to replicate. It relied on a lot of chance and recessive genes."

"It was destiny." Shai's eyes met mine in awe. God of fate appeared excited by the prospect when he wasn't the one controlling it for once. That was good. Having Fate accept Polly's existence was good, considering Shai played no part in creating her.

"Yes," I affirmed. "I hope it changes destiny to allow me to have a future with Apollo and our child, to have a family." I uncharacteristically threaded my fingers in his, not ever a woman who showed affection, in any small amount, toward a man while in public.

Lucien's eyes went big. Didn't he know by now that I wasn't the type to rock the boat; I was the kind of goddess who tipped it over? Quickly, he recovered and gave my hand an affirmative squeeze. He knew it was no small concession of mine. It was tantamount of me declaring my love for him for my entire family to hear and see.

They all stared at our joined hands as if that small action were louder than the words that declared my wish to marry a god from another pantheon.

"Let us meet this child." Bes winked at me. I did not expect his full support in this but was glad to have the protector of children watching over my girl.

"I'll go." Lucien's hand left mine. He was out of the room fast, a ball of nerves who wanted to be anywhere but here. So far, my family had been kind. They had not imprisoned him, murdered him, nor given him the third degree about his intentions toward me…yet.

"Mmm-hmm. I see why you want *that* scoop of Greek." Hathor, my mother, said, making a few others laugh as she fanned herself as if Lucien's looks had made her sweat.

My father shifted uncomfortably in his seat. "You truly want this path, Ma'at?"

I met his gaze. "I love him. I want to be with him, but I must go with whichever path keeps my daughter safest. If you reject her, I must go with the Greeks. My choice lies with our daughter. Lucien would die to protect her. I do not say this flippantly. He did die for his family, and they brought him back."

My father blanched at that comment. My big mouth. In defending my choice, I had taken the tangential road. I quickly explained the story to them, and my father, our closest god to Lucien's uncle Hades, relaxed. "So, Hades gave Apollo's soul back in return for freedom?"

"Yes." Wanting to get back on topic, I asked directly, "Will you protect my child?"

My father looked to Amun, who sighed, weary of being seen as a ruler still among a democracy. "We vote as always, but in my opinion, we cannot let Greeks spill Egyptian blood. If Zeus wants to kill any being connected to us, merely because he has not sanctioned the birth, I believe it is our duty to protect that being. Your daughter has our blood. We protect our blood. What say you?" Amun asked the room.

There were concerns about war, some excited at the prospect and some reluctant. There were questions of whose house of gods she would belong to and other questions that were pointless at this stage except for one thing: it told me they had accepted Polly.

How wrong I had been to not come to my family sooner. Somehow, though, I had a feeling Thoth had been right to advise me in the way he had. Perhaps on hearing about Lucien's death and resurrection, they grew softer toward him, or perhaps the idea of Zeus smiting any Egyptian was enough. I had not known about Zeus's domination and ruthlessness when Polly was younger. Perhaps they only learned recently how he overstepped his power too.

My rumination and the chatter in the room died suddenly. I turned to see Lucien holding Polly's hand in the doorway, Thoth and Seshat holding the doors open.

"Sorry. Polly was listening to Sheshat's story about Ma'at, and I had to let them finish." Lucien's smile told me it had been comical at my expense.

They approached me. I draped my arm protectively around Polly's shoulders. Soon—too soon—she would be as tall as me.

They stared at her. Most wore soft expressions of intrigue on their faces.

"Polly, this is my family. Everyone, this is Apollinaria."

"Are her eyes blue, brown? I cannot tell from here," my father asked.

My bold and brave girl answered. "They are green, sir, like my father's."

"Sir?" He looked flustered. "I am your grandfather, child."

"Well, how was I supposed to know that?" Polly put her hand on her hip.

That was all the icebreaker she needed to win them over. She was a mini me, sass and spite, and that made them reminisce and laugh. The room turned more into a mingling party. Everyone interacted, most wanted to meet Polly, a couple to chat with Lucien, and many reprimanded me for hiding my daughter. Still, I could not regret raising Polly so far without family influence. She had been mine, and our bond was strong. Now, I would give her to her families, and then one day, the world.

It seemed to be a time of celebration, a new chapter in the world of gods. Tomorrow would be the discussion of war, logistics, and plans, with an official vote. I knew the answer already. Everyone's kind eyes and smiles appeared when they spoke to Polly, which told me they would protect her.

It was one of the best nights I could imagine. My man and our child were accepted. I could not describe a better feeling than that. I had come home.

We had an amazing night with my family, and my parents would not part from Polly. She stayed in their rooms, talking up a storm, and they told her stories about me until she fell asleep on the couch. I did not want to wake her, and Mother insisted on letting her stay put till morning.

Lucien whisked me away to our rooms, and finding ourselves child-free, he planned on taking advantage of every moment of that. I could not complain—not in the least. I finally felt free to love him without any inhibitions. I fell asleep couched in the comforting thought that all would be well.

One moment, bliss. The next, things fell apart.

"Shit!" Lucien was up and out of the bed at immortal speed and dressed before I had fully wiped the sleep from my eyes. "Shit, shit, shit…" And then he rapidly fired expletives in ancient Greek I could not keep up with. He rarely did that.

I sat up, covering my chest in the sheet. "Lucien!"

He looked at me as if he had forgotten I was in the room. "Ten missed calls. Even more texts. My family."

My stomach dropped.

Despite the gravity of the situation, he sat on the bed and closed my mouth that had been ajar with a twinkle in his worried eyes.

"Attacked? Are they okay?"

"I think they are okay. The messages just said Zeus is on the move. They need me. They're mad at me for not responding. They want to know if your people are in…" He scrolled through the messages. "Worse, now they are worried about me, and—"

"Call them now," I ordered.

He dialed and whipped the phone to his ear, yanked open the curtains, then door, and slipped out onto the balcony. I got up, wrapped in the sheet, as he closed the door. I dressed myself in the bathroom. When I came out, he was pacing.

"Well?"

He shook his head. "The worst. Zeus is in New York. They need me, right now. I have to go." He grabbed me and pulled me against him, kissing me soundly, his tongue slipping into my mouth with a moan, showing a desire that he wanted to stay.

I gently pushed him away. "Then we must go."

THE IMMORTAL TRANSCRIPTS: GLIMMER

"Polly." His face scrunched up in concern. "Stay here, please, with her. Beg your people to send reinforcements immediately. Athena is racing across the world, calling on allies to move. I need to get back to New York, immediately."

"If you think I'm staying put and letting you die in some family feud—again—you have another thing coming to you—"

He kissed me.

I froze.

"With all due respect, be quiet for a second. Polly is a liability for both of us. Come fight by my side if you'd like, but how distracted will we be if she's there, and if they get ahold of her…" He cringed.

I nodded. "Go. I will be behind you. I don't know how long. I must gather those who want to fight, explain things to Polly—she won't understand, but I'll make her—and ensure she will be looked after in my absence."

His hands cradled my face. "I love you."

"Don't do that. Don't say it that way." He was scaring me, like it was goodbye.

"See you soon then." He smirked at me and winked before he hurried out onto the balcony. He disappeared in a tunnel of wind.

Dread filled me as I stared at the spot he had just stood before one of his wind gods swept him away from me.

Then I snapped out of it.

Now was not the time for sentiment or worry. It was time for action, to get things done to get to his side, to protect him. It was to protect Callie too, for she represented what Polly was, a free world where no gods would bat an eye at a relationship like me and Lucien's.

If we lived through this, I would secure him for good. I'd marry Lucien, give him a child, and fulfill his dreams of settling down. It was something I wanted as well. It was something worth fighting for.

CHAPTER 32

Zeph dropped me off in Dionysus's bar. It was safer for the wind god, and I could get the scoop from D about what was happening. The bar was empty, with the lights out and the open sign facing inward at me: closed. It was dark outside, the middle of the night. Was he even here?

Zeph gave me a look, his eyes tired. Likely, I was not the first or last ally on his list. I put my hand out for him to wait a moment.

I called him. "Dionysus!"

"Hang on!" He called back from upstairs.

Zeph looked like he was about to leave.

"Hold up, Zeph." I went behind the bar and pressed on the hidden side panel next to the keg cooler to get to the godly stock. I pulled out three nectar bottles, mild in concentration. I needed a clear head, but the boost of health would help. "Here." I gave one to Zeph.

He sighed, grabbing it. I could imagine how exhausted he would be from so much traveling.

I chugged the elixir, annoyed Dionysus was taking so long, but I had to know the lowdown before entering the fray. He hurried into the room, two duffle bags strapped over his shoulders.

"Oh, help yourself, then." He scowled at me.

I held up a bottle for him.

"Why not?" He shrugged, taking it.

"Fill me in."

"War in New York, again. I've got the best healing stuff in this one. I've got some weaponry in this one." He shrugged each shoulder with the bags respectively and sighed. "It'll take me ages to replenish my stock."

"Hopefully, it ends today—" I clanked my bottle against his. "—in our favor. What are their numbers?"

Dionysus shrugged. "I only got a couple texts about help and what was going on. An attack, Zeus, his demigod-spawned and godly Olympus army. Rumors of others helping, such as the Mayan sector. Gods only know what he promised them. North American territory? A few gods from Africa, Asia too—disgruntled minor deities wanting more power. You get the Egyptians on board?"

"I was only there a day, trying to keep my head attached to my body and my kid alive. Akila's coming behind me with reinforcements—I hope. The Norse?" I shifted the subject because I wasn't sure the Egyptians were definitely coming on such short notice.

"Chase texted they arrived just before you."

I nodded. "Take us to my apartment," I instructed Zeph.

He touched both of our shoulders, and we reappeared in my living room. There were worried voices and someone running down the hallway.

"Let's do this," D said as he yanked open my front door.

Zeph vanished onto his next trip.

Aroha was running down the hall into Callie and Archer's apartment.

Raphael was in his doorway and beckoned us inside. "You can see everything from here."

We hustled into his room. Destruction was below. Cars were upside down all down 74th Street, glass everywhere from smashed windows. I looked out the other window onto 1st Ave. Mortals had cleared the area for the most part, but a few were crouched, hiding in the bus shelter. Poor Mnemosyne had her work cut out for her if she was planning to erase this battle from mortal minds and media. Even worse, how would we explain any mortal deaths that occurred as collateral damage? Excluding Chase's wars, it had been thousands of years since we gods got mortals killed on an epic scale due to our problems.

Raphael's voice trembled. "They came down from the roof, a couple of them, going straight for Callie—she's okay. Chase annihilated them, and he and his boys moved the fight outside."

"My son, the medic?"

Raphael nodded. "He's here, set up in the lobby."

"Who's up here protecting Callie?" Dionysus asked.

"Athena and Aroha."

Dionysus snorted. "Bet Athena is pissed she's not out there. C'mon Sunshine," Dionysus mocked me.

We took the elevator down to the lobby, which felt like it took ages. The lobby was a disaster zone. In the back of it, Asclepius was tending to Aios's arm.

I hurried over. "Are you okay?"

Aios flushed up red, my concern humiliating him. "I'm fine. One of Janus's personalities wanted me dead. I don't even think he knows what side he is on."

I tousled his hair, ignoring his sullen face at my affection.

"Dad," Asclepius greeted as he held Aios's half-severed arm in place as it started healing, the flesh and sinew mending back together.

"Here." Dionysus plopped a duffle bag down.

"Thanks for the quick response." Asclepius moved Aios's arm around. "You're good."

"What's in the bag?" I asked Dionysus as the three of us headed to the door.

He fished inside and handed me a mason jar that had a cloth sticking out of its punctured lid. "Molotov cocktails."

I whistled. To kill my kind turned my stomach. One thing to incapacitate them in a mortal way; it was another to kill them indefinitely.

"Zeus killed a score of mortals already. This ends tonight."

"Just watch where you throw those." I thought of Archer and how he had killed Thanatos to save Callie. Love made him light the former death god on fire.

Dionysus handed Aios a bomb too and then me a lighter. "If you see Helio or Heph, send them my way. I want to do something big." He went right toward the intersection. Aios, armed with a sword, went left onto 74th. I stuck to my kid's side in search of a weapon. The first people we came across were two Muses battling Poseidon. Away from water, he was at a disadvantage, but the way he wielded his trident, you'd never know it. He slammed one to the ground, while Aios slashed his other aunt. As she faltered, I tore the quiver off her body, slipped the alcohol bomb inside and wrestled her for the bow. A flaming god ran by, screaming in agony until he fell and crumbled into a pile of ash. No Chaos—no Olympian deaths yet.

Poseidon gave me a wink as he backed up, seemingly retreating, but with the East River only a couple blocks away, he had power and reinforcements there.

A group of unfamiliar gods rounded the corner, and one snapped the neck of a mortal who had been trying to run away. I stood stunned. This war was making the battle at Liberty look like child's play.

"Dad, snap out of it!" my son shouted, swinging his sword to deflect an arrow that had been headed right for me.

"C'mon," I told him, running after Poseidon with an idea.

Aios followed, and I yanked him into a walking garden-plaza between buildings right before the next intersection.

At immortal speed, I pulled out the Molotov cocktail, unscrewed the lid and cloth wick. I tied the broken straps of the quiver around me. I handed the lighter to Aios, who was lost at what I was up to. I pulled out an arrow and dipped it into the jar of D's most potent-smelling liquor. Catching on, Aios lit the head as soon as I had it nocked.

I peeked out, seeing the gods and a couple more Muses ganging up on the retreating Poseidon. Now that they were past our hideout spot, I could get them from behind. I fired, the arrow finding purchase in Clio's back. She screamed and ran around, trying to pull the arrow out as the flames spread onto her clothes. Aios and I repeated the process. It wasn't enough fire to kill them, but a nice way to scare them into retreat.

We rushed out, and Aios covered me until we reached the next place we could hide: a parking garage entrance. I kept leaning out, delaying the enemy, giving Poseidon coverage as he joined Prometheus, who was just ahead of us. They were fighting like mad toward the well-protected Zeus, who was at the dead end by a high rise. I picked off as many as I could in front of my two allies, but Zeus was out of range.

Poseidon's retreat was well orchestrated. He now was closer to Zeus and the water. A massive wave flew out of the East River, over the highway, and onto Zeus, almost knocking him and those who protected him down.

Then she was in my sight. *Mother.* Fighting Euterpe. They had come from my right, Zeus on the left, further down the street. Torn on whom to help, I watched my ex take on my sadistic mother, who made all our lives Hades. She had drugged me to make me tell on my friends, knowing well it would lead to my death.

"Light it up, Aios."

"Don't hit my mother." Aios's voice was strained.

Before he could light it, my head felt like it exploded. I fell to my knees in pain, my mind unable to stomach images of all of time—past, present, future— Chaos reigned. An Olympian died. I was up and aiming again, my hands shaking.

Euterpe had fallen, a knife in her stomach, scrambling toward cover, to us. I fired the arrow as my mother turned, not trusting myself with the fire. She screamed out as it pierced her side.

Leto turned to glare my way. I gave her a smug grin to show my contempt.

She stormed our way, knife in hand. I fired another into her shoulder to slow her down. Aios pulled his mother around the corner of the building to the safety of the garage.

Out of the corner of my eye, I saw fire, which stopped me from firing again. Distracted, I glanced down to see Aios's Molotov cocktail alight in Euterpe's hand.

"I was never good enough for you? How about now?" She chucked the bomb at my mother, who stood wide eyed as it came flying at her.

I watched in horror as the fiery cloth came loose, dropping to the ground. The glass jar smashed into Leto, dousing her in alcohol.

She laughed. "Yes, Euterpe. You just proved how useless you really are. Useless, weak, pathetic woman, who birthed a useless runt of a son."

"Light me up, Aios," I hissed.

"What? You're going to kill your own mother?" Leto asked incredulously.

Arrow on fire, I aimed at her torso. *Damn right.* She forced me to betray my friends, family who were there for me when she wasn't, those who risked their lives to bring me back from the dead.

I fired.

It felt like slow motion as it flew toward her. Her knife came up just enough to knock the arrow off course. Rage filled me. My entire life, everything had been about her, about suppressing me, about making me feel like I was the problem.

Hatred burned in her eyes. "How. *Dare.* You."

I reached for an arrow, finding only one left. I nocked it as she came toward us.

"Useless child of mine. Disappointing. Worthless."

Aios lit the arrow. I immediately released it without even aiming.

The arrow punctured her chest, my instincts guiding my hands to fire and make purchase in the part of her that was already dead: her heart. Flames bloomed across her torso as she staggered back, the glower turning into shock before the pain hit her.

A bubble of a sob came from behind me, but I heard Euterpe soothing my son and urging him to look away. She had always had a way with him and was the best one to help him through his conflicted feelings toward his grandmother's demise.

I did not look away to even blink. The woman may have birthed me, but I could not remember a time in my long existence when she loved me. As I met her gaze before the flames consumed her face, I felt nothing but relief. Everything made sense. The part of me that was broken, that failed at relationships, at maintaining intimacy, of fully giving myself to someone, stemmed from her and Zeus. Neither parent had shown me how to love or had even given me a shred of respect to make me feel more than worthless.

The form that had been my mother was now a pile of rubble and slowly puttered out. Chaos did not reign for a Titan in celebration; she mourned for her descendants. She'd be the only one to mourn—and maybe my conflicted son.

"Dad!" Aios drew my attention. He was pointing at Zeus, who was being attacked on the other side.

That's when I saw the terrifying helmets of jackals, birds, cats, and more climbing over the wall that divided this street from the highway parallel to the river. The Egyptians arrived. My girl came through for me. Pride, longing, and love wiped away the bitter sick feeling I had from killing my mother.

"Akila!" I shouted, stepping out into the street.

Euterpe grabbed my arm. "What are you doing?"

"I'm in love with an Egyptian." I shrugged.

She smirked. "Good to know someone finally got through to you. Here." She handed me the knife that my mother had embedded into her. The handle had an *L* carved into it. A morbid souvenir. "Arm yourself at least, you lovesick fool. You're out of arrows."

I didn't get more than three steps on the street when someone slammed into me, hugging me tightly. My eyes met those beautiful blue ones.

"You're alive," she whispered.

Unable to form the words of what I felt for her in this moment, I kissed her.

"Uh, Dad—" An exasperated Aios broke my moment of bliss. "—you think you can make out later?" He deflected an arrow with his sword.

Akila lifted her shield to protect us.

"We can push them back toward our building, get your family inside, replenish your energy. You're out of ammo, and she is unarmed." Akila pointed at Euterpe.

I shook my head. "I stay with you."

She gave me a censorious look.

I gave her one back. "You want me to fight away from you? I have your back; you have mine."

Her face scrunched up looking at her people, who now pushed Zeus past us and down the street. Lightning streaked the sky beyond, the Egyptians pushing them toward the Norse.

Her people swept her up in their crowd, and I hurried after her, realizing Aios was no longer with me. I stopped, unable to see Akila anymore. I fought through the crowd to find Aios, who was frantically looking for me.

"I lost her." I shrugged. "She can take care of herself quite well."

"I don't doubt that for a second. You, Dad, need a weapon."

We made our way back to our building to get some weaponry and some nectar before we entered the fray again.

This was going to be a long night. At least, coming from Egypt with the time zone difference, I was well rested.

CHAPTER 33

Archer

Allies. We were lucky to have them. The Titans and some of the Chinese gods were defending our backs from Zeus's demigod army. I stuck to Dad's side as I'd promised Ma, who was worried he'd get killed—and she and my unborn sibling would die as well, due to immortal marriage. That very threat for Callie, Philo, and me made me cautious on the battlefield. Epimetheus was closest to me, with his annoying commentary about what I should've done instead to incapacitate my enemy. Atlas was on my father's other side, distracting me with his antics.

Prometheus was able to spring him, and the sky didn't fall. It had all been a punishment Zeus had inflicted to control the Titan. But after years of holding such a weight, he was strong, beyond that. He was tearing limbs off gods and then using those limbs to beat them unconscious. I hoped he'd chill after this war, or maybe it had been a terrible mistake to free him.

"Yes, it looks like a terrible mistake, doesn't it?" Epimetheus said, stabbing someone behind me.

"Can you get out of my head? It's distracting."

"Don't have regrets, then."

I pushed forward, trying to get away from the Titan, but the line in front surged forward into us. A knife or sword sliced my side, but I turned in time for it not to stab me.

Dad growled with a knife in his belly and an arrow in his shoulder. Still, he wildly hacked at those in front of us, swords in both hands. "Get us out of here before we get crushed."

I sheathed my sword and grabbed Chase. I pushed off the ground in a giant leap, defying gravity. I landed us on the roof of a two-story building across from our apartment building.

Dad sheathed his swords, then ripped the arrow out, mangling the flesh before it healed.

I turned and looked down 74th Street as he grunted, removing the knife. Not wasting a moment, I pulled my bow off my back and nocked an arrow. I was much better in this fighting position than using a sword in a crush of seasoned warrior gods. I picked off Zeus's army one by one.

THE IMMORTAL TRANSCRIPTS: GLIMMER

Then I saw him. The white hair, the ring of protectors around him, the lightning striking any god who came near his circle of protectors. He was surrounded by our side, and they were pushing him toward us, who were protecting our homestead. He was far from me still, but I was a damn good shot. I quickly calculated the distance. It would make it.

I released the arrow.

It struck Zeus in the shoulder. He fell back a step. I nocked another.

"Archer," Dad warned.

I aimed.

Dad yanked me back, and the arrow went off wildly up in the sky.

I rounded on him, furious. "What are—"

Lightning struck behind me so close, the hairs on the back of my neck stood on end.

He pulled me back out of sight of the battle and Zeus. "Callie. Your child."

Wanting it all to be over, wanting the looming threat of Zeus to be gone forever fueled my adrenaline. We—my wife, child, and I—could be free to simply *live*. "I could end this right now."

"And you could end your lives. No rash actions. Zeus's weapon is the sky. He can get us if he knows where we are, from a greater distance than your arrows can fly. I need to get close. I need to be there right in front of him. I can handle his lightning. The gods know how much he used it to toughen me up as a child."

An idea struck me. "I got it. Zeph."

My wind god friend appeared, looking tired. "I'm no fighter, Archer."

"I'm sorry I'm asking this of you, but..." I filled him in on the plan. Reluctantly, he agreed, the most dangerous part being the last step of it.

I nocked my arrow, nervous about how fast I could aim. "Go."

I was pressed in Zeph's wind and reappeared on a building a hundred feet from Zeus. I got two arrows fired before Zeph relocated us. Hera and Hermes faltered. I felt a tiny bit bad since they had spared Callie and our baby, but here they were defending Zeus again.

From the next location, I aimed and got three off since Zeus had struck the last building I had fired from. Artemis and a couple of her girls went down, but the goddess was up and aiming back at me instantly.

Zeph already had us traveling to another building. Artemis was the biggest problem. I fired four off just at her.

We relocated, and I felled Hera and Hermes again. Why wouldn't they just abandon him already?

"Chase," I told Zeph.

We went back to my dad. Zeph let go and grabbed Chase to take him inside Zeus's circle and immediately come back for me.

The second they were gone, I fired off arrow after arrow, immortal speed, taking down the line, and before Zeus could retaliate, I hesitated, aiming carefully, and released.

The arrow struck him exactly where I intended: his right eye.

Zeph grabbed me, and we reappeared right outside the ring. I unsheathed my sword. "Go."

Zeph shook his head and took out a knife. Only once had we fought together, but we took it up like it was yesterday. He bent down low and stabbed my opponent who was clashing swords with me.

Past our fray, Zeus screamed out. There were gasps, and people froze.

An Egyptian took out the Mayan god whom I had been fighting.

I spun around. Dad had one sword embedded in Zeus's abdomen. Zeus struck Dad with a bolt of lightning, which made him stagger. The sword he had been swinging toward Zeus's neck froze inches away from its target as my father writhed in pain. Growling and fighting the pain off, Dad forced his hand forward, but too slow. Zeus was shoving his lightning bolt—the splintering metal weapon, which was a more powerful conduit for his electricity—upward toward my father's abdomen. He could electrocute Chase until the ichor in his blood ignited.

Ma. Dad. Their child. My sibling. I didn't think.

I acted.

CHAPTER 34

Callie

Athena was staring out the window at the battle far below, and her banter was making me anxious. The deserted streets were free of mortals who might get killed as collateral damage. According to her running commentary, it sounded like Zeus was losing the war now. The Egyptians and other allies had arrived, and Olympus was highly outnumbered. It was a staggering feeling that most of the immortal world was here at my defense or just to stop a tyrant.

"Athena." I sighed. "I don't need the stress of hearing every single battle move." I rubbed my belly. I didn't have any prophecies or visions about any impending doom considering Philo, but I had some dread that something might go wrong.

Of course, it would. We were at war. Athena and Aroha almost collapsed three times now. Chaos "reigned" when an Olympian died. According to their reactions—ones my blended heritage excused me from—three were dead, and we had no idea who they were. We only knew that Chase and Archer were alive because Aroha and I were still, and Prometheus had only mortally married Athena (waiting for their return was debilitatingly stressful).

Athena looked at me, confused, until it clicked. "Sorry. I just want to be out there. Being stuck in here is so sexist and demeaning."

"For the fifth time, Athena, it's because we all have a baby to protect. All of our family and friends are out there. Do you think we want to be stuck here too?" Aroha's hormones had made her a bit snarky (well, very snarky). She was as far along as me, but I'd had those intense emotions early on, and she was having them now.

Athena inhaled quickly, her eyes darting to the door. She ran at it. Before I realized why, the front door burst apart, shards flying. A woman was there, bow and arrow pointed at Athena's face. Before the archer could release the arrow, Athena knocked the bow upward, and an arrow shot into the ceiling.

"Athena, really?" The goddess cracked her neck and stared down at Athena's abdomen. "Challenging me when you know I can wrench that thing from your womb as Father destroyed your other abominations?"

Childbirth goddess. Not Hera, though. Artemis, Lucien's twisted sister. Of course, she came for us. Hurt us all where it counted the most.

Artemis looked worse for wear, tattered, a clear loser in this war. She was coming for one last attempt at my life.

Athena smashed one of my vases on Artemis's head. "Never again."

Aroha went in and yanked Artemis's hair. This seemed like the typical fighting tactic for the beauty goddess.

Was I supposed to join in?

"Where are your sad little worshippers to do your dirty work?" Aroha snarled and twisted the goddess's hair until she screamed. Clumps of hair came out in her hands. I'd be sure to never start a fight with Aroha.

I redirected my attention to weapons. I was good with a knife, but what good would that do against this goddess? Still, I grabbed the butcher knife. Athena had backed off from the hair-pulling fight and took the knife from me (okay, then). I grabbed a smaller knife. The two-on-one battle was going in their favor.

I looked through drawers and cabinets for something that would *end* a god. Nothing flammable in our house came to mind. I grabbed a wine corkscrew and slipped it into my back pocket in case. (Was wine flammable?) We didn't even have any. I yanked open the fridge. The dufus twins must've drunk Archer's Dionysus brews. Next, I looked under the sink. Cleaners. I grabbed a bottle of disinfectant.

"Here!" I shouted.

Aroha had backed away, holding her head.

Athena was wrestling Artemis, plunging the knife expertly into her a couple times, while bending to avoid the goddess touching her abdomen.

"Aroha."

She snapped out of it and looked at me.

"We can't light her on fire in your apartment without risking us all."

I pulled out the small fire extinguisher from under the sink. She cocked her head and grabbed the cleaner, unscrewing it.

Athena smashed into the wall, making an indentation.

Aroha threw the cleaner at a charging Artemis but only got her face, which made her furious. The goddess reached for Aroha's belly. I lunged and slashed Artemis's hand as Aroha retreated into my bedroom. I could not let her touch my child.

"We need no more of your kind." She reached for Philo, but I slashed her hand again. This time, she grabbed the knife, yanking it from my hand, blood dripping on my floor, hissing as it landed. "I'll take that."

She threw it into her other hand and thrust it toward me, but Athena yanked her back by the neck, pulling her to the ground. "Bedroom, now." (It was an order.)

I hurried into the bedroom. "Nothing?" Aroha looked at me. "No matches, lighters?"

"Why would we have them?"

"Scented candles?"

"Do I look like the scented-candles type?"

Aroha scoffed. "Anything hot that could start a fire? A curling iron? Anything?"

The fight between Athena and Artemis was getting intense and now in my doorway. Artemis pulled another hidden knife out of her waistband and swung toward Athena's abdomen. The experienced war goddess was able to dodge every swipe, thankfully. Their battle headed back out into my living room.

"That beauty kit you gave me, under the sink." I pointed at the en suite and took the corkscrew out of my pocket, hardly a weapon, but Athena might need help.

I hurried out into the living room to see Artemis's hand just an inch from Athena's stomach. She could not lose another child. I wasn't thinking but ran up, my rage boiling. I went for the only place I thought the corkscrew could do damage from my angle.

Artemis screamed and fell to the ground, the corkscrew embedded in her ear all the way to the handle.

"Thanks," Athena gasped. She pushed me toward the bedroom and retreated with me. She went to close the door and lock it to give us a second to figure something out.

But Artemis was up and shoved her foot in the gap. Then she shoved it open. She pushed her way into the room, the corkscrew still in her ear. She twitched as if the weapon had affected her brain.

"Artemis." Aroha drew her attention, then threw liquid at her torso. Nail polish remover I had never used.

Without warning, Artemis slammed into me, and we fell down. I struggled, and right as Athena yanked her off me, her hand brushed my abdomen.

Sharp pain laced through my stomach. As she was pulled away, a crazed joy filled Artemis's face. (What had she done?)

I screamed, holding my stomach. Pain cramped in my abdomen in spiking waves. A deep ache and a ton of pressure pushed down on my pelvis.

Aroha scooted me away from the fight between Athena and Artemis. "You're in labor?"

"I'm not. I shouldn't be. I don't understand." I barely got the words out when another gripping pain shot down my abdomen.

My face must've screwed up, for she gasped. "Those contractions were like thirty seconds apart!"

Contractions. *No.* Lucien had estimated I was about thirty weeks along. It was too early.

Artemis laughed, her bottom lip split and both eyes blackened, but the wounds were already healing. "I don't need arrows to kill you and your baby."

"Bitch!" Aroha screamed and flew at her, kicking her so hard in the face that head and shoulders slammed through the drywall. Still, my abdomen crunched in pain, making breathing difficult. I lost track of what they were doing as I scrambled up, despite how I felt, and backed away from the danger.

Artemis. The goddess of childbirth was hastening mine. Could it even be stopped at this point? My entire abdomen convulsed, and warm liquid ran down my legs. That was my answer. If my water just broke…

CHAPTER 35

Archer

I collided with Zeus, flying at him with my powers. We fell, the bolt clattering to the ground. I rolled away over it, snatching it up, and leaped into the air, not wanting to let him get ahold of me.

"Archer!" Prometheus screamed, his dark eyes glaring as he pulled me down and behind him. He whipped around, his eyes wide. "You die, and all this is for nothing. Don't be reckless." He shoved me down next to my father, who was grimacing down on bended knee, recovering from the lightning bolt's sting.

Dad grabbed my arm, squeezing it. "Thanks." He smirked.

"Zeph."

He rushed over. I handed him the bolt. "Go far and stay there."

Zeph stared at the legendary bolt spike in his hands and vanished. Zeus still could pull lighting from the sky, but the bolt had been a weapon that spared him energy while having more power and accuracy.

I pulled Dad to his feet.

"You, inside. He's right. Don't be stupid. We need Callie alive via you." Dad grabbed my neck and butted his head gently against mine in that way he did to show quick affection.

"And I did that something stupid for Ma, you, and my future sibling." I turned away and let an arrow loose at Erato.

She scowled at me. Our friendship, bonding over love poetry back in the day, apparently was over.

"I said thanks," Dad chided as he swung his sword to stop anyone from interrupting the one-on-one battle behind us. "You made me see how stupid I was being."

"Dad." I drew his attention to Prometheus, who was fighting to get to Zeus, who had snapped off the arrow shaft, leaving the point in his eye, and pulled Chase's sword out of his abdomen to arm himself.

"Cover him." Dad went in with his sword, trying to take out the one side of protectors.

Hera and Hermes were missing, leaving the front thinly guarded with Artemis's crew, who could not get arrows off so close and were less skilled with a blade. Their leader was missing as well. Had Artemis abandoned them?

The same was true for me. My arrows were useless from this vantage. I pushed up off the ground, nocking an arrow. I fired from above and made an opening for Prometheus and then started taking out the side my father was not working on.

A scream full of bloodlust drew my attention, and I floated back down in the crowd before the archers could retaliate. Prometheus swung his sword at Zeus. All that rage, pain, and horror Zeus had put him through for thousands of years came tearing out of his mouth. He was more formidable than my father.

But Prometheus went down, Zeus's sword embedded in his stomach.

Prometheus laughed as he yanked it out as if it were nothing. "You think that does anything to me? That I can even feel pain?" He was up right away, two swords, one in each hand. "You had my liver pecked out of my body daily. What can a sword do?"

Prometheus was talking, stalling, because he needed to heal to finish this.

I nocked my arrow. Too close. I backed up in a recessed area that led into a parking garage and defied gravity just a bit. Instead of going with my instinct for the heart, I shot Zeus in the foot. The Achilles heel, to be precise—Lucien would love that one as it mimicked his crowning moment in the death of Achilles when he'd guided Paris's arrow.

Zeus roared in pain, so I shot his other heel.

I landed and rushed out into the crowd.

Lightning struck where I had been standing prior. Close call. *Callie.* Prometheus was right. As much as I wanted to exact revenge and to free us of Zeus, I needed to be with her, protecting her. I could fire from the top floor and still do something.

But I was transfixed. Prometheus slashed at Zeus, slicing into each of his arms with both swords. Lightning struck Prometheus, who faltered back but held on to his weapons. Dad yanked Prometheus back a few steps—not a second too late—as lightning struck the ground in front of them.

Then Prometheus pushed my father back and leaped through the air. I nocked an arrow, but there were gods between me and Zeus. I pushed up off the ground.

Zeus yanked something from his belt. A shining object—a dagger or knife—moved toward Prometheus.

Pain sliced through my shoulder as I fired.

My arrow hit Zeus first. I had aimed for the arm holding the weapon, but missed slightly, hitting his abdomen.

I landed, realizing I'd missed because an arrow had struck me.

My shot was enough to throw off Zeus's aim, though. Prometheus stabbed both swords into him, pinning Zeus to the ground.

THE IMMORTAL TRANSCRIPTS: GLIMMER

Zeus screamed out in agony.

In his face, Prometheus screamed, "For my daughters!" He yanked the swords out and stabbed one in again. "Athena!" Then stabbed the second. "And me!"

Darkness curled around my feet. I staggered back as Dad did the same.

Eyes wild, Zeus shouted, "Hermes!"

He appeared behind Zeus but made no rush to help. "Yes, Father?"

"Get me out of here."

Hermes stared him down with contempt. "I don't think so, Father. I don't have to follow your commands any longer. I. Am. *Free*." He gave Zeus his classic sneer and vanished, appearing behind me, hand on my shoulder.

I gave him a quizzical expression, not sure whether I should trust the trickster. He had freed Callie yet showed up here defending Zeus. Now he was abandoning him.

"Archer, Artemis…" Hermes stopped talking, eyes wide at something behind me.

I had to turn to see. Artemis's hunters were backing up, but she wasn't among them. Before I could ask Hermes to finish speaking, I noticed what stopped him. Darkness enveloped Zeus on the ground. Crackling laughter resounded. Hades's form grew out of the darkness.

He laid his hands on the hilts of Prometheus's swords, wiggling them around. "Hi, *brother*."

Zeus glared at Hades, trying not to show his pain.

"I learned something as soon as you trapped me in the darkness. I *was* the best to punish wrongdoers. I can stop their power, freeze it, for lack of a better word. Completely. That's how they cannot do a thing from the depths of Tartarus." He put a foot onto Zeus's chest when he tried to move.

Zeus sent a bolt up at his captor, but Hades turned into a shadow, a wispy black form. The bolt passed through him and wildly shot up into the sky.

Hades formed back into himself again.

The fighting had stopped. No one—not even our enemies—seemed to bother now. Everyone had either fled or were watching this unfold, transfixed. Many of them had never seen Hades above ground.

Weakness filled Zeus's voice, "How are you…here?"

"I had so much power. More than you. So did Poseidon. That is why you locked us down into our domains. I was trapped but could freeze powers by transferring them into things. I could not wield them, but I could channel them into things. My trophies, I call them."

"Helm of darkness," Hermes muttered by my side, astounded.

Prometheus's head whipped around to Hermes behind me. "Hermes, Athena. Bring her here now."

Hermes vanished.

Hades glowered at Zeus. "Objects you could destroy, but I got my wife out of the first experiment. Then, I realized I could put them into living—well, undead things. I put all of Kronos's rage at your deception into three beings."

Athena and Hermes appeared, the former thrashing around until he pushed her into Prometheus's arms.

Hades gave her a wicked grin. "Pray, Athena. If any one of his children deserves it the most, it is you."

Athena looked down to Zeus, to Hades, to Prometheus. Her quick-thinking mind caught on immediately to what Hades referred to despite not hearing him say it a moment ago—likely the same moment I figured it out: the Erinyes. The winged Tartarus-spawn women who almost trapped Callie and me in the Underworld for robbing Hades. Their role was vengeance to wronged gods, able to leave the underworld to steal mortals who did so. But they had other roles and orders from Hades.

Athena apathetically stared at Zeus, who writhed under Hades shadows that seemed to hold him down powerless.

"Kill him," Prometheus demanded. "Helios. Hephaestus. Burn him!"

I had never seen the god so angry.

It had no impact on Athena. Even when he came up to her, pleading to have Zeus killed, she did not move.

Hades, glowering still at Zeus, said, "Prometheus. Death is too easy a punishment. Trust me."

No one spoke for a moment. Then Athena bowed her head, muttering a prayer, her lips moving, but no words came out.

The Erinyes swooped in. Some gods gasped. Some gods ran. But those of us close enough knew what was happening.

Athena, daughter of Zeus, called upon vengeance for the injustices her parent had cast upon his child. What Hades took from Kronos, he put into his winged scavengers—defiance. Hades had accepted Athena's dead daughters in the Underworld, where he and Persephone cared for them or helped them move on. He knew she was the one with the most power to call for vengeance—and as the goddess of justice could instill it. The fact Nemesis was not here was telling. She might've been one of the three Chaos moments.

The Erinyes came in like birds of prey, swooping down.

They, Zeus, and Hades vanished.

It was over. No one spoke or moved for a moment.

THE IMMORTAL TRANSCRIPTS: GLIMMER

I sighed with relief. Dad slapped my back, grinning.

Hermes was in front of me. "That distracted me. It's Callie, Archer."

The concern on his face made my stomach drop in horror.

CHAPTER 36

Archer, I pleaded, hoping he would feel my panic and get to me.

My precious child. What happened to premature gods? What happened to goddesses with interrupted births? Would Philo "heal"? Would he live?

I bumped into something and felt a hand press upon my back, warmth radiating from it, easing the pain. I whirled around. Hera, behind her, Hermes. They had freed me because of Philo. As the goddess of childbirth, she would not harm Philo. Hermes was too squeamish to murder another child. Still, instincts made me scramble away and onto the bed. Hermes was gone in a split second.

Hera hushed me in soothing tones as a wave of contraction pain hit me. "It's okay." She waved her hand over me, and the pain faded to a dull pull on my ligaments. "I am not letting a baby or mother die whom the Fates have not assigned death to. It's that bastard spawn of my husband's fault." (I liked that reference to Artemis, actually.) Hera stood between me and Artemis.

"Turning sides?" Artemis glared at Hera, then spat at her as Aroha pinned her arms behind her back.

It landed on Hera's boot. She made a displeased face. "Zeus is losing this war. You saw defeat coming and hightailed it up here, desperate to do something to make him love you. Only a spineless god attacks the most innocent. Only a traitor to her role and nature would attempt to kill children to feel some shred of affection from a god incapable of loving anyone or anything but power and control."

I shuddered at the mention of killing children.

"Spare me the speeches, *Stepmother*. You're no saint."

Hermes reappeared and grabbed Athena around her waist and vanished. My own dire situation did not stop me from worrying about her, likely to join the battle. What side was Hermes on? And Hera? I was unsure.

This distraction was enough to kick things off again. In a blur of movement, Artemis was free of Aroha, who staggered back gasping, a knife embedded in her thigh.

"Callie," Aroha gasped, limping to the bed. "The flat iron. Bathroom."

A ripple of pain went through me.

THE IMMORTAL TRANSCRIPTS: GLIMMER

I could not run to the bathroom; I could hardly walk, the spiking, cramping pain making each step unbearable. Hera had Artemis in a headlock, wrestling her across the room.

In the bathroom, the flat iron was plugged in. I raced out, weapon in hand. Seeing what I was up to, Artemis kicked the flat iron out of my hand. It thudded across the room.

Artemis shoved Hera back across the room. She landed next to the iron.

Everything happened so fast. Artemis was upon me, and I struggled out of her grasp, tripping and scrambling to Hera.

Artemis came toward us but roared, screaming out in pain. Aroha had thrown the knife she yanked out of her leg right into Artemis's back, between her shoulder blades where she could not reach it.

It was all the time Hera needed. She wielded the flat iron and clamped it on Artemis's soaked clothing. "I. Am. *The* goddess of childbirth."

I could not breathe. Was it still hot enough? In answer, fire spread quickly, up her chest and face. Artemis shrieked.

Hera gave her a double-footed kick.

Artemis flew into the window, smashing it. Then she was gone. The air whistled and whipped inside, but louder was Artemis's scream as it faded away and stopped.

Hermes appeared next with a writhing, fighting Archer. He stopped, gazing around our destroyed bedroom.

No one moved. No one spoke. All but Hera and I grabbed their heads in pain. (Chaos.) She was staring solemnly out the window.

It meant Artemis was dead.

I had no time to ponder that, because I had another contraction, this one longer. The pressure below was telling me I was having a baby. Soon.

My pain sobered Archer from the Chaos vision first. He went to scoop me up until he realized he had an arrow sticking out of his chest. (How did he not know?). He snapped it off like it was no big deal (supposed it wasn't) and swept me up into his arms. He rushed me from the room into Athena's apartment across from ours. He placed me in the guest bedroom.

"What is it? What's wrong?" He brushed a kiss against my brow.

"It's too early. Artemis forced my labor."

He sat down next to me, rubbing his hand soothingly down my belly. "It'll be okay. Philo will be fine. I'll never let anything happen to him or you."

"Why now?" I cried. A war at our front door, Zeus thirsting to kill me, and Philo was on his way. The pressure down below was becoming unbearable.

Hera entered. Archer stiffened.

LISA BORNE GRAVES

I squeezed his arm. "She was helping me. She freed me, remember?"

"Archer." Hera's eyes teared up. "I could not help you. I was trapped. But in this, I can."

Archer was frustrated. "Why didn't you simply not save him in the last battle?"

"I have been trapped in this relationship for millennia. I can go into the many reasons, Zeus's many versions of abuse and psychological warfare, but your child is about to be born."

Hermes came into the room, his face lost. He had no idea what to say, I supposed when he was used to being a jerk so long to the others. Archer simply nodded at him.

Archer gripped my hand tightly as I squeezed his hand to rid myself of another crippling contraction.

Hera went to the closet and came back with towels and a sheet. She draped the latter over me and slid some towels under me. She checked my dilation, which made me buck up from the pain and pressure. Instinctively, I kicked at her, and Archer apologetically held my leg down. I suddenly wanted a hospital, drugs, an epidural—something, anything.

Even with my limited knowledge, Hera's next statement told me I'd have no pain relief until Lucien was here: "Ten centimeters. It's time to start pushing."

CHAPTER 37

Pure exhaustion. I had just chased off the last of the Mayan gods with Heph and the Charities. A building down the street was on fire. Heph's work.

The sun was rising, starting to ease my fatigue slightly.

Dread filled me, as well as panic. Aios. Akila. I had lost track of her, and then Aios and I were separated later.

"I'm going to D's bar. Who's in?" Heph started lumbering away as if he just got off work and was heading to happy hour.

The Charities agreed. I turned down the invitation, needing to see my family and friends were safe.

I rushed around the building from 74th, turning onto 1st, to see the Titans gathered with grim faces as traveling gods took small groups away. I'd find out whom else they had lost later because they were not upset about my mother, who had fought against them.

I kept running down the street, turning the corner onto 75th Street, finding the Norse celebrating on York Avenue like they were at a block party, not a war. Pollux was with them, and a young man next to him raised his glass to me.

"Castor?" I had no clue who he was, except he was with Pollux. Nor did I recognize what god's body his soul now possessed.

"The one and only. Like the new bod?"

"You're much more attractive now," I teased. "An upgrade."

"Ha ha."

"Good to see you back." Not good for whatever demigod Zeus had made immortal and Hades sent Death for, but now was not the time to ruminate on ethics.

They tried to ply me with a drink, but I was on a mission. I continued the loop back to our building. Stuck not knowing where my people were, I hurried inside. I ignored the frightened doorman, desk person, and terrified residents. I was a sight to see.

The elevator ride all the way up was maddening. I dialed Mnemosyne.

"Yes, I know. I'm here already. There are lots of mortals to deal with, and I have to start with the news, but there are way too many mortals who filmed it," she complained.

"I'll text Hermes to take care of the internet and to later send you a major bonus for all your work."

"He's back in business?"

"Yes. He's free. You're free. The surface Titans are free."

"No more day passes out of jail?"

"Zeus has no power, and you're out right now, aren't you?" I pointed out.

She squealed into the phone, making me pull it away from my ear. Once she stopped, I felt it important to add, "Hermes and Hera turned on Zeus and helped us in the end. They are not to be harmed."

"Understood. Till we meet again." Then she hung up.

As soon as the elevator door opened, though, anxiety rushed through me. "Aios! Akila! Archer! Anyone!" I screamed out.

A door opened at the end of the hall—Prometheus and Athena's place. Chase's face was etched with worry, but when he spotted me, he rushed to me, not stopping until he embraced me in the most crushing hug I have ever had. I thought a bone snapped, but a quick scan of myself only showed a small stress fracture that would heal instantly.

"You're alive?" He pulled away and tapped my cheek with less vigor. "He's alive!" He shouted, although a bunch of my family members were already clogging up the doorway.

"Is everyone accounted for? Akila?"

Chase placed his hand on my shoulder, gripping it. "Yes. And, brother, we have an additional life on board. You are a great-uncle, and I'm a *pappoús*." His grin was huge and not the typical expression I was used to seeing on his face.

All of us. All of us changed because of Callie, but now we were changing even more. She must've freed us, but when Hades's…I had no word for it aside from "nullified" Zeus, his power over us was completely gone. I lost my mother and father—but I had zero regrets. This was my brother, my family. Aroha, my sister. Archer, Callie, Aios—all of them were my family and everything I needed.

Chase pulled my shoulder to steer me toward the apartment.

Akila came running out, her eyes wide. She said something in an ancient tongue, the only word I discerned was "love." She would've tackled me had I not pushed back against her as she kissed me. Her hands cupped my cheeks as she repeatedly kissed me. I had to kiss her back, ignoring the comments down the hall.

"Enough, enough." Himerus came out with two large bottles of Dionysus stock in hand. "Let's leave the li'l munchkin and his exhausted parents alone and open up this floor into a party."

I broke away from Akila but held her close. "This is the family you want to live with?"

"Absolutely." She kissed me.

"Polly."

"I'll call her now. After we were separated, I wasn't sure where you were. Then Aios got separated from you too. I didn't…" Her eyes welled up and she blew a breath out. "I thought—"

"I worried about the same. Where's my son?"

"Two of them are here with Euterpe. She said you had to kill your own mother?"

I nodded. "It's fine. She was…"

"Like your sister."

"Yeah."

"A bitch."

"Yep." I nodded. "Yes, that. I was teetering more toward 'insane,' but she never was kind since my first memories."

"Hera killed Artemis."

Hearing the news was strangely relieving. It was liberating to know my sister could never come after my kids again. I could not think of many moments between my sister and I that warmed me or made me feel any sense of great loss.

Hermes and Hera stood awkwardly against a wall, clearly not belonging. She met my gaze, her face weary because she'd slain my sister. They had switched sides, helped us with Callie, and did not help Zeus in the end.

I nodded at them, choosing forgiveness. "What will you do now?"

Hera spoke first. "Run *my* resort how I see fit. All will be welcome, all my children, including you, *son*."

I was so stunned, I had no idea what to say. She had never accepted Zeus's bastard children before. Now she was offering that olive branch to all of us. Perhaps she had been suppressed, controlled, abused—too scared to leave.

"Mother," was all I could say.

She gave me a tentative smile.

"You?" I directed at Hermes.

He stood wide-eyed, his gaze fixed on mine as his mouth upturned into his typical sneer. Then his lips broke into a genuine smile, making him look entirely different. I could not remember him as a happy god, but there was an inkling of a memory that, once upon a time, he had been. "Anything I want to do."

He had served Zeus as a punishment for so long. He was now free. "I don't think any of us will mind what you get up to as long as you send us some of your bounty now and then. You know, as a thank you for freeing you."

Hermes winked, his smile slipping into a mischievous one. "With pleasure." Then he looked to Hera. "Shall we go to Olympus? You have a lot to do, and I deserve a vacation."

She nodded, smiling.

Hermes took Hera's hand, and they vanished. Even if any other gods wanted to punish him for theft, I had a feeling they would never find him, and all our bank accounts would grow.

We unleashed the trickster thief. The mortals would not know what hit them. The idea made me smile.

Akila squeezed my hand. "Hera delivered the baby, but I think Callie would love it if you gave her some pain relief."

"After fighting a war, easing some pain is child's play." I smiled, but my mind churned with worry. How would the rest of the world's gods, the others, react to the war and deaths? Could they come down on us and accuse us of murder? We had to do something. We had to tell our side so they would know all of this, the *how* and the *why*.

"Dad!" two voices said in unison as doors were unlocked and opened, and gods left the end room, where I guess Archer and Callie remained. Both Aios and Asclepius hugged me, although the latter blushed and backed away quickly. He'd called me "dad."

I grabbed his neck and pulled his head to my shoulder. "Don't be ashamed of your feelings."

"It's good to see you're still on this side of Hades," he mumbled before I let him and Aios go.

"Stop almost dying, Dad." Aios put his hands on his hips, shaking his head at me.

"I didn't almost die—thank you very much—I chased away some Mayans and did a perimeter before I came in." My boys were safe, the third being far away from the battlefront with Demeter. My daughter was safe in Egypt.

We were engulfed with happy Greek gods, some who didn't even live here.

Akila smiled at me. "I'll tell Polly all is well, but I thought we should let her stay with my family for a couple days."

I nodded. I was exhausted, but I was looking forward to spending time alone with her. Before I could escape to her room away from the bustle up here, there were people to see. "If you want to go down, I'll meet you soon. I have to see my friends, my family."

"I know. I'm not going anywhere but by your side." She gripped my hand in hers.

THE IMMORTAL TRANSCRIPTS: GLIMMER

We walked through the open door of Prometheus and Athena's apartment. My guess was Archer and Callie would live there until their apartment was repaired. There wasn't even a door anymore to their apartment. We were fighting against the grain of others walking out, and many stopped to make small talk.

When I got into the apartment, Aroha was shooing people away. She gave me a warm smile and hug, her baby bump in the way. I dropped Akila's hand to hug one of my best friends back.

We pulled away, and she patted my face gently. "I'm so glad this is over."

I didn't want to tell her there could be repercussions to our actions. "Me too."

"Go see them, and then urge them to rest." She patted my chest and gave Akila a warm smile.

I went into the guest room as Akila shut the door behind her, and most of the noise out. Archer was in a chair by the bed, staring at the bundle in Callie's arms. Both of them looked up warmly at me, despite the exhaustion on their faces. Childbirth was as exhausting as war, and they'd faced both.

Despite how haggard he looked, Archer was up and hugging me. He pulled away quickly, too eager to show me the early new addition to the family. Grinning widely with paternal pride he said, "Philo." His eyes glowed with love as he peered at his son.

I bent down over the beaming mother to examine the little squawking bundle in her arms. Being so premature, they had him swaddled in layers of blankets. His little face peeked out at me, his eyes wide open and already focusing on me. Then he surprised me by smiling a huge toothless grin—not that newborn gas-relief expression, but a huge grin followed by a squawk.

I touched my thumb gently to his forehead to ascertain his condition. He was okay. The ichor in his blood was on full alert, healing his tiny body of issues mortal preemies sometimes have with breathing and temperature regulation. Still, I used my gift to pour some healing energy to speed it up for the little warrior, making his lungs develop fully and healing a minor brain bleed. Then the little bugger reciprocated his powers to me: a rush of love for my friends.

I removed my thumb, smiling, as his eyes peered into mine. Archer's eyes, glowing with warm friendliness. "Nice to meet you, new friend."

I met Callie's gaze as she held him close. "Is he—"

"He'll be fine. I healed him, but the ichor is doing its job. He gave me powers back. A little god of friendship is exactly what we need for godly world peace." Then I sensed the pain radiating off Callie. "But you could use some help."

"I had ambrosia via Hera and nectar via Asclepius."

That was good but something was still off. I scanned her and saw the issue neither concoction had cured. Not all the afterbirth had come out. Over time, even a goddess could bleed to death if the issue was not one that healed on its own. "Archer, a complication. Take the baby out of the room. Akila, will you get Asclepius?"

"What?" Archer was up and taking the baby. The happiness on his face dropped.

My tone of voice made Akila rush away while I explained things to Archer and Callie.

I was thankful Euterpe came in with my son, and they took over. I loved my friends and would do anything for them, but performing a minor surgery on Callie in the female region would've been awkward for a hundred years at least.

Akila held Philo, which kept distracting me because it made me want to see her holding our child or wish that I had seen her with Polly when she'd been born—both. Archer paced, running his hand through his hair so many times, I'm surprised he hadn't made himself temporarily bald.

"Archer, she will be fine. If I thought she wouldn't, I would be in there."

Anteros and Himerus entered next, the latter one staring at the floor, not meeting Archer's gaze.

"How is she?" Anteros asked.

I explained for Archer, "A complication. She'll be okay."

Himerus's gaze darted up as Philo made a little fussy groan in Akila's arms. "Is that my nephew?" The pure joy on Himerus's face was wiped clean when Archer's hard gaze met his.

Himerus looked down at his feet. "I'm sorry, Archer. There's nothing more I can say. I can't undo my actions, but I can promise I'll never repeat them."

Archer sighed. He was a lover, not a hater.

"Yes. This is your nephew, brother." Archer placed his hand on Himerus's shoulder and gave it a squeeze. "Philo."

Himerus smiled, and then, to get rid of the awkward silence that was forming, he cooed and baby-talked to the little bundle in Akila's arms. It was odd to see the lusty, super strong god turn to mush at the sight of a tiny baby.

Archer started pacing. "What happens now?"

"What do you mean?" I was lost.

"No Zeus. Athena's gone to try to start some international government who will punish gods who did wrong."

235

THE IMMORTAL TRANSCRIPTS: GLIMMER

I knew his guilt for taking another god's life because I felt it too. I looked to Akila for help. Thanatos and Leto were not good immortals, unhinged even, but taking life was not in Archer's or my natures.

Akila gave us a soft smile. "My people have been in a democratic situation longer than you—well, you haven't had that at all, sorry. Athena knows law, justice. You'll get a chance to say your side of things."

A thought struck me. "Why don't we write it down?"

"Huh?" Archer stopped his pacing.

"Our accounts of what happened. It would exonerate you from murder and show it was self-defense, that Zeus enforced the unjust attacks. Not just about Thanatos but any others. We can proactively defend ourselves while they assemble this government. All of us involved write up their own account of what happened—you, me, Callie, Chase, Aroha, Athena too, and whoever else for the blanks of me being temporarily dead and all that."

We had the right to prove we were defending ourselves, trying to survive. There was the attack on the Brooklyn Bridge; the Battle of Belize; the Battle of Liberty Island; minor skirmishes for Chase, me, and others, and then this full-out world war of the gods. It would take this newly forming international government months to sort out what happened, whereas a detailed account could do that for them.

Archer shook his head. "I wouldn't even know where to start."

"From the beginning." I grabbed up a sheet of paper out of Athena's printer and a pen from her desk and sat down.

Asclepius and Euterpe came out, nodding. The latter said, "She'll be fine."

Archer rushed in to check on her. Asclepius gave me a wave as I thanked him, Euterpe clung to his arm.

Akila only had eyes for the baby in her arms.

I took up the pen, thinking about when Callie arrived and upended our world but ended up liberating it. But that was not the right place to start. I contemplated.

Akila sighed. "Don't know where to start?"

"No."

"With you, my love, it always starts with women or prophecies." She laughed quietly as she had just gotten the baby asleep.

She was wrong about "or." I knew exactly where to start.

I started to write at an immortal pace, from the beginning, the catalyst that changed everything for us Olympians:

I found myself adrift in a sea of fog, so I knew it was one of my repetitive dreams. Trouble for me always starts with dreams—and women—but women in dreams is the worst combination...

END OF TRANSCRIPTS

CHAPTER 38

Archer

It took us two months to write and type up our accounts. You'd think a story would be easy to write at immortal speed, particularly when it was the truth about what happened. It was four volumes long. The holdup, to be honest, was Callie and me. Being new parents, we hardly slept. Although Philo was the calmest and happiest baby I had ever seen, he was a preemie, and Lucien said he had to eat every two hours, even if we had to wake him. At least he helped us, coming to feed him when we needed a nap. He was weirdly protective of Philo and was acting that way about Ma if Dad did as much as tease her. She was due any day now.

It went that way for a couple weeks until we figured out what had happened. Lucien had inherited his mother's powers—protector of children and motherhood. Overburdened with roles, he was hoping Ma's or Athena's babies would take the roles from him. He probably would have to wait for his own. The fact Polly stayed more at her brother's place than her parents told us all that Akila and him having another kid was not a long way off.

Now that Philo had caught up in size to an average newborn baby and the writing was finished, we got more rest, and so did he. We nervously waited for the IRI, International Republic of Immortality, to discuss our case.

One last thing I did, out of sheer concern about the upcoming IRI verdicts, was to make a copy and pen a note in each volume. I gave them to the only person who could preserve our story if I was executed: Raphael.

Our story deserved to be heard. They would likely think it a fictional piece, but at least Callie and my story would be out there somewhere in the world.

The official transcripts were taken to Fiji via Iris, where Hera was hosting all the gods in the IRI, one representative from every culture around the world who had wished to join. A week had passed without a word—

Ping.

It was a text from my father. **Come over now.**

Callie was feeding Philo, who was looking drowsy.

"Dad wants me to come over."

"Maybe your Ma is in labor?"

"Maybe." I got up.

"I'll stay here and get Philo down. Just let me know if I'm needed."

I kissed her gently and brushed the baby's head with the back of my finger. I didn't want to leave them for a second.

I went to Ma and Dad's, the door opening as I approached. He yanked me in, his eyes wide.

Athena was in the room, her face serious. "The verdicts were made."

I burst into our apartment. "They gave—"

Callie shot me a death stare, Philo asleep in her arms.

I pinched my lips to stop myself, feeling as if I'd burst if I didn't tell her the news. She got up slowly and went into the baby's room, placing Philo into his crib. She came back out, closing the door quietly.

I was right there, making her jump. "Come," I whispered, taking up her hand, leading her into the kitchen. My other hand snagged the baby monitor. I switched it on, placed it on the counter, and indulged in a small smile of paternal pride as I saw our little god sleeping peacefully.

Callie smiled when she looked at him too, but immediately, the anxiety came back to her face. She had been through so much and feared retribution from the IRI. Zeus was still alive too, which didn't help her fear that he'd escape his temporary prison in the Underworld.

There was a lot to tell her, so I grabbed a bottle of nectar since my wife hated all of Dionysus's fermented brews. I poured two glasses.

"Some kind of news?"

I nodded. "Athena's back. The IRI gave their verdicts."

"And?" She rolled her wrist impatiently for me to get on with it. "The transcripts?"

"The IRI read them all. We are not being held not responsible for anything: the battles, the blame, and the punishment is solely leveled at Zeus. My killing of Thanatos was ruled as self-defense. With you, Polly, and some others who already exist, any remaining laws in some cultures about regulating bloodlines have been abolished. Anyone is free to marry anyone. It just made sense since Titan and Greeks already intermingled. If you think about it, the second generation of us— my dad, Lucien—they all were products of two cultures that merged together in the beginning."

I lifted my glass to cheers.

"Zeus?"

Archer put his glass down, sighing. She'd want to hear it all before we could celebrate. "The IRI decided not to sentence him to death but to be rendered powerless and have eternal punishments. The Moirae shall decide. We are all to attend the decision."

"I can't cheers to this. I don't want to go anywhere near him or have Philo anywhere near him." I thought she'd be much happier about it, but I couldn't blame her.

"Philo can stay here with Linda, Akila, Polly, and Raphael. We'll be gone for what, an hour? It'll be awkward but fine. We are safe now, Callie. That is something to celebrate." I toasted. "To getting closure."

"Okay," she lifted her glass. "I can drink to that."

The next morning, we were all summoned to Hades. The wind gods of many cultures met us on the roof.

Zeph came over and hugged me, then Callie. "I'm meeting the little one when we come back." Then he swooped us up in his squeezing wind, and we reappeared in darkness. It took my eyes a moment to adjust, but we were in Hades's courtyard garden.

"Eros! Callista!" Hades's face was alight, excited to have so many guests. But then he swept my wife up in his arms in a huge hug, whispering something in her ear. When he let my wife go, she was grinning.

"Where's Persephone?" I looked around for our hostess.

Hades was already greeting my parents and others.

Callie took up my hand in hers, threading our fingers. "She will not be coming back to the Underworld for roughly six more months."

It took me a second to put two-and-two together. "Are you sure you're not the goddess of fertility?"

"I hope not. Don't you already have Aroha and Dionysus for that?"

She didn't even want to know about Pan. It would take way too long to explain exactly what he was, how he was created, and where he ended up.

Soon enough, we all stood in front of the entrance to Tartarus. Athena faced us.

"Are we going in there?" Callie asked.

I vehemently shook my head. Before I could explain that no one could leave Tartarus once they entered, except for a few exceptions such as Hades, Prometheus hushed us all.

Athena spoke up. "It has been decreed by the International Republic of Immortality that all punishments by Zeus are now null and void. Those in Tartarus already must remain there unless they ask Death to take them onward. Their punishments will stop."

Hades closed his eyes, and his hands danced around in the air like a conductor of a symphony. Behind those doors was a pit down into an abyss of darkness. There was a loud bang from beyond them.

"That would be Sisyphus," Hades informed us.

Callie was racking her brain trying to remember who he was, so I whispered, "Big boulder guy."

She nodded, recalling the story about Sisyphus, whom Zeus punished several times, and he'd evaded it each time. Trying to prove himself smarter than Zeus was not a good idea because he sent him to Tartarus, the place of torture for his enemies he could not control. Likely, that was his ultimate goal in kidnapping Callie unless it was death. I shuddered at the thought.

There was some screaming from behind the doors, some of joy, but most sounded like screams of the insane. I doubted any Titan or other "resident" still had an intact mind after all this time. Zeus was headed to a madhouse likely hellbent on revenge.

The crowd of us parted as the new Death led Zeus toward Hades and the doors. Three women trailed him—the one in the front looking us all over, the other two following with vacant stares, the Fates. Only one could use the gift of mortal eyesight at a time.

Zeus had that cold sneer on his face, his cold, unfeeling eyes trying to meet each god in turn. When his gaze alighted upon Dad, Chase straightened his posture, and his eyes glowed with hatred, something I rarely saw from him these days. Ma smirked at Zeus and drew his attention to her belly by rubbing her hand down it.

Irritation spread across his features as his head whipped around. He was trying to find us. When his eyes danced over me to my wife at my side, pure, unadulterated wrath poured out of his gaze. He lunged at Callie, who bravely didn't flinch. Before any of us could act or Death regripped his shackles, Callie punched his face, bones cracking.

She winced, shaking her hand. Blood poured out of Zeus's nose.

Lucien, on the other side of Callie, took up her hand, healing what probably was a couple of broken bones. "That was badass," he murmured.

Zeus and the entourage were nearing the doors.

He barely spared a glare at Prometheus, who stood with Athena. Zeus was coming to terms with entering a place he'd never leave again, facing the fact he had no power over any of us anymore.

Prometheus smiled. "Checkmate."

"You," Zeus accused.

"Yes, me. It has been a long game, Zeus, but I won." Prometheus slipped something small into the chest pocket of Zeus's shirt. It looked like a chess piece, a king.

Hades walked right up to Zeus, face-to-face, a smug grin on the former's face. "The Titans and other of your victims will be granted death when they tire of watching your torture. Except you. You will not be granted death."

"Yes, Hades, thanks. I wasn't sure what 'eternal punishment' meant. Thanks so much for clearing that up." The sarcasm was so thick, I thought Hades would get angry at the insult.

But he laughed, loudly and uncontrollably.

Zeus looked around, confused. "Lost your mind, have you?"

"And so will you in about four thousand years. At least now, thanks to Callista, I can find my mind again."

"I tire of this. Just get it over with." Zeus spat on the ground. There was blood in it from Callie's right hook, but the nose had healed.

The Fates spoke in their odd way, a mix between talking in unison and sometimes finishing each other's words and sentences. Born as triplets, they were more like one collective mind in three bodies. "We will choose the punishments to be doled out by the ones he has wronged the longest. We will gift the ones whom he hurt the most. Poseidon, what punishment will you dole out for eternity?"

His face stern, but not taking enjoyment in the suffering of anyone, he answered: "To drown daily."

"Prometheus?"

He seemed surprised at being a choice, but he recuperated quickly. "To have his liver plucked out every day."

I shivered, realizing they were each giving him the torture they had endured because of him: Poseidon not having fresh air; Prometheus having his liver grow back just to have it plucked out for a thousand years. We awaited Hades, but I already knew what it would be.

"I will gradually grant light in Tartarus so those you tortured can watch your torture, but you will be forever shrouded in darkness to never see the torture coming." That was a twisted one, but Hades's cat-eyes would take eons to return to normal—if ever.

Zeus's gaze darted around wildly as we watched the horror of his eyes clouding over until they were completely white. His face was terrified, but instead of screaming as expected if suddenly blinded, he let out a little whimper that made me cringe.

The doors were opened, and he was led in by Hades, who then gave him a shove. He fell down the hole of black abyss, screaming, making us all somber despite knowing this punishment was well deserved.

Well, all except Hades. "Onto the gifts if you will, because I'm ready for the after-party." He locked the doors.

"Hear! Hear!" Dionysus tapped a large wooden keg he had brought with him. Of course, he had.

"Hera, long-suffering wife, what unclaimed power do you choose?"

This was interesting. I'd thought that only Zeus's were up for grabs. But there had been casualties, and the Fates had powers beyond any of us.

"To be motherhood goddess that I am, but to take on the portions that Leto and Artemis had taken."

The Fate who was using the sight in that moment nodded at her. Hera smiled, content.

"Thank you, Hera." Lucien sighed, happy to be relieved of some of his new maternal powers.

The Fates turned to Chase. "Ares, as the eldest child, what power do you choose for yourself?"

Dad overeagerly blurted out, "Lightning. I mean the sky—all of that." I made us chuckle and lightened up the mood. Dad made a fist, and the crackling electricity ripped over it.

Oh man, that might've been a bit much. He'd be unbeatable in battle, and I was sure Thor and him would be sparring soon.

The Fate stopped. "We feel the lightning is enough."

"C'mon. I'd be unstoppable."

Athena crossed her arms. "That's why, Chase. Maybe compromise with thunder as well?"

The Fates took a moment and nodded at him.

Dad shrugged, putting his fingertips near each other to make the lightning crackle between them. "Best ones anyway."

"Hebe?"

"Protector of children and chastity, please."

Lucien pumped up a yes-fist into the air. He had gotten rid of all his mother's powers.

"Apollo?" The Fates asked next.

He shook his head, his hands up in surrender. "Pass, hard pass. I have enough on my plate. Give someone else my share."

Down the line, all of Zeus's children chose. Hermes took shapeshifting, likely to up his theft game. Iris, controlling the Skies, shaking her head at Dad, who was motioning for her to call him. Iris was the best to keep Dad in check. She hated war. Dionysus just wanted Zeus's bedroom prowess, which confirmed all along that Zeus's charisma to get women in bed had not been a personality trait but a power. Hera gave him a disapproving look when Dionysus started trying to chat up Iris. Athena chose hunting and wilderness. Prometheus looked at her, surprised.

"What? Animals are better than people, and I don't want the responsibility of the moon."

With all the children and Hera gifted, the Fates turned to Lucien. "Who do you gift the moon to?"

Lucien smiled and gripped Aios shoulders. "My son already had some good practice with the sun and many of mine. He can wield the moon, and it is only right it sticks within the family rather than going to someone yet to be born."

"The last gift will be given to the grandchild who will be the best to wield this power. Eros."

My brain was not computing what gift was left and the shock about being chosen to take on a power.

"Your immortal marriage to a goddess who can cloud omniscience makes you the best to carry the burden."

"So, you're giving me a power so no one can use it, not even me?" It didn't feel like a gift, or a burden, more like a mean trick. I was excited for a moment that I'd be gaining something, after all that I had been through.

"We think you'll figure it out," they said in unison as they nodded.

A bolt of energy rippled through me. Suddenly, I felt like I was floating outside of my body as I did when I searched for mortals who needed love. No one except Callie was around me. I yanked myself back into my body. The Fates were walking toward the large group of traveling gods behind us, ending their stay.

"You okay?" Callie asked.

"Yeah, just trying to figure it out. It's the opposite of what you'd think omniscience would be."

"Because of me, free will?"

"I'll figure it out. The Fates are never wrong."

CHAPTER 39

After we stayed at Hades for a polite amount of time, Aroha escaped home with the excuse that she was tired. Archer and I made excuses that we hadn't been away from the baby until now. Both our excuses warmed the expectant father's heart, and Hades had no ill will of us ditching a party.

When we got home and Zeph met the baby, we thanked Linda for babysitting. Aroha and Chase came over instead of staying at theirs. Then, in little clusters as the day went on, everyone in our building returned but came directly to our apartment. At some point, Zeph left, and Philo fell asleep in Archer's arms, so he put him in his crib for a nap. The last of our crew to show up was Lucien and Aios, without Akila and Polly, who were at Central Park, enjoying the pocket of warm second summer before fall officially set in.

I didn't realize how crowded our apartment became until Linda had trouble cutting through the group to get to Aios. He took her hand, smiling. (Aww, cute.)

Linda said, "I wish I was able to go with you. I've been so worried."

"I'm glad you were not there—for your safety." Aios was adorably nervous. (Sooo cute.)

Himerus and Anteros were smirking and whispering to each other. I shot them a glare to not do something stupid to embarrass the bashful couple. They looked down at their feet, faces losing their mirth. I kind of liked my sister-in-law status with them. Okay, it felt like a bit of a power trip on my part.

Linda shrugged. "Well, I didn't belong there anyway."

"You did. You *will*," Aios said with emphasis. "You'll be an Olympian too one day, Linda." He weaved his fingers in hers as if none of us were present. Then he kissed her.

Admittedly, we watched them kiss for a moment too long until Aroha said something about snacks and drinks. I think we all needed to see that moment of bliss to get over the heavy and mixed-emotion events that had occurred and to ignore our many unanswered questions. There was some shuffling, some people leaving to grab things, people sitting at the table, the breakfast nook, pilfering our kitchen—Archer's brothers, of course.

After everything that had happened, we needed to be together. I think we all needed to unpack it to understand it. No one would function or sleep at night without figuring out how easy it all was in the end—no punishment, gifts given, and Zeus eliminated from our lives? I could hardly grasp the concept of not looking over my shoulder every moment of my life.

Linda and Aios sat down, whispering to each other. I snagged a seat on the end of the couch, pulling Archer down between me and them; I was getting us a seat in our own house (thank you very much). Food and drinks crowded our coffee tables and the breakfast bar, where Archer's brothers took the stools closet. Some dragged over our dining chairs to sit across from us. Without seats left, Lucien was stuck standing as if he lost musical chairs by not being attentive. Our apartment was packed, but Philo slept peacefully in his crib when I looked at the monitor screen. I shouldn't worry. The baby slept as deeply as his father did.

"So…" Lucien said as he sat down on the arm of the sofa next to me. "Where to start?"

Athena stared off at the wall, the gears in her mind churning. "How about with 'checkmate'?"

Chase crossed his arms. "Yeah, Prometheus, explain." Chase's words might as well have been a punch to the face, the anger in his posture as his narrowed eyes were telling.

Prometheus sighed. "Can you throw the punches later after we leave?" He leaned back against his chair without a care. "You got lightning. You're welcome."

Athena stared at him incredulously. "I left you out of the transcripts to protect you when, all along, it sounds like you and Zeus played some game with our lives."

"Yep. I'm reading layers of deception over here," Lucien added, scrutinizing him.

"Are you all done? I'll tell you now. Yes, I had a hand in all this. You knew this. I told you in Iceland I had planned for this—"

"For Callie!" Athena shouted, "Not to beat Zeus in some game with our lives so you could usurp him. You denied that in Iceland."

Prometheus looked strained. "Thena, it wasn't a *game*. That was a metaphor for something way more than that. You'll be angry with me now—some of you rightfully more so than others—but none of you could've known how we would overthrow Zeus. Not even Callie, who saw pieces of what I saw all of. Anything any of you might've done could have destroyed this moment, where we are now. We might be under Zeus's rule, punished irrevocably, or many of us dead. Start with Callie, and follow the trail of who would die for her or to avenge her."

All of our eyes went to Archer, then Lucien, Chase, and danced around following who might've died if Zeus had killed me. If Lucien had not made his noble sacrifice, what would have happened? Likely, Chase, Aroha by proxy,

Archer's brothers… I could continue. We were a family. A real tapestry of beings who cared about one another, with the love retinue in the center, the heart of it. Prometheus was right—not that everyone else would see it that way at first.

Athena crossed her arms, scrutinizing Prometheus. "So, you orchestrated the fall of Zeus, wielding Callie like a weapon, no worse, bait?" (Gee, thanks Athena.)

Prometheus stood up, most likely to get away from that accusatory stare of hers. "I told you, I had a lot of time chained to that rock to think, to plan a way to save Callie. I figured out a path to do so much more than just that. Callie was not a weapon or bait, but a shield and an emblem to draw us allies."

Athena frowned. Likely her emotions were battling against the logic of his planned war much as mine were. I didn't want to be the cause of a war, and he had helped that happen.

"She was bait," Athena pressed. "The mind connection you had with Callie was not there. You had to have known she was taken and that Lena was an imposter."

He sighed, looking at me. "Forgive me Callie, Athena," he added and gave her a hurt look. "Archer and Himerus." He ran his hands down his face in frustration. "Tartarus, sorry everyone. Callie had to be taken to pull Hera and Hermes to our side. They were key in the war."

I thought of Hera killing Artemis, of delivering my baby. How Hermes apparently abandoned Zeus, his only means of escape. I felt used.

"And a reason to attack a weak Zeus in Fiji," Athena accused.

Prometheus continued, as he walked around the coffee table toward Lucien and my side of the couch, "That was not the plan. I half lost my mind being so close to the weakened god. I had thought to change the plan, to end everything then and there. Thankfully, you all talked sense into me. You see, plans get ruined. Not everything can be foretold. Before, I had tried to save my daughters and failed. This time, I knew Callista was the key. It told you all as much." Prometheus pointed at me, making me feel like the weirdo. "But it wasn't a vision. How I saved her from Zeus when she was five wasn't either. I got those prophecies from my mother, Themis."

Everyone grew quiet and confused. I hoped they'd explain why they appeared shocked, particularly Lucien, who tensed. I tried to probe Prometheus's mind, but he was only thinking about what he was saying.

Prometheus continued, "She knew all. Along with my half sisters, the Moirae, who foresaw everything, yet they could not intervene. You saw the amount of power the Fates have to mold us. They could not let Zeus know what they could see. He would hunt them down and kill them. You already saw what he did to me for withholding one major secret. On the other hand, my mother was dead, safe in Elysium, away from Zeus, and she loves her children enough to fight for me the only way she could, by communicating with me."

Lucien shook his head. "But your mother was always in my prophecies."

"Your sleeping ones, right? They started when you were how old?"

"Eighteen." Lucien's expression was an array of emotions I couldn't pinpoint, confusion seeming the strongest. "My oracles?"

"*My* oracles." Prometheus sighed. "Zeus could never know things came from me, from my mother. He had to believe you had that power." Prometheus gave him a sympathetic look. "Lucien, you were no god of prophecies. Zeus manipulated you all more than I could ever manage."

His eyes darted over to Chase, who uncomfortably cricked his neck, then looked down at his hands, flickering the lightning between his fingertips, a somber expression on his face. Archer had told me stories about how Zeus had "conditioned" Chase to be a war-god through many forms of abuse, one being shock therapy.

Prometheus went on, "He tried to push the prophecy gift onto you in hopes to wrestle it away from me after my mother's death. He did not know I could still communicate with her. I sent her to you and let Zeus think he had succeeded in stealing part of my foresight abilities and given them to you."

Lucien stood up. "I just can't." He walked toward Prometheus, who backed until he was pressed into the wall roughly by Lucien. "You used me like a puppet— no, to use your chess analogy, a pawn. You say Zeus is a manipulator. You played god with me, and I can't forgive that."

"I didn't ask for your forgiveness. I don't expect it. We all play god, Lucien. The difference is that your subjects are mortal. You must know that you were elemental in all this. One of Zeus's biggest mistakes was targeting you as the prophecy god. It made sense to him because you couldn't lie to him like I could. But Truth prevails, Lucien."

Prometheus placed his arms gently on his shoulders. "I trusted Truth. You were impeccably unbiased and just. You could not—back then—let emotions sway you. You were the perfect conduit for prophecies. When Callie freed you, you felt more acutely than ever. *That* was the most important part."

Lucien let go of him.

Then it dawned on me what Prometheus was getting at, and I needed to say something to soothe my friend. "Lucien, if this all didn't happen the way it did, had you chosen truth over feelings, you wouldn't have died for me, so—"

"All of us would be dead, a prophecy said as much." Lucien's anger slipped away, understanding why he, Prometheus, and I had to be careful about the future.

Prometheus gave him a pointed look. "Lucien, do you want your prophecies back? You gave up your awarded gift to your son, thinking you had prophecies on your plate too."

"What? Why?"

"By facing my mother every time despite how painful it is to me, I can keep my powers, not send her to you. No oracles, no dreams. It can all stay away just as it has since you returned."

Lucien's eyes flickered to me, to Archer, to his son. "I enjoyed the break. Moments ago, I would've said yes to let you keep them. But now…if I have done it so well as you said, I should continue for all our sakes." He sighed, nodding. "Yeah, I'll take them back."

Prometheus smiled widely. "After all you've been through, I think you deserve the ones headed our way." He tapped his temple. "I have a feeling they will be much better than what you have seen in the past. You will need to go find your new oracle, give her your blessing."

Lucien nodded and sat back down on the arm of the sofa, next to me. I squeezed his hand, and he gave me a small grin, squeezing back, a best-friends-forever squeeze.

Athena shuffled her feet. "Can we get back to the point, now that you feel better, Lucien?" I didn't think she realized how rude that was, but no one said anything. "I know you too well, Prometheus. If you used two of us, you did with many of us. I think it's best to lay down how you used each of us."

"So, you're saying *all* of this was set up by him?" Archer's brow furrowed, his gaze on Prometheus. "Like you banked on me falling in love with Callie, foresaw it, even though I have not loved another in thousands of years?"

"No, Archer. You almost botched all my plans. That I was not counting on at all. I saw you, Aroha, and Lucien as a good way to mask Callie's powers, so I sent her father to New York by showing him the doctors who'd give him more time, got him that apartment so close to yours so Zeus would not sense her growing powers. In Iceland, when I said I had seen all your and Callie's kids, it was a lie to keep up your hopes. She had told me that tidbit, and I trusted her vision while my own was foggy by her proximity. I'm sorry to you all for lying, hiding things, and if I made you at all feel powerless. I had to beat Zeus at his own game and to do so, I had to act like him, try to control you."

Archer's brow crinkled, and I knew what he was feeling. We were used, like pawns in some chess game between Prometheus and Zeus. *Ouch.* Even me, most of all. My power did all this.

The others listened with interest, except Athena, whose eyes were now closed as if she could not bear anything else. Aroha draped a comforting arm around her, and Athena clutched her hand in thankfulness.

Prometheus paced the small area along the wall for lack of room to walk more. "I thought it was all over when rumors reached me that you, Archer, defied Zeus and said you would not give her up. I feared Zeus would realize her power of freedom, that if Love was so deeply in love that he would and was able to disobey his elders, it would expose Callie's gift earlier than I had hoped, and everything would unravel. Frankly, it did, but Zeus thought she was a demigod to our benefit. The biggest strength, the one thing that got us through this all was how so many of you banded together. You were drawn in by her will to let you be free from Zeus's power, by her need for protection, or through many forms of love. Your teaming up together is what made me outmaneuver Zeus this time. That was—perhaps—what had been missing all along. Familial and romantic love, friendships."

"Couldn't we have had—I don't know—a warning?" Aroha shook her head, feeling manipulated. (Same, girl, same.)

Chase leaned forward in his chair, hands on his knees, "No, we couldn't. Had he told us or asked us to defy Zeus directly, we wouldn't have. We'd be scared. We had to know who Callie truly was and what she meant for us symbolically. No one could tell us she was a ticket to freedom. We had to *see* it, *feel* it. While fighting for her life, we instinctually fought for our autonomy. Don't get me wrong; I was fighting for you, Callie, because I cared, but also to keep my son alive. I would've always chosen to fight my father, but others…" He looked around at Archer's brothers and Aroha, who ran a hand down her due-any-day-now stomach, then to Lucien and Aios. "If she had only been a measly mortal, I doubt many of you would be so compelled—"

Lucien protested. "That's not fair—"

Chase became animated, likely excited to be the one piecing it together, the logic, over Athena, who was beyond overwhelmed. "Think hard back to the beginning, Lucien, when you were first able to lie. Wasn't that power to be able to withhold and hide the truth addicting? To be able to focus on love and family over war was for me."

This whole conversation was making me feel uncomfortable. "Can we stop talking about me like a drug?"

"Sorry, my love. Think about it, though. I don't think Lucien was ever *in* love with you," Archer said quietly.

Lucien moaned. "First, I'm a pawn who feels too much, and now I don't know my own feelings? Can anyone give me some credit?"

Archer put up his hand in protest. "Lucien, listen, I think you loved that feeling of freedom she gave you. I tried to tell you it was the opposite for me. I love her so much, I feel powerless." He squeezed my shoulder to assure me he had some point, because I was starting to hate this conversation, and he could tell I wanted him to shut up. "When we brought you back, you didn't love her anymore. I think it might've been because you were reborn free from Zeus, so why be drawn to a freedom you don't need?"

"That's a likely theory, Archer," Athena announced, finally coming back to us after her need to check out for a minute.

"Can we stop talking about me?" I asked before I'd lose it.

Archer gave me a sheepish look and was about to speak, but Prometheus interjected. "Sorry, Callie. We derailed. My intention was to free *you* from feeling responsible. Nothing is your fault, and none of this was done because of you, just what power you gave all of us. I know you. You don't want to be locked into some savior type for hundreds of years, have people grovel over what you've done. You just want to live a normal life…with him."

He was right. I did. Just existing to free them from Zeus was okay. Yeah, the future floated around in my brain, and I saw into their minds more than I wanted, but I could just be me now. I could live.

Side conversations started, and Prometheus pulled Athena up by her hands, his eyes concerned as he led her out of the apartment. They had to make their peace together, talk it all out, and I hoped they would be okay.

Archer looked at me with a smile. "I think I figured it out."

"What now? My brain is about to burst if I get any more info."

"We'll try it out tomorrow."

Now he piqued my curiosity. "What?"

"My supposed omniscience. If we masked you, you masked us from Zeus. So, in Hades, I couldn't see anyone but you. I always can see you, find you though, because—"

"Immortal marriage."

"I think I can see the rest of the Olympians not in your range, which is what I need to test out tomorrow."

"What help is that? No offense," I added quickly.

"Well, if I'm right, I might be able to see those far away from us. Hera and them in Fiji, Hermes antics, and more importantly—"

"If Zeus somehow gets out." It was a useful gift, but because of me, it would be limited. It was the right thing—not that Archer would ever abuse power like Zeus—to keep it safe from anyone else who might abuse it.

Archer nodded, his beautiful face full of excitement. "Later, I can keep track of our grown children when they move away from home."

I kissed him. He stared at me, fully content. I sat with Archer, half exhausted, half stunned. I could not be sorry for how things turned out, the fact we were controlled by Prometheus, because I ended up here: safe, with the love of my life, and a huge family that cared about me. There would be time to digest the information, plenty of time. And with me safe, my power would not allow any of my loved ones to be controlled ever again.

After a while, despite loving their company, I was ready for them all to leave, wanting to be with my husband and son, alone in our little bubble.

I closed the door behind Aroha and Chase, the last to leave, sighing from exhaustion. There was so much to clean up that I just wanted to ignore it until morning. Two arms wrapped around me, one around my waist, the other my shoulders. Archer lowered his lips to peck my neck in that spot that gave me chills, right where my ear and jaw met.

"What now?" I asked, leaning into him.

"Whatever your heart desires." His voice was thick, but I wasn't talking about where his mind was venturing, typical guy.

"I'm being serious." I turned around in his arms and met those incandescent eyes, full of regard for me.

Archer smirked and ran his hand down my back to join the other at my waist. "You're the one who can see the future."

"I don't see everything."

"Good. Some spontaneity can be a good thing," He murmured, stealing a brief kiss. "You're the one who freed us all to have choices. We can do anything."

"I don't know where to start, how to relax."

"Considering the mortal world is pretty much at a standstill, you have plenty of time to spend with me and Philo until you decide about school or work or anything really. It's time to just…relax."

"How do I do that? I forget." From having an ill father who died, finishing high school through depression and illness, transitioning into goddesshood, going to the Underworld to bring back my friend, a kidnapping, and—oh yeah—two wars, a near drowning, being in hiding, forced early labor, almost dying a few times—forget it, I was not rehashing anymore trauma. In short, I hadn't relaxed in a couple years.

Archer laughed lightly. "I get what you mean, but Callie, we have *forever*. Forever together. You and me, and apparently hundreds of kids."

"I never said that many, but it might feel that way if we add in your entire family and if the whole fertility thing is left unchecked."

"Dionysus should reign it in after a baby boom. But no matter how big our family grows, this building will be our Olympus now. We'll slowly take it over. When you met me, I was away from Fiji with Lucien and Ma. We can go off together for hundreds of years—just you, me, and our children. They will eventually go off on their own. We can hang with Ma and Dad for a while, Lucian and Akila. Even my brothers. Or we can stay here in this apartment for a little while. Every decade or so, we'll have to relocate, but for now, it's wherever you want."

"What about what you want?"

He took my chin in his hands, needlessly memorizing my face because it would never change. Then he met my gaze. "This decade is all you, Callie. You've been through Tartarus since I entered your life. Now, it's time to spoil you."

"Spoil each other," I returned, leaning into him. "I made you love me after all, which put you through Tartarus as well." I kissed him.

He made more of the kiss, and I opened my eyes to see we were inside our bedroom. "Starting now." Archer's vibrant eyes glowed.

Philo started crying in the next room.

Archer growled in frustration. "Or not."

"You said it. We do have forever. Unfortunately, his hungry belly does not."

"But…" Archer pulled me in. "He's a god. He doesn't *need* the food." He went to kiss me, but I dodged it, pushing his chest away.

"Archer," I scolded.

"I know. I know." A sigh of defeat left his lips as he gave me a smoldering gaze full of promises. Then he was out of the room at immortal speed, and Philo stopped crying.

Exhausted, I changed into my pajamas. It was only when I had left the room and saw Archer in the rocking chair, holding a bundle in his arms, did I realize I was acting out a dream I'd had before I'd known I was a goddess. It was a vision of the future, the same one I'd shown Archer on our wedding night.

When I crept up and leaned over to see Philo swaddled in a blanket, only revealing his round little face and a soft warm brown curl loose. He stared up at me, smiling, and from the blanket's movement, he was kicking with joy. He was such a happy baby, only crying shortly for his needs, but as soon as we came to get him, he'd stop. Those little eyes beamed at me with love, glimmering with emotions, just like Archer's eyes. Seeing the bottle in Archer's other hand, he flailed, ruining Archer's "perfect" swaddle—the little Houdini was an escape artist.

Archer kissed his little fist and tucked it back in, then looked up at me when I put my hands on his shoulders. His eyes were filled with such love, adoration, respect, making all these hardships worth it to have this foreseen moment that felt much like a turning point. I prayed to all the gods for years of mundane bliss. No more drama or death-defying situations.

Archer's lips crashed into mine. All his feelings poured into me with that kiss, sharing my sentiment, calming my worries with the balm of love.

Philo cooed loudly for attention. Archer broke from the kiss first. Not tearing his eyes away from me, he popped the warmed bottle in the mouth of Philo, who drank greedily.

Archer's expression was quizzical, feeling my array of emotions through our bond. "You okay?"

My hands still on his shoulders, my dark hair over his shoulder, I looked back and forth to the matching blue gazes that both stared at me with love. I was more than okay, but the words to express my feelings were hard to formulate. Everything here on out would be wonderful. This moment was everything we had fought for. "I feel like I'm in Elysium."

Archer's lips upturned in an adorable smile, making me think of that first day, by the elevator, that shy smile of interest in me while I ogled the hot guy in my building. It was the day both our lives drastically changed, and I had never expected all of this. In this moment, I could not be mad at Dad or Prometheus from hiding things and plotting for this future. I could not ask for anything better than this.

Archer's gaze understood me fully, his mind likely back in that elevator with mine. "Forever, together," he assured me.

"Forever, together," I repeated as if to form a pact between us. I sealed it with a kiss.

CHAPTER 40

Fog all around. Stone walls and gilded gates. I knew exactly where I was. Not long ago, I would have dreaded this situation. What god would want to visit Elysium in his sleep to hear doomsday prophecies?

It never had been a choice. Since I was eighteen years old, my sleep had been plagued by these dreams. I would appear in a strange but beautiful place. My feet would propel me forward; unable to fight, I would be forced to meet with Themis for a prophecy I never wanted to hear.

I now knew Prometheus had done this to me. I was no god of prophecies, but merely the messenger of them.

Unlike before, I walked forward with haste and confidence. I chose this. That made all the difference.

I opened the gates and entered, leaving the fog behind.

I had always thought the Elysian Fields were glorious, but when weighed down with dread, I couldn't fully appreciate them. They were indescribable. I itched to write some poetry down to give it justice, but feeling the pockets of my jeans, I had nothing earthly with me but my clothing.

I took it in. The air moved in a slight breeze, smelling of honeysuckles—nectar. The sun poked through the clouds and warmed my flesh. The barley rippled, making soft undulating, soothing sounds, making me feel at peace. I heard the trickling brook in the distance.

I had almost ended up here. It was terrifyingly intoxicating because I wanted to stay. Most of the time I had ended up here, though, I was chased out by Hades's dogs, or I fell through the fog beyond the gates. This place felt so soothing and yet terrifying at the same time. After I'd died, Hades had prevented me from moving on here.

I cringed at the thought. To never see my family again? To have never reunited with Akila and learned of Polly. I belonged in the alive world.

So why was Themis bringing me here in my sleep tonight?

Per usual, Themis appeared out of nowhere. Her hair in braids, her dark eyes, and curvy figure—they once had sparked lust in me. Wanting her for millennia, I had tried to get closer and closer, till finally achieving that long awaited kiss.

Nothing stirred today, not one thought of her, aside from admiring a pretty interruption to the perfect scenery.

I thought of Akila, home, in bed next to me. She was staying over as of late, Polly with her brother, and I wondered when I should simply ask her to give up her place and never leave mine. After the war was over, I tried to get her to agree to a hasty marriage, but now that there was peace, she didn't seem to be in a rush.

Themis smirked. "The womanizer is in love? That's what I call poetic justice."

I smiled, not denying it in the least. "Themis."

She cocked her head. "Still, you came back. There's no reward of my lips, no reason you should be here. My son should be the one getting the prophecies from me. Why did he send you?"

"I sent myself. I kept the prophecies, not to spare him, but because my truth protects them, protects us all. This is a burden I choose."

She nodded. "You have done better than my son. His emotions clouded his mind in the past. What now?"

This confused me.

She laughed at my likely bemused expression. "Apollo. Is this what you truly want, the gift of prophecies?"

"Of course, as I've said."

"I see the truth in your eyes."

It was my turn to laugh as I let the barley tickle my palms. "I *am* truth."

This made her grin widely, an expression I had never seen due to the gravity of the messages in the past. I could see Prometheus's features a bit in hers, the dark eyes, the same almond shape and color, the broad smile, and bronze skin.

"Come here." She held her hand out.

I was expecting a prophecy, so I was surprised when our hands joined and no images shot forth. She tugged my hand, leading me through the barley. I had never been this far and could now see vines of grapes—a vineyard maybe—and olive trees in the distance.

We walked in silence. I took in the new scenery as she led me forward. Feeling tension in the air that wanted to push me backward—much like in these dreams the fog pulled me to the gates—there was that feeling that I was not in control.

We came to the bubbling brook, and the water looked so fresh and cool. I knew it would be the perfect temperature to wade into.

"No," Themis said sternly as if she read my mind. "Never touch the water. If you cross it, you will never return to your loved ones.

So, the brook drew a line between the real Elysium and whatever type of reception field I was allowed in.

A *kylix* appeared in her hand. She hooked the curved handle of the wine cup on her fingers and dipped it into the water, careful not to let the flowing water touch her skin. Once some pooled into the cup, she pulled it up, grabbing the other handle. She held the cup up to me. "Drink."

"Uh…" After her instructions never to touch the water and the threat never to see my loved ones again, I wondered why in Mother Gaia she was asking me to consume it.

She laughed. "I will miss you, sun god."

"Miss me?"

She took a deep breath and gazed around the field. "I have waited in this field, alone for thousands of your years out there, I think. Time is not discernible, but the memory of so many prophecies tells me it has passed. Alone. I will cross the river. I will never come back. I will join the heroes and gods and finally go home to everyone who came before us."

"But…"

She moved the cup to her one hand, and the other touched my face gently. "Apollo, drinking this water will bring you here in your sleep without me. Another oracle will take my place here. But one will not be needed for some time."

"That's it? No parting prophecy to get us through the meantime?" Funny that. I cursed this gift, wished it away, and saw it as a depressing chore. Then, when I learned I could lose it and fly blindly through life, I clung to it.

"Do find your mortal oracle. She no longer needs to be protected from Zeus, but she has an interesting genetic makeup and powers."

"I heard. Psyche and my lines crossed."

Themis nodded. "Until you locate her, I'll give you a parting gift."

She smiled, then touched my temples. Images raced through my mind in that zing I was so accustomed to. Happy images flittered through my mind: *Aroha styling her daughter's hair, Athena helping her son wield a sword, Aios marrying Linda, Archer and Callie celebrating her college graduation with three kids in tow, ending with Akila in bed, holding a bundle, with me next to her, a baby with dazzling Egyptian blue eyes and black hair.*

Then the images stopped. Frustration laced through me. I wanted to see more. "Was it a boy, a girl?"

Her brow quirked. "Does it matter?"

My face split into a massive smile I could not subdue. I shook my head. I was going to get that happily ever after I'd mocked Aroha and Archer about when they discussed mortals' love lives. I would get to raise a kid and be a father, a good one this time around.

This glimmering future full of hope stretched out for me—that was my Elysium.

I took the cup and drank. The water was sweet and cool, but refreshingly so.

"Goodbye, Apollo."

The water churned in my stomach but not in a nauseating way, spreading warmth through me.

"Thank you, Themis."

She walked into the brook, turning her back to me. As she crossed, she faded as if she were particles of dust on the breeze being blown away. They say that prophecies are heard on the wind. Forever, I'd remember Themis when the wind blew.

My stomach cramped unpleasantly. I stumbled backward as the pain sliced through me...

...and woke up in my bed, gasping for air my immortal lungs technically didn't need.

Akila moaned, then mumbled, "You okay?"

I put my hand over my racing heart. "Yeah. Prophetic dream was all."

She groaned. "I don't want to hear about it until morning."

A laugh bubbled out of me. "Sleep, love, sleep. It wasn't a bad one."

She opened her eyes, gazing at me, looking beautiful in my pale sunlight of early dawn that glowed through the windows.

I smiled, my heart finally beating back at its immortal pace. I leaned down and kissed her lips gently. "It was good, great actually."

"Mmm, tell me tomorrow then. I'm tired." She closed her eyes.

The covers had been tossed off by me. I checked out her lithe body, clad in a skimpy satin cami and matching shorts. So beautiful. I ran my hand down her top to her lower abdomen, wondering how long I would have to wait for that vision to come to fruition. I lifted her top and kissed her belly, then rested my head upon it.

Akila's hands weaved through my hair. She breathed out a happy sigh.

Yes, love, this is everything.

With love and hope, life is simply...

Elysium.

ACKNOWLEDGMENTS

I'd like to thank friends, family, and every loyal fan who read this far and urged me to keep writing it. Thank you to Authors 4 Authors Publishing for the opportunity to publish the Immortal Transcripts series. Biggest thanks to my parents and husband, who pick up any slack and duties I cannot perform so that I can bring readers these books.

Thank you to Reflections Book Club for your ongoing support and inviting me to speak with your group as well as Our Next Chapter Bookstore for hosting signings and launches; we local authors truly appreciate the support.

I want to thank every reader. I hope you enjoyed the ride.

Eros's OLYMPIAN FAMILY TREE
(from the journal of Dr. David N. Syches)

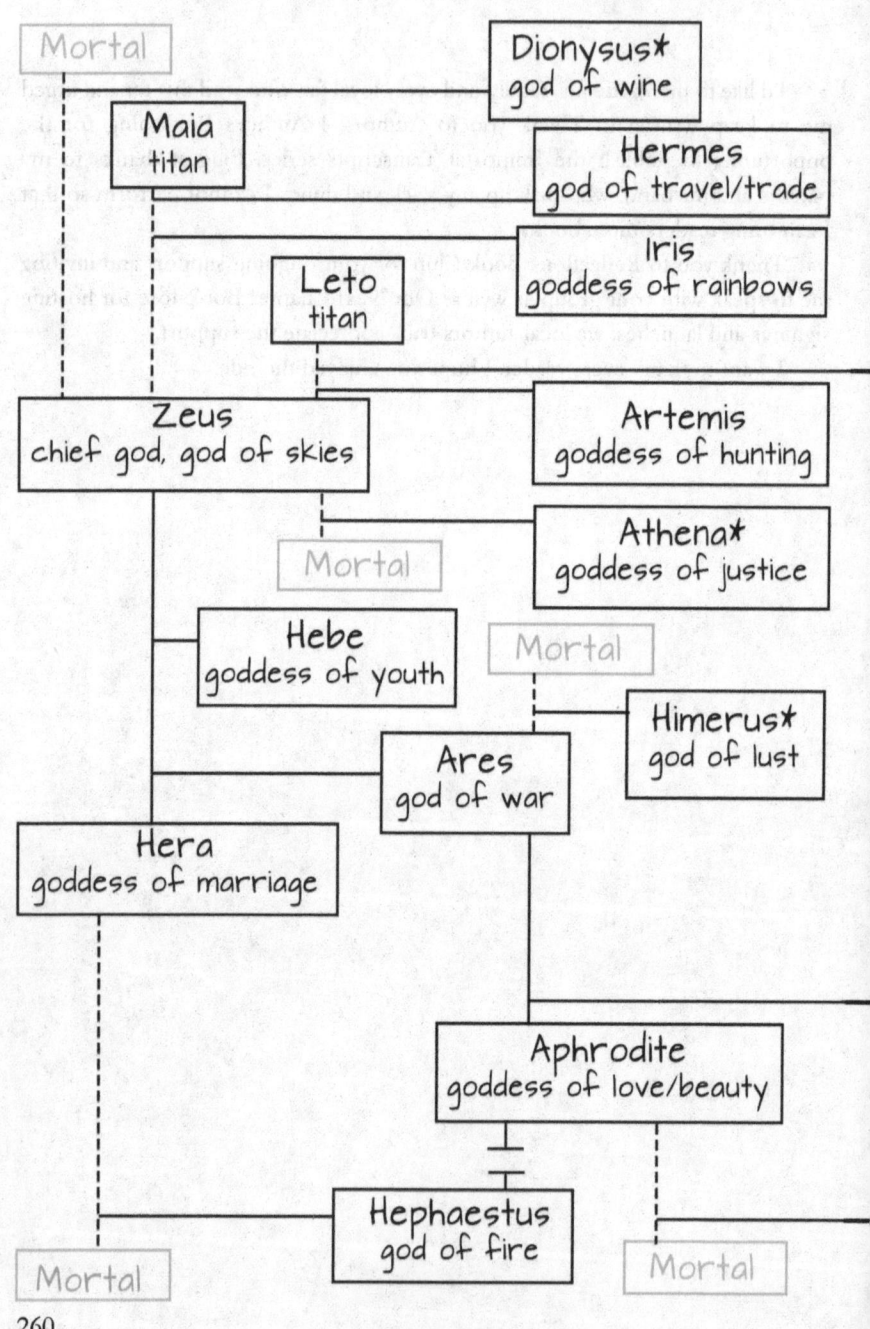

Mortal

Dionysus*
god of wine

Maia
titan

Hermes
god of travel/trade

Iris
goddess of rainbows

Leto
titan

Zeus
chief god, god of skies

Artemis
goddess of hunting

Athena*
goddess of justice

Mortal

Hebe
goddess of youth

Mortal

Himerus*
god of lust

Ares
god of war

Hera
goddess of marriage

Aphrodite
goddess of love/beauty

Hephaestus
god of fire

Mortal

Mortal

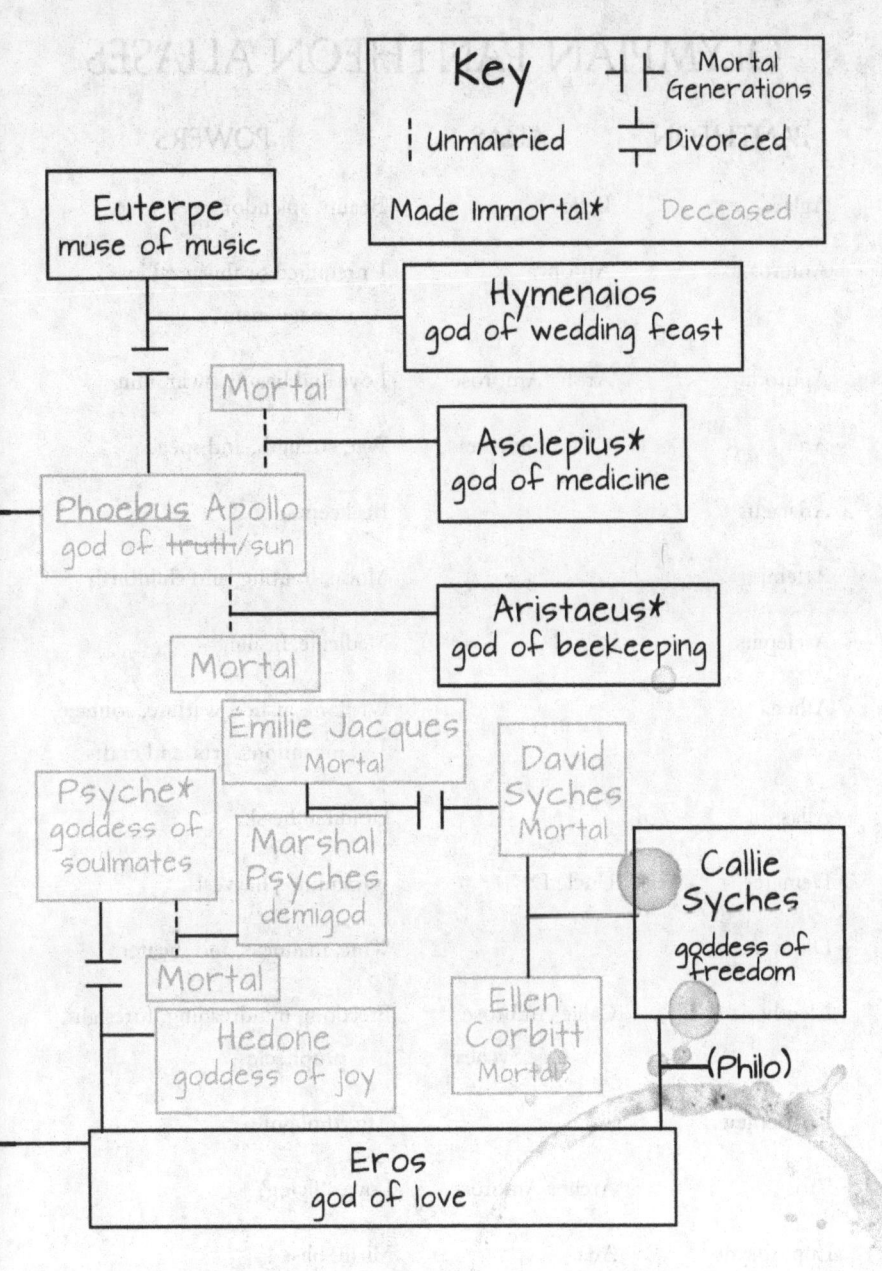

Key

┤├ Mortal Generations

┆ Unmarried   ╪ Divorced

Made Immortal★   Deceased

Euterpe
muse of music

Hymenaios
god of wedding feast

Mortal

Asclepius★
god of medicine

Phoebus Apollo
god of ~~truth~~/sun

Aristaeus★
god of beekeeping

Mortal

Émilie Jacques
Mortal

David Syches
Mortal

Psyche★
goddess of soulmates

Marshal Psyches
demigod

Callie Syches
goddess of freedom

Mortal

Hedone
goddess of joy

Ellen Corbitt
Mortal?

(Philo)

Eros
god of love

Anteros★
god of counterlove

261

OLYMPIAN PANTHEON ALIASES

PANTHEON	ALIAS	POWERS
Aglaea	Belle	Beauty, splendor
Anteros	Antony	Unrequited or thwarted love, "magnetism"
Aphrodite	Aroha Ambrose	Love and beauty, swimming
Ares	Chase Gideon	War, strength, and speed
Aristaeus		Beekeeping
Artemis		Moon, hunting, and childbirth
Asclepius		Medicine, healing
Athena		Wisdom, justice, warfare, courage, inventions, arts, and crafts
Atlas		Holding the sky
Demeter	Uncle D	Agriculture, harvest
Dionysus		Wine, madness, and theater
Eleutheria	Callie Ambrose (née Syches)	Freedom, mindreading, foresight, prophecies
Epimetheus		Afterthought
Eros	Archer Ambrose	Love, "flying"
Euphrosyne	Ada	Mirth, bliss
Euterpe		Music, lyric poetry
Hades		Underworld, scotopia, and invisibility

PANTHEON	ALIAS	POWERS
Hebe		Youth
Hedone		Joy, pleasure, "flying"
Hephaestus	Heph(ie)	Fire, forging
Hera		Marriage, family, pregnancy
Hermes		Messenger, teleporting, theft
Himerus	Russ	Lust, strength, speed
Hymenaios	Aios	Marriage ceremony, soul fusing, and Phoebus Apollo's powers
Hypnos		Sleep
Iris		Rainbow, teleporting
Janus		Duality, passages
Leto		Motherhood
Ma'at	Akila	Truth, justice (Egyptian)
Mnemosyne		Memory
Moirae	The Fates	Birth, destiny, and death
Muses		9 sisters of the arts
Persephone		Spring, plant life, and death
Phoebus Apollo	Lucien Veras	Sun, light, truth, prophecy, music, poetry, medicine, and healing
Poseidon		Sea, earthquakes
Prometheus		Foresight, prophecies

PANTHEON	ALIAS	POWERS
Proteus		Shapeshifting, foresight
Psyche		Soulmates, mindreading, and "flying"
Thalia	Thalia	Delight, charisma
Thanatos		Death, soul bearer
Themis		Justice, law, prophecy
Zelus		Zeal, ice, and "flying"
Zeus		God of gods, lightning, thunder, sky, and omniscience

ABOUT THE AUTHOR

LISA BORNE GRAVES

Lisa Borne Graves is a YA author, English Lecturer, wife, and supermom of one wild child. Originally from the Philadelphia area, she relocated to the Deep South and found her true place of inspiration. Her love for all literature led her to branch out from the academic arena to spin her own tales. Lisa has a voracious appetite for books, British television, and pizza. Her inability to sit still makes her enjoy life to its fullest, and she can be found at the beach, pool, or on some crazy adventure.

Follow her online:

lisabornegraves.com
Twitter: **@lisabornegraves**
Facebook: **@lisabornegravesauthor**
Instagram: **@lisabornegraves**

AUTHORS 4 AUTHORS PUBLISHING

A publishing company for authors, run by authors, blending the best of traditional and independent publishing

We specialize in speculative fiction: science fiction, fantasy, paranormal, and romance. Get lost in another world!

Check out our collection at https://books2read.com/rl/a4a or visit Authors4AuthorsPublishing.com/books

For updates, scan the QR code or visit our website to join our semi-monthly newsletter!

Want more fantasy romance? We recommend:

KISS OF TREASON

by Brandi Spencer

Two forbidden lovers share the rare gift to heal others with a kiss—but at a cost. Odelia's life has been a lie. When the queen tries to remove her from the palace, Odelia uncovers the truth. Now she must decide whether to forsake her people or embrace a destiny that would pit her against the current heir to the throne...her best friend. Though her only hope of avoiding a civil war lies in winning his heart, revealing her secrets too soon could cost both their lives.

And a kiss might not be strong enough to save them...

books2read.com/kisstreason

www.ingramcontent.com/pod-product-compliance
Lightning Source LLC
Chambersburg PA
CBHW010515100726
47903CB00009B/2761